THE
WARD

JORDANA FRANKEL

KT KATHERINE TEGEN BOOKS
An Imprint of HarperCollins Publishers

Katherine Tegen Books is an imprint of HarperCollins Publishers.

The Ward
For information address HarperCollins Children's Books,
a division of HarperCollins Publishers, 10 East 53rd Street,
New York, NY 10022.
www.epicreads.com

Library of Congress Cataloging-in-Publication Data
Frankel, Jordana.
 The ward / Jordana Frankel. — First edition.
  pages cm
 Summary: "Set in a futuristic Manhattan after a catastrophic
flood called the Wash Out, sixteen-year-old Ren must race against
a conspiracy to find freshwater springs and a cure for the deadly
disease that has stricken her sister and many others in the
Ward."—Provided by publisher.
 ISBN 978-0-06-209534-3
 [1. Adventure and adventurers—Fiction. 2. Virus diseases—
Fiction. 3. Sisters—Fiction. 4. Water supply—Fiction. 5. Science
fiction.] I. Title.
PZ7.F8543War 2013   2012051733
[Fic]—dc23   CIP
                                                              AC

Typography by Erin Fitzsimmons
13 14 15 16 17   LP/RRDH   10 9 8 7 6 5 4 3 2 1
❖
First Edition

For my mom and dad and grandparents

PROLOGUE

This is no ordinary flea-bitten day—not for me, it ain't.

The other kids don't know that, though. Which is how it's gotta stay. If any of them found out I was going to the races, they'd tell Miss Nale on me and I'd get stuck washing dishes for a week.

Just go to sleep already, I whine from under the industry-standard I'd-rather-be-cold-than-itchy blanket. Getting the girls in the corner to quit their gabbing and conk out has got to be harder than scoring extra rainwater rations in this joint.

Even after Miss Nale left the second time around, their machine-gun giggling kept right on.

Boys. That's all it ever is. Well, let them waste those perfectly good heartbeats.

If my heart's gotta beat itself to death, I'd like for it to go out with a bang.

Or, at the very least, a checkered racing flag.

Another thirty minutes, and I hear the healthy kids' telltale easy breathing. Ten more after that to make sure it's for real. The girl next to me snores slightly, her whole body slumped and buried under the covers.

Four months ago, she walked into a room full of empty

beds and chose the one next to mine. Then she started sitting with me at mealtimes. Then free time. I never talk to her, but she keeps on trying. Always chipper. Odd, too, rummaging around abandoned buildings looking for copper pennies to give away.

She seems nice enough, and that's exactly why I don't get attached.

Kids like Aven, they don't last long in an orphanage. Not with so many parents losing their own to the Blight. Provided she keeps herself from getting sick, she'll be out of here, adopted in a minute, guaranteed. And if she does catch it . . . well, it's still a quick turnaround. Dying will do that.

I learned early on, it's best to keep to yourself. Everyone leaves eventually.

Except for me, of course. I'm the lucky one who gets to watch everyone else go.

Slow moving, I slip out of bed. Bare feet against the floor make me want to yelp—it's always a bitter cold—but I keep my trap shut. Can't have anyone waking. On the floor between my bed and Aven's are her leather clogs, filled to the brim with pennies.

She could sell those things. People love buying pennies 'cause they make nice thank-you gifts. Like giving someone a bit of luck to show you're grateful for something.

I consider taking one—

Nah. Who am I kidding? I don't need luck.

I do, however, need some water, I realize, eyeing the canteen next to her shoes. She always shares her rainwater rations anyway. One swig, I think, uncorking the bottle and downing two instead. I'll need the extra boost for tonight. Tomorrow, assuming I make it back, I'll thank her.

I put the canteen down on the floor and head for the window—my escape route to the races. As I slink past, Terrence opens one eye.

Don't say nothing. You better not say nothing, Ter. He wants to be a racer too, someday. He'd understand what I'm about to do, but I still freeze, like in that dumb game.

He winks, and closes his eye.

Good boy.

I tiptoe on. One of the girls in the corner wheezes, stops me dead in my tracks. I hold in my air out of habit. The virus starts just like that, before you get the tumors.

Bet she'll be gone, off to the sickhouse, by the time I get back.

I plug up my nose and keep walking, though I've been in this place thirteen years, without even a sniffle to my name. Miss Nale used to wonder how I never got sick.

"I don't breathe no germs, that's how." That's what I'd say.

I didn't know it, but I was wrong.

Just yesterday, Nale sent me to see the orphanage doctor for being "too healthy." Apparently my not dying was cause for suspicion. Rightly so, as it turns out, 'cause according to Dr. Hartigan, I got something funny in my blood that makes me *immune*. To the Blight. At first, I thought that meant I was gonna die. I started bugging out, and then the doctor explained: Turns out I'm *not* gonna die. Not from the virus, anyway.

Still, I keep my nose plugged until I'm able to lift up the

window through the bars and inhale the grimy, salty city air.

One of the girls squeals from behind.

Good grief, don't they ever sleep? I think, whipping around.

"Ren! I knew it!"

Faster than a racing Omni, Aven rushes me, her white-blond hair glowing in the dark. "It's been you making that scratching noise every night, hasn't it?" she asks, squinting as she clutches my bicep.

I flinch—she's digging her fingers right where Dr. Hartigan's needle went.

Her grip loosens when she sees my face pinch up. "What is it?" she asks, and grazes a finger over the leftover bruising.

I shake her off. "Nothing."

I can't tell her, or anyone, the truth. Miss Nale and the doctor both said so. He was putting my blood away in his briefcase and that's when Nale looked at me dead serious. "Do you remember the frog from your science class last year?" she'd asked.

I gulped hard and answered her. "We cut him open and looked at his heart."

Nale nodded. "He was an experiment, just like you would become. Keep your secret. Avoid the Blues—if they take a blood test and know what to look for, you'll be at their mercy. You don't want to be at their mercy, Ren. They have none."

The doctor nodded with her. Their words still give me the shakes.

And here I thought immunity was a good thing.

Ignoring Aven like usual, I feel around for two slits in the metal near the top and bottom of the window bars. Traded three weeks' lunches for enough razor blades to make these cuts, but it's going to pay off. If I can just get out of here . . .

"Go to bed, kid," I say finally, yanking at the loose spot I've kept stuck together with gum.

"You're leaving? For good?" Her face downs like I punched her in the gut.

"I wish." Once more, I tug at the bars—that gum is sticking a little too well. "No, this time I'll be back," I grunt.

She smiles, relieved. "Good," she says quickly. "You can't *leave* leave."

Aven places her tiny fist over mine on the pole—I don't quite know what she's doing, but when she nods, then I get it. Silently, I count to three for the both of us, and together we pull. The bar flies free from the frame and we stagger backward, noisy.

"You're welcome." She grins, though I don't recall saying thank you. "Where did you say you were going?"

I raise an eyebrow. This kid's got more nerve than I thought.

Guess I could tell her. *Someone* should know where I am, just in case I die and all. "Can you keep a secret?" I ask.

Aven claps her hands. Her extra-long sleeves stifle the sound and she nods her head, bouncy as a ball. "Tell me."

"The races."

"Ohh, no." Her eyes go wide. "Dragsters are crazy, I've heard. They won't slow if you get in their way." When I grin but don't answer, she says, "Ohh," again. Then, "You're not going to watch, are you? You're actually racing?"

"That I am." I puff up some, and pull at the second bar. It's looser than the first, thankfully. "I've got a mechanic waiting for me and everything."

"Just . . . be careful. Please don't die."

I stop what I'm doing. Look at her head-on. "Aven?" I say, thinking of the science class frog, dead on its back. "Did you know that the heart only gets one billion beats in a lifetime?"

Cocking her head, "Okay . . . ?"

"Point being, I most certainly will not be careful. Now, I'm not going to be reckless either. But not going all out is the same as standing in one spot, counting down from a billion, you understand?"

"But you're a . . ."

"Girl?" I finish.

She nods.

"True enough. Guess I need luck then," I say, sarcastic, ignoring how I almost took one of her pennies.

"You won't need it," Aven tells me matter-of-factly, and I can see she's thinking something—her pale brows go all knotty. "If anyone can win a roofrace, it's you. You're the toughest, bravest person I know."

Then *I* do a double take, thinking she must not know many tough or brave people.

Neither do I, I realize.

She smiles and hugs her arms close to her body. "You're gonna beat everyone. I just know it. You'll tell me everything?"

For a moment I forget that I'm straddling the window, one leg out in the open, and that I'm about to race for the first time ever.

See, *I* always knew I could win—but to have someone else think it too?

Always knew I liked this kid.

"You know it," I tell her like we've done this before. She beams back at me. Don't know why I'm so surprised by the fool grin on her face.

I swing my other leg out the window and make a jump for it, dropping down onto the fire escape. The metal clanks and I have visions of the Blues coming after me. Just as I'm about to book it, Aven's face peeks out of the window, her long braid dangling.

"So . . . I know you're not going to be careful and all," she mumbles awkwardly. "And that's fine. But . . . could you try not to die? You see, I was sort of hoping . . . I was sort of hoping you might come around to it, being my best friend, that is. It'd be nice, don't you think?"

I can't quite believe her—is that how people do it? Is that how people get to be friends? I'd sort of avoided the whole shebang. Not worth it when they get adopted and want nothing to do with you anymore, or when they die and you want nothing to do with them.

She sees me hesitate. "It's not like it hurts. What are you so afraid of?"

The challenge in her voice, it's enough to make me reconsider. Maybe she's right. It might be nice. To try.

Arching my neck to face her, I whisper, "Yeah, why not? We could be friends. I'll be sure to stay alive."

"Yeah? Really?" she asks, disbelieving. The fool grin is back, and she squeals "thank you" about a half dozen times.

7

"Great, 'cause I like you. It's going to be fun, Renny. Promise."

Renny?

Aven disappears through the window and just as I turn away, start the climb down, she pops her head out again.

I pause on the ladder, waiting.

"Good skill!" she calls down in a breathy voice.

Now I'm the one cocking my head. "Skill?"

"It's the opposite of luck!" With that, she throws me an excited wave, and tosses me a penny, before disappearing again into the dorm.

I like that, I think, rolling the penny along my fingers.

Good skill.

Atop the roof of the Empire Clock, right where my mechanic told me to meet him before the races, I jump from drainage pipe to drainage pipe. Up here it's a tangled knot of them, built when the United Metro Islets was part of a state, and the state was part of a country, and everyone was paying money to someone else, and no one liked it.

A heavy wind sucker punches me to the left—I stumble onto the copper-plated rainwater collection panels. *Glad no one's watching*, I think, kicking my boots against the puke-green metal and looking out at the skyline. Most of the buildings are pretty ugly. But standing tall, like a steel seven-layer cake—the Chrysler.

She'd be fun to race on, for sure.

To pass the time, I try and imagine what the Ward was like pre–Wash Out, before ocean levels rose and contaminated underground fresh. Asphalt roads instead of canals, and none of our boardwalks or suspension bridges mazing through the city. People driving cars. On land, not water. Even traveling underground.

I can't begin to picture it, though. Everything is too different.

Where is he?

It's just me and the wind, and the boxy, concrete buildings rising up from the canals. I'm not nervous being up here alone, but I don't much like waiting around. Ain't like I'm about to leave, though; it took me nearly six months to hunt this guy down. Benson "Benny" Gates, the only outsider to win at the races. He don't live in the Ward—a West Isler, born and bred—but he owns a garage on Mad Ave where he hardly works.

No one, not even the Blues, wants to come to the Ward since the Blight got bad.

I look across the Hudson Strait, beyond the Ward to the West Isle, and I scowl. That's his home, in all its perfect, electric glory. I try not to think less of him for it. Shiny skyscrapers touch the sky, built after the Wash Out for wealthy refugees. Some are even brimming over with light . . . at this hour.

Makes me want to eat my fist. I hate them for it. Who are they to have everything? They can afford black market bottles of Upstate fresh for the price of a kidney. Don't even have the cancer virus over there. No need to funnel rainwater off *their* rooftops.

And all they did was get born on the right side of the Strait.

Why do we get the short end of the stick?

It ain't fair.

The clock gongs straight to my brain—I bang my hands against my ears and wait for the eleventh chime, after which Benny Gates will officially be late.

"Renata."

I spin around.

That'd be him—from across the rooftop, gruff and tough sounding. Benny may have been born on the other side, but his voice belongs here. It's made of spark plugs and carburetors. He tried like hell to talk me out of racing, told me I was too young to get into it. I wore him down though. Showed up at his garage every day for a week and bugged him till he cried mercy. Finally, he said I had "pluck."

I spat on his shoe, and he laughed.

"I've told you before—the name's Ren," I say, short. "Renata sounds like an Isle name. Can't have my mech calling me by an Isle name. At the races, nothing would brand me worse."

Benny ignores me, hands clasped behind his back. "How do you feel about a quick test?" he asks, pointing to the clock tower. "You'll have ten minutes to climb up, then down that tower. No pressure, I'd just like to see how your mind works." He pauses, then chuckles. "*Some* pressure, perhaps. Who wants to fail their first test, am I correct?"

My throat goes dry; I'm glad I took that swig from Aven's canteen or I'd be crazy with thirst right now. Maybe I am nervous.

"What happens if I can't do it?"

"Nothing horrible," Benny assures me. "Tonight's race will

be a no-go, though. We'd spend the time going over where you went wrong."

I swallow, and I walk to the tower. I'm racing no matter what. The tower's no higher than fifteen feet . . . *easy.*

Carefully, my fingers graze the siding, feeling for tiny cracks to dig into. Bits of concrete crumble off, and when I look to my hands, I'm shocked. They're shaking. . . .

I *don't* shake.

I lift myself and begin the climb.

I pretend I'm that radioactive spider kid with supergrippy skin from old-time comics. At first it works. But no less than a minute in, the pads of my fingers go tingly and raw. I'm not used to climbing, and everything from my shoulders to my knuckles cramps. My legs have it a little better—they just burn. I keep going, and the feet drop away.

Then I look down.

That's when I slip—gravity pries my fingers from the cracks. My feet kick against the wall and I suck in air. *Don't fall, don't fall*, I tell myself, and I don't.

A few feet higher, I feel my palms fold against a skinny ledge. Trying not to show how happy I am about that, I elbow myself over till I'm belly down on the overhang. It's so narrow, half my body dangles off.

Then I curse myself at what I see—

Along the far side of the tower, someone's stacked a pile of boxes and extra piping. Alls I had to do was climb up, instead of ripping my palms to shreds.

Guess that's lesson number one: scope around for the best route.

Holding on to the overhang with one palm, I crane my neck and put the lesson to use: Still another six feet to go, with no other route to the top. And then I have to make it down.

"Time?" I call out to Benny.

"Six minutes."

It'll take just as long to make it to the top, much less to the top and bottom. Of course, if I'd looked around to start, the climb wouldn't have taken half as long—I'd have had those boxes to jump on.

I could have used them to help me up the second half, too.

Ugh, I groan, finally understanding that I actually need those boxes to make the climb in ten minutes.

Which means I have to get them.

I whine, facedown, little shards of concrete digging into my forehead. *Can't waste any more time*, I remind myself, dropping my legs back over the side. I lower myself down, then let go of the ledge, falling the last few feet.

My feet hit the roof's copper panels and I hear Benny laugh. Without looking, I growl at him, and rush to the farside of the tower. There, I begin stacking boxes. As they pile up, they lose their balance, so I reach for a long copper beam and prop it against the higher ones. That will keep 'em steady, I hope.

Done—everything's in position.

I'm gonna do it, I'm hours away from being a real racer. I grin to myself and hop onto the first box, then the second, all the way up to the first ledge.

As I hug the tower and step up, the boxes jiggle underneath me, but I keep my foot firm on them. My fingers feel the brick for more cracks, and I keep climbing. When I look up, I see the final ledge. In order to reach it though, I have to lift my foot and let the boxes drop.

On the count of three, I jump. The boxes give me one last boost, and my hand finds the ledge. Then they tumble down, and I'm left hanging here, feet dangling in midair. I kick against the siding; I throw my elbows and shoulders onto the overhang. Knees swinging, teeth gritting, I clamber up the wall.

And then, I've made it—*I'm at the top!*

I whoop and I holler, punching the sky with both my fists. Remembering that this was only half the test, I look for Benny. "Time?" I call out again.

A moment passes. He doesn't answer. Once more: "Benny, how much time?"

Still nothing . . .

Then the air starts to shake. Vibrate. Under my feet, the brick shudders.

"Renata!" Benny immediately calls. "Get down . . . Now!"

I don't have to ask why. It's the Blues—one of their helis, I'm sure of it. Though I've never seen one with my own eyes, everyone knows the warning signs. Somewhere, there's about to be a raid. Could be a water theft, or maybe a black market drug bust—who knows.

I sit on my butt and swivel around. With my stomach to the wall, I shimmy down and drop the remaining few feet onto the next ledge. There, I repeat the process once more till I hit the ground.

At the bottom, Benny wastes no time—he grabs my elbow,

drags me to a corner. Together we duck behind the brick wall that surrounds the rooftop, and wait.

"Why do you think they're here?" I whisper, watching the dust get kicked up by the angry air. If I strain my ears, I can even hear the chop of propellers. We've got a clear view of the Blues' headquarters on the West Isle from here too, but it's useless; the heli's already on our side of the Strait.

My skin gets the prickles.

We see it: one beamer crawling across the horizon. It's headed for the Ward's residential district, nicknamed the U 'cause from a bird's-eye view, the Ward is a big ole horse-shoe-shaped island of squat, mostly gray buildings. Once it was called Midtown. Now it's in the middle of nothing, 'cept for the Hudson Strait.

Benny follows the light with his eyes until it hits the U's western arm. Shaking his head, he answers, "Not for the races, that's for sure. Ever since we've had a designated 'racing district,' they've turned a blind eye."

He nudges me in the elbow, then points to the Ward's southern racing quadrants, Seven through Ten. No one lives there now—it's just an island of abandoned skyscrapers. After the Wash Out, the government left them to crumble. The buildings were so huge and so high, it was too expensive. The Restructuring teams didn't even bother.

Now they're a racer's playground, good and dangerous.

"It's stopping," Benny says.

Just north of us, the heli hovers over Quadrant One. Then it picks up again, travels down the arm of the U. At Quadrant Three, again it stops. If I'm right, Five is next—us.

Benny and I stay silent. We watch the heli lift up and continue south. Its props blow the air wild, rocking the suspension bridges that zigzag east to west, rooftop to rooftop. For many, they double as laundry lines, and right now, thanks to whatever business that heli's got going here, entire neighborhoods are losing their clothes. Bet the Blues haven't even considered how much it will cost us.

I was right . . . Quad Five is next. The aeromobile is so close I can make out its slice-em dice-em props and disk-shaped belly. And the words *Division Interial* painted on its side, though we just call 'em the Blues.

One guy in blue dangles out the pit, a megaphone to his mouth, and moments later we can hear him. "Attention, citizens!" he shouts.

Benny and I exchange glances.

"Due to the rampant spread of the HBNC virus, also known as the Blight, Governor Voss, two hours prior, has declared a state of emergency in the Ward. Effective immediately, he has enacted the following two Health Statutes for the good of the United Metro Islets."

I scoff at that—the cancer virus is rampant all right, but not on the West Isle. This is for *their* good. We've already got it bad.

"Statute One," the man with the megaphone continues, "declares transmission of the HBNC virus a statewide offense, punishable by arrest. The DI will be establishing a local Ward task force responsible for randomized public testing.

"Statute Two orders the suspension of all outbound,

civilian trade and travel from the Ward to the West Isle until further notice.

"That is all. Please turn to your local radio channels for more information. Thank you."

With that, the heli churns upward, back into the sky. We watch it hurtle off into the dark, more laundry scattering in its wake, but I'm still playing over the words in my head. Didn't quite get all of their meaning, about health statutes and whatnot.

Benny falls back against the brick siding. "I don't believe it. . . ." he whispers to himself.

"Believe what?" *He sounds so terrified.*

"A quarantine. Over the entire city. In not so many words, but that's what it is." He pauses, brings his hand to his mouth. "I, I can't . . . I can't leave," he murmurs.

Is that what that meant?

"I'm sure they'll let you cross," I insist. "You live there—"

Benny shakes his head. Mutters, "Perhaps . . . perhaps," as he runs a hand through his wiry, gray hair. "I'll contact someone tomorrow. No doubt the lines will be busy all night." But his eyes glaze over, he's lost in his head, and I wonder if he really is stuck here for good.

We sit together, side by side, silent.

"How can they arrest people for being sick?" I ask, 'cause that part I mostly understood. Everyone knows the word *arrest*.

My question shakes him out of it, barely. "Transmission," he clarifies. "You can be sick. You just can't get anyone else sick."

"Oh."

We're back to quiet again. Above our heads, the hour hand on the clock ticks closer to eleven thirty. I don't want to sound like I don't care—Benny's in a rough spot—but my mind is stuck on whether I get to race tonight. I keep quiet, though. Can't stop my mind from being rude, but I can stop my mouth.

I don't have to say nothing, turns out.

Benny sees me hawk-eyeing the clock, and pats my knee gently. "You'll race tonight," he says, though his voice is tired and sad, like he's not really here. "After all, you did make it to the bottom in just around ten minutes."

"You sure?" I ask, biting my lip. "I'd understand if you wanted to take care of stuff and forget about the race. Really, I would."

And I would, I guess. If I had to, I would.

He places a palm on my head and tousles my wild, wiry black curls. "I'm sure. You knew when to turn around and start from square one, and when to keep going. You're ready. Just be careful of those guys," he says, pointing in the direction of the Blues' headquarters on the West Isle. "They may not like patrolling the Ward because of the Blight, but if they catch you—if you do anything stupid—no hesitation, they'll jail you."

I look up at him, confused. "But I heard sometimes they try to make a mole out of you if you're useful?"

"And would you like to become a mole?"

I see what he's getting at. "Moles are sellouts," I spit. "I'd never turn mole."

"Then don't do anything stupid, like stealing from freshwater stores, or nabbing treats from the Mad Ave vendors. I know what you orphans do."

At that I grumble, checking the sky. "They won't catch me," I say, confident.

"Ha." Then he looks to reconsider. "No, I'm sure they won't. And if they did, they'd probably throw you back into the sea, such a pain-in-the-arse fish you'd make."

I nod, hoping he's right.

PART ONE

1

Three years later

1:00 A.M., SATURDAY

My breathing quickens and I realize I'm panting: pre-race jitters. *Racing is your job now,* I remind myself, readying my game face in the bathroom mirror. It's not a mask—I've worn it for too many years now. It's a knife. A blade. All angles, sure to cut. I'll smile. I'll keep all my fear undercover.

You're invincible, dammit.

Who else—aside from Benny, back in his prime—has won every race they've ever entered?

No one.

Who else is immune? Who else could ask to be tested any day of the week and pass, always?

No one.

Too bad that last thought does me no good. I'd give my

blood to Aven if I could, alone and sick at home. She's not contagious anymore, so we don't have to worry about her getting arrested. But the virus is no less deadly just 'cause she's not contagious. In only two months, her tumor's grown bigger than an egg, bulging out from the base of her skull.

Someone as good as she is shouldn't be dying. Someone like me . . . *I* should be dying.

You're a sellout, my mind hisses.

At my wrist, my DI-issued cuffcomm trills: thirty minutes till flags go down. Time to check in.

The Blues don't like it when their precious moles are late.

One quick glance to make sure the bathroom is empty, and I duck into a stall. I play around with my brass headset till it fits comfortably—a few purple and lime kinks of hair boing out the sides, but there's no fixing that. I stopped trying for pretty long ago. Pretty won't win races. Pretty don't get respect.

I take a deep breath to still my nerves. I'll never get used to this, I think, and flip open the comm. Crouched over the toilet seat, I punch in Chief Dunn's number at headquarters, and look down into the murky water. To think—people used to fill toilet bowls with fresh. Pissing into a pot you can drink out of. *Unbelievable.*

The earbud crackles as I talk into the mouthpiece. "Come in, come in, Chief Dunn at HQ."

Mole. That's what I've become. The very word makes me shake, even after all this time.

Three years ago, Aven and I planned our escape from Nale's. Aven had just started to wheeze, and we could feel the tumor. She'd be unadoptable. And no one was going to pick me for their daughter, so it made sense. I botched it all, though, "borrowed" fresh from the orphanage stores—for the road—and Nale called the Blues on us.

I was the only one they caught—Aven got left behind. A great big heli swooped down, netted me, but never even saw her, dizzy and tired a hundred feet back. Flew me away like a stork with a baby bundle, all the way to the Division Interial's headquarters for jailing.

I wasn't bothered by the jailing, though—no, I was more bugged that they'd take my blood, figure out I was immune, and turn me into a froggy experiment. So I offered to work for them—whatever they needed.

I *asked* to be a mole. Still makes me want to spit.

As it turned out, they needed someone who knew the lay of the land and could scout the Ward's dangerous quadrants for freshwater. A racer, for instance. And here I landed in their lap: an orphan. A ward of the state. Totally disposable. If I got sick, they could find someone else.

The line sputters, levels into a low buzz. "Quadrant?" a recording prompts, and I punch "10" into my cuffcomm. Like always, the recording reminds me to report to Chief Dunn immediately after the race. As if I'd suddenly forget.

The bathroom door creaks open. *Brack*, I curse to myself, flipping my cuffcomm shut. *Who's in here?*

I wait for the line to go dead, then hop out of the stall before anyone could've heard me. My mole status stays a secret. Even if I'm just looking for fresh, no one likes the Blues. I'd be hated by the other racers. More than I already am.

In walks the Dreaded Duo. Dragster girlfriends. Their platform shoes knock against the floor, and by way of the mirror's reflection I see Tanzii first—fauxhawked, with one ear full of metal hoops, bars, and studs. Then comes Neela—all infinite legs and waterfall hair. All flaunt. No confetti-spiral do like I got. No dusky, freckled skin, or eyes that are half-open, half-closed all the time.

It kills me to say it, but the other racers have hot girlfriends.

I bet they're even nice . . . to people they don't hate so much, that is.

"That's right . . . scamper off," Tanzii, the taller of the two she-devils, hisses, running a hand through her tawny do.

And I do leave. But not because she told me to.

I step out onto the rooftop, ready.

Two feet out of the stairwell, a fist grabs for my shoulder and steers me to the rooftop perimeter.

"Not again," I grumble, turning to see a muscly guy wearing the telltale yellow-and-black jacket. Don't need to see his back to know what's written there: *HBNC Patrol*. He's one of the Blues' goons, a Bouncer, here to randomly test people and then bring anyone who turns up contagious to a sickhouse.

Commission-based earnings, it's called. Each infectious person they pick up earns them money. That way, the DI rarely risk getting sick, only hitting the Ward to make Transmission arrests.

I pull back the right sleeve of my red leather catsuit to

show how many times I've already been tested. It don't matter, they keep on dragging me. "Look," I say to the guy, and wave my forearm in his face. A row of small, white X marks have been branded into the skin—proof of every VEL test I've ever been given. Of course, my Virus Exposure Level is, and always will be, nil.

The Bouncer ignores me as he searches my arm for the date marked under my last X.

"Not recent enough," he growls, dropping it. Then he slips on a pair of white latex gloves and sticks me in the forearm with a tiny needle—a blood scanner—to see if I've got a certain amount of the virus that would mean I'm contagious.

Which I don't.

I roll my eyes and start to tap my feet, impatient. This is a waste of my time, and even after a dozen VELs, getting the brands still hurts. Not to mention how I hate getting tested before a race—I actually use these arms. For pretty important stuff. Like, ya know—racing.

A moment later, the scanner beeps and the Bouncer takes back the device. "HBNC negative," he informs me.

No kidding.

Flipping the scanner over, he presses a button, and we watch the tip—no bigger than my pinkie nail—glow until it's red. I make a fist and try not to wince as he presses the blazing X and today's date into the white of my arm.

It lasts less than a second, and then I exhale. One more welt, raw and pink, to add to the mix.

"Ren!" a voice calls from behind me. I turn around and spot Terrence to the far left.

My stomach bottoms out. He's beneath the undercarriage of a brand-new racing mobile—an Omni, of all things. Makes me think I must've heard wrong, that it can't really be Ter, but I know his close-shaved, brown head of hair too well.

His Omni's a beaut—not to mention almost impossible to beat. But I can't lose. The money I get from the Blues keeps Aven stocked in pain meds. My earnings from the races keep us fed and alive.

Take one away and life goes from hard to impossible.

"Ter!" I shout back, ignoring the cold trickling through the zipper of my catsuit as I maneuver my way to the other side of the roof. The whole thing lays at a slant, perfect for all our mobiles to gain momentum before the first jump, but a bit awkward to be running on in my beloved Hessian boots, tassel and all.

Soon as he waves, my jealousy over his new mobile fizzles away. It's something about his eyes, I think, that does it. They're a bright, West Isle Astroturf green that would be shocking even if his skin weren't a bit darker than mine, and they're always laughing. Not to mention his baby face—Ter's still pudgy-cheeked from childhood. It doesn't exactly inspire fear.

No, he's not the big bad wolf of the races. More like a lamb, if you ask me. But with this kind of mobile . . . well, anyone's a threat. I can't hold it against him, though. He's never won a race in his life, and if I had the money, I'd buy an Omni to fix that too.

"Holy sweaty socks from Hell! Terrence, how did you pull this off?" I wrap my arms around him in a bear hug.

Good thing he's one of the nice guys, or I'd never let on how green I am.

"Oh, this old thing?" His dark hand gives a casual slap to the orange exterior, and he walks around the cone-shaped body. Gently, he presses his fingers into each of the front wheels, testing their pressure. Then he moves to the single back wheel. "Well, my birthday's coming up, and my dad wanted me racing safe. Since I was gonna do it anyway."

I nod—that's what I think I miss most about never having had parents. The gifts.

Since I like pushing buttons, "Why don't you tell me about your new vegetable," I ask.

"S'cuse?"

Terrence looks perplexed.

"Your carrot. She's orange, ain't she? I would've given her a paint job before the big day, but that's just me. Plus the shape, it's very . . . carrot-like."

"Well then, she'll be a swimming carrot," he says with a smile, and I should've known better—Ter has no buttons. Always been hard to anger. "This is a grade A Omni6000 mobile. Retractable wheels, airtight interior. Even got a backseat."

"Fully equipped?" I ask. It's not for nothing that they're called Omnis—*Omnimobiles*. All terrain. Land, sea, and air, though flight capability don't come standard. Anyway, flight during a roofrace isn't allowed, but I'm curious nonetheless.

He shakes his head. "Just land and sea," he answers.

I look at his Omni again and the realization settles in: this race is no longer in the bag. My Rimbo's a good mobile, no doubt, but I don't quite see how it can match Ter's carrot.

For one thing, mine's no boat. A Rimbo—short for *rimbalzello*, the Italian word for that game where you skip stones—just skips across water, like a pebble. You add enough thrust from the propellers and you can keep it skipping. Stop the thrust, the mobile sinks hard.

Terrence's is airtight; it can move underwater. And because it's airtight, without momentum it just bobs to the surface like an apple. Nice and safe.

If I get stuck on a canal or a gutter, it's a big, fat Game Over—I can't let that happen.

I swallow my envy. Ter made it out of Nale's home alive, and with a rich new dad to boot. Rich by Ward standards, at least. Ter doesn't need this money like I do. Losing is not an option for me. Ter's shiny new metal is nothing.

Metal can't think.

Metal can't gauge how fast you need to drive if you want to fly.

I'm the better racer. That's what matters.

Turning away, "I've got to get mine ready," I tell him quietly, and stalk off, headed in Benny's direction. I can just barely make him out on the other side of the roof.

"Don't be a sore loser!" I hear Ter call from behind me. But I haven't lost. Not yet.

As I storm across the roof, I can feel the remaining two racers' eyes glued to me from under the brims of their derbies.

Jones and Kent. Both descendants of Manhattanites who wouldn't leave when the Wash Out struck—didn't want to stray too far from their skyscraping palaces. These guys come from old money. Money so old it ain't even around anymore, but they like to play make-believe. Act rich, get treated rich. Those are the Derbies for you. Still thinkin' they own the place.

Kent moves toward me, slow, waltzlike, whiter than a ghost. Lifts his derby to tuck a stray black hair behind his ear, then pins me with his eyes. He steps closer, stopping not two feet away. Faces me. Towers over, his body long and thin. Uses height to intimidate.

Jones follows suit. He is Kent's pastier-looking shadow, after all. Wears his greasy blond hair just the same way and tips his hat to the exact same angle. Of course, Kent wears it better; Jones is hardly taller than I am.

They circle me, vultures.

"I'm feeling lucky tonight," Kent says. The corners of his lips curl. He draws a line with his eyes straight up and down my body. He's too close. I don't like his words. Don't like their double meaning. If I back away, he'll see my fear.

Times like this, I wish I were wearing something less flashy. Less red. Something maybe not leather. *This is a show*, I remind myself. *And you're the main attraction*. Besides, leather does wonders for girls who are small up top, and I don't need any help making my backside look good. Plus, the bigger the audience, the bigger the winnings.

I move closer to him and look up, meeting his gaze, though my eyes are level with his chest. "Too bad you need skills, not luck."

I'm thinking of Aven, and it helps. Gives me courage. She

may not be blood, but she's family—my sister. I reach for the penny around my neck. Three years, and the old coin has started to feel lucky, though that was the opposite of the point.

"You never did." He scowls, then nods to a few bystanders watching our tiff.

Crowds of people have started to line the perimeter, all gussied up for the postrace party at the Tank. Girls in short skirts, braided hair coiled high on their heads. Guys in their best patched-up denim. Pleather jackets on both.

I wave big. People come for this part of the show too.

"Then why do I always win, Kent? Can't blame it on the mobile; you've got a fancy postflood Honda and I've just got a Rimbo. Must be the driver."

Through a smirk, Kent spits, "You've got no place in the races. No reason to be here. Go work a sickhouse, or the rooftop planthouses with everyone else."

I turn to face him. "You don't mean everyone else. You mean the girls."

"We all have our jobs." He shrugs.

"Tell that to my fans. They'd be mighty disappointed if I just disappeared."

"I'm willing to take that risk—one of these days, I'll see that you do 'just disappear.'" Kent takes one last lingering look that makes me flush with anger. "Poof," he whispers into my ear.

He's all talk, you know he's all talk, I tell myself as he laughs, but this I know: say something enough, eventually you'll try and make it true.

2

1:15 A.M., SATURDAY

Walking toward Benny, I don't even feel the tap on my shoulder. Only when this guy gets right up in my face do I stop. Look at him. His coat ain't patchy, his hair's too short to get mussed, and his face is too clean. He's an outsider, no doubt.

I check his neck, and sure enough I see a small, adhesive patch there—the K-dot. It's white, too, so he's only just arrived. Each day, the dot gets blacker, until it's totally filled in, and you know the medicine's all used up. You've got no guard against the Blight.

No one round here takes it, though. It only works for about five consecutive days, and if you try wearing another one right away, you start going loopy from the side effects. Not really useful if you value a little thing like sanity. That's why none of the locals wear 'em.

"Sorry to bother you, but it's getting down to the wire," the guy says. He's young, not much older than me, but the way he holds himself—tall and self-assured—makes me think I could be wrong. Pointing to the Empire Clock, "I need to speak with you."

"Who, me?" I ask, looking at the clock myself. Still fifteen till the flags go down.

"You're Miss Dane, correct?"

When I laugh in his face, he seems genuinely confused. Like people come up and talk to me sweet every day. No one but Chief Dunn uses my last name. "I'm a representative of the United Metro Islets' Division Interial—"

Cutting him off, "*You're* with the"—I whisper the next word—"Blues?"

I'm shocked; the Blues are never out and about in the Ward. Only a few days a month, they'll slap on a K-dot and arrest some contagious folks for violating Health Statute One. They call it "policing the neighborhood."

I give him the up-down, not even bothering to hide my disbelief . . . or my disapproval. The boy is lanky, reason enough to be suspicious.

"Officer Justin Cory, miss." He shifts his slick tasseled shoes and grins when he looks down at his poorly endowed arms. "Thanks for the vote of confidence in DI lawmen." Flashing me his badge, "I'm just preliminary recon, only here for a few days. No need for brawn," he adds, excusing his lack of muscle.

There is no excuse for lack of muscle, in my humble opinion.

I keep my mouth shut and continue to give him the stink eye, not out of unfriendliness though. More out of professional interest in seeing how he acts under stress. He seems like the type who'd wither.

Justin looks down at me, his baby blues caught like a gnat in a bug zapper, and he goes quiet. Then he stays quiet. I wave my hands a bit, trying to shake him out of his brain lapse.

I was right. He's a witherer.

When he remembers what he came here for, he stammers, "I . . . uh, we need you to deviate from your intended route."

I laugh. Maybe he'd like a pummeling instead. "No way. The route is set, and if I deviate, I lose."

His face is blank as a fish's.

"Money," I clarify, expressing the obvious. "I'll lose lots and lots of money. And with the way your guys pay me, I really can't afford that."

Neither can Aven, though I leave her out of it.

Justin nods. "That's why we are prepared to offer you generous compensation. We have a lead on a freshwater source, and you're headed in that direction anyway. Throw the race, survey Quadrant Nine, and you'll get what would amount to your winnings, plus some."

Tempting.

I don't like what a loss will do to my rep, though. I've worked long and hard, and not to mention, I'm sixteen, a girl, and five foot two. It was a full year before people started taking me seriously. To lose my first race in nearly three years? That's no easy thing.

Then Aven, nothing but a skeleton with skin, appears in my head. What am I thinking? Of course I should do this. It's money, for us. And who says I have to lose? I'm good, right? Prodigy and all that. If I buy all that junk about *believing in myself*, then this should be a breeze. I just have to reroute and scan quickly, get back on track, and watch my competition eat water.

I can do this. I can still win. And get twice the earnings.

For just a moment, I'm delirious. All that green . . . Aven and I, we could eat like queens for a month. I wouldn't have to ration out her pain meds.

"What if I don't find anything?" It's a distinct possibility . . . likely, even.

"You will still be compensated for your effort."

I can handle that.

I look around the rooftop, watch the circling onlookers as they check out the dragster's mobiles. Then I realize something strange—I'm under the DI's thumb, whether I like it or not. So this whole game of him asking me? Well, it's a charade. This isn't a conversation, though it may look like one.

I don't have a choice.

"Fine. Where do I pick up the money?"

Justin exhales, as if he's relieved. Excited, even. "Where will you be later?"

"An after-party. Postrace shindig at the Tank—"

"Perfect," Justin says, cutting me off. "I'll meet you there."

I shuffle my feet, considering. It's convenient, sure. My bookie usually meets me there to pass along my winnings from the race. I'd be killing two birds, but it's not ideal. If I do lose, I'm going to have to go to a damned party afterward. In front of everyone. May as well dress myself in rotten tomatoes, I'll be so tyrannized.

Only one answer: I just won't lose. "Very well, sir. If you'll excuse me . . ." I say, pointing to my mech, nearly invisible, hiding under my X19 postflood Rimbo Steamer.

"Sure, sure. Good luck—I hope the search proves fruitful." He pauses, almost awkward, then turns on his heel to join the rest of the crowd.

Fruitful? Who says that? What's that even mean?

Shaking my head, I jog to meet my mech. "Benny!" I yell, forcing my mind back into gear, because a nagging guilt has started to put me on edge.

I can't tell him about the route change. He'll want to know why, and that's a can of worms I have to keep airtight—my being a mole is supersecret. No one likes the DI, no one likes people who work for the DI.

Which means I have to spring the change on him during the race, at the last minute. He's going to love that.

"How's it lookin'?" I ask his shoes, poking out the side of my Rimbo.

My mobile's not the swankiest of the bunch, but I think it's as dapper as can be. Even with the out-of-fashion delta configuration: one wheel up front and two in back. More dangerous than the Derbies' four-wheelers, I'm proud to admit. And it runs off the brackish river water. Engine works fine, but you have to unclog it from time to time.

"All's dandy, boss."

"Good, good. You checked the boiler? Blow out the salt accumulation?"

Benny slides out, and the blast radius of his Einsteinesque

gray hair nearly has me on the floor doubled over in a giggle fit. "What do you take me for?" he huffs, but I can't take him seriously, not with his hair, looking like he stuck his finger in an electric socket. I swear, he hasn't cut it once these last three years.

"Just covering my bases, taking precautions," I answer, laughing. "I know you're the best of the best, Benny."

I glance around the rooftop once more, this time looking for that infamous copper head of hair belonging to my bookie. "He's not here, is he?" I ask, wishful.

Some might say it's bad form to bet on oneself. In legit sports, it's even illegal, as there's the possibility that you might throw the race to fix the outcome.

In wall racing, no one throws the race. Throw a race, you could die.

"Derek has, not once, been present for a race. And yet you always ask." Benny throws me a look, one that makes all the blood rush to my cheeks. "How curious."

I hide my face.

I think the only person who doesn't know I'm somewhat, only slightly, infatuated with Derek . . . is Derek. "Just asking," I drawl.

"Course you are. No . . . Derek did help out with a few things before you got here, but he left early. As usual. He said he'd be at the Tank later, also as usual." Benny passes my utility belt for me to put on.

Great. One more reason I have to win. Can't have Derek see me like that, a loser, tail between my legs. As I buckle my belt, *Focus*, I remind myself.

Running through the list, I feel each pocket and strap to make sure everything is there: Canteen, check. Flashlight, check. Lighter, check. Protein bar, check.

"You're awesome, Benzy. Stuck under my Rimbo for hours making sure that she's all fired up and ready to go." I pat my belt. "*And* you even make sure I'm fed."

"Damn straight, I've been here," he says in his ragged old way, then waves a wrench at me.

In the distance, the Empire Clock sounds. Along the perimeter, even the fans are getting fidgety, checking cuffcomms and whatnot. They've grown silent.

It's nearly time.

With Benny's back turned, I circle my mobile to do one last thing before the race. At the front wheel, I take a quick swig from my canteen and kneel. Make like I'm inspecting the headlights.

From my bra I pull out a small, DI-issued freshwater detection light filter—it turns any freshwater pockets I might run into a neon purple. Don't have to take samples or anything. I carefully fix on the filter and take a deep breath.

This is just like any other race. With one foot on the front hood, I hop into my Rimbo through the scratched moonroof and close it above me. In the pit, the first thing I do is sync my headset to my cuffcomm so Benny and I can communicate.

"Good to go," I tell him, once I hear static. Then I say, "Patch me in to her, would you?" He knows who I'm talking about—this is tradition.

Moments later, Aven's voice is in my ear.

Bubbly, she says, "Good skill, Renny," and I smile as soon as I hear her. Either she's got more energy today, or she's faking it for my sake.

She doesn't have to, though. After my month of DI training was up, I came back. Searched every sickhouse in all six residential quadrants. It took months. Gave me the worst memory I've got: Aven, ragged and too thin, but worst of all, she was alone. Every time, it slices me open.

And still, I would do it all over again.

"See you later, Feathers," I say into the microphone, and then the line cuts out.

In front of me, Neela, Kent's girl, arranges herself in the middle of the four mobiles. She stops between Jones and him, and winks. Leans forward to give him an eyeful—her dress is less dress, more handkerchief. I bet Kent doesn't know that her breasts aren't naturally that gravity defying. Or maybe he does.

What nonsense.

To keep from gagging, I repeat my personal racing rules over and over again in my head, even though I don't need to.

Get your ass in one piece from A to B—now to Quad Nine. However your heart desires. Easy peasy. Keep to the walls and roofs. Water skip only when need be. Get your ass in one piece from A to B, keep to the—

The checkered flag is down.

3

1:30 A.M., SATURDAY

I push the neon-green button—DETATCH—and in an instant, my Rimbo jolts forward, speeding down the roof, the momentum sucking me backward into the seat. The next thing I know I'm halfway down, followed by Kent, Jones, and lastly, Ter. Not too surprised by that; Omnis are decent out of water, but he'll pick up speed in about thirty seconds. For the time being, I'm leading.

But I haven't had time to come up with a new route that gets me to Quad Nine, then back to the last roof.

All four of us are approaching the ramp that will send us over the edge of the roof and onto the next building of our choice. I'd bet good money Terrence is going to dive straight for the water. Kent's Honda steals up behind me and I swerve closer to the outside of the roof.

The bastard.

Not only would my metal be crushed if we were to have a collision, though I'm sure that's his intention, everyone knows the first roof is a grace period. You don't mess with other mobiles until you're off the first roof. Too many people watching. Spectators have died that way, found themselves up close and personal with a fresh set of tires.

Not that Kent cares about racing etiquette.

All the Derbies would rather make mush of me than watch me win again, and if that means killing a spectator or two, I guess he'd be fine with it. He's also probably tired of losing. Looking for a change of pace.

But he isn't going to get it. Never had the brains for this sort of thing. Racers need to prepare ahead of time. Maybe that's a little-known secret, though it seems fairly obvious. It's even Benny's favorite mantra: "How can you get where you're goin' if you don't know how?"

True racers scout the territory beforehand so we know the routes.

For example, we are headed straight north. I know that when the roof ends I need to swing my mobile sharp left, a heading of three hundred degrees, to be precise, according to the compass that's smack center of my steering wheel. That way, the mobile will land on the roof of another building, one that is covered in only about an inch of water thanks to the low tide. Normally that building would be entirely under-water, and I know none of the other racers will go for this route; they don't watch the tides like I do.

That—and I'll make an educated guess here—is why they always lose.

Of course, all that planning would be wonderful if it were still the plan. At least the quad isn't too far out of the way of my original route. I don't have time to deviate too far just yet, so I'm still going to run the roof at three hundred degrees for the time being.

A voice cuts through a wash of static on my headset. "Ren, how you doing?"

It's Benny, watching from the roof dock, probably grumbling more than I am about Kent's little stunt.

"I'm fine, B. Kent's just trying to get me shakin' in my boots."

My Hessians have never seen me shake, and they're not likely to.

"Mama's boy. I should have put maple syrup in his tank when he wasn't looking!"

I don't reply—too much else on the brain—but I chuckle as I imagine Kent trying to start up his mobile and finding it better suited to a hotcake breakfast than to a Ward roofrace.

Here it comes—the end of the building.

Readying myself for the jump, I grip the steering wheel. My knuckles whiten. I watch as blackness eats its way toward me until the nose of my mobile dips into the dark mouth. This is, oddly, when my queasiness disappears. When there's nothing but . . . nothing.

Shooting off the edge of the building, now halfway in midair, I hit a red button. My favorite button of all: ROCKIN'

Music shoots out the stereo—bass vibrations from an old pre–Wash Out classic. Mostly muffled, but loud enough to keep a girl's head on straight. I'm sure even the people watching from the first roof can hear something. *Yes. This is what it's all about.*

Being airborne is nothing short of bliss. Nothing to worry about. I can't drive, and I can't die. A moment of pure painlessness. Head banging along with the music, I yell the lyrics—"I'm on a highway to hell"—and then close my eyes as the mobile drops, probably ten stories.

My stomach can tell—it's used to it. When I first started racing, it would rise into my throat like I was gonna upchuck. Nowadays, this feeling of weightlessness, even for only a moment, is addictive. My stomach plays along.

I open my eyes—three years of racing have developed my sense for things like how long the fifteen-story drop should take. I can tell I'm nearing the next roof when I catch a glimpse of the other racers out of the corner of my eye.

I was right about Terrence—sort of. He's driving *down* the building. All wall-racing mobiles have propellers on the front to slow down the momentum for a vertical drive like that. He must have slowed to a crawl before the first roof jump. Both safer and dumber, if you ask me. Safer, as he's not going to nosedive into some unknown building underwater. Dumber, as he's dragging way behind, all in the name of caution. He reaches where the water meets the building, and his mobile slips into the channels.

He's going to have his own obstacle course though— underwater rubble and wreckage from before the Wash Out. Hundreds of buildings that you can't see from the air. An entire city, even larger than this one, tucked out of sight—a watery ghost town. Nearly impossible to map, too. I'm beginning to think I don't envy his snazzy water-adaptable carrot.

My mobile hits Roof Two and is immediately cushioned—

too much—by the water pooling there. Everything starts to drag and slow, my wheels fighting against the pressure. I do not have the time to friggin' dog-paddle through this muck. I must not have measured properly—the water is too deep to keep my wheels down.

Though the mobile has already slowed considerably, it's not too late to reach for RETRACT.

I do, and all three wheels tuck into the body. The flat underside skips against the waterlogged roof, and I step on the acceleration. Having a limited supply in my H_2O tank makes this a bit dangerous to do so early in the race, but I have no choice.

Propulsion shoots my Rimbo forward. Within moments I'm back to an acceptable speed. It's a blur, speeding toward the roof's end, straight for the canal. My Rimbo makes the terrain shift, skipping along river just fine, but I see I'm using more saline water than I'd expected. I'll have to increase the temperature of the boiler to make it. I need to find Roof Three, and if my sense of direction is good—which it is— Roof Four will be the one that gets me into Quad Nine.

Now comes the tricky part. I need to gauge my skips just right. On the last skip before reaching the next building, I'll hit the release button. The wheels will extend out, and then I'll lean away from the wall to get my mobile on its side, and just like that, we'll be driving along the wall of the third building.

"Ren. Come in, Ren!"

I'd completely forgotten. "Benny, hey. All's well. I'm eating up my supply fast, though." A quick peek at the reader tells me that I've got about a half tank left.

The comm is quiet, then Benzy's voice returns through the static. "Well, Plan B is always there if you need it," he replies.

If I have to use Plan B now, there's no way I'm making it to Quad Nine, and I can forget about the win.

It's time. Last skip—I put all my weight into my left side, trying to raise the right. Then, release.

Sparks fly. The wheels extend just a moment too late—the mobile swings sideways to drive along the building's exterior, her suspension causing a load of jostle. About twenty feet ahead, Kent comes barreling down the wall. Damn. Must have lost more time than I thought back on Roof Two.

"B, come in." I swallow my breath. He's not going to be happy about this. "There's been a change in plans."

Static rolls through the headset—there's a pause that's just as disturbing as a scream or a cuss.

"Ren, what kind of stunt are you thinking of pulling?" he asks slowly.

Think quick—he needs to believe that I'm doing this for myself. Why would I be going to Quad Nine?

"A stupid bet I made with Kent. Don't worry about it."

His voice rises. "You're going to toss this because of a bet with that . . . that—"

I cut him off before he gets too riled up. "I need a position on our potential Four, but headed toward Quad Nine."

My guess—I'll need a heading of about thirty. Though I scout ahead of time so I know the area pretty well, it's easy to lose your sense of direction when you're driving at a ninety-degree angle.

The crackle of the radio comm screeches in my ear, then

Benson's voice returns. "You've got a few options, but none of them will get you first to the finish."

He's pissed. Clearly. But not as pissed as he would be if he knew why I was really doing this. So I guess that's a win. "Just give me the heading, Benny."

Before he can answer, Kent jerks his car in a zigzag to keep me from getting ahead of him. If I can't gather enough speed before the edge of the building, I'm not going to make the jump to the next roof and it won't matter where it is. The pit of my stomach starts to do a jig, and not in a good way, like that time I first raced Kent and tore him up.

The mic is silent. After what feels like hours, B gives me my move.

"If you're aiming for Quad Nine, the next roof is far. A heading of forty degrees northeast."

Close to thirty degrees. Glad I asked.

Benson adds, "The race isn't the only thing you lose headed in that direction; Kent won't follow you. Too far off course. He's not going to go for it. It's a long shot for you too, but you're bent on a suicide mission. So enjoy." The mic goes quiet again. I know he resents me right now, but all I can do is move forward with the plan.

A bright red light on the dash catches my attention—it's the water-tank reader, and it's nearly empty. How is that possible? Just a moment ago I was at half tank. That should have taken me to building five or six, at least.

"Benson—my tank is flashing a bloody red E in my face. What do you make of it?"

"You sure?" His reply is quick. Confused.

I sigh, rolling my eyes even though he's not here to see me.

"Yes, Benz. I'm sure. I'm not blind, am I? I can see it flashing, clear as day."

"Well, you know what to do." He sounds resigned. "B it is."

My knuckles are pressed hard, cramping against the steering wheel. *How is this happening?* "No way," I respond, jaw clenched. I can't lose both the race *and* the surveillance money. "I need to make it to the next roof."

"And what are you going to do when you get there?" Benny growls—I can hear his anger loud and clear. "Sit down and have a tea party?"

He does have a point.

"I'll just have to make it to Quad Nine. After that, I'll have more options. You can find a route via the canals, right?"

I can see it now, Benny hunched over his handmade topographical maps of the modern NYC. Contour lines mark the varying heights of the buildings that survived the Wash Out, so he can tell me at a glance whether or not I can make the next building from this one's highest point. As much as we plan, we improvise too. A flashing red *E* is textbook "improvise."

He hasn't responded yet. I'm not waiting any longer to make a decision. "I'm doing it, whether or not—"

"Yes. You have more options after that." Static. "If you make it that far."

"I will." I just love the vote of confidence. Heartwarming, really.

Up front, Kent is still playing around, trying to keep me from getting up to the speed I need in order to cross to the next building.

"Benson, confirm. It needs to be a roof jump? How high is the next one?"

46

I'm running out of time; the edge of the wall must be coming up.

"Ren, you can make it from your side of the wall. But you're going to have to cut a hard right, like I said. A heading of at least forty degrees."

"Optimal speed?"

"One nineteen."

He can't be serious. "Why didn't you say that in the first place?" I yell with no small amount of wrath into the comm.

My speedometer reads "95." Peanuts. If only Kent would get the hell out of my way. What is he doing anyway? How can he afford to just fiddle around with me like this? He's got to have a plan of his own. . . . Or maybe he doesn't care who wins, so long as it ain't me. I jam on the acceleration.

I'll just have to make him move.

My mobile zips forward and clips his bumper. Kent veers right. He starts crossing the wall diagonally, heading back up toward the roof. Good riddance.

102.

I've never taken her past 115. My only fear right now is that she just might not have it in her.

"Faster, c'mon, *faster*!" My foot is now pressed against the floor. *109.*

The red light on the dashboard is still flashing like a Christmas tree, but I've got bigger worries right now, believe it or not.

112.

The steady acceleration draws my back into my seat, making it near impossible to move. I'm almost there—the edge of the wall is within visibility. I add some of the boiler propulsion and it gets me to 116.

RETRACT. Hopefully, the wheels tucked in will make my Rimbo more aerodynamic.

I hurdle over the edge, but I'm still at 116. I would try to use the props to give me the edge, but by the time they start up, I'd have to turn 'em off again.

There's no way. No more options. If I make the jump at this speed, I'll squash myself into that building like a juicy bug.

Instead, I drive straight.

My mobile hurtles off the building, and I don't have to look down to know that the Hudson channels are flowing beneath me, capped with ice, jagged and painful looking.

Whatever. Hello Quad Nine. I might have missed building four, but maybe I can still survey the area and get my earnings.

My mobile holds steady for a good while, then starts to plummet into the channels.

Good thing I have Plan B.

With a bit more propulsion at precisely the right moment, I can water skip *and* refill the tanks, thanks to Benny's clever suction thingamajigger. All it does is suck up the brackish water already in the channels and redeposit it into my tank.

Filling my lungs with much-needed air—I'd been holding my breath—I ignore the possibility of imminent doom. This is what life is all about, right?

As the mobile drops toward the channels, I try and keep it as straight as possible. Just before it collides with the smooth surface, I turn on the back prop, setting my mobile skipping like a schoolgirl. Strange though—considering how low my tank is, I'm surprised the prop even works.

Heck, if it ain't broke . . . who am I to complain about some good, old-fashioned luck?

I need to fill up the tank—fast. On the far right are two more buttons, side by side. The first just has a picture on it: Ø. The second reads SUCTION. Benny told me what to do when he installed this bit, but now I'm drawing a blank. I hit the Ø and wait.

If I thought the dashboard looked like Christmas before, it's like Christmas on steroids now. Distracted by the blinking reds and greens, I swerve to avoid a spire reaching out of the channel like one of the Derby girlfriends' stilettos. I clip the spire on my left side, sending my mobile sideways. Out the window, I can hardly believe what I see: a steady stream of water flowing *out* the tubes.

Frantic, I press the SUCTION button.

It's too late. The tank's entirely empty, and from my Rimbo's erratic jostle, I'd say Mama Death Spire took out my front prop.

Gauging from the motion and weight of the mobile, I have about six more skips before—

Brack. More underwater rubble, and it's knocked the rear of my mobile up into the air. Instead of sinking nice and easy, it's going to be a nosedive. Perfect. How am I going to get myself out of this one?

For the first time, I feel it.

I'm used to turning my nerves to metal, but now they're molten and liquid, every cell buzzing. Fiery. Fear isn't just a feeling in your head. It swallows you whole.

Racing is dangerous. I know. I've always known it. But the *when*—the real end—that's been unknown. And in case it was ever in question, I'm well aware of my immortality complex—orphanage psych evals were good for something. I mean, I've never lost a race. Or broken a bone. And I can never get the Blight. Course I act like I'm immortal.

But with my options dwindling faster than the water in my tank, I remember I ain't made of metal. And if I do make it, not only do I lose the win, but there's no way that I'll be able to survey Quad Nine, so I'll lose that money too.

Aven can't afford my losing. Nights of hearing her howl from headaches caused by the tumor, me knowing it's my fault she's hurting . . . it'll be too much for us.

My Rimbo's nose slices into the water. Against the window, a great splash crashes. I remember too late that I should have tried to open it before going under.

Will the glass hold? Maybe I should have had it replaced . . . maybe it really is too old.

Right, I remind myself. *Like I could have seen this coming.*

Any moment now I bet it will crack directly over my head. Bust open, sending a dozen pointy daggers down on me.

For the briefest instant the tail nods against the surface, readying itself to sink. Then the nose and front wheel suck slowly underwater.

My Rimbo ain't airtight and so, within moments, water begins to flow through the unsealed spaces. I tug at the moonroof, trying to slide it open, but the water's weight is too heavy. Nothing budges. My Hessians feel the leak first, poor things, and then my toes feel cold and wet.

The water is rising.

4

1:40 A.M., SATURDAY

I'm pounding against the glass, now wishing it *would* crack. Water splashes inside the mobile, all around me. Grimy, icy slush finds my mouth. I close my eyes, struggling to get out through the moonroof, pushing against it. My Rimbo drops into the sunken city. I open my eyes despite the cold and the water. Beyond the roof, giant-sized buildings loom, towers of brick with the windows crashed in. I can't stop looking—I can't stop trying.

It takes less than a minute for the water to reach my neck.

Despite it all, I'm thankful for my leather jumpsuit. It's keeping me warm. Relatively speaking, that is. I press my mouth against the glass and take a deep breath, one that I hope will last me long enough.

As the water starts clinging to the ends of my hair, moves to soak the roots and all of my scalp, Aven appears in my mind.

Like a punch to the gut. A sister who is not my sister—as close a resemblance to each other as a swan has to a pigeon, and I'm the pigeon. Take everything about me, flip it on its head to get its opposite—that's Aven. She's too good . . . for me, for the world. Why did she pick me? Of all the people in Nale's orphanage, she picked me.

Did she think I could protect her?

Selfish, reckless . . . I didn't even want her around to start.

Panic starts ticking away in my chest until I can actually feel my heart bombing around in my rib cage. What have I done? Losing the money would have been bad, but was it really worse than her losing *me*? Without thinking, I open my mouth just a little bit. A trickle of water flows in. Fear is in my mouth too, with an aftertaste like acid.

The thing I can't leave—it isn't life. It's Aven.

The inside of the mobile is now filled. I tug again at the roof—it doesn't budge. The pressure inside should have equalized against the outside right about now. My arms move too slow; I slog through the water, my hand fumbling for the knife I keep strapped inside my boot. Above, the watery ceiling has turned so dark and I can't tell how far I've sunk. Has this taken seconds? Minutes? I can't tell. . . . My mind's all dizzied. I can't panic. I *won't* panic.

Using what energy I've got left, I spear the tip of my knife into the glass window.

Nothing.

I pound again on the window, trying to weaken the spot.

Still nothing, but I think I see a slight webbing. The blade's cracked the window, barely.

Hoping the third time really is the charm, I go full force. I hurtle myself and the knife into the window.

It works.

The glass cracks, breaks into pebbles. They float toward my face. I shield myself and shimmy through the side window, avoiding the fragments jutting from the frame.

Out in the open channel, my body feels weightless, drifting.

Next to me, my Rimbo slams into a building, loosening some of the bricks. Debris barrages down, a slow-motion shower of stone and concrete pieces. I can't avoid them all. All I can do is dodge them, one by one. Dog-paddle. Push myself backward. Then, somewhere along my forehead, sharpness and fire are all I feel.

A bloom of red appears before my eyes.

A square shape bashes into my shoulder. Eyelids grow heavy; I can't make myself want to stay awake. The swirling underwater city fades into jagged shapes and shades of brown. Navy, too. It's as if the sky is somehow underwater, and I'm sinking into a galaxy of black.

Air hunger forces my eyes open. My body heaves, convulses. I ignore the need to open my mouth. *How long was I out?* It don't matter. Instinct overrides thought. My body knows what to do, even if exhaustion has made my brain useless.

I swim. Up.

Can't get there fast enough. Arms grow heavier. I can barely feel my legs, though my Hessians are still on, I think. Thank goodness.

Then I can't help it—I open my mouth. Water rushes in,

salty and cold. So cold, it makes my teeth ache. It trickles down my throat, knifing my lungs. I gag, I push myself up.

It feels like hours since I came to. Years since I went under. Years till I reach the surface.

Aven. The race. The money. My Rimbo. All of it pulls me back to myself like the riptide of a tsunami. I need to get out of the water.

Each stroke tears at my muscles. Something as light as water has never felt heavier to anyone, anywhere. It's lead. My body is lead. It's like lead pushing lead, and I can't even be sure I'm moving.

Am I moving?

Then, a slow shift in darkness. From the black of a raisin to the black of sun-bleached asphalt.

I believe it only when my hands shoot out of the frigid water. Next, my elbows. Then forehead. My nose. My mouth, choking and retching, is last.

Hard and fast, I suck the sharp air into my lungs. It stings. Heady with relief, I close my eyes. My body is so tired, though, it forgets to tread water. Again, I go under. *Stupid.* I push myself up, once, twice. *Swim.*

I'm numb to the cold now, but my brain knows enough to tell my arms to paddle and my legs to kick. Once more, I force my head above the surface.

Beside me, the brick siding of a wall, and not too far off, an escape ladder.

I swim—flail, more like it—through the dank canal, inching my way closer to the ladder. When I reach it, I throw myself out of the water, trying to catch the bottom rung so that I can pull it down. I catch it in my grip, and the ladder collapses down. Chips of white paint and rust flake off.

Ignoring the ladder's shake, I pull myself up. Never did like those chin-ups they made me do during DI training, but now I'm grateful. A few rungs later and I'm level with a huge window, cracked open wide and covered with algae. It tinges the sharp edges with green, makes them look smooth.

Finally, I'm close enough to the windowsill that I can swing myself half in the building, half out of it. Glass crunches under my fingers. I can hear it, the only reason why it registers on my radar, not because I can feel anything. Well, there's one perk to being nearly paralyzed from cold, I guess. Shards rip the leather at my thigh—skin too, possibly, though I can't feel it.

Both feet touch ground at last. I collapse onto the floor, grasping for flimsy, disoriented threads of thought. My blood pools on a mildewed carpet, and my teeth dance around in my mouth. I clench my jaw to still them. One look at my hands shows me they're shredded from the windowsill and have turned a delightful shade of blue. I imagine my lips are about the same.

A heavy panting—*my* heavy panting—brings me to myself. I wipe my face of the brack water and my hand comes back red. Only then do I notice the deep sting of a gash somewhere around my temple. I flex my hands, watching the red squeeze from each cut. I may as well be a robot, nerve free. Don't feel a thing. On my wrist, my cuffcomm blinks a fluorescent red through a cracked screen. This one is water resistant, but the crack must've allowed some in. Still, it's a reminder that so long as I've got a heartbeat, I've got a job.

I feel for my video comm, though it wouldn't do me any good with my cuffcomm not working. It's gone, anyway. Must have lost it in the crash.

Benny will be able to approximate my location from the GPS in my Rimbo, though, so he'll send someone for me, I'm sure of it. Which means I don't have much time. I may have lost the race, but I can still scout for that Justin guy. At that thought, a wave of adrenaline courses through. Makes me forget for a moment how broken I am.

I try to stand but my legs wobble and I lose my balance. Then I feel myself shaking from the bottom up. This irritates me—I've got to scout before anyone gets here. But my thermal homeostasis has just been given an icy-cold middle finger, and I need to get warm. That's step one.

I force my Hessians to carry me around the perimeter. Until I can arrange heat, movement is key. Get the blood pumping. I pass old bulletin boards, whiteboards, and wooden chairs, too, scattered along the floor. Peeling paint and tiny, scampering critters tell me that this place has been deserted since the Wash Out. With each step, the floor creaks. Hope this building doesn't collapse with me in it— they can go under so easily, and my Rimbo hit the thing real good.

Feeling for my utility belt, I remember the lighter and my flashlight—it turns freshwater neon, but I can still use it. I pull the lighter out of my belt, removing it from some elastic lining that seems waterproof.

Don't know for sure, as I've never needed to look.

To get the lighter started, I roll my finger over the metal.

Nothing but sparks. With a few more flicks, I have a flame—
a small one, sure, but it will do. My utility belt has already
proven handy and I say a secret thanks to Benny for making
me wear it all these years. "For your protection," he'd say,
and I'd take the belt and hook it on to humor him. Never
thought I'd actually *need* any of this junk, aside from the
flashlight. And even that, well . . . it's been years since we've
found a local freshwater spring in these parts. I never expect
I'll *need* the flashlight.

Now for some dry fabric. I start opening all the doors on
this level, hoping that one of them is a closet. When I find
one with a few coats, I toss a whole pile of musty, moth-eaten
fabric to the ground and light the edges on fire. I'm not worried about the building burning down—everything here is
damp from tide fluctuations.

After some blowing, the coats go up in flames. I get as close
to the growing fire as I can without burning my jumper off,
then step out of my Hessians to let my feet roast.

The blood creeps back to my extremities, and every sensation is magnified. Painfully so. It's worse than being numb,
I realize. I know it won't last long, that my skin just has to
get used to this new and improved, fully functional body
temperature, but that don't make it any easier.

I give myself two minutes, then slide my Hessians back
onto my feet—they're still wet and I'd rather go barefoot, but
I'm not stupid. I stamp out what's left of the glowing, charred
coats with my soles.

Grabbing one of the last coats from the closet, I make my
way down into the stairwell. If freshwater is going to be

anywhere, it'll be either ground level or under the basement—
Blues training, and common sense, taught me that.

It's dark so I flip on the flashlight, clutching the banister
the whole way. I'm in no shape to be doing this; my knees
rattle like a madman's and the cold is creeping under my
skin again, but on the upside, that gash on my temple feels
like it's clotted.

Need to keep moving.

The plan is to first find out if the lower levels are underwater.

I step out into the ninth floor, officially below the water
level. The stairwell isn't flooded, so I'll make an educated
guess and say that the lower floors probably aren't as well.
The ninth floor looks much the same.

But there's one key difference: the windows. Every single
window on this floor has been patched up with bricks and
mortar. Why would someone do that? If they wanted to pre-
serve the building, why is this place deserted? And why stop
just at the water level?

It don't make much sense.

Back in the stairwell, I pick up my pace. By now, the race
is probably over. Someone should be coming for me.

Level after level, staircase after staircase . . . my head starts
to spin and nausea sets in just as I realize I'm going to have to
walk back *up*. I groan out loud—the sound rebounds off the
stairwell, a reminder that I'm the only one in here.

For some reason, this makes me nervous. As though smashing my mobile into the canal and busting up my face haven't
already made me nervous . . . But the quiet—a deep, echoing

kind—lets me know how alone I really am. How I could pass out here and never come to, and no one would find me. Just some crazy dragster, turning to bone in a rotting stairwell. That's the kind of realization I don't need to be reminded of at every turn.

When I finally reach the ground level . . . well, when I reach what *was* the ground level before the waters rose, I see signs dangling from the ceiling. They've got letters and numbers on them, reading "uptown" or "downtown."

This was a subway—one of those underground trains people used to get around on. The Blues taught me about subways early on, during my scout training.

The tunnels continue a ways in the distance, lines of rusted track laid out for miles. If I strain my ears, I can hear droplets of water sounding off, rhythmic, like a busted faucet in the underground. Seeing as I'm fifteen stories underwater, there's probably a leak *somewhere*—I don't want to get my hopes up.

Still, I glance around, listen for a direction. Though I don't expect to find anything, at least this way I'll have something to tell Officer Cory. The building is, after all, in Quad Nine. He never specified *where* in the quadrant I needed to look.

This flashlight is so genius right now.

I flip it on and head right. Random pools of water—brack or rain, I don't know—gather under the tracks. The beam turns them bright and I follow the *drip-drip-drip*-ing way back into the dark.

Every few steps I slow. Stop. Listen—to the droplets and their echo.

I continue walking, then I pause. *Wait.*

They're doing more than that. . . . I hear something at the tail end—a final sound, like water trickling into a full-up bucket. The sound of water as it falls into even more water. For a moment my heart does a jig. *It could be . . .* I think, almost allowing myself to hope.

I inhale, and I let the steady rhythm of its falling lead the way. Like it's calling to me, speaking.

5

2:00 A.M., SATURDAY

I keep on moving—the sound is so loud, it must be next to me—but the farther I walk, the farther away it gets. *Where'd it go?* I backtrack until I can hear it again, but there's nothing in front, and nothing behind.

Next to me, maybe?

I press my ears to the tunnel walls. Sure enough, I find it: the spot where the sound is loudest. But what am I supposed to do, walk through walls? I shine the beam along the grime-covered tunnel looking for a crack, a crevice . . . anything.

Then I see it: a hole. Made from a different material than the tunnel walls.

The hole is, of course, filled in with bricks.

Ugh. I'm really starting to hate bricks—first the knock on the head, now this. I steady my foot and aim to kick the things, when I realize one crucial difference. This time there is no mortar.

These bricks were meant to be removed.

And who better to remove them than me? I get down on all fours and start hammering away at them with my flashlight. After each swing, it shakes on and off like a strobe light. The flashing makes me dizzy, so when I give the final blow that ends its life as a flashlight and turns it into an official hammer, I'm almost happy. Darkness coats the tunnel again.

I pull all my air tight between my lungs—hadn't realized what a comfort the light was. . . .

You won't get lost. . . .

There's left, there's right, and there's up.

The segments loosen, and since I don't want to have to crawl into a pile of bricks, I try to push them to either side of the hole using the flashlight turned hammer. When I've removed enough of the bricks that I can crawl through the opening, I take my coat off to get rid of some of my bulk.

My kneecaps crush into the gravel and whatever else is sharp and pointy underneath me. I slide forward, inch by inch. Without the light, I have no sense of how large the interior is. I whistle. The sound doesn't carry far—it's cramped in here. There's a dripping, and it's coming from a few different sources along the ceiling, but I can't see where. I keep on inching, continuing the crawl. My palms pick up pebbles as I slide along.

An ache in my wrists tells me the ground slopes. I put my left hand down, then my right, then left. . . .

A slippery wet against my fingertips. My wrists, all the

way to my elbows, sink down, and then—

It's too late. *More water.* Hot water, and a little bit slimy, too—I'm in it headfirst, flailing around, splashing and kicking and trying to right myself. Out of habit I choke out the stuff, expecting sour, dank, brackish bitterness.

Only I find none.

This water, it's *sweet.*

I get my head back to where the air is—tonight's theme—still choking from the surprise of it all. It's hot, and it's sweet, with no trace of the saline that's made the local reservoirs undrinkable. I bob around for a few moments, allowing myself to luxuriate. This is about as close as I've gotten to a bubble bath in years. Who cares that it's made of ancient subway mud?

As I dog-paddle to get a sense of the space, I can tell it's small. Not much wider than seven feet across. I can tell, because though the tunnel is mostly dark, a tiny orb of light is glowing neon just a few feet below the surface—my flashlight. It's shining like new, clinging to a ledge. *Great.* Now *it works*—I reach for it, and then realize: It's glowing. Not just glowing . . .

Neon purple. The thing is glowing neon purple.

I don't believe it.

I dive down, thanking the subway gods for the warmth of the water. I don't think I could've taken any more cold. Keeping my eyes open till I have the light in my hand, I find myself wincing out of habit, expecting salt water to burn my eyes. But no, nothing.

Soon as I have the flashlight back in my hand, the fact of

what I have, literally, fallen into hits me. A hot spring would have been bizarre enough, though there is a fault line around these parts, somewhere. But that's not all: *freshwater.*

I never really believed I'd find it. Hoped, sure. In a probably-not-gonna-happen sort of way. Do I even remember the procedure for what to do after finding it?

Wait . . . Yes, I do. My flashlight . . . I'd totally forgotten— that's where the test tube is stored.

And I used the thing as a hammer. *Brack—how could you have forgotten?*

Hey, head trauma? I remind myself. If ever I deserved a little slack, it would be now.

I unscrew the back of the light. . . . A cork falls out, followed by teensy glass pieces. Wonderful.

To the canteen, then.

Removing the cap, I dunk the bottle into the spring. Once it's filled to the brim, I almost can't help myself . . . I have to taste it. I shouldn't. Who knows what's in the stuff? But I've already swallowed gulpfuls, thanks to falling in. If I'm going to get sick, the damage has already been done.

I bring the canteen to my lips. Pull it away before it touches. Then, I drink.

The fresh tastes so much better—cleaner, purer—than the rainwater from the dinky drainage systems everyone in the Ward has.

One gulp follows another. I didn't realize how thirsty I was. I chug until my stomach feels jiggly as a water balloon, and when I'm done, I refill the canteen for Boss.

A slight nausea sets in and I want nothing more than firm

ground beneath me, so I swim around the edge of the spring. Digging my fingers into the slippery, spongelike surface around the pool's edge, I steady myself and with one push, pull myself from the pool.

Still heady with the taste of the spring water on my tongue, I begin the awkward, plodding wriggle back through the crawl space into the tunnel. Exhaustion has begun to settle in—thank goodness for these walls, they keep me balanced, but I have to remember to lift my feet or I'll trip on the rails.

And then a tingling sensation starts behind my eyeballs.

Not uncomfortable. At first. The tingle soon becomes a prickle, which in turn becomes a burn. My eyes water. Salt tears coat my cheeks, the cuts—all of which have started to sting. But it's worse than that. Across my entire face, the scrapes and the fresh cuts also begin to burn.

Like a bonfire, the fire grows and it grows, and soon enough the fire starts to itch, and hell, do I want to scratch. I don't know what's going on. My lips, my forehead . . . if I had nails I'd be raking them over my skin right now.

I'm about to rub at my cheeks, but then my hands, my arms, every microscopic cell in my body also feels like they've been doused in gasoline, then lit on fire. I think I hear myself calling out to the stairwell, but I know I'm alone. *Lit on fire.*

And here I am. Fifteen stories underwater, but with no way to quit the burn.

6

2:20 A.M., SATURDAY

I'm calling into the stairwell, or I'm hearing a noise from the stairwell. I don't even know . . . the scratching . . . *I'm doused.* I'm hallucinating, I must be hallucinating. None of it was real—the hot spring, the freshwater. That's the only thing that makes sense. . . .

If none of it makes sense.

But in the stairwell, a noise. *Am I making it up?*

I speak out, voice hoarse and quaking, just in case. "Hello?"

The word comes out too weak for even me to hear. Again, "Hello?" I yell, louder this time. I'm draining my energy, shrieking like this, but I don't care about that either. If someone is there, I want them to hear me loud and clear. I open my eyes, but everything's blurry through the tears.

Boots—*Thunk, thunk. Thunk, thunk.* Two at a time, then silence. A scraping, the squeak of palms gripping a wooden banister.

It's gotta be Terrence. Benny would've told him where my Rimbo crashed, and Ter's got that Omni now.

The thunking noise closes in. "Stay right there, Ren. I'm coming for you."

That voice—I know that voice. It's not Terrence's.

Please don't let it be him . . . please don't let it be him, I whisper to myself. *Derek can't see me like this.*

But here he comes, finally in my line of sight, his coppery head of hair bright and glinting, even in the dark of the stairwell. Or maybe it's not that it's so bright. Maybe it's just that I'd know him even if I were blind, which isn't too far from the truth right now. I can barely open my eyes—the feverish feeling is gone, but not the itch.

"Derek," I mumble. My bookie. The only guy who makes me forget my words with no more than a look.

He hurtles down the stairs, trousers slick, white collared shirt soaked and hugging his skin. He must have swum from the mobile to get into the building.

The thought makes me warm.

Then he leans over me, lacing his fingers behind my back and knees. That's when I get really hot. I'm about to resist—I can still walk, I have legs after all—but he lifts me up so easily, as though I weigh no more than a small bird. And I may be small, but I'm not light.

"How on earth did you get all the way down here?" he asks, almost to himself, voice muffled.

When I start to answer, he tells me, "*Shh* . . . it's okay. Save your energy."

His breath on my face—it burns my cheeks, already scalding. I'm closer to his skin than I've ever been, millimeters between us. I could press my nose to his tattoo. A small, graying circle symbol just under his earlobe that I've always known was there, but I've never been close enough to get a look at. I could touch my lips to it if I wanted, nip at it the way the orphanage cat used to give Aven and me love bites.

I must be delirious.

I see all his tiny, almost invisible freckles, too. Dozens that I never knew he had, dotting his cheeks and nose and jaw. I want to say something—I have freckles too—but, like always, my thoughts are mealy mush when I'm around him.

Avoiding his eyes is the only way I can keep my head straight with him near. I turn my gaze to anything else, though there's not much to look at. Some lovely banisters to my right. And left. Stairs, too. Those will do. Just not his eyes.

For some inexplicable reason, much as I don't want to, I lean into him. My body sinks against his arms and chest. *Okay*, I tell myself. *It's okay—you're tired. You've had a rough day. This is your survival at stake, right?*

Immediately my cheeks feel better against the wet of his shirt. The itch fades.

He carries me the whole way to the top, his breathing barely labored. *Boy's in shape.* When we come to the windowsill that I came in through, I push away from him, signaling to him to put me down.

I'm not going back in the water. . . . Already too wet. Cold. *No.* Derek takes some more coats from the closet and drapes them over the windowsill. I don't know what he's doing—I watch him straddle the sill, sitting on the coats. My heart's beating like it does before the races, but for an entirely different reason. I'm still wrapped up in his arms.

Then an orange Omni's headlights break through the darkness under the water, setting the channel aglow. If I weren't feeling like absolute crap, I might find it sort of pretty.

Terrence steers closer to the window, and Derek swings one leg into the moonroof, steadying the mobile. He does it just like he's mounting a horse, like they do in the pictures I've seen during my history classes back in the orphanage. He sets me atop the roof, careful, straddling himself behind me. My spine curves into his abdomen.

I may feel terrible, but I'm not too far gone to take a mental note of his nice, strong muscu—*Stop, Ren.*

This attraction I have is from afar. He can't know I'm into him, he's my bookie. Our relationship is strictly business. He gives me my winnings from the races, we make small talk, and I go. I know he cares about me; he's always warning me of the "dangers of racing," something I'm sure he doesn't do with the other racers. And I know it's not 'cause I'm "just a girl"—I'm always winning.

But there's caring and there's *caring.*

My energy seems to be returning now that Derek's obscenely hot—*ahem . . . warm, as in temperature*—body presses up behind me. I begin to lower myself into the Omni, but Derek's hands cup under my armpits, dangerously close to other places, and he helps me down. Normally I'd be chafing at this sort of thing. I'm a girl who can handle her own, but right now I'm content to play the damsel. And to be honest,

I'm not entirely playing. I might even blush, and I wouldn't be playing at that either.

"Yo, Ter," I croak, seeing him up front at the wheel. "Th-th-thanks for coming to pick me up." I smile weakly. He looks in the rearview mirror, brows knitted together, clearly anxious. "Who won?" Curiosity always gets the best of me.

"You worry about getting warm," Terrence tells me from the front seat.

I grunt. He probably won. Better than Kent or Jones winning, though, I remind myself.

I open my mouth to tell him about the spring, but then I remember—it was a scouting mission, and no one, not even Ter, my closest friend, can know I work for the Blues.

Besides, the *Codes and Violations Handbook* states that any findings on a scouting mission must first be reported to the Blues' base. Never tell civilians anything. Makes sense, I suppose, not telling civilians. Can't have hordes of people fed up with crappy rainwater drainage systems—draining acid rain, at that—flocking to a structurally unsafe abandoned building all at once. Recipe for disaster.

I keep my mouth shut, but that giddy feeling about my discovery, combined with Derek's warm, muscled body all pressed up against my side, makes me feel nothing short of bliss. I choose to ignore pain at this particular moment. And then, of course, reality does its thing.

My postrace report to the boss. I've never missed a report. I don't even know what the procedure is. . . . Will Chief punish me? A subzero fear works its way up my spine. *It's okay,* I tell myself. *It's okay.* He must've heard about the accident by now. He'll know I haven't bailed.

Still, I can't help the shivers once they start in.

Derek rubs his hands together nervously. "You should really get out of your . . ." He coughs a little, as if not wanting to finish his sentence.

He thinks I'm shivering because I'm cold. . . .

"Terrence brought a pair of sweats you can change into."

I almost gather the energy to full-on belly laugh. Now, I'd be lying if I said that the thought of being in a state of undress with Derek hadn't crossed my mind at one point or another. But this is a whole different story. No way, I am *not* getting naked in a mobile full of boys. "Psht. You wish," I spit out. I'll stay cold in my shredded, shrunken leather getup, thank you very much.

A line of static comes in through Ter's headset. He holds down the green button by the mouthpiece. "Come in?" He releases the button, then looks back.

"She with you, Terrence?" Even through the low-grade mic, I can hear Benson's fear.

"Sure is," Terrence replies with a heaving sigh.

"You okay, kiddo?" Benny asks.

He never calls me "kiddo." I race with the big boys, and I get treated accordingly. But the way he says this now, well, he must be feeling especially mushy.

Terrence passes the headset to the backseat and I slip it over my ears, clicking the green button. "Fantastico, B. Just a few scrapes." I pause, remembering how I have to meet up with Justin. "I'll see you at the Tank in an hour," I say, my hand instinctively moving to the tender gash on my forehead.

At least it's not dripping anymore. That was annoying. And painful, obviously.

"The Tank, Ren?"

The line goes silent, and Ter and Derek exchange glances in the rearview mirror.

I groan, embarrassed that I forgot. A racer goes down, the after-party gets postponed a night. A nice bit of respect in a not-so-respectful industry. "Oh. Right," I mumble, unhappy. I don't like delaying my meeting with Officer Cory.

"It's a good thing, Ren." Derek's eyes catch mine, and I glance away. He pulls a scratchy wool blanket from underneath the seat and drapes it over my shoulders and around my waist. "You need rest." And though it doesn't do much to warm me, I'll admit that it's nice when he starts to rub the blanket over my leather sleeves.

Looking up at Terrence and Derek, I'm amazed. It still amazes me . . . having people who care. The only missing piece is Aven. For a second I'm angry she's not with me, even though she's home, barely moving these days, and couldn't make it here if she tried. Still. I nearly died.

She's the only person I really want with me right now.

"Let's hitch your mobile now, too. . . . Will you last that long? I can come back for it if you'd rather," Terrence asks.

"Let's just get her home, Terrence," Derek responds. "She needs to get warm. I think the worst is over, but still."

"No, really, I'm—"

"Later. He'll come back for it later," he interrupts.

I do not want to leave my Rimbo all crunched and crushed at the bottom of the channels, but I have no choice. "Fine,"

I grumble. Whatever. It's clearly not fine, but so long as my Rimbo gets to Benson's garage, I'll be okay. Then he can fix her up, find out what happened to "Plan B" and why it bunked out on me.

"Ter, you know where Ren's place is from here?" Derek asks.

My fists ball up instinctively. "*No*—not like this. Aven . . ." I cry out.

For a moment, they're both quiet. Tense.

I never talk about Aven. Not even to Ter, and he knew her from the start, at Nale's. They learned early on not to bring her up unless I did. Which I usually don't.

"If she sees me like this she'll be so worried. I have to get cleaned up first. Someplace else . . . please."

Terrence nods, but answers sheepishly, "I still live at home, with my dad. So unless you want to go to the hospital, which is exactly where my pops will make you go, my place is a negatory."

I know where this is going. I need to get myself some girl-friends.

"Fine. Ter, take Ren to my place."

7

4:15 A.M., SATURDAY

All this clean water, and here I am just *floating* around in it. I've always known Derek was rich; he's *my* bookie after all. But this is obscene.

Is this what it will be like for everyone in the Ward once the Blues get to piping off that spring?

Thanks to Yours Truly.

I allow myself a bit of brag time in my head, because hey, I did almost die on that mission of theirs. That's worth something. I laugh to myself, buzzing from tonight's events. The sound echoes like gunfire against the marble bathroom walls. *Derek's* bathroom walls.

Man, do I love bubbles. I love bubbles so much that if I could be anything in the whole universe, it would be a bubble. Prepop, of course. Postpop and they're, well, gone.

Bubbles just float around, not a care in the world, multi-colored *and* clear, would you believe it?

There's this one bubble doing a balancing act on my big toe right now. I dip my fingers in the sudsy bathwater and, sticking my tongue out as I do when aiming really, really hard, I flick my finger, sending a splash its way. But it's a persistent bugger. *No!* it says. *I will not go down without a fight!*

It's nice not being dead, you know?

It's especially nice not being dead, in Derek's tub.

The bathwater starts to feel cool, so I reach for the shiny porcelain handle and add more hot. Indulgent, I know.

The water comes streaming from the faucet like pure gold. And all this water! He must have a drainage system the size of Africa. Bet it takes up his entire roof, which means he owns the building.

Come to think of it . . . which building am I even in?

Leaning my head against the hammered brass tub, I try to remember the ride back, during which I was completely zombified. Last thing I recall is dozing off on Derek's shoulder.

I have no idea where in the Ward we are.

I do know I was half-asleep by the time he set me in the tub—the only way to get my temp up. He must've been fretting about the possibility of my getting hypothermia. Eventually, when I realized I was being lowered into even *more* water, I woke. And there Derek was, sitting over me in my birthday suit.

So yeah. There I was, naked in front of Derek. Me. Naked. In front of Derek.

And I didn't even get to enjoy it!

That's when I screamed like a banshee outta hell.

"Okay, okay! I just wanted to make sure you didn't drown. Again."

"OUT," I'd said, not bothering to correct him that I did not, in fact, drown a first time. And out he went.

What an effed-up night. It's like all my dreams are coming true—finding freshwater, getting closer to Derek—but in this really messed-up way.

My mind drifts to other things, like how I'm gonna handle Officer Cory, and the logistics of this freshwater discovery. And the fact that I missed my report to boss man. I bet he's already messaged my backup cuffcomm at home to reschedule. I've *never* missed a report before—I don't mess around with these guys. Never wanted to give them a reason to cut my pay. We couldn't afford that.

I sink my head underwater, eyes open. Let the heat flood over, watching a watery mosaic of light and soapy blue. Sound becomes cocoonish, as if the world only exists within a few inches of my skull.

I found fresh.

I found *fresh*.

Then why does it feel like nothing's changed? Why does it feel like nothing's better?

The answer is easy.

My sister is still going to die, whether or not Justin Cory quadruples his offer, whether or not everyone gets their fair share of the spring. Whether or not I work for the Blues, or race, or live, or bite it. Whether or not anything. She just is.

All the fresh in the world can't keep Aven alive.

I look at my arm without thinking, to the raised Xs there.

She has only two. Indoors, the Blues don't test. We talked about bringing her to the hospital, but there's just not enough money. Cheaper to buy the pain meds black market, and have the doctor make a house call when we're flush with green from hefty winnings.

The last doctor gave her three months.

I dig my nails into my palms. How dare he give her an expiration date? She's not an effing carton of milk.

And when she does "expire"?

I'm back to being alone, just like how it was before I met her.

Whatever. She's already a corpse. You're not losing much.

I force myself to unclench my fists, hating myself for even thinking that. It's not true, not always, though these days she's less and less herself. There's a rock in my throat—if I cried it would go away, but I can't.

Water trickles into my ear canals, replacing the air. The sensation, so small but so distinct, it's too much. I open my mouth and choke back a wrenching gulp, taking in the sudsy bathwater.

I shoot out of the tub; my chokes become gasps. The drops on my face are no longer just from the bath, I'm sobbing. With the echoes, there are a hundred of me, each one a blubbering mess. I'm so loud, I have to sink back underwater.

The bathroom goes blessedly quiet. Walls can't hear a girl bawling from under here.

I can still hear me, though.

A light *rap rap* jerks me back out of the water, just in time to hear Derek calling through the door, "Everything okay in there?"

Everything *should* be okay, but I'd like to say bugger off, because obviously everything is not okay. "Fine," I shout back just a little too agreeably.

Pulling myself together with a few even exhales, I'm tempted to reach for the water once more, but decide not. It's already cold, no use making it warm again. My fingers are prunish, and that combined with the red scratches makes 'em look like they belong to the undead.

I step out of the tub and slip on Ter's sweatpants. Left next to them, a white T-shirt, small enough to fit me, which makes me wonder where Derek got it. Next, I make sure my canteen of gold is latched, secure, to my belt.

I'm about to leave when it occurs to me—I may want to make full use of whatever else Derek's got up for grabs in this bathroom.

Like, maybe deodorant, if I'm lucky.

On the shelf: soap in the shape of a seahorse (why would anyone have that?), a shiny pink seashell, and a glass bottle of clear liquid, speckled with tiny gold flecks. I push down on the cap and spray the air in front of me.

The smell . . . at first it's just boozy, like a bottle of alcohol that hasn't been opened in too long, but after that, it's sun on water, grass for miles, and a bouquet of real flowers. I imagine, at least. I've heard that stuff is great.

Now this, *this* I want to steal.

And it's probably worth more than a cure for the Blight. But after I spray myself, I leave it be.

I turn to make sure everything is in its place before heading out. I haven't unplugged the drain in the tub—not sure he'd want me to. Gray water can be reused. Derek seems like the type to have plants; he could water them with it. Or maybe he's just rich enough he doesn't have to. Hell, I'd take it with me if I could. Wash some of my clothes.

Voices at the door stop me short.

"Why did you bring her *here*?" It comes out as a hiss. A girl. An angry girl by the sound of it.

I stifle a groan. Only a girlfriend would be over at four in the morning, pissed that another girl was naked in his bathtub.

How could I not have known?

Derek says something in reply, but his voice is too low to pick out the words. I should get closer.

Careful not to make too much noise, I crouch in front of the door.

"I can see it plain as day, Derek," she says. "I know what it looks like, remember?"

"You're paranoid." Derek pauses just as I'm about to twist the brass doorknob. Instead of risking it, I stay close to the tile, craning my neck so that I can hear under the door. "She's just a friend, Kitaneh. Barely that. I'm her bookie, no different from any of the other guys."

My stomach bottoms out, worse than cruising off the side of a building, because that's a feeling I actually enjoy. I always knew I never really had a chance with Derek, but to hear him say it like this . . . it makes me want to puke.

"There are rules," the girl, Kitaneh, says.

I'm sure she's talking about bookies and racers not mixing affairs—no one would like that, but it doesn't matter. He's just said I'm "barely" even a friend. My neck is starting to hurt and the voices sound like they're moving farther away, so I reach up for the door handle—I want to see this girl. When I peek out, I catch a glimpse.

Once more, I'm sick to my stomach.

She's beautiful.

See, I never wanted to be five foot ten, have buttery-yellow hair like Aven's or the kind of baby blues that turn guys into puddles. I never wanted to be pale-skinned, though I could have done with a few less freckles. What I *have* wanted was to be able to run a hand through my hair once in my life, and not always have my own personal spiral skyscrapers on my head. I've wanted my body, small and dense, to be small and willowy. My eyes to be dark, but still interesting.

I've wanted to look like myself, just different.

So, basically . . . her.

It's pretty awful, coming face-to-face with the person who is your version of perfection. Which means Derek didn't bring me here because he *likes* me, he just felt bad.

I swallow the realization like swallowing needles—*I never stood a chance.*

I don't want to go out there. See him. But I know my priorities: Aven. Officer Cory.

Giving in to that silly, stupid feeling I get when Derek's around is not on the list.

If only feelings listened to a list.

8

When I step out of the bathroom, I harden myself before seeing Derek. But I stop walking. Gasp. Too easily distracted by the fact that he lives in a bloody palace: oriental rugs, a brass chandelier, instruments that I don't even think we have names for anymore. So what if it's all a bit threadbare? You don't come by this stuff mint.

He glances up from his spot on a red velvet sofa-looking thing. "How are you feeling?" he asks, eager, and I follow his gaze. It rests for a slow moment on each limb and each scrape, inspecting my injuries.

His looking at me like this makes me feel naked. Even with his hair mussed and tattered clothes—he's still a mess from the rescue—it don't matter. I go lock-lipped and awkward. No idea what to say . . .

Normally, I'd fake it. Act comfortable, play around. Be one of the guys. That's when I was the premier dragster. A winner. Right now, I've never felt more like a little girl, even when I was a little girl—beaten down, saved by a silly white knight from a mess I couldn't get myself out of.

"Good," I say, because it's all I can think of, though I'm fully aware how ridiculous it sounds.

He scowls. Even that looks good on him. Somehow, knowing that he's got a girlfriend has actually made me want him *more*.

"You can tell me that you feel like death, Ren. I'm not your competition." He doesn't even give me time to react to that before pointing toward the table. "Here. I picked up some food. Let's eat."

I eye the goods. "Lihn's," I say, approving. I know Lihn herself. She runs a smart business. Bought up a few abandoned roofs in underpopulated quadrants up north for growing things on.

I like her especially 'cause she gives me free winner's grub. And this food is *real* food. Expensive, and hard to come by. Half homegrown, half air-dropped by her family on the Isle.

"Excellent choice. I'd know these cartons anywhere."

Derek laughs, passing me a pair of porcelain chopsticks and a random carton. "Of course you would. She is right downstairs, after all."

Wait a minute. Lihn's Take-Out is the holy gateway to the betting hall Derek runs. Every time I come to place a bet, Lihn acts as gatekeeper.

"She's downstairs? You live above Lihn's too?"

"The betting hall is a few flights down. I own the build-ing," he tells me.

Well, that answers the question of his drainage system.

"The other racers don't know, though, that I live where I work, and it could be . . . problematic . . . if they found out. So keep this quiet, if you would?"

I cross my heart. "Scout's honor."

Without warning, the TV hologram flashes in front of us.

"Autoupdates," Derek says, when I jerk around, surprised. Most folks in the Ward don't have one of these things—they eat up too much electric, if you even have electric. Which most don't.

Projected onto a canvas of scattered light in front of us stands the 3-D image of a middle-aged man. He's at a podium—Governor Voss. I know him from pictures hanging at DI headquarters. Crowded in front is a group of dapper men and women, some sporting those posh, itchy vests they love to wear on the Isle.

"Governor Voss," one man calls out. "What do you have to say regarding yet *another* outbreak of the Blight on the West Isle? How does it continue to spread? And why can't you stop it?"

Simultaneously, Derek and I roll our eyes.

"Not this again," I mutter. "Whenever some old rich family from the West Isle contracts the Blight, it's news. People in the Ward get sick every day. You don't see us calling press conferences over it."

Still, I can't pull myself from the light screen. The gov-ernor looks much older than in pictures. His face is hard, gaunt. You could cut sheet metal on the angles that make up his jawline. But his nerves betray him—he fidgets at the podium, then catches himself. His body goes still. "A team of scientists is looking into how it continues to spread to the Isle, despite Statute Two." He's slow with his words. "Transmission of HBNC is illegal and still punishable by arrest. Additionally, the local task force conducts random testing for contagious members of the Ward's community.

"To the people of the West Isle: I am doing everything in my power to limit the spread of this disease."

With that, his fist drops down like a hammer.

"What about the water crisis?!" one man yells. "Perhaps it's time for another Appeal to Upstate?"

'Cause that ended so well the first time. People shake their heads and look at him like he's crazy.

The NYC Appeal of 2054 may, or may not, have included heavy-duty artillery against Upstate New York. Upstate just laughed and turned into their own country on us—taking their freshwater with them. Easy enough after the Wash Out.

"There will not be another Appeal," Governor Voss answers, dismissing him with a hand wave. "Unfortunately, Upstate has no intentions of lifting their water embargo, and they continue to auction off the stores. Therefore, until we find a local source, the Division Interial has been working with an undercover scout who conducts regular searches for freshwater. Next question."

Holy brack. That's me he's talking about. It's just . . . it's funny. Me. Important, *outside* of the Ward. Sure, in these parts I'm known, but the West Isle? I almost laugh, but stop myself, hardening my face. Using one chopstick, I spear a dumpling and eat the thing whole. I glance at Derek—he's totally absorbed.

A woman calls out, "Governor Voss, how does Mrs. Voss fare?"

The governor's breathing stalls, his nerves clearly taking a hit. He scratches his chin, rubs at his temples. Of all the questions, this is one that gets to him. "She's not faring any better, but thank you for asking, Lauren. This conference is over." The governor steps down from the stand and leaves the room, followed by his advisors.

The pixels of light from the image scatter on their own.

"What's wrong with his wife?" I ask Derek.

He looks at me, surprised. "The Blight. You hadn't heard?"

"No electricity, remember?" I shake my head, then wince. "Ow," I groan, kneading the nape of my neck with my knuckles. Whiplash is a beast, though it's hardly the worst. Every time I move my face, even just a little, the split skin on my temple pulls open.

"Finally." Derek laughs, his mouth full of noodles. "She's human!"

"What do you mean?" I poke at my gash, looking up, even though I know I won't be able to see it.

"Ren, I think that's the first I've heard you complain all night. You nearly . . ." His expression drops, and he stands up from the sofa. "I should sew that up for you. Might even be able to make sure it doesn't scar."

I'm feeling bold. Maybe it was almost kicking the bucket. Hell, I almost went and demolished the bucket with a two-by-four. "So, you wanna doctor me up?" I ask, one eyebrow raised. "I can play nice."

He laughs, surprised, then confusion registers, and his expression sours.

Too bold, perhaps?

"We almost lost you," he says, serious, his back turned.

We. Not I.

"What about Aven?" Derek goes on, and still I can't see his face. "What would've happened to her if you didn't make it?"

There it is: the one card in the deck that makes me feel guilty about racing. I sink into the plush velvet, suddenly very tired.

He turns. I don't want to look at him, but I can't help myself. He's standing so close to me, I could count his eyelashes if I wanted. I find myself looking up, noticing things like how his eyes match his hair, which makes no rational sense—his hair is as coppery as a penny that's been around the block a few times, and his eyes are perfectly brown. But somehow, all his colors work together.

"You only get one life, Ren. Why are you so damned ready to die?"

I choke back breath, words, and don't even notice when my fist is no longer balled up by my side but close to his body. He's reached for it, turned it upward so that my palm faces the ceiling. My lifelines stretch longer and clearer as he extends one finger at a time.

"Don't you want to make it here?" he asks, drawing a fingertip along the crease of my lifeline. The sensation of just one small square inch of his body pressing against mine is too much—a cross between a tickle and a bonfire. "Or here?" His touch is still on my life, somewhere in the future. The corners of his lips turn down, and I can tell he's eyeing my temple. "I should sew that up for you."

"You said that already," I whisper.

Then he shakes his head, like he's waking up from a dream. I watch the moment end right before my eyes, unable to stop it. Something just broke, and even though I can see him pulling away my hand is still in his, he's still holding it.

"So you *do* wanna play doctor?" I grin, trying to get back whatever we lost.

He steps backward. "I'll get the needle from the med kit."

I really wasn't serious about *that* part of the doctor bit. As much as I might have imagined his hands on me, that particular dream never involved a sharp needle and thread.

"Bleeding's stopped," I insist, now that my head is corked back on. "It's fine. Looks worse than it is. Besides," I say, pausing a moment, "your lady friend wants me gone."

Why did I just say that?

My head must be more uncorked than I thought. You do *not* mention the girlfriend after a Relationship-Defining Moment with Taken Boyfriend! *Bad form, Ren, bad form.*

Derek stops midstep and spins around, two little lines deepening between his brows. "What?"

Well, the damage is done. "I overheard her."

Derek has gone quiet. *Say something else. . . .* "You must have a giant filtration tank."

Wow. I almost want to add "baby" to the end of that to make it sound like a bad euphemism.

"I don't—she's not—" he stammers, not looking at me. "She's my friend Kitaneh. We've known each other for forever."

Jeez, I didn't ask for her frikkin' biography. And really, do I believe him? Maybe they're not "official" or whatever. Hoping to change the subject, I just mutter, "You sure you should've wasted all that fresh on me?"

Derek looks at me like I'm made of stupid. "Your temp was too low. And don't be ridiculous. It wasn't a waste."

I look around for the stairway—things just got too awkward. "I should go. Aven . . ." I start, without any intention of finishing. "Thanks for dinner . . . and everything else."

"You can't thank me for that." His face is sad, like he didn't just save my sorry butt.

"No?"

"No."

I leave it.

Derek backs away, and his gaze drops to my shoulder where, I imagine, it lingers just a little too long. Turning from him, I wish I knew what to say. How to not turn into an tongue-tied mess. I walk to the door that leads out to the stairwell and feel his eyes on me every step of the way.

Forget him, I tell myself, even though telling yourself to forget something is the quickest way to make sure you remember it.

Aven is waiting. Aven, alone, wondering where I am. Not knowing why this race has taken so long. She must be worried.

If she's still . . .

There it is, the only thought that could make me forget all the others. And after a night like tonight—especially a night like tonight—that worry . . .

Home, get home to her.

It's stronger than diesel fuel.

9

6:00 A.M., SATURDAY

Crossing town is a pain—ramshackle rooftop suspension bridges the whole way. Old, rickety things, thrown together early on, when no one knew if the waters would keep rising. And though I'm only one quad north of Derek, the 'Racks are as far east as possible before you hit open ocean.

So . . . lots and lots of bridges.

I grip the cord on either side, fighting against the wobble, and try to ignore how old these planks are. I try not to look down, either. A hundred feet under the bridge, a wide-open canal flows where a street used to run. Instead I look ahead, to a view that's clear for miles. Miles and miles of water. Glancing left, just a few blocks south, I can see where Ter lives. A massive black tower, fitted with electricity. The

Trump Card. Its windows are dark at this hour though, even if it is the Ward's swankiest residential building.

Our well-to-do citizens aren't *that* well-to-do.

I face my route once more, continuing the slog across one bridge, then another, until thick smoke ahead stops me short. Following its trail, I find the fire, then I listen.

I groan when I hear it, the sounds of woozy laughter.

A beggar campout up ahead, atop the roof of a sickhouse for patients who are no longer contagious. They've set up tents pitched from old, holey blankets, around a metal pit filled with burning planks stolen from bridges or boardwalks. This sickhouse isn't much different from a homeless shelter—sick with family don't end up here. Mostly these folk are drifters, hopped up on pain meds that work a little too well—"daggers," they're called, and they're pricey. I should know. Meds don't come free, not even at the sickhouses.

The nearer I get, the tighter I hold on to the canteen at my belt. Of all the times I've had water jacked, this would be the worst. I quicken my pace. As I walk by, I hear them calling out to me for "just a drop."

If they only knew where I got this fresh.

When I'm a hundred feet from the 'Racks, I breathe easier. Up ahead, they loom dreary and gray, but it's home. One tall building built atop an even taller building, entirely of stone slabs. The government erected it right after the Wash Out, keeping few comforts in mind. It was a place for dryness and warmth, no more. No waterfront views for us, not the first four floors anyway—all built without doors or windows. A safety precaution.

Rough to get into, though, seeing as Aven and I live on the first floor. Gotta climb the fire escape up five levels, only to climb down five. Don't usually mind it myself, but after the night I've had, I'm not at my best.

Placing one foot after another, I hoist myself up the ladder to the fifth floor, where I can cut through a window. A little nudging and it unjams, and I swing myself into an old, empty storage room. From there I make for the hallway, where there's a trapdoor for access to all the lower-level corridors.

I climb down those skinny stairs another four flights, landing on the first floor. Apartment 105, only three doors down on the left. A few candles in glass jars line the hallway. Instead of light fixtures, periscopes line the ceilings. Some show views of the roof, the others, views of the boardwalk. I take Aven out here sometimes to remind her what the sun looks like.

Reaching into my pocket, I remember: my suit is at Derek's; my key is in my suit. *Ugh.* It's not even like we really need a key; that would mean that you have something worth locking up. No one's going to be stealing a sick girl like Aven, that's for sure. Beyond her, I've got nothing of value.

Nonetheless, we keep the door locked, which means I have to knock.

I don't like making her walk on her own—she's not steady on her feet these days—but the alternatives are limited: sleep on the floor or go back to Derek's.

I tap quietly, then a little harder when Aven doesn't come. After five more minutes of light knocking, unruly paranoia sets in.

What if she's gone? What if the doctor overestimated how much time she has left?

An image of her sprawled across the floor—she could have been there for hours and I'd never have known it—ties knots in my stomach. A jolt of adrenaline powers up my legs, even though I have no place, no reason, to run; I just want Aven to open the door. I lean into it, rapping harder.

Finally, it creaks open and five twiggy fingers wrap around the edge, dotted with the purple nail polish she found years ago during one of her abandoned-building penny searches. In spite of the Blight, there's still a hint of the old her. Just as quickly as it came, the adrenaline drains away and I'm left with that burning feeling like I ran a marathon. Then I can breathe, and I realize that I hadn't been.

"Hmm?" She's disoriented. Her eyelids droop so heavy it's a wonder she can see at all. A curtain of wispy hair, so blond it's nearly silver, dangles across her face and hides her from view. Even as she is—skin too sallow, features too sharp from poor nutrition, eyes too large—she's beautiful. None of that matters. I love her so much, everything on the outside is irrelevant.

"Morning, Feathers," I say too cheerfully, trying to gauge if my obscenely early wake-up call has somehow placed her closer to death's door, though I know it's irrational.

Aven doesn't say a word, just moves away from the door.

I step in and close it behind me, flipping on the flashlight from my tool belt. The strange egg-shaped beam bounces round the room, and I use it to draw Aven a path to her bed. We walk together, one of my arms wrapped around her waist, the other steadying her by the shoulder.

She crawls in, angling her head so that there's no pressure on the tumor.

"How's the noggin?" I sit on the bed next to her, pulling the covers up so that she's warm enough—the night's still cold.

No answer. Not a good sign.

"Why didn't you comm me?" I ask. "That's why you have the thing. I could've had a neighbor check in . . ."

"It's not so bad," she insists, but her chin drops ever so slightly and her eyelids flutter open and closed.

I know Aven's every gesture. This one means the hurt is worse than she's letting on. "I'm getting the Dilameth," I tell her, and I reach my arm under the bed and grab the orange bottle.

Daggers. Just one of these pills costs more than a month's worth of protein bars. They're so potent, Blight victims, along with half the city's beggars, love 'em, if they can get their hands on the stuff.

I fish one out of the bottle. Aven opens her mouth and I drop it under her tongue.

The pill dissolves almost instantly, gets circulated into her bloodstream. Within minutes she'll be comfortable. I watch it start to work; the furrow between her brows relaxes and she's smiling, almost.

This will last about eight hours. Dilameth shuts off the brain's pain receptors—it does something so that the body registers pain as pleasure. That's why it's such a popular drug. You can have the tumors anywhere, at any stage, and it works just the same. Daggers won't fix anything, though. The tumor's still a death sentence.

"Is it summer yet?" Aven says, through a yawn.

If I didn't know her so well, I might think that the tumor lodged in her brain has finally taken its toll on her mental faculties. But I do know her. This is her. What's left of her, anyway.

"Hate to disappoint, darlin'."

She looks at me through still half-closed eyes. "Yes, it is summer," she says, resting her hand on my knee.

"I'm sorry I woke you," I say quietly. "You feel better now?"

Aven ignores the question. "The race went late tonight." Then she sees something disturbing, like my face, for instance. "What's this?" She looks a little closer at my temple, pulling her tangled, whitish hair to one side. Her hazel eyes go wide. She stifles a gasp. "What happened?"

I want to tell her everything. The race, the accident. *Water.*

And isn't this awful . . . but most of all I want to tell her about Derek. Would it be too much to ask? To be a girl for five minutes? I'd tell her how he *saved* me, sort of. How afterward I was naked, though it was much tamer than it sounds.

But I can't tell her this, because she's dying, and somehow that means I need to shut my life up in a box from her. *For* her. How do you tell someone who's three months from dead that you're all boo-hoo because your crush doesn't fancy you? You don't. They'll always have bigger things to worry about than your sorry love life.

Aven eyes the largest of the cuts on my face, her fingers dangerously close. Instead of answering, I just say, "Hey, easy—you don't want to touch," and dodge the graze of her hand. I slide off the bed, thinking I should take a look at the abstract art that's been made of my face.

I decide against it. Only going to make me depressed. Not only do I have to go to the Tank tonight as a loser, but I have to go looking like this. Now, I'm not vain, but a girl's gotta draw the line *somewhere.*

"Ren!" Aven snaps with more gusto than I thought she had left in her. "Earth to Ren?"

"Hmm?"

"What's wrong with your face?"

"What's wrong with *your* face?" I answer, knowing she'll laugh. But I'm in a bind. I don't want to tell her how close I was to The End.

"An accident. No big deal." Not quite a lie, but nearly. If she knew how bad it was . . .

"You hurt?" Her voice is thin as a breeze, but I can tell she wants to ask more questions. I cut her off before she gets too worked up.

"Don't worry, I'm made of bricks." I almost died of them, too. "I lost the race. . . ."

For just a moment, Aven scrunches her face up tight, confusion registering. Then she shrugs. "We'll get by." She says it with such confidence that I have to think my bedridden fourteen-year-old sister is stronger than I know.

Am I really not going to talk about the fresh find?

Screw the *Codes and Violations Handbook.* Something tells me a fourteen-year-old girl, nearly dead from the Blight, might compromise the mission. I may not feel right talking to her about Derek, but this . . . this I can tell her.

"We won't have to." I kneel down on the floor and cross my arms over the quilt, resting my chin on my wrists. "Aven, I've got a secret."

"Oooh." She smiles, barely. "I hope it's going to make me feel better about your face looking like a scratching post for Moo."

"Don't make me sad," I say. "I miss Moo." She loved the spotted stray tabby more, I'm sure of it. The cat came around when we lived in the orphanage, and we haven't seen him since we left.

She doesn't say anything, just closes her eyes, smiling. "Mooooo." A giggle breaks away from her, thin and gone too fast. When she opens her eyes again, all she says is, "Secret."

I unclip my canteen from the utility belt.

"I've found it," I whisper.

"Found what?"

Pulling one of her hands closer, I fold it into mine, and rub my thumbs over her candy-colored nails. "Fresh."

Even while burying my face into our clasped hands, the word sounds as clean as the thing itself.

Her eyes widen, her brows lift up. "You're serious."

"I'm serious."

"Did you taste it? What was it like? When will it be—" She's grinning as the questions tumble out. Almost immediately, though, she falls into a wheezing fit. Months in bed have destroyed her stamina. Doesn't stop her grinning, though. The gasping becomes laughter that dissolves into another bout of rasping. Every time she so much as snickers, it morphs into a cough, and the ludicrousness of it all—her utter inability to even break down in giddy, side-splitting joy—sets her laughing-wheezing, laughing harder into the bed.

I follow her lead, cracking up from watching her unable to talk, unable to laugh, unable to not laugh. Once I finally get control of myself, the fits start all over again. It's sad and horribly funny at the same time, and we're cackling like maniacs, because I've found one of the two things that life cannot exist without, and yet it does. Right here. *In the Ward.*

This goes on until I have to remind her to inhale. "Deep breaths," I insist, which seems to calm us both down a bit. "Yes, I drank it. Tasted like pure nothingness. And no, I don't know when it will be piped off."

Then the fit dies down fully, and when Aven speaks again, her tone is sober. "I won't be around to taste it, will I?"

Do I give it to her? The *CVH* would say an adamant "no." The fresh should really be tested—I know from memory what section 72(a) states:

Any and all findings from Government scouting missions* [*see 21(a), (b), and (c) for term "Government scouting missions": [(a) approved, (b) financed, or (c) assisted]] must be registered immediately with DI Headquarters, where it will be sent out for testing of infectious foreign bodies.

I shouldn't give it to her. *Infectious foreign bodies* don't sound like a barrel of fun.

On the other hand, I did taste it, albeit accidentally. And I'm fine. If there were something wrong with it, I'd be upchucking over the john right now.

Okay, then.

I unscrew the cap to my canteen. Drops of water trickle along the sides. "Taste," I say, pushing it into her hand.

Aven sits up slowly. "You have some?"

"No, I'm giving you liquor and getting you drunk. Yes, I have some, silly face. Drink. Not too much . . . I need some as a sample to send to headquarters."

She takes a sip; it dribbles down her chin.

Pulling away, "It *does* taste like nothing," she says. "Why, it doesn't taste too much different from our drainage water." But she drinks the canteen nearly dry nonetheless. Leaves me just enough to get to Dunn.

"Fine, then," I say in mock insult. "Give it back."

"No." She laughs. "It's wonderful. I'm sorry. I know what it took to find this. And now you don't have to work for them anymore." She smiles, and it dawns on me.

What happens now that I've found fresh? I need this job. . . . Without it I can't care for Aven. The DI has to keep me on as a mole. We can't afford otherwise. *And the report I missed . . .*

What's he gonna do? The thought makes me lose my balance, sends fear all the way to my feet. Glancing down at my wrist for my cuffcomm, I remember it's busted.

My backup. It's around here somewhere.

The mattress. I flop onto my bed and reach between the popped springs and the stuffing falling out on one side.

Finding it there—*whew*—I pull it out, see the neon-blue screen blinking frantically.

The comm beeps twice.

Brack—it's *been* beeping for the last three hours, but stuffed in my mattress I couldn't hear it. Quickly, I flip it open—I've got one message, from Dunn:

> Potential Stat. One Violation at the 'Racks, 17:00. Prepare to report afterward.

A raid? *Here?*

I don't like the DI this close to my home. Despite the fact that I work for them.

Aven and I are silent. Still, I don't consider telling her about the raid. She'll insist they're coming for her, even though she's not contagious, and never fall asleep. Instead, I set my alarm for ten to five, so I can warn her just before it happens.

"Ren?" she calls to me from the bed.

I arch my head back so I can see her better. "Yeah?" I answer, watching her as she stares at the ceiling like there's a movie playing up there.

"I can feel it getting closer."

In my throat, a sigh catches, stuck there. Waiting. Every once in a while, something dark gets the best of her, like it is now, and I hate it.

Aven talking like this kills me. I go teary and numb, all at once. As though my brain shuts down at the very thought of her . . . not being around anymore. It can't even think that word. It's a curse.

I watch the ceiling too, but I see no movie. "No, it's not," I say. I insist. I'll force it to be true if I have to. "That's just tired you're feeling."

"Okay," she says. Then, a little bit more determined, "Okay."

"Water, Ren?" Aven groans only an hour or two later.

I jerk awake, body buzzed from too little sleep, and stagger to her bed. I feel her palms, try to calm the razor-sharp queasiness I get in my stomach whenever she randomly wakes up like this. Her hands are usually cold as glass, but not now. They're hot. Sticky. She's red-cheeked and breathing through her mouth. When I nudge her slightly, she clutches at my wrist.

"It hurts?" I ask, confused. The Dilameth should still be working. . . .

She shakes her head. "Hot."

I nod, and hurry to bring her rainwater from the drainage system.

In the bathroom, I light a candle to see the glass tank. This is how the cheaper buildings do it. It's a simple setup: tank + sand = filtered water. The rain passes down the roof pipes, into each home's individual filtration system to be cleaned by the sand. Too bad it don't work with brack. Funneled rooftop rainwater makes up 100 percent of our water supply.

I fill a glass under the spigot and return to her in the main room. Pushing it into her hands, I feel her forehead again. There's nothing I can do. Not right now, anyway. Without last night's winnings, we've got no money for another visit from the doctor. *A few more hours*, I tell myself, thinking of my meeting with Officer Cory, when I can get the green he promised.

I crawl back onto my mattress and listen to the uneven rise, then fall, of her breathing.

Maybe it's from lack of sleep, but when I shut my eyes again, I start to imagine Aven's a plant—rosemary, or mint, something that grows in land. I give her water because that's all I can do, but air and water ain't all a living thing needs.

I want to give her sunlight, but no one bottles that.

10

5:00 P.M., SATURDAY

The building's foundation shakes straight through to its bones, and I snap awake as if I'd never fallen asleep in the first place.

Damn. Looking at my cuffcomm, I see that it's five on the dot, and that the DI are right on time. I'm the one who's late—I slept through the alarm. Close to ten hours. *How the hell did that happen?* I think, but I shouldn't be surprised after last night.

"Aven—" I whisper, pulling myself off the mattress and moving to her bed. The brass frame shakes with her in it, forces her awake. "They're coming . . . they're coming to the 'Racks."

She tosses the lower half of her body closer to me. I see her struggle to sit up, eyes still closed, reaching for the water at her bedside.

"Here," I say, getting it for her. Bringing the glass to her mouth, I tilt it down for her to sip. Normally, she hates when I do this, says I'm "hovering." Then she'll swat me away like I'm a mosquito. But not now. I don't like it—the swatting at me means she's okay.

Her eyes snap open. "What if . . . what if," she mumbles, and tries to pull the glass from my hand. Her hands shake, though, and so does the glass, so she gives up.

"They can't be here for you, Aven. You're not contagious anymore, remember?" I remind her, but when she gets panicked like this, there's no talking her down. She may be wiser than your average fourteen-year-old, but she's also been indoors for nearly three years. My sister is still a kid in so many ways.

Simultaneously, our heads turn—outside, we hear voices murmuring, the buzz of neighbors congregating in the hallway.

"I'll check the scope to see what floor," I tell her, and rush for the door.

The way people from some countries grow up knowing earthquakes, we've also been trained to know what a vibration means. But for us, it's the Blues' helis, and everyone knows the sound.

In the hall, I'm met with the faces of people I've never seen before. After all, the 'Racks is home to more than a few of the Ward's ne'er-do-wells—mostly folks with connections Upstate and on the Mainland who source the UMI black market with water and meds. And though the Blues let that stuff slide (and other criminal activity, like murders and theft and such), they will cross the Strait to make Transmission arrests. Some residents even have periscopes installed in their homes for checking the hallway before they leave.

I can't get to a scope; they're all taken.

"What's the deal?" I ask anyone who'll answer, my heart upping its pace. Fear catches, too—not just viruses. "They coming?"

"Inside. Now," my closest neighbor, Mr. Bedrosian, tells the crowd. "You as well, Ren," he urges, eyes narrowing behind square-framed glasses.

Like I need the reminder.

The air hums with a muted panic, as if the sound's been turned off. You don't even need it. You can hear what people are saying on the inside—*not me, not me.* The halls empty, the doors click locked, and ladders drop from a few flights up. Boots pound the floor overhead.

Just like that, I'm alone in the hallway. My arms are shaking, and I can actually feel the blood knocking around in my chest, through my body. I may work for these guys, but that don't mean I ain't scared. Maybe that's even why I am scared—I know full well what they can do.

Dashing back into our apartment, "It's our floor," I tell Aven, and bolt the door behind me. When I sit beside her on the bed, run my palm across her forehead, it comes back slick with sweat. She's hotter than an engine.

"Have more water." It's all I can tell her to do right now.

The walls shudder. A troop of guards stampede the corridor outside. When they knock on a door, the sound is so loud

I can't tell whose apartment they're in front of.

My blood stops in my body—I hear a man's gruff voice call, "Inspection! Open the door." A Bouncer, here with the Blues. Only after someone's filed a complaint can they test in people's homes. And even though I know they can't be here for Aven, I feel myself freeze up. I imagine the what-ifs. . . .

I want to see for myself. I need to make sure. . . .

Heel to toe, steps weighted evenly and quietly as possible, I walk to the front of the apartment, then peer through the peephole. I can't see nothing, but the silence is thick and eerie—the sound of too many people making too little noise.

Feet shuffle, a door creaks open. A woman sobs. "Wha—what do you want with us?" she asks. "We've done nothing wrong."

She's stammering, frantic. *Wheezing.*

Another scuffle—

"Mr. and Mrs. Bedrosian!" The same voice. "Step back! Stay inside the apartment!"

Footsteps enter the apartment, then fall silent. The only sounds on this floor come from two shrill beeps.

"HBNC positive. Contagious, both of them," the man says. "But the complaint's only been made against the woman."

I rest my forehead to the door, pushing away my sudden rush of anger. *Contagious?* All along they've been next door? Aven might not have been able to catch it anymore, but what about everyone else?

"Mrs. Julia Bedrosian," a new voice barks. A familiar voice—I know him. "You are being placed under arrest for Transmission of the HBNC virus. According to an anonymous complaint, the witness heard you, Julia Bedrosian, overtaken by a wheezing fit on Broad Walk two weeks prior. Within two days, said victim developed symptoms of HBNC and was tested positive for the contagion. I'm sure the victim will be pleased to know you're being brought to justice. Mr. Bedrosian, HBNC Patrol will be here momentarily to bring you to the nearest sickhouse for the contagious."

My boss . . . that's my boss out there.

More scuffling.

"There is no justice in this!" Mr. Bedrosian yells. "You cannot criminalize a disease! You cannot take us from our home—"

"Leave it alone, Armand," his wife pleads.

Then, the unmistakable sound of metal against bone—metal *cracking* bone—and the slump of a body as it slides quickly to the floor.

Aven gasps from the back of the room. The candle flickers, and I see her cover her mouth.

"Armand?" Mrs. Bedrosian's voice sounds low, stunned.

The blow . . . did it kill him?

The snapping of handcuffs as they bolt into position. A body pushed forward. Feet stumbling—she's being taken.

Behind the door, in this pathetic crouched position, my face begins to flush so red and so hot, warmth radiates against my legs. I can actually feel the temperature of my shame. I may not be happy that the Bedrosians were living next door all this time, but that don't mean I think they should've been punished.

I work for them. *Them.*

If I were a better person . . . I'd do more than just hide here, a coward, while the people I work for hurt people for being sick.

But that's how it is here. Every man for himself. You do what you need to. You protect your family by any means. Besides, I'm not doing anything wrong. I'm one of the good guys—I scout for fresh. Even though I work for them, I'm not one of them. Right?

What else can I do?

Nothing.

My palms press sweat into the floor as I keep my neck craned, listening for the weighty footfalls to pass our door. Soon, when I think the hall is quiet again, I choke back a sigh. Get my head on straight.

There's a new guilt building in my chest and I don't like it. It's relief. I'm relieved. Relieved I didn't have to do anything. *If I were a better person.*

"Ren?"

Aven . . . I should get her more water. Put some food in her before I leave for the Tank. I uncurl myself from my spot on the floor and return to her bedside. One more time I feel her forehead. The sweat beads are still there, though now her temp seems even.

"That was awful," she whispers into the dark. Our candle is out.

"How do you f—"

Cutting me off, "I'm fine. You should check on Mr. Bedrosian, Ren."

Because she knows no one else can.

I don't want to leave her. "I'm fine" could mean anything. But she's right—I'm the only one. Our neighbors sure won't risk seeing if someone who's been diagnosed as contagious HBNC positive is still alive.

I stand and walk to the front door, but make it no farther than the knob. *Another knock.* Heavy, hammer-like knocks. And this time there's no mistaking it. *He's here. Chief is here. . . .*

My muscles fire up, and stupidly, I find myself scanning the room for a place to hide. Like I could avoid making this report. Like that wouldn't get me in even more trouble. But my brain's not doing the thinking anymore. My guts are.

What's he going to do to me? A thousand possibilities race through my head: he could dock my pay, send me for correctional training. Beat the living daylights out of me.

I just don't know.

I'm so dizzy, anxious, I almost forget—my trump card. The fresh. Maybe I missed the report, but once he hears about the spring, how angry could he be?

Gathering myself, I open the door a crack, find myself standing face-to-face with Chief Dunn.

He's a tower in blue fatigues. A skyscraper, steel made flesh. Chrome and black hair, mustached, with a face that looks like it'd been flattened by bricks. When he sees me, he turns to one of the Bouncers, shouts, "Inspection here, too!" and pushes the door wider to let himself in.

It's just a cover . . . it's got to be—so that my mole status stays top secret.

With his hands clasped behind his back, Dunn strides

into our apartment, followed by a yellow-and-black-jacketed Bouncer. I throw Aven a look. They don't know about her. I thought it better that way—no one likes the sick. She'll know to keep quiet. If we're lucky, it's dark enough in here that he might even miss her.

The door closes. Dunn surveys the room, stance wide-legged. Militant; he's chief of the DI—he *is* the UMI military, after all.

"Dane. You missed your report." He snorts, and as the patrolman shuts the door, the room goes pitch dark. Dunn's first words are even, composed, but the way he enunciates every syllable gives it away. Something tidal is underneath.

A lump has gone and lodged itself in the back of my throat, but I can't seem to swallow it. "Yes, s-sir. I'm sorry, sir," I answer.

The patrolman clicks on a flashlight and a yellow glow floods the room.

I can see Chief again. Even in shadow his glare is razor edged, but he looks worn down too. "You think this job is a game?" As he speaks, he carves each word. "Something you can forget about when it's convenient and come back to later?"

"No, sir . . . I don't think that." I avoid his eyes. "It'll never happen again, I swear it. . . . I'm sorry, sir." I'm pleading now, but I can't stop myself. I don't know how to do this, how to make him believe. "There was an accident—my Rimbo smashed into a spire. . . . I almost didn't get out—"

Chief steps closer. Shuts me up with no more than a look. Across his forehead, the line of a vein rises up, red and full. I need to tell him about the fresh, but there's no right time.

"That is not the point, Dane!" he shouts into my face, so

near I see each brittle hair of his mustache, and the white K-dot stuck to his neck.

He's too close. . . . My nerves short-circuit. His words are on my skin, and I want to step back, but it's more than that . . . I want to break. *That's not the point.* My almost dying is not the point.

It's not like I expected a hug. Didn't even expect him to ask if I was all right. I did, however, think that it would matter.

Just the tiniest bit.

He's not done—"You missed your report, and you never contacted headquarters after the fact. Yet." He pauses, the blacks of his eyes fixed on me. "Here you are. Perfectly fine." He drawls those last words.

I'm about to open my mouth, say something, anything, but another voice beats me to it.

"It was my fault. . . ." Aven says, urgent. Unwavering. "I got sick."

No, my head cries out. *Stay quiet!* I stumble backward, positioning myself between Dunn and Aven. As though I could somehow block her from his sight. "It was my fault, sir," I insist. "She's not speaking sense right now."

"Who is *she*?" Dunn points, seeing the sickly girl—my Aven—on the bed for the first time.

"A friend." No need for him to know more than that. "She's not contagious. . . ." Except for that.

He motions to the Bouncer, like he wants him to test her. Only out in public is random testing legal without a complaint. Not here in private. But this is Dunn. He can do what he wants.

The Bouncer pulls out the needle blood scanner, and I see

Aven's mouth open in fear.

I could distract him. *Now, the fresh.*

"Sir," I start, anxiety pitching my voice a dozen octaves too high. I sound panicked. . . . I am panicked. I can feel my heartbeat everywhere, from my toes up to my throat. "My report. I found this—"

I reach for the canteen dangling off the edge of the bed frame and push it into his hands. Chief Dunn takes the canteen from me, not understanding, and I lead him away from Aven's bed, closer to the door.

In a hushed voice, I tell him, "It's fresh, sir."

He unscrews the cap, eyes on me. "You know as well as I do, it's been years since we've found an uncontaminated groundwater source," he says, taking a whiff. His face registers nothing.

"Tasted it myself," I insist, confused. Yet another reaction I'd never expected: doubt. Maybe I should have, though. Years I've been searching for fresh with no luck.

Shaking the canteen, he listens to hear how much is in there. "The governor would be pleased, to be sure. Location?"

"Quad Nine. A building with a red star painted on it, under the subway system."

"You said Ten on the recording," he reminds me.

"I had a tip. One of your guys, actually. Officer Cory. Officer Justin Cory," I tell him, happy to offer credit where credit is due, give the officer a slice of the pie. Without him, I wouldn't have found anything at all.

Chief shakes his head. "I know the name of every man

112

assigned to me, Dane. There's no Justin Cory in the DI."
Then, aiming his finger at me like a gun, he says, "Find out
who this guy is and report back. Could even be a reward in
there for you if he turns out to be someone interesting."

I nod, but my head's on a roller coaster, confused, even
though it all lines up. . . . *Justin Cory was lying?*

I mean, of course he was. The way he spoke to me, too
polite. And his lack of brawn. So the question is, who is he?

Chief opens the door, and he doesn't look back at Aven.
"This goes to the lab immediately," he says. "If it turns up
good, I'll send a scout team out to gather more samples first
thing tomorrow, five a.m. Don't get your hopes up, though.
More than likely, it's just a pocket with low salinization levels. Not enough to pipe off for mass consumption."

As the patrolman follows Chief out, he takes the light with
him. Leaves us in darkness.

"I'm sure you're right, sir," I say, from just behind the door,
watching as they leave, all the energy being sucked from my
limbs. I'm exhausted. After hours of sleep, I'm exhausted.

Soon the sound of their footsteps is too far away to hear, and
I look down the empty hall toward the Bedrosians' apartment.
Even the body is gone. Everything is back to normal—the
candles replaced, flickering like they never died out. *Almost.*

If only the bloodstain were gone too.

11

9:30 P.M., SATURDAY

I don't know what to do. . . .

It's been more than four hours since the raid. Afterward I rehydrated Aven with some soup—she couldn't keep it down at first. Then she could, and it seemed like she was feeling better, too. Now though, even in sleep, her breaths are short and erratic. And when I take her hand, it feels clammy in my own. Cold.

But the Tank—

If I go, I've still got a chance at meeting with this "Officer Cory" guy. Since he's not really with the DI, he won't know I just met with Dunn—no reason for him not to give me the green he promised. And if there's a reward for passing on information about him to Dunn, so much the better. Aven and I will need more to make it to the end of the month, especially if she's sick.

But as I move to her bedside and feel her cheeks—I don't like it. They strike me as too warm.

I inhale and rub the bridge of my nose, racking my head for an answer.

I'm only *sixteen*.

How am I supposed to tell when she *needs* the doctor? If we had the money, I'd call him every time her temp hit 98.7. But we don't. . . . I have to make the calls. I have to tell "bad" from "worse." Right now, I don't think this is the worst. She's sleeping—that's gotta say something.

If I stay, all I can do is make her comfortable: feed her daggers, get her water.

But if I go, we'll have the money to pay for the doctor by the time I get back.

I don't like this plan.

Leaving her alone turns my stomach like swallowing motor oil. Squeezing Aven's hand, gentle, I head to the bathroom. If I'm going to leave, I should at least not look like I almost died.

I pull a paste pill from the cabinet and brush my teeth; no need for water. The foaming action is activated by the saliva in the mouth, and when I'm done, all I have to do is take a minty gulp. It occurs to me that I should probably clean my head wound before leaving, so it doesn't get infected. After all, we don't even have enough money for one sick person in this apartment, much less two.

Using some filtered rainwater, I soak a tiny corner of our washcloth, readying myself for the damage. I don't particularly want to look at myself. From the barbed sting going on above my eyebrows, my face feels like the kind of ugly that's best left in nightmares.

Good thing we don't have a real mirror.

On the wall, hanging from a nail, we keep a tin lid. Aven pulled it off an empty coffee tin way back when, and it works all right so long as we keep from denting it.

I bring my temple closer, but it's hard to see for myself. Rarely do I find myself wishing someone was around to take care of me; now is one of those times. And it would be especially nice if that someone were named Derek.

Oh, how his girlfriend would love that.

The thought makes me queasy, so I dismiss it, and squint to examine the wound.

Where the brick got me—the largest of the cuts by my temple—the blood's crusted. I wipe away the dried, flaky reddish-brown bits. After a few dabs, I have to pull back. Not from pain . . . from surprise. I'd expected the two flaps of separated skin to be, well, separate, but already they've joined together. Formed a seam. Only in a few spots, where the slice was deepest, can I see tender, pink flesh underneath.

I've always been a fast healer, it's true. This is *really* fast, though. Not that I'm complaining . . .

I toss the cloth onto the laundry pile and walk back quietly, careful not to wake Aven, then look around for something to wear. Normally, I'd just sport my red leather suit since the festivities usually get rolling after the race, but that's at Derek's. And destroyed.

After a few minutes of scrambling, lifting trunks, and tossing aside pants that haven't fit my butt for years, I find my outfit for tonight's soiree. In a lovely pile, accompanied by only a few dust balls. Perfect.

Black tank, check.

Grommet-and-buckle black leather vest, check.

Tan suede leggings, check.

Spare canteen, check, as Dunn now has my other one. I run to the bathroom, turn the spigot, and fill it only halfway. Don't want to over ration.

Back in the main room, I find my Hessians: check, and check. Last, I throw on my utility belt.

Knowing that I'm going to be cold for the walk, I buckle on both my sleeves. A jacket's around here . . . somewhere . . . but I'd just take it off when I got to the Tank anyway. Then I'd lose it. Better to be cold for a little while.

One last time, I look to Aven. On her wrist is the cuff-comm I've given her, just in case. I reach under the bed for the orange bottle and take out another Dilameth, which I leave on the bedside table with the water.

"Feathers?" I whisper, kneeling closer.

Her eyes stay shut, but she musters a "hmm" so I know she's heard me.

"I'm going to the Tank, but I'll be back soon. You have the comm. Don't forget?"

She tilts her chin, up then down, an even weaker response than the last.

I stand up, walk to the door. Hope she doesn't open her eyes just then. Leaving her hurts, physically hurts. In more ways than I can pin. Guilt twists itself in my gut, insists that I'm not doing the right thing . . . going to a party, of all places. Even though I'm going to help us.

But that's not even the worst of it.

My imaginings, they're what do me in. Every time I step out the front door, I picture what coming back could look like. Because if my worst memory is of the time I found Aven alone but alive at the sickhouse, I can think of only one thing that's worse—finding her dead in *our* home.

Alone.

PART TWO

12

9:45 P.M., SATURDAY

The cracked, Mad Ave solar-powered streetlights shed an eerie, fragmented bluish glow over the boardwalk. I'm trying to pass a family of four on either side, but they're buying seeds from a vendor, probably for a private roof plot up north, and they're lollygagging. It's damn near impossible. Though the Tank isn't far from here—a straight shot down—tonight is so crazy, it'll take me twice as long.

As I finally weave through them, my spare cuffcomm buzzes on my wrist. I look down, see a message from Benny:

> Towed your Rimbo back to the garage. Looking into the problem, may take a while.

Sure, sure . . . Benny says it'll take a while, but if I know him, he just doesn't want me to hound him every ten minutes. He'll have an answer soon, no doubt.

I keep on through the market, slowing when I spot Zora's cart. She's my favorite, a gap-toothed little punk kid with a red afro and so many freckles on her face, you'd never know what color her skin really was. She's the smartest sneak on the walk. Always offers to check for airdrops from her wealthy West Isle grandma. Then, when her dad goes on break, she'll call me over—ladle me a bit of bona fide black market Upstate fresh, for Aven. Her grandma gets it by way of the Mainland, and I doubt there are even a hundred people in the Ward who can afford the stuff.

But living off rainwater ain't so bad. So long as it rains.

"Hey, Z!" I shout across the avenue.

She sees me and waves.

I start to walk closer, but a push to my shoulder sends me rolling forward. I spin around, angry, and spit, "Watch it!" before realizing that the push was by no means an accident.

It's Kent. . . . He laughs at me, lazy, thin lipped. Threads of his ink-black hair fall in his face. With his hands in the pockets of an oversize trench, he drawls, "If it isn't the 'Red Rider,'" and strides up with rubber-band legs—all loose and relaxed, ready to mess with me. "I was so hopeful, and look here, now you've ruined my whole night." He throws up his arms. "Of course, your being alive is an easy enough problem to fix."

Jones passes me by and nods, smirking, his ponytailed sandy hair pulled tidily out the back of his round cap.

"Sorry to disappoint," I say, and turn around, hoping for a smooth getaway. *I'm not in the mood for this.*

But Jones is there, cutting me off.

I face Kent again. He's been joined by the Dreaded Duo. Tanzii's and Neela's arms are looped around each other like shadows. The girls watch me, adjusting their tops to reveal a bit more flesh, and they snigger. It kills me. More than the Derby guys, even.

All I'd need is one of them . . . just one other girl at the races would even the balance enough.

"You've got some fuel on your face, honey," Neela says when she sees me looking at her. Coyly she points at me, bowing her knees together. Then she goes wide-eyed, fake as those dolls with the movable eyelids.

I know better than to touch my face though. We've been through this one before.

"Don't you have tulips to plant, Neela, or whatever it is that you do all day?" I pretend to flick her away like she's a bug on my thumb.

If only it were that easy.

She rolls her eyes, and when she looks at Kent, I see her barely nod in my direction.

Uh-oh—she's calling in the big guns, and Kent's been dying for an excuse to pummel me as it is.

I look up; they're still there, and Kent's just getting closer.

"Hope you enjoyed your lucky streak while it lasted," Kent says, laughing as he nears and cracking his knuckles. "After tonight, I'm not sure you'll be fit to hold a steering wheel."

His eyes always target me like he's looking down a gun

barrel, so why do I always wonder if he's actually going to do it? Kent hasn't clobbered me bloody yet, but each time we get into a row like this, it feels more and more likely.

I ain't gonna find out if tonight's the night, though.

I smile, and I wave, and then—though I sorta hate myself for taking the coward's way out—I turn on my heel, and I run like an animal.

Booking it through the labyrinth of steel-wheeled wagons, with the old fabric warehouse in view, my breathing goes too ragged and I have to stop. I pull over, nearly tripping on a girl I swear I know—shortish, dread-headed, wearing fairy wings and probably on her way to the Tank. I don't say hi; I just duck under one of the striped umbrellas that dot the boardwalk.

From here I can spot the HBNC Patrol hornets. They're buzzing around the building's exterior. Crouched farther beneath one of the vendor's carts, I watch them through the wheel's spokes, waiting to see if Kent or Jones catches up.

No one comes.

I grow impatient—the Tank is less than five minutes away, so I slide out from under the cart and start walking. A hundred paces out, from behind me, I hear a swishing noise.

Someone's following? The thought makes me stop short. Staggers my step.

Another pair of boots staggers after me, too.

I whip around, squatted low to the walkway. Instinctively, my hand goes to my ankle where I've stashed my small blade. From this vantage point I can't see much through the stalls, but I'm not dumb.

Kent, maybe? My blood runs just a little bit quicker, hotter, than before.

It wouldn't be the chief. . . . He's long gone, I'm sure. Anxious to leave the Ward quick as possible.

I don't know who's back there, so I slide beneath a few stalls to throw whoever it is off track. The sooner I make it to the Tank, the better. Once I'm inside, whoever is following me will have a hard time keeping up.

I break into an easy jog, feeling the beats tremble up the boardwalk and into my knees. They're so heavy, they're the partygoer's audio bass version of a breadcrumb trail. But it's not even necessary.

Just follow the Patrol hornets.

It's still early, but those guys go where the crowds will go. And just like at the races, the Bouncers aren't just here to act as musclemen. These guys don't check IDs, neither.

They're checking blood.

"Ro!" I call out when I'm close enough, slowing as I near. I push through a few guys my age, all wearing patchy, pleather pants and sleeveless tees, with dog collars around their necks. It's like the uniform for badassery around here.

One of them curses at me, but then he sees who I am and shuts his mouth. Even the tough guys step aside when the dragsters come through.

The biggest of the big Bouncers turns my way, arms folded over his chest, looking rough.

"Glad to see you're in the land of the living," Ro comments through blackened teeth. Even under the weak solar lamplights, his jacket reflects a bright and shiny neon yellow, so everyone can see he's a Bouncer. He blathers on for a bit about how the Derbies were sure I'd kicked it, sure I'd finally bit the dust.

I zone out, scan the crowd, first to see if Kent is around. Then I find myself looking for the one person I'm always looking for. Hoping he's here. Without the girlfriend, of course. She's a wet blanket if ever there was one.

"It wasn't that bad." I brush him off. "You've been listening to too much Derby gossip." Just as I'm about to stick out my arm so Ro can see the date of my last test, I see a young girl wandering round the outside of the entrance to the Tank.

"Who's that?" I ask, but Ro just shrugs, says he's never seen her. She looks familiar, but under the damned lights it's so buzzy and dim, I can't tell.

"Be right back." I wave Ro away, and he calls after me. He could tackle and Taser me for being in the yellow zone. Only those confirmed with zero, or undetectable, viral levels can hang here. But the girl. I know her.

She's in the yellow zone too, about to get tested.

Waif of a build, skin too sallow. Blond, near-white hair.

Aven . . . ?

My heart lurches in my chest, pushes itself against my very rib cage. *She's supposed to be in bed.* My instincts revved, I have to protect her, I have to get to her. I have to bring her home. . . . She's sick.

That can't be Aven, though. It's just not possible.

I don't care. My muscles are kicked into gear—I dodge the Bouncers already positioned, a wall in front of me. Good thing big guys don't look down much.

"Aven!" I holler, still not entirely sure of myself. There's no way she could've left the 'Racks.

I've got to be wrong.

The girl turns around to face me. She's still sticking out her arm from the test, as a Bouncer pulls away the needle.

"Stop!" I call, sprinting up, ready to yank her away.

"Renny!" The girl smiles.

The Bouncer drops her hand, focuses his attention on the scanner.

It's her . . . but it's not her. This girl is shining, wearing a grin brighter than an electric moon. Not to mention, she's upright. On her own. Wobbly on her feet, yes. And her skin still has that algae-green tinge to it that makes her look not quite right. But she's *here.*

All my tongue can do is loll around in my mouth, sluggish and thick—I've got no words.

I watch her get her X—the Bouncer takes her arm and turns over the scanner. He waits for it to get white-hot, then down it goes. Aven bites her lip and I see her eyes are watering, but she doesn't cry out. Not even a peep. I don't know what to be confused about first when nothing makes sense.

Somewhere in the tunnels of my brain I hear the Bouncer declaring that she's "good to go" and she should "have fun," but no, that can't be. My sister is sick, deadly and irreversibly sick, because there's a tumor—*a giant, bracking lump of a tumor*—lodged against her skull, so really, *what the hell kind of alien is this new girl, anyway?*

Aven snaps me out of my stupor with a hug. Her mittens find their way underneath the tight corkscrews of my hair to the back of my neck. There they rest, warming me up as I hold her tight.

We're still in the yellow zone, my VEL unconfirmed, so when I feel a hand on my shoulder I'm just thankful that I've got enough pull here that they haven't Tasered me already.

"What are you doi—" is all I can manage. I show Ro the latest X on my arm, never—not even once—taking my eyes off Aven.

"I'm better, Ren." She says this like she had the flu, not a death sentence.

"How did you even get here?"

Before she answers, my mind wheels back to the walk over. "It was you. . . . You were following me?"

She nods fiercely, like she's gotten away with stealing cookies from one of the toughest Mad Ave vendors.

I take her wrist, a thing so thin my fingers wrap around with room to spare. "We need to get you home."

She pulls away, twisting herself from my grip. I wasn't holding hard, but I don't know if I'm more shocked by the fact that she *could* do it, or the fact that she *did*.

We don't disagree. Ever.

"But my VEL? I'm not contagious," she whines, like that explains everything. "I can be here, I'm allowed. He said so." She points to the Bouncer, whose hawk eyes watch us, suspicion creeping in.

"Aven," I whisper through gritted teeth. Looping an arm through hers, I lead her out of the yellow zone. "I don't care what that test says. You. Are. Sick."

"Blood doesn't lie." Her hazel eyes are steely, her expression

128

harder than I've ever seen it. "And I feel fine."

And I'm about to say something I've only heard adults say. "This isn't a discussion. We're leaving. Now."

Yeah . . . that tasted as bad in my mouth as it sounded. I think I even pointed at the ground when I said "now."

Aven unloops our arms without saying a word. She walks back into the yellow zone, sticks out her arm for one of the Bouncers again.

I run up to her, grabbing her by the shawl. The last thing I want to do is make a scene here of all places, but I can't let her stay.

She spins around, twisting herself away. "No, Ren. I won't go back!" Her eyes look wild. But then she stands still, only her white-blond hair moving with the wind. "I feel all right. The scanner thingy says I'm good to go. Please, Ren. I've never had a night like this."

Everything about her changes right then. She wilts, no anger left in her.

"Look at it." She pulls her hair to the side, revealing the spot where the tumor should be.

But it's not there. Not much of it, anyway. I bring one finger to her hairline behind her ear and feel around. One small lump, no larger than the size of a coin, peeks out, barely noticeable.

How is it possible . . . ?

Tumors don't just spontaneously shrink.

I rub my forehead, confusion settling in my brain, boulder heavy. My fingers peel something crinkly off the skin near my temple. I realize I'm rubbing at the gash where the brick hit. The scab . . . it's already flaking off.

"You see?" she whispers.

"Aven . . ." I want to stop her, explain what's going on.

But I don't know.

The last few hours rewind through my head: I met with the chief. There was the raid. Aven's fever. I told her about the fresh.

I let her drink from the canteen.

We both drank from the canteen.

It's not possible. But I didn't think she could be here, and here she is. And I didn't think that her tumor was gone, and it is.

Mostly . . .

"I want to live before I die," she continues. Her eyes find mine, serious. "One night of fun, Ren. That's all I need. The tumor's not gone. I know it. But if it comes back, I'll want to make it. I'll want to hold on."

She'll want to hold on. The words pierce my other thoughts. Put the questions on pause. Whatever's made her better, I don't want to think about it too hard. You don't question miracles.

I can't say no to her; we don't have forever. We only have now.

Reluctant, I nod. Arm in arm we walk into the warehouse.

The elevator arrives. It takes us down, well below water level—we drop so far our ears crackle.

Aven tugs at her lobes. "Weird!" She giggles.

I want to laugh with her, but the whole ride, I'm in a daze. Too confused, too frantic to even think. *Breathe*, I remind myself, and together we feel the bass beats rising up through the soles of our feet. The elevator walls vibrate in time with the *ding-ding-ding*-ing from floor to floor. Aven smiles at me and clasps my hand in her mittened ones, rocking on her heels.

Should I not have agreed? She looks so . . . happy.

I push aside the gnawing fear that comes along with anything good—that it will leave just as quickly. *She's here now. That's what matters*, I tell myself, but it doesn't stop me from wanting to freeze-frame this moment.

Aven and me, walking into our first party together. Ever.

Like we really do have our whole lives ahead of us.

13

10:00 P.M., SATURDAY

The doors open.

We're in a fish tank. And that makes us the fish.

The Tank didn't get its name from nowhere—it's a basement, gutted and fitted anew with floor-to-ceiling concave sheets of glass. One of the few lucky buildings in the Ward to be restructured after the Wash Out. Never completed, though. Upstate pulled the plug on any rebuilding 'cause of the Appeal, and we got left with half-finished buildings, like this one.

Installed with some mighty fancy technology, but no faucets in the bathrooms.

Aven and I both look around, though she's the one with wonder on her face. "This place is incredible!" she yells, spinning in a circle to get the full 360. "I can't believe you get to come here every month. I think this is heaven."

The mucky water's been set aglow with underwater lighting, and Aven is plastering her face to the glass to get a better look.

It strikes me as funny that for us in the Ward, heaven is down, not up.

"Can you believe I've never seen it from Before?" she asks.

I don't answer, and my appreciation for the view right this moment is minimal. It just conjures up less than glamorous memories from last night. Reminds me how, for the first time, I've come to the Tank as a loser.

I turn to face Aven again, and catch sight of her running off, skipping from glass panel to glass panel.

"Wait up!" I call through the music, but she never stops for longer than a few seconds. Not even the whirlwind of colored lights overhead has time to catch her. I run after, zigzagging myself through a dozen dancing bodies, until finally, she's winded.

Her breath leaves a circle of fog on the glass in front of her face. She looks at me, all seriousness. "How come . . ." I see her asking, but her voice trails off and I can't hear any more.

I move us a few feet to the left, under one of the antinoise beams—they cancel out the music using opposite sound waves, or some other science voodoo of the sort. It's quiet under here, but I can still feel the heavy, electronic beats 'cause they make my nose hairs buzz.

"How come you never told me how wonderful this place is?" Aven asks again, looking around our invisible bubble like it's magic.

I'm quiet. Outside this window, we watch the sad remains of a parked truck as it does nothing but rust. "I didn't want to make you feel bad," I say at last. "That's all. Didn't want to make you wish for things that couldn't be."

Aven sighs. "All I had was my imagination. Hours to do nothing but wonder when it was finally going to be over."

At that I flinch, though she's not saying it to be mean.

"It would have been nice to have something like this to think about."

The realization stings—I'd never thought of it that way. All these years, I could have been treating her more like a sister, telling her things. I'm about to say that I'm sorry, but she tugs at my hand, and I know she knows.

"Some friends are here," I say, thinking how now is as good a time as any to catch her up to speed on the last three years. I glance around the club, landing on every near-reddish head of hair I see. None of them are him, though. "You want to take a loop together?"

"Lead the way. But first . . ." Aven riffles around for something in her shawl, opening a small pocket in one of the corners. "You need makeup."

I really don't know this girl. Is *this* what she's been thinking about all these years stuck in bed?

Parties and makeup?

"Where did you get that?" I examine the stick of kohl eyeliner like it's a black bullet gone astray that could hit my face at any moment.

"One of my scavenges. Been saving it since Nale's. Can I . . . ?" she asks, leaning in with the weapon of cosmetic destruction.

"Noo way." I shield myself with my hands. "That's all you."

Aven leans her head on my shoulder and gives me her best puppy eyes.

That's all it takes: just one tear-jerking iota of unhappiness on her face—even the fake kind—and I'm a goner. I lean my back against the cool glass and close my eyes. "Fine. But please don't make me look like one of those girls on Broad Walk."

"What girls?" She looks at me, confused, and unscrews the stick of compressed coal. I open one eye.

Oh. Right. "Forget it. Just . . . you know, go easy."

We're quiet for a few moments, and I try not to squint while she prods over my eyeballs with that black junk.

"Open."

I open my eyes.

"Close."

This is exasperating.

She uses her fingers, presumably to blend the stuff. "Ren, you need moisturizer." I'm mentally giving her the middle finger.

You know when your eyes are closed, but by way of some freaky sixth sense you can tell you're being looked at? Well, that's the vibe I'm getting right now, so when I hear Aven tittering like she's trying to be quiet, I know it's bad.

"That's a good look for you." It's a guy's voice. Deep, kinda husky. I can't quite tell because he's standing outside the anti-noise beam.

Oh no. He's not here. He's not here. He's not . . .

He's here.

"Derek," I groan. "Don't you dare laugh." I make like I'm

going to throw him a left hook.

"You look haaawwwt, Renny." Aven nods her head with altogether too much cheer. "The liner makes your eyes really exotic. Like Cleopatra. Or Mata Hari."

Both sluts who died gruesome deaths. At least they were pretty.

Though I did just suffer a major blow to the head, I think Derek is kinda . . . gaping? His mouth is open and yet there are no words there. Oh, this is too good. "No making fun," I say, pointing at him.

Derek laughs and touches his hand to his chin. Aven mimics him. Together they look like they are examining a confusing piece of art, like that one of the toothy shark in the formaldehyde.

The Physical Impossibility of Death in the Mind of Someone Living.

Saw that one at the New Met with the orphanage. Everyone stared at it just like that, how Aven and Derek are staring at me.

So . . . I guess that makes me the shark. And whaddya know? I'm in a tank too.

I turn and try to catch my reflection in the glass, but a seven-inch-thick pane of glass isn't the best place to look for accuracy. Still, Aven's handiwork appears . . . not awful.

I'm caught in a moment of unadulterated girlyness when Derek taps me on the shoulder. "Don't I get an introduction? I didn't know you had friends who are girls." He points to Aven—the girl he's heard about for three years but has never met.

Brack.

How the hell am I going to explain this?

"Derek," I say, pulling him under the beam—we're pushing it to capacity so we have to speak louder. "Meet . . . Aven." I draw a deep breath. I certainly can't tell him that I think some miracle water shrank her tumor. Then he'd think that brick to my head did enough damage to send me to the loony bin.

We didn't even have time to think of a story. And really, what kind of story would help in this situation? *Meet my sister, Aven, who, as you know, has been deathly ill for quite a few years. Kidding! She's been fine. P.S. She's a certified club bunny!*

"*The* Aven?" His eyebrows shoot up, the whites around his irises practically glowing purple under the black light. I can see the suspicion there. He looks at her. He looks at me. He plays ping-pong with his eyes. To me, "And what happened to your face?"

I thought we'd established that, and so I point at Aven. "Uhh, memory loss much? This one had to turn me into an art project."

Aven grins. "You'd get an A. Actually, *I'd* get an A—"

With a flick of his wrist, Derek silences her, which makes me want to silence him with a flick of my fist. "No, Ren," he interrupts. "Your face . . . Yesterday you needed stitches—remember that giant-sized gash by your left eye?"

I bring my hand to my temple, covering where the wound should be. A few minutes ago, the scabs fell away. And only a few hours ago, the flesh had seamed together.

This is bigger than my being a "fast healer." It's got to be. Because both Aven and me drank the water.

Unbelievable, that's the only word for it. I have no answers, no explanations, but I know one thing. My gut's sending a message loud and clear: I have to play it off like it's no biggie. Can't have anyone knowing about the fresh find . . . and if it's more than that, even more of a reason to keep quiet.

"I'm a quick healer," I answer, falling back on that, despite how weak it sounds. "Remember that time I sliced my arm on the carburetor? I was better in days."

"Days, Ren. Not *a day.*"

I avoid his eyes. If I look at them, there's no way I'll be able to lie. Across the room, Terrence has just stepped out of the elevator. His gaze fans around but doesn't land on us. "Ter is here, guys."

The moment I step outside the sound bubble, music floods my ears. Derek follows me, then Aven. Thankful for the distraction from questions I just can't answer, I stick my fingers in my mouth and whistle. Ter sees us and shakes his head as he shuffles over, addled by the attention.

After the high pitch cuts out, I realize there's a loser spotlight on me. People stare, a few point. I slink closer to the glass, trying to find a corner where all those eyes can't reach.

Ter strides across the room, eyes not on me but behind me. By the time he's near enough, I expect him to stop, say hi, I dunno, address the girl who just hailed him with a hundred decibels of finger whistle, but he just ignores my ass. It's only when he stops behind Aven that he turns toward me, mouthing and pointing, *Who's that?*

I shouldn't have let her stay.

Terrence is going to remember her from the orphanage. Had quite a crush on Aven too, if I recall, though it's been a while. I'd say it was too bad that Ter was adopted before a real prepubescent relationship had a chance to blossom, but that's ridiculous. He found a home.

"That's Aven," I say helplessly, ready for the sky to get on with its falling.

His turf-green eyes widen. "What the . . . She's . . ." He stammers, just as confused as the rest of us. "She's . . . here?"

"T-Bone!" She squeals his orphanage nickname, a name I'd just about forgotten, and pulls him into a bear hug.

Terrence looks to me, undecided about hugging her back.

"I'm not contagious," she assures him. She raises up her arm, showing off her fresh, red welt in the shape of an X. It's a prize to her, not a brand. Says with a smile, "Confirmed green."

"I don't understand . . ." He shakes his head.

"I always told Ren that miracles exist," Aven says knowingly.

Ter ain't entirely convinced, but a few seconds later he returns the hug, wrapping his arms around her, squashing her tiny frame against his chest. "You're okay?" he whispers into her hair, dazed as I was. Am.

Aven giggles. "How have you been? Do you still like your dad? Did you ever get a mom too? I want to hear everything . . . from the moment you were adopted up until this very instant. Don't leave a thing out." She takes him by the wrist and pulls him under one of the free antinoise beams in the corner.

"Don't go too far?" I say first to her, then to Ter.

Aven rolls her eyes, and I swear it's like I'm looking at myself. "This is T-Bone, Renny," she says through a grin. "You don't have to worry."

"I'll watch her," Ter calls back, and they duck off.

I'd trust Ter with my life, but I don't like this—not one bit. A palm on my arm forces my attention. "What?" I huff, even though I know it's Derek, and whip around.

He takes me by the arm, leads me back under the antinoise beam.

Technology is cruel—no one should be denied the right to give "I can't hear you" as an excuse not to talk at a party.

Pointing behind me, "I really should stay with Aven," I say.

"What the hell is going on? How is she here? Why would you bring her?"

I swallow the insult—my jaw clenches. "I didn't *bring* her—she followed me. And why are you acting like I'm hiding something? I don't know how she's here. I just know that she is. Can't you just be happy, like the rest of us?"

I wish *I* were just happy.

Derek's eyes are stuck to my face, clinical and detached. He even leans in, like he's going to examine the wound.

"When did Aven get better? And when did you notice the cut starting to heal?"

The questions—they're so specific. Like there's an answer that makes sense, and if I give the right one he'll figure it all out. A twinge in my gut stops me from answering straightaway. I feel myself wanting to lie—why, though? It's more than not wanting to break *CVH* guidelines and tell him about the fresh, and it's more than being afraid of him thinking I'm crazy.

To be honest, I can't put my finger on it. But I'm not one to ignore my gut. "This afternoon," I lie.

Muttering to himself, "That doesn't make any sense."

"What doesn't make any sense?"

"This whole thing . . ." he answers too quickly. "You think that a cut healing in twenty-four hours—less than that—makes sense?" He seems almost angry now, and I'm not sure what to make of it.

"No," I answer, and look away. Of course it doesn't. And part of me, a nagging in the back of my brain, wants to dig deeper. To understand how any of this is possible. But I'm also afraid of looking too closely. Some things, especially good things, disappear once you start picking them apart, trying to understand them. I don't want to explain miracles.

Then they stop being miracles, and can be undone.

"Look," I tell him, still avoiding his gaze. "Alls I care about is that she stays here. Alive. Healthy. Happy. Look at her, Derek. I've haven't seen her like this since Nale's. I'm not going to question it. What I am going to do, however, is make sure she stays healthy. She's probably thirsty. Hungry, too. I won't have her passing out because I forgot to feed her."

"Right," he mumbles, dropping his eyes. The questioning, the irritation, it all leaves his face. "I'm sorry. That was insensitive. Of course I'm happy she's better. I'm just concerned, that's all. Let me get her something from the bar."

His voice is so earnest that I want to put my arms around him, to hold him. I don't know why it occurs to me in this moment, but I realize that whenever we have any kind of spat, it's always because he cares about me. It's always because he worries. But with Aven healthy and my head wound healed, what could he be worried about?

"I'll get it," I tell him. "Will you watch her for me?"

Derek nods, glancing back at the two of them. Then, before I turn to step out of the antinoise beam, someone else steps in. It's her. . . . *Kitaneh.*

She cozies up to Derek's side, drink in hand, and ignores me completely. I can't ignore her though. Now that I'm closer, I see . . . it's not that she's just beautiful, it's like she's made of different stuff. *Magnetic.* Naked-faced, too, unlike most of the girls around who'll primp themselves unrecognizable.

In a singsong voice: "And what's going on over here?" Kitaneh asks Derek, her cheeks dimpling with the sly half smile she gives him. Makes me want to puke.

Derek rubs his jawline and the nape of his neck. His nerves are all over the place. "We were just—talking," he stammers.

He may have said Kitaneh isn't his girlfriend, but he's sure acting like she is—it's as though he's been caught with his hand in the cookie jar. *Wait . . . does that make me the cookie?*

"Won't you introduce me to your friend?" Kitaneh asks, still not a glance to spare for me.

Derek's silent for a moment too long, and so I introduce myself instead. "Ren," I say, waiting for her to look at me. In the eye, preferably.

Smirking, she actually gives me the up-down. "And how old are you, Ren?"

Oh, she's good. Her voice is whipped cream, nothing but sugar—I can see her laughing on the inside. It's right there, in the corners of her eyes.

I won't let it get to me, though I understand the gibe—Derek's a few years older than I am. Twenty, maybe. I just shake my head, show her who the immature one is for asking such an obviously dumb question, and turn to Derek.

"You'll watch Aven?"

"Of course," he tells me, and as I step out of the antinoise beam, I hope for his sake he and Kitaneh aren't together.

She may be magnetic, but you've got to be crazy to actually *want* to be around her.

Away from the others, people pin me more easily. I hear the whispers. I'm the one that nearly died. I fold myself into the crowds, hoping I don't see the Derbies, and try to disappear below heads much higher than my own. Except that makes my next task somewhat difficult.

I wasn't lying about wanting to get Aven some food and drink from the bar, but I have another reason for leaving her alone: Officer Justin Cory.

He led me to the fresh—he's got to know something about its unusual "side effects." And where did he get his tip? If he's here, I've got to find him. Fast, so I can get back to Aven.

"Miss Red, the Undead Rida!" a voice clucks from behind the bar. Never one for subtlety, this lady. "Step right on over and take yer round, darlin'. On the house."

I guess being the survivor of a recent near-death incident has its perks (aside from, you know, the survival part).

I squeeze through the pushing bodies, ignoring the occasional "wachit" or "uggdh."

"Heya, Pidge," I call out, tipping my head up. Way up. Pidge is tall enough to give the Empire Clock a height complex.

She smiles, toothy but kind, and claps a hand over mine. "Let's celebrate, eh? To not dying. Something bubbly, I think." Then all I can see is her pigeon-gray hair as she rummages behind the bar.

"Not much in the mood for spirits," I say. "But you can help me out another way."

Pidge doesn't listen, too busy fighting to free a bottle from the evil clutches of its cork. "Our near-dead racers always get a special round o' the house. Only polite, it is. Drink up."

She passes me something fizzy and green, and I hear her mutter about the "change in times." How kids my age couldn't drink legally before the Wash Out, and we'd do just about anything to get liquored up.

Always thinking about the customer, that's what I love about Pidge.

I take a sip and she's satisfied.

"Now. How can I be of service?"

"You seen any out-of-towners?" I ask casually, glancing back to where I left Aven.

"What, who? Out-o'-towners? Naw." Pidge shakes her head. "Wait, maybe, I have." At that she pauses, chuckles knowingly.

"Either you have, or you haven't. Which one is it?"

"I'd say, yes. Yes I have."

Exasperated, I spin around on the stool.

Standing right in front of me, one hand about to tap my shoulder, I see Justin Cory.

14

10:15 P.M., SATURDAY

"**Y**ou . . ." I start, unprepared, jumping off the stool. "You're
here."

*So he has no idea I met with Dunn, or that I know he's
not really with the DI.*

At least until I get some answers, I'd like to keep it that
way. Whatever he knows about the water, I want to know too.
Not just 'cause Chief asked me to, either—so long as Aven's
involved, it's information I need. For myself. For her.

Though I wouldn't turn down the green. It's not like we
don't need it.

Justin cocks an eyebrow, clasps his hands behind his back.
"You thought I might not show?"

I realize I don't know what I'm thinking, because it hits me
that Justin Cory could be anyone. He could be worse than

the DI—a corporate bigwig with money to burn, looking to be the first to get his hands on a gold mine.

My throat parches. Wish I hadn't sipped on that drink. Suddenly, meeting up with him seems like a very bad idea. . . .

Anxious, I scan the dance floor for any hired help he might have tagging along. A muscleman, maybe. Then I look to the corners of the club. Coast seems clear, but with so many people around, there's room for error.

I keep my eyes down, away from his. Pointing in the direction of the bathrooms, I yell, "Follow me," over the music, and lead the way through the pulsing lights.

Heads turn as we pass. I'm already known in the Ward, and this guy sticks out like a sore thumb. Shoes shined, suspenders for holding up his pants—he's dressed the way the Derbies wish they could but don't have the money to pull off. My chest buzzes with all the attention we're drawing, and not in a good way.

Inside the bathroom, glad to be away from the crowds, I swallow my relief and check under the stalls to make sure we're alone. Then, I lock the door.

Almost immediately, Justin leans his back up against it.

In my throat, my breath catches, and I hope he don't notice. I don't like this, him cutting off the exit. Feels like a threat.

Then, all politeness, he says, "I'm sorry to hear about your accident. It must've been terrifying. I can't imagine doing what you do."

He's so clearly not with the DI, I don't know how to even reply.

Spotting the cuts on my face—what's left, anyway—Justin leans in. Gives me the same look Derek did. Only his reads more amazement than anger. "You didn't have this scar yesterday. . . ."

"No," I answer, wary. "Slight scrape from the crash."

"And it's already healed?" His stance is casual—back still up against the wall, knee bent—but the words sound shrill, tense. Excited.

He knows something.

Tucking his hands into his front pants pockets, "So. Let's talk," Justin begins. But then he stands up straight, says, "Oh, yes—" and reaches in his breast pocket.

The envelope he pulls out is crisp and white. Tells me how loaded he must be, since neither the Isle nor the Ward harvests trees. That's only done Upstate, or on the Mainland, and imported goods are pricey.

"For you," he says, passing it over. "I'm one to keep my word. I said you would get your money. Whether or not you were successful."

Who is this guy? Even the tassels on my Hessians are amazed—he's keeping his promise.

I open the envelope, count the money. It's all there, neatly paper-clipped together. A sum that would amount to my winnings if I hadn't thrown the race. Stuffing the green into my bra, I relax a bit. Whoever he is, he seems decent. More decent than most of the Derbies or dragsters. Far more decent than the DI.

"You'll get the extra." He eyes the scarring across my temple and with a nod adds, "Depending on whether or not you tell me what you found."

He seems so sure I found something. . . .

A rap on the bathroom door cuts my thoughts short.

"Occupied!" I shout back, while I replay the last thirty seconds in my head. The way he nodded to my cut—there's no doubt about it. He believes the two are connected.

To Justin, in a whisper: "It's not just freshwater, is it?"

Someone is still banging their fist against the door. "Ren? You in there?" Ter's voice calls from the other side, a sharpness that I'm not used to. Like he's afraid.

I reach for the knob, but Justin blocks it with his body.

"It's Aven," Ter shouts, and now the sharpness makes sense. "She's not feeling well . . . something's wrong. You should come out."

No . . . I think. *She was fine not ten minutes ago.*

I reach for the knob again and look up at Justin, expecting him to try and stop me. I'll fight him if need be. But his clear, baby-blue eyes drop, concerned. There's worry there. Without hesitation, he slides out of the way. Even opens the door. *He's letting me leave?*

Again, his decency is a shock, but there's no time to wonder at it.

Immediately, Ter drags me by the arm. Cuts straight through the dance floor rather than walking the long way around. The way he grips my wrist, his speed, how he pushes people aside—he wouldn't be rushing like this if . . . if something weren't wrong. Really wrong.

Panic clenches my stomach, the slow fuse of a bomb, waiting, waiting. Combined with the heavy beats pounding away, my heart's pace rises too many notches, too fast. I have to force myself to breathe.

We reach the other side of the Tank, and I spot her. She's crouched against the glass wall, head hanging low. Her near-white hair glows, a purple halo draping around her shoulders, hiding her face.

I drop to my knees, clutch the tiny bones of her ankles. Using the back of my hand, I push the long, pale strands over one shoulder. Tipping her chin, "Feathers?"

"Renny, you're back," she mumbles, breaths heavy. A feeble smile. "I'm okay. . . . It's nothing. Just a little weak, that's all." She leans her head on the wall, glances from Derek to Ter. "See, guys? I'm fine."

Fine. She's definitely not fine . . . but maybe it's not as bad as I thought. Of course she's weak, she's been in bed for months. Her muscles ain't used to any of this. It was too much, too fast. Still, the panic ticks in my gut.

Gently, I wrap my arms around her, lift her to her feet. "Let's get you home."

She sways, falls against me. Two years younger, my sister is still a few good inches taller. I stumble backward, catching both of us. A hand low on my back, firm, steadies me. From over my shoulder, Derek yells for Ter to help and rushes to grab her waist.

Aven's knees buckle; she collapses onto Derek's side. I watch as her eyes roll back in their sockets, leaving only white behind.

"Aven?" I choke out.

The panic in my stomach detonates. Shock waves rock

my body. I can't breathe, there's nothing for me to breathe. It's like I'm back in the Strait, ice water flooding my lungs, numbing every muscle and bone from the outside in.

No, it's worse.

That I could control. I could swim up, I could find air. This, now . . . There's nothing I can control. I can't help her—

Her limbs stiffen; she starts trembling, shaking. Convulsing. It's too much to watch.

What have I done? How could I have let her stay?

My fault . . . this is all my fault.

At the realization, my brain pixelates. Turns to static. A blank, gray-white screen with nothing on. Somewhere else, a world spins in its orbit without me. The club funnels into darkness. Distant, faraway music wails in my eardrums, liquid metal spilling into a mixing bowl with computers. Notes drag, everything skips.

Even in my mind, only one image skips, stuck on repeat: Aven's eyes rolling, rolling, rolling back into her head.

I can't stop it.

"Your shirt!" a voice yells from behind me, right at my ear.

The closeness of the words, their strangeness—it draws me out of my stupor. Grafts me to the present. A shirt? Why? *I don't understand. How is any of this happening?*

Then Terrence's top is off, and I'm back in real time, still watching, still not able to stop anything. Aven's body writhes on the floor.

She's on the floor? How did she get on the floor . . . *Your sister is on the floor and you didn't even see it happen?*

Ter tilts her head to the side. He holds up his T-shirt while vomit falls from her mouth. Drips down her cheek. She's blank faced, irises invisible. She doesn't even know that she's just thrown up. Her mind's not there, she's not there.

She is, though—I let her come down. I said it was okay. Only an idiot would've done that, I never should have agreed.

But she was better.

This whole time I've been blaming myself for allowing her to stay, when there's so much more. Fresh guilt floods my face with heat—I let her drink from my canteen. *What kind of a sister am I?*

Who would let anyone—much less their sick sister—drink untested water?

"What should I do?" I think I ask. No one hears me, and I realize the words never made it past my lips. Everything feels so heavy, my limbs, the air, the music. There's a lump, a brick, in my throat, but I'm too ashamed to cry. I want to move to her, to push her hair away, or rest her head in my lap like I do at home when the headaches get real bad, but my feet are anchors. I don't move. Can't move.

Go to her, I tell myself. *She needs you.* This may be my fault, but she's still my sister. . . . I have to force my guilt to take the backseat, and I do. But when I try to take a step forward, I realize that someone's been holding me up this whole time.

In my ear, Derek whispers, "You're back. . . ." and unfolds one arm from my waist.

I can only assume he's talking to me as I stagger forward. I can't reach her, though—one of the Bouncers pushes me to the side. He doesn't even push, not really. One moment I occupy the space, and another it's his. Like displacing air.

The Bouncer pulls out his scanner and lifts her arm. Anytime someone falls sick in the Tank, it's standard protocol for Bouncers to take their VEL, even though they already did. The scanner flashes green: NOT CONTAGIOUS.

He shakes his head—the brackhead isn't even bothering to hide his disappointment as he calls into his cuffcomm for an ambulance. To him, the fact that she's sick at all is irrelevant. He's not making any money on her.

He'd probably be happy if she turned up contagious.

Red, molten anger bubbles to the surface.

"She's going to Ward Hope. Step aside," he says, motioning for me to move as another Bouncer wheels over a stretcher. When I don't budge, he places his two huge hands on my hips, like he's going to move me by force.

"Don't put your grubby hands on me," I spit, fighting back a slow, swelling rage. "She's my *sister*—I'm going with her."

He laughs, his grin uneven, like one side of his mouth got caught on a fishing line. "Sure she is."

I can't help it—all the fear and guilt and shame of the last fifteen minutes wants an outlet. It needs a new home, and it lands on a perfectly good target. Instinctively, my hand balls up. It also instinctively pulls back and flies into his arm.

Okay, if I'm being honest with myself . . . this is more about poor anger management than about instinct. And the moment my knuckles make contact with the shining nylon black-and-yellow fabric of his jacket, it occurs to me that this was not entirely well thought out.

I barely feel bone. It's all mush and muscle under there.

The Bouncer, he don't even flinch. Not a dent, a scowl, a sign that yes, my fist did in fact make contact with his body. Nothing.

He's ignoring me.

He *can't* ignore me—I have to go with her. *He has to let me go with her.*

He's lifting her onto the stretcher, wheeling her away. I rush after, bodychecking him to the side.

With him out of my way, I lean over Aven. I hardly see the Bouncer behind me as his knee buckles and he staggers backward.

When he holds on to the stretcher for balance it rolls out of his grip, and then I see him. He's right behind me—

We collide.

He elbows me in the ribs at first, tries to push me to the side, but I've got Aven's hand in mine now, and I won't let go. Then I feel the bulk of his elbow like an anvil as it connects with my temple.

I go down hard and heavy, hearing a chorus of curses with the use of only one ear. In the way, way back behind my eyelids, starlike fish swim in the void. And I'm underwater, and I'm underwater.

15

ding-ding-ding-ing brings me back to the world.

I open my eyes to a blur of light so thick, every other shape is reduced to haloed shadows. My palms dig against these hard silver dots, a floor that looks like bubble wrap, if bubble wrap were metal. I don't know exactly where I am, but the space is small, and I'm moving up. And that rhythmic dinging—I'm in an elevator. Not for the average partygoer, either. It's the Tank's service elevator, I think.

Then I remember getting elbowed in the head, and the rest of it comes back. My lungs prove that they're in working order, and I start heaving, making myself dizzy.

"Slow breaths," a voice says, standing over a stretcher. *Aven's stretcher.*

Too quickly I rise to my feet, stumbling into the side of the elevator.

She's not moving.

My gut hurts, and I'm not sure if it's from the feeling of everything coming to pieces or from that blow to my head. Both, probably. I push the hair from her forehead, wishing we were both back at the 'Racks, curled up in bed, telling each other stories. I'd rather her sick like she was yesterday. Not sick like she is now.

"Is she going to be okay?" I ask, watching her stillness. Then I realize, I'm not even supposed to be here with her. Aven and I ain't family, not by blood anyway. How am I allowed here?

I look up, and it's Justin's face I see. "What—?"

"Am I doing here?" he finishes, eyes glued to another, more complicated-looking VEL scanner. Then he leans over Aven, tilts her head with one hand to examine something.

The tumor. It's back, visible again. Not as large as before, but I can see it. We both can. I stifle a gasp, shaking my head. *Not possible.*

"She's stable, for now. I've given her an anti-inflammatory and a heavy dose of Dilameth for the pain. No longer contagious, I presume?" He doesn't say it the way the Bouncer did. The way his brow furrows, his jaw tenses—it's like he cares. Dangling from his neck, a blue dog tag with the hammered image of a snake coiled around a rod.

A doctor.

"Who are you?" I ask, gripping Aven's hand. She doesn't grip back. Her hand is limp, which just makes me hold on tighter.

"My name is Callum Pace," he answers. "And I'm sorry to have mislead you."

"You don't work for the Blues."

He sighs. Looks around the elevator. I guess he decides it's safe enough, 'cause he says, "Not anymore, no. We had a sort of . . . falling-out. I now go by the name Justin Cory, Dr. Justin Cory," he says pointedly, and I get the hint. Call him Dr. Cory. "After you left the bathroom, I saw this young girl collapse. I knew the Bouncers wouldn't provide her with the medical attention she needed, being that she's probably not contagious. So I stepped in." A pause. "I hope that's all right with you?"

Of course it's okay. . . . A doctor helping my sister, not asking for pay.

"When did you first notice her symptoms?" He wraps his fingers around her wrist to take her pulse.

"Three years ago . . ." I mumble, avoiding his eyes.

"And she's still able to come to parties at the Tank?" Then, when he looks at me, something like understanding dawns on his face.

I don't answer. All I can do is look at Aven's face, watch and imagine movement there.

Then I'm no longer imagining it. Her eyelids flutter, just barely. I'm sure of it—

"Feathers?" I say, bending closer.

A tiny smile grazes her lips. "I ruined your night." Her words are so quiet I have to lower myself inches from her mouth to hear.

"Shhh," I whisper, and I kiss her knuckles.

"Are you mad?"

"No, no, no. Of course not," I tell her. Even though I am. *At myself.*

"Ren?" Aven tugs at the hem of my shirt, her breathing thin. I shush her, but it doesn't matter. "You think T-Bone could like me again?" she asks seriously, like her very life depends on the answer. "Even though I'm going to . . ."

"Hey, you're not going anywhere. And yeah, I think you and Ter would make an adorable couple."

One final *ding*, and we're at sea level, the ground floor. Callum wheels Aven out of the elevator, into a shock of cool night air. I follow. Terrence and Derek wait for us there, pacing and arguing with each other.

"Finally!" Derek calls out, covering the distance between us in only a few strides. "It's been forever."

"Service elevators," Callum replies curtly, even though Derek wasn't talking to him. Looking at me, he says, "We're going to Ward Hope. Hop in." He gestures to the hulking red marine transport that waits at the edge of the dock.

We jog together—two of my steps matching one of his.

Callum lifts the hatch, but Derek calls out, "Wait!" just as I'm about to jump in. He runs to catch up, and when he's close enough, he leans toward me. "Ren, I want to come with you." His eyes flick to Callum. "Aren't you suspicious? Why is a West Isle doctor hanging around these parts?"

Why, indeed. I thought I knew who he was. Now he could be anybody.

I look down the hatch into the red emergency-transport sub. There's barely enough room for Aven, much less Callum, me, and Derek. "I don't know why he's here," I answer, speaking the truth. "But . . . trust this guy or not, I'm going with. So is Aven."

Derek shifts his body slightly, covers the hatch of the submarine with his arm to stop me.

"Derek," I plead, and my voice breaks. "I don't think you understand. I won't leave her again. For three years I've been leaving her, and this last time, she almost . . ." I don't finish the sentence. Never before did that reality seem so close. "I never shoulda left her, not ever." The words tumble out too fast, and then silence is the only thing to listen to. I'm about to cry—the muscles in my throat burn, I'm holding it back so hard.

Derek brings his hand to his forehead, runs it through his hair, worry all over his face. Then, almost as though he needs it as much as I do, he folds his arms around me, resting my head against his chest.

I'm too shaken by everything that's happened tonight to think about it, but dim recognition dawns that this feels natural, comfortable in a way it wouldn't have yesterday. I curl up against him, allowing myself just a few moments, and breathe him in.

I also allow myself to believe that maybe he was telling the truth. About Kitaneh.

I pull away before the thought lasts too long. No time to waste on me. "See you at the hospital?"

The smallest movement—his fists balling up at his sides— makes it clear he doesn't like my leaving. But it also shows he's fighting to keep quiet, which means he understands.

I hop down into the transport sub behind Callum, and when I lower myself into the cabin, the doctor's hands steady me by the waist.

"Your file didn't say you had a sister," Callum notes as the sub sails through the underwater city.

Always knew I had a file. But I don't like that this guy thinks he knows me 'cause some lights on a screen gave him my stats. "We're not blood. And anyway, it ain't your business," I say quietly, watching Aven. "Bet the file didn't say a lot of things."

My tone smarts in my ears—I'm being too harsh on him. It's just, small talk hurts more than silence. "I'm sorry," I say into my hands. "I'm sorry. Thank you. You know I mean thank you. I'm just . . ." I cut myself off, choking the rest of the sentence by biting into my fist.

"You don't have to say anything."

So I don't, and the only noise comes from the soft whooshing of the steam engine and Aven's air flowing in and out. As I press my forehead to hers, she reaches for my shoulder, clutches it tight.

Too tight.

"Where are you?" she rasps, too sudden. "Ren? Where'd you go?"

I get closer, leaning in so my face is clear in front of hers. "Right here, I'm right here—"

"What's going on? Why can't she see me?" I ask Callum, all the fear racing back.

"Her brain is swelling," he answers. "I gave her all the

anti-inflammatory medication that the Tank had on hand, but she needs more, soon."

"Well, why don't you tell it to that guy?" I cry, waving my arm toward the driver.

Callum pushes a red button on the side of the sub, which obviously means "speed the hell up," because the driver suddenly grows a pair and we're really moving.

Aven smiles. It drops away too quickly. Her eyes roll back into her head again, and then fix on me. "Can we fly home now? I have wings, too. Just like you. See?" She lifts her arms; this isn't one of her games.

"Why is she saying that?" I'm trying to stay calm, but my heart becomes a wild animal. Starts slamming against my rib cage like it wants out of my body, fast. My vision even goes black around the edges, and soon I'm looking at everything through a funnel of darkness. *Breathe. You're no good to anyone if you pass out too.*

If only Derek or Ter could have come with us—this would be so much easier.

Callum moves me aside and places a mask with a breathing tube over her face. "She's hallucinating. The swelling is depriving her brain of oxygen. If we don't get her there fast . . ."

The sentence dangles there, but I know how it ends. Comatose.

16

11:45 P.M., SATURDAY

Standing up.

Sitting down.

The waiting room is the color of old pigeon crud, white and yellowed and crusty, and I'm wondering if I can peel the paint off the walls.

Biting my nails down to their beds.

They took Aven away, wheeled her off into the great crap-colored yonder, and left me sitting here.

Up.

Down—

No, wait. Pacing. Pacing is the way to go, most definitely. I keep moving to hold the guilt at bay. Every time I stop, I feel it closing in, and my eyes start to fill up with salt water. I go back to the moment at the 'Racks when I give her the water.

I rewind. Make the right choice, the smart one. The one that doesn't send Aven to the hospital. My mind tilts and gravity no longer works like normal—I feel like I'm in a constant state of sideways free fall.

So I keep myself moving, read the signs around me. Anything to distract. Tacked loosely to the whitewashed walls hang poster after poster, each one aiming to convince you to get tested.

Are you experiencing shortness of breath?
Have you blacked out with no apparent cause?
Do you sometimes see blood when you cough?
If so, you may have contracted Hyper Basilic
Neoplasma Contagion, or "HBNC,"
and you could be contagious.
Get tested.
We can help.

They leave out the bit where you could get arrested for transmitting it, of course. Which is impossible to prove, by the by, but the Blues don't care none. So long as someone's getting blamed, and it's not them, they're happy. If that's not incentive to find out you've got a deadly disease, I don't know what is.

Minutes pass, hours pass, decades and centuries—*Where are the guys?*—then it becomes universes and galaxies that pass, and with all this pacing, it's as though I'm running through the space-time continuum, but when I look up, nothing has changed. I'm alone. Alone.

Soon enough, that's how I'll be all the time.

I try and steel my mind to the thought, except my mind

and body are on two different planets so even if I harden one, the other is off doing its own thing. I'm so in my head, I don't even notice when Derek and Terrence finally come bounding into the hospital.

"Where is she?" they ask in unison, and when I look up, Derek walks close—too close—and pulls my hands into his.

"What are you doing to yourself?" he asks.

Here I'd thought I was keeping it together pretty well. "What do you mean?"

He brings my hands in front of my face—shows me my bloodied nail tips, raw and red smeared.

"Oh . . ." I say, not really caring. "I hadn't noticed."

"You need a Band-Aid," Terrence comments, running to a nurse behind the counter.

"Go wash the blood off," Derek tells me, putting his hand on my back and pushing me in the direction of the bathroom.

I can't see why any of this matters.

I go to the bathroom anyway. It's easier than thinking for myself.

There's a rusty faucet in here, and even the hospital doesn't spill its filtered rainwater for visitors—just chlorinated brackish water. Only patients get fresh. The murk runs over my hands, mixing together with my blood, then whirlpooling down the drain. I wait to feel something, some pain to bring me back to myself. But I guess biting my fingernails wasn't enough, 'cause I feel nothing. That, or everything has shut down.

I walk back to the waiting room and sit beside Derek and Terrence, all three of us quiet. After a few moments of the mind-numbing silence, Derek tugs my hands away again.

I'm back to gnawing at my cuticles like they're dinner.

"I can't help it," I growl, exasperated. This is not the Important Thing that's going on right now.

Derek won't let go of my hands, though, when I try and move on to chewing at the nail beds since the nails are mostly gone. I meet his eyes and glower, yanking my hands, but with his solid-as-cement grip, it's useless.

"She needs you right now." Our eyes are still magnets—mine angry and filled with venom, his weary but calm. Polar opposites that can't let go of the other.

And it occurs to me: those are the only words anyone could have spoken to me that might've had any chance at keeping me sane. Somehow, he knew. He didn't tell me to calm down, or to relax. That would've just pissed me off. It's a comfort, when someone knows you like that. Would I know what to say to him, if the tables were turned?

I quit the tug-of-war and force my hands to slacken, which is when I realize that Derek's holding them for good, and he ain't letting go. I try not to focus too hard on what that means, or doesn't mean.

A radio blares from the receptionist's desk, even though they've got hologram TVs overhead. Cheaper that way, keeping the radio on for nighttime use. We've all fallen into a tense silence, so with nothing else to listen to, we're forced to hear news of yet another West Isle Blight outbreak.

Derek rolls his eyes in Terrence's direction, then opens his mouth to speak. The next piece of news stops him before he starts.

". . . the West Isle citizens are even planning a rally. At dawn tomorrow morning, in front of town hall, individuals are encouraged to attend and voice their discontent with Governor Voss's inability to address the two major issues facing the United Metro Islets: a viable freshwater source, and the spread of the HBNC virus."

"They're rallying," Derek says. "Things must be getting serious."

"A rally won't help nothing," I say. "You can't make water appear where there's none, and you can't disappear a sickness."

Those last words make me queasy. For one perfect moment, I thought it was possible—a sickness just disappearing. Nothing's that easy. I knew nothing was that easy. Water can't heal, especially not the water I found. It's dangerous, and I handed it to my sister on a silver platter.

I shut my eyes to keep the tears away.

"Miss Dane?" the receptionist calls out. "Please step to the front desk."

I snap my head up, slip my hands from Derek's. Their sudden coldness makes me tuck them under my armpits. I stand, nervous. Never liked being called by my last name. It's always bad news.

At the window, a woman seated in a low chair points to a laser projection, red against the white counter. At first I don't know what she's asking of me. That is, until I see the dollar sign.

Aven's first hospital bill. The first of many.

I pull the cash Callum gave me earlier out from my bra and slide it across to the woman. There goes the money that was supposed to get Aven and me through till the end of the month, when I get my stipend.

If I get my stipend.

Who knows—the chief might suspend my contract if the sample I gave him turns out to be a viable source of freshwater.

The doors swing open and Callum—Dr. Cory—strides though, a white mask dangling from his neck. I look for signs of what he's about to tell me, and straightaway I notice his hands. They're tucked into the pockets of his lab coat in a comfortable, relaxed Good News sort of way.

"How is she?" I blurt, leaving the counter to join him.

Don't say "coma." Don't say "coma."

Please don't—

"She's awake, but the growth . . . it needs to be removed. Quickly."

"That can even be done?" I ask. I'll find a way to cover it. However I have to, I'll find a way.

"It's risky, but it's her only option."

"And it'll fix her?"

Callum pauses. "It's a patch. And that's provided she doesn't bleed out on the table. If successful, however, she could live another year, depending on how fast the tumor grows back. HBNC-related growths have a hundred-percent return rate, but they sometimes return more aggressively than they did at primary onset. She could live a year. She could also live a month, or less."

Boy doesn't mince words.

Last question. The one I need to ask, though the answer changes nothing.

"How much will it cost us?" I hold my breath and wait for an answer.

When Callum finds my eyes again, something like guilt catches in his expression. "I don't know, but I'd like to try talking to some people. I might be able to do something for you. No promises, of course."

Is he saying he can get her the surgery for free? Is that what he's saying?

I don't feel comfortable outright asking—always said I'm no one's charity case. But for Aven, I'd eat my pride, I'd take whatever they're willing to offer. Got to wonder why he'd stick his neck out, though, for a roofrat like me.

"Aven's surgery has been scheduled for tomorrow morning, nine a.m.," he continues. "You can see her in a few moments, if you like. The nurse will be with you shortly to assist from here on in. Oh, yes . . ."

Callum takes me by the elbow, leads me out of earshot of the others. "Two things. First, a reminder. Do not offer my real name to anyone," he says, then eyes the name tag pinned to his coat. "I've been working under the Blues' radar for about six months now, and I'd like to keep it that way."

The whys come back—there's so much I want to know—but now's not the time. So I just say, "Sure. Dr. Cory," and I keep the questions to myself. I'm going to get some answers from him. Just don't know how. Yet.

"Also," the doctor says, checking his cuffcomm for the time. From his lab coat pocket he pulls out a shiny, fancy pen. I can't help but wince, watching as he tears off the corner of yet another envelope and writes something on it.

When he's done, he holds up the piece of paper and pushes

it into my fist. "They can tap the cuffcomm they gave you too easily."

In a low voice: "Aven was very sick before tonight, wasn't she?" And then, his face a mixture of distress and hope, he whispers, "You found it," and watches me for my answer.

I drop my chin the slightest bit, meeting his eyes. For a moment our gazes are locked. I nod.

"Find me. I can help her," he insists, his tone soft. Desperate, almost. "And bring a sample. It's the only way."

But I don't have a sample—I gave it to Chief. . . .

"I think we got to your sister just in time." One last pleading look and Callum tips his chin, much the same as I've seen the Derbies do, but with respect. First to Ter, then Derek, and me last. Once more he looks at me, before heading down the corridor.

Still turned from the others, I look at the piece of paper, then stuff it into my bra for safekeeping. It's his address.

We got to your sister just in time.

A gentle reminder that without his help, she might be dead.

But then, a voice, small and angry and irrational, gnaws at my mind: without his "help" I never would have found the water, or given it to Aven in the first place.

The fault is just as much his as it is mine.

I walk back to Derek and Ter, chewing on my lip, suddenly full of anger. Not at myself anymore, though. Now, now it's toward Callum. If he'd never found me . . . or lied about being with the Blues . . .

"It's just so weird," Terrence comments. "She seemed fine. Did you change her meds or anything?"

Sitting down, I cradle my head in my hands. His question rings in my mind.

The guilt comes back, tidal. For a few measly seconds I'd been able to forget it, put it on someone else, but I'm glad it's back. Because that sort of thing is too big, too important to forget. Or deny. Even for a second. I should feel it—the sick, gut-twisting knife of my stupidity. I should feel it over and over and over again.

And I should make it right. I gave her the water, I'm responsible for making sure she gets better. Which means she needs to have the surgery. I can pay for the surgery with the extra Callum promised.

Not hiding his suspicion, "What did that guy hand you?" Derek asks.

"*Dr. Cory* handed me the names of some herbs I can pick up on Mad Ave to help her with the pain." It could be true. Herbs ain't offered in hospitals, but that don't mean they won't help her. Pricey, though, like anything grown in soil.

Derek looks down at his cuffcomm like he's reading a message. Then he stands up, face drawn and grave. "*Brack*—I'm so sorry, Ren. I just got a call from a friend. I have to be somewhere."

"You're serious?" I ask, stunned. A friend? I swallow, knowing full well what that means.

Her. He can't leave. He can't. . . . If there's one thing he could do to make every feeling I've ever had for him die a quick, early death, it would be this.

"Yeah, man," Ter says. "Stay . . . we should be seeing Aven any minute."

Almost on cue, the double doors open. A woman in white

calls my name while reading from a clipboard.

"Look, we're headed in now. Let's go." Ter rises to his feet.

I search Derek's face, as though I might find out what could be so important that it would take him away. At this hour. From here.

And from me, a hurt, wishful part of myself adds.

But his face is no better than stone: hard, without expression.

"I'm sorry. . . . It's an emergency," Derek pleads, looking at me. "Please, tell Aven I hope she feels better. Ren, I'm sorry, I am. . . . I'll come back with you tomorrow. Promise." He backs away from us, then turns and quickens his pace out the hospital doors.

I stand, and Ter and I watch as Derek practically races away. We exchange looks—shocked, confused looks—and without a word follow the nurse.

17

12:30 A.M., SUNDAY

My insides turn to water when I see her—I'm going to be sick.

Tubes snake around Aven's body, laid out too still on the small hospital bed. A curtain divides the room, bluish lights buzz overhead, and the smell . . . it's the smell of dying. Of people waiting to die. That alone shakes me.

"You have five minutes with her." The nurse speaks to us like Aven's not even here. "It's a good thing you were able to bring her so quickly. This is the most aggressively growing tumor I've ever seen. Between the time she was admitted, up until about thirty minutes ago, its diameter increased a full six millimeters. Seems to have slowed now, though, which bodes well. I've never seen anything like it." She shakes her head and, looking over her glasses, adds, "Dr.

Cory said this is primary onset?"

Primary onset . . . Callum said that she wasn't sick before tonight? Must not have wanted to raise any questions, like what she was doing in a club with a baseball-sized tumor pressed up against her skull.

"Yes," I lie. No reason to change the story and raise even more eyebrows. And her situation is already strange enough.

"Ren . . ." Aven moans from her bed.

With a nod the nurse makes for the door. "Five minutes," she reminds us, which makes me want to throw a dart at her face.

Ter and I walk to opposite sides of her bed. "Shhh," I say, and I take Aven's hand in mine. "Don't talk."

"You don't need to talk anyway. We've got Ren in the room," Ter jokes, trying to lighten the mood. He hasn't seen her in years, but it doesn't seem like it matters. His shoulders are hunched, tense. He looks nearly as anxious as I do.

Though Aven's chest rises and falls like it should, I can see that the air tank at her side is doing all the work. Her eyes stay closed, but I hope against hope she can hear me again, that her mind's clearer than it was back in the transport sub.

"I'm sorry we fought. . . ." she says. Pale blond lashes flutter and she opens her eyes slightly, tilts her head in my direction. "Forgive me?"

The question undoes me. Tomorrow they're going to cut her open and she might die, and she's asking forgiveness. That hard lump I'd been fighting off for the last hour finally breaks its hold.

Don't lose it, I tell myself. *If she sees how worried you are, she might not want the surgery.*

Too bad there's no pep talk in the world I could give myself right now that would do any good. I push my palms into my eyes, find water there, and choke on a sob I can't hold back. "There's nothing to forgive, silly." I sniff, my nose suddenly crying too. "We're sisters. Sisters fight. That's, like, half the fun. We should celebrate, actually. I think that was our first fight ever. It's finally official. Really, we should get a certificate of authenticity or something." I laugh and wipe away the salty wet from my cheeks.

Aven giggles, then stops 'cause it makes her breathing too hard.

I smile, kiss her forehead. She always liked my sense of humor. If there's anything I've ever been good at, it's making her laugh. "They're going to make you better tomorrow," I tell her.

"I'm nervous. . . ."

"Don't be, Feathers—"

The woman in white returns, owning the place in just a few steps. "Time for meds," she crows. "Which means it's time for you two to be off. This *is* the critical care unit." She raises an eyebrow and taps her cuffcomm.

"No way, it's only been five minutes, lady. Just a few more, please?" I try to leave the edge out of my voice. This woman is a gatekeeper. I should be buttering her up, but right now I'm just no good at faking nice.

"Visiting hours have been over since eleven. You only got those five minutes because Dr. Cory said it'd be good for the patient," the nurse says, not budging. "Besides, this one needs her rest, what with her surgery tomorrow." She prepares a dose of some liquid that looks like it's going to get fed through one of the dozens of tubes Aven's hooked up to. When the nurse sees her slight crinkle of fear, she says lightly, "Three injections. One for the inflammation, one to help her sleep, and one's a pain reliever. All good things."

All those meds . . .

Within seconds, Aven's zonked out.

"When can I come back?" I ask, still holding her hand.

"Like I said, this is the critical care unit, so visiting hours are limited. If she stabilizes, you can see her more often," she says without answering my question.

"So . . . when can I come back?"

"Right before her surgery tomorrow, if you like." The nurse steers us through the room and out the door, her hand on each of our backs. "Now, off you go."

Ter's Omni barely sways as he brings her dockside. "Drive you home?" he offers, standing over it, ever the good guy.

I didn't notice just how snazzy the carrot was before, being half-dead and all, but now I do—fancy-pants nav system. Autostabilizing props. I nod my thanks and climb in, sinking back into the red leather interior.

"The 'Racks?" he asks.

I swallow my surprise—didn't think Ter knew the 'Racks existed, much less where they're located. He's never been; I've never invited him. Though we were both in the orphanage, once he landed himself a rich dad, we grew up very differently. Doubt his pops would've wanted him hanging around the 'Racks, and no doubt Ter woulda felt mighty out of place there too.

"Mad Ave is fine, actually. I can walk home from there," I answer, thinking of the address in my bra. Callum's place is right off the main drag. I know he said he could only help if I brought a sample . . . but I have to try. "Just want to pick up a bite to eat," I add.

"Mmmm . . ." Ter grumbles and pats his belly. "Jealous."

I'm jealous too. I'm jealous of the lie I just told. My stomach tightens, but I know it'll be a while before I can get my hands on some grub.

As Ter steers the mobile east though the gutterway, I let my mind wander for distractions, watching the underwater city as it rolls tape. History, right in front of us. Deep in the silty, muddy canal, we see just the torso of a sculpture. One of his arms holds up what I think is supposed to be fire, because he's just stolen it. That's how the story goes, at least. Supposedly, we could brush him down and he'd be gold underneath. I never believed it.

Then, when I look around again, we've hit Mad Ave.

"Stop here, if you would," I tell Terrence. I want to ask if he's planning on visiting tomorrow, but I don't. Don't want him to feel obligated or nothing.

Ter gazes wistfully out at the boardwalk. "Eat some dumplings for me, will ya? I'd totally come with if I weren't positive that my dad's been having a two-hour heart attack, wondering where I've been."

I laugh, but I can't help wondering what that'd be like, having someone at home worrying about me. The one person

175

wondering where I am is lying in a hospital bed. It'd be nice though.

Maybe. *Nah*. The word *parents* sours in my head almost as soon as I think it. Better off without. Can't be worrying about any more people dying on me.

"Extra on the grease, just for you," I say with a short wave, wishing I were telling the truth.

The roof clicks closed and Ter smiles his good-bye and the Omni spins out along the canal. As it disappears into the dull, graying morning I glance at the address, now wrinkled and scrappy: *51 Rough Block and Mad Ave #1A.*

Callum Pace. He may have lied, but he also saved my sister.

I have to trust in him, for Aven's sake. Much as I don't like it.

18

2:00 A.M., SUNDAY

Fifty-one Rough Block and Mad Ave.

Prime location, right off the most popular boardwalk east of Central Bay. Prime apartment number, too: 1A. First floor. No walking up any stairs, or across any suspension bridges; sea-level apartments have use of the narrows—planked sidewalks for first-floor tenants. So they don't step out onto water, and all.

The walk is maze free, as most of the vendors are sleeping. But in a few hours, they'll all be selling hotcakes and oatmeal. My mouth can practically taste it, I'm so hungry. Thirsty, too. When I see Rough Block, though, I can push aside the wanting.

I turn left into the gutterway, where the only sounds come from the groaning narrows underfoot. At 51, I knock. Loud.

I'm not going for quiet. Callum's probably sleeping, and I want him to hear me.

A few more knocks, but no one comes. I can't help but examine the padlock.

Maybe he's not even here.

The cuffcomm at my wrist reminds me that we don't have much time—three hours before Chief gets to quad nine. I need to know if Callum can do anything for Aven; otherwise I'm not about to go switching teams. Making enemies with the DI ain't on my to-do list, but if it'll help Aven . . .

In which case, Callum won't mind if I have a look around. Get some answers on my own.

Most apartments use the same standard type of lock, as the original keys for the knobs got lost. First I tug, making sure he hasn't left it unlocked, which he hasn't. Not surprised at that; he's a West Isle boy. Probably thinks the whole of the Ward is crawling with criminals. Which it ain't. Just *some* of the Ward.

I pull out that paper clip he used for the money and fold it up so that the loops make a T. If he's as desperate for this information as I think he is, I doubt he'll hold a little lock picking against me. Not with what I've got to tell him.

Then I take off one boot and use the edge to push the steel wire together. Sliding my foot back into the boot, still snug from its earlier dunking, I push the new-and-improved paper clip turned lock pick into the padlock. After some jiggling around, the lock pops open, and I walk right in.

The room is dark. It feels empty. When I flip the light switch, nothing happens—he did say he was trying to stay off the grid. Soon my eyes adjust, and I cross the apartment toward what looks like blackout curtains. I throw them open, letting just enough light from the walk in so that I can see, and I turn around.

The walls . . .

They must be under there somewhere, but I can't see them. Every inch of space is covered with topographical maps, not just of the city today, but of the city under the water. Manhattan. Pictures, too. From over the years. Black and whites of the skyscrapers, only three of which I recognize. The Empire Clock, the Slant, the Chrysler. Color photos in neons, the buildings lit in ways I've never seen. Like electric three-tiered cakes, each frosted in fluorescence. Awful waste of energy. But imagine racing with those lights on. Damn.

It'd be like running at light speed. Intergalactic travel here on Earth. Brainbuzzed with just the idea of it, I scan the rest of the walls, distracted. A photo catches my eye.

It's me.

Age thirteen. Scrawny, no build, no muscles. Barely even the beloved ass that follows me around everywhere. The good ole days. Hair wild as ever, though, and the same freckled, dusky skin. Black eyes.

The picture is three years old, taken right before I got netted. Before I offered to work for them and Aven found her way to a sickhouse.

Looking at it feels slimy. Like he's been watching me. I understand why Callum has this photo—while he was working with the Blues, he must've taken it from my file so he'd know who to approach. Far as I know, I'm the only mole in town scouting for fresh. The others, whoever they are, keep tabs on potentially contagious citizens who could be spreading the disease around.

Still. This picture reminds me that Callum's in this for his own reasons as well.

Looking at it unnerves me, so I tug the picture from its tack and shove it into my boot. He don't need it anymore, and I want it back.

Where is he? As I look around, it occurs to me that there isn't even a bed. There must be another room. I can't find another door though, with every square inch covered in paper. I step backward—my calf hits something. Something heavy. I feel it tip over with a dull *thump*, and when I spin around, I see a cloth laundry bag open on the floor.

But there aren't clothes inside.

Articles. Spilling out, everywhere. They're each enveloped in see-through film, probably for protection. I pick one up, the one that looks the oldest. Through the film I can see the yellowed paper, its edges rippled from water stains. Says it's from 1940.

MINETTA BROOK GONE FOR GOOD?
No Sign of the Brook in a Decade

The Minetta Brook, which only a decade ago
reappeared in lower and mid-Manhattan, seems to have
gone underground for good.
The spring, once called "Devil's Water" by the

natives for its poor taste and foul smell, plagued lower Manhattanites in 1930.

It is hard to believe that Dutch settlers would have fought over such filth, with other freshwater sources in the vicinity. Originally, though, the Minetta water seemed pure. It was only found to have a sulfuric odor after flowing to the surface, local surveyor Diederick Hoff noted.

Thankfully, the fountain in the lobby of 33 Washington Square West is no longer plagued, and perhaps we may all say, "good riddance."

I place the article back in the cloth bag and consider this "Minetta Brook." Is that what Callum thinks I've found? The location is off—that's not the quadrant he had me survey—but in DI training I did learn there were once whole rivers flowing underground, covering miles. But that was years ago, even before the Wash Out contaminated the reservoirs.

Even if I found the Minetta, it can't explain what happened to Aven. Or me.

When I touch the gash on my temple, all I feel is the thin raised flesh of a scar—it's healed entirely.

Aven, meanwhile, is worse.

From a far corner, a door creaks open—that's gotta be Callum. I need to move, hide, get the hell outta dodge, but all I got time for is stooping behind the worktable.

"I see you!" he shouts, with more force than I would have expected. "I have a gun—show yourself."

Sure enough, from my vantage under his desk, I see he's got his finger on the trigger of a semiautomatic and here I am, a sitting pigeon.

I have no choice. Both hands up, I grumble, "Fine," and back away from his desk. "Hi?" I wave.

"What the hell are you doing here?" he asks, understandably peeved, but he lays the gun on the table.

"Lost in the neighborhood?" I offer. "You *did* give me this." I wave the envelope corner like it's a white flag of surrender. "Remember?"

"You don't just go . . ." he blusters, looking for the right word, "barging into people's places of residence. That's quite insane, you know?"

I step in front of the moonlit windowpane. "Sorry. Just thought you'd want to hear from me sooner rather than later."

"Yes! Yes, of course," he says, and his face lights up, not hiding his excitement. "I'll get the extra. . . ." He fumbles with the lock of a drawer hidden away beneath a small table. From it, he pulls out yet another thick white envelope, which he holds in the air for me to take.

I reach for the envelope. "I found a freshwater spring," I admit. Soon as I hear Callum laugh his disbelief, though, I stop myself from saying more.

What about the Blues?

Working with Callum changes everything. Working with Callum means working *against* the Blues. I'm their mole. Means I keep on getting that monthly paycheck—money Aven and I need now more than ever.

If anyone at the DI finds out I'm working against them, I'll be at their mercy. *Not a good place to be, as they have none.* Miss Nale's words echo in my head from years ago, when she told me to keep my immunity a secret.

But . . . there's another voice in my head. One that, despite everything, hopes against hope. 'Cause that's what hope is: belief against the odds. If Callum can cure her . . . really, truly cure her? For good?

It's a risk worth taking.

I pull back my hand, ignoring the envelope for a moment, and make sure Callum's looking at me. "Aven. You said you could help Aven."

After a pause, he says, "Yes . . . I believe I can."

"You also said you needed a sample."

"Without it, there's not much I can do, I'm afraid."

I glance down to the time on my cuffcomm again. "I don't have it. Chief Dunn paid me an unexpected visit and I told him what I'd found. He's headed for the site in three hours with a whole team."

Callum sits down on the floor, bites at his thumbnail. "I was afraid of that happening," he mumbles.

"Hey—you're the one who claimed you were with the DI," I say.

He just shoots me a look. Thinks for a moment. "We have time though. You could take me there. To the site."

"Tell me what you can do for Aven—I want to know who you are, and why I should trust you—and then, maybe. Maybe I'll take you. I've got a lot at stake, you know? Been relying on my income from the Blues for quite a while."

Callum looks down, solemn. "I understand. I do." He taps his fingers on the table, like he's weighing options I can only guess at. "But how do I know I can trust you? You work for the DI, after all."

"I work for whoever can help me help Aven. If that's you . . ." I shrug.

Callum gestures to a chair. "All right. Take a seat."

Shaking my head, I lower myself onto the floor instead, and cross my legs. I'm more used to sitting this way. Chairs make me uncomfortable.

"My name—my birth name—is Callum Pace. I was part of the Blues' Young Scientists Curriculum. . . . You've heard of it?"

I shake my head.

"A program headed up by Governor Voss. With the Blight spreading, he needed more doctors, so he created an accelerated program for promising youths. Some of us examined geological surveys, theorizing the locations of underground freshwater. Others though, my group, we were studying the HBNC virus and looking for a cure."

"Ambitious for a bunch of . . . wait, how old are you?"

"I was seventeen; this was less than a year ago."

"A little young to have the fate of an entire city's health resting in your hands, don't you think?"

It occurs to me that I'm a dragster working for the government, looking for fresh. Not much different. The DI likes hiring them young, I suppose—cheap labor.

Callum waves his hands. "Oh no, we weren't the only ones working on it. Though I am proud to say that I was doing some of their most promising work," he says, beaming a bit. "That's why the higher-ups gave me superior security clearance. I overheard some of the in-house gossip. One scrap was about you—a girl scouting for fresh in the Ward. A couple of times I overheard my boss's bosses, the chiefs, joking about the governor. How he was hoping that moles like you, who worked for the Blues, would actually find a real, live fountain of youth." He even says it with a laugh, like he knows how daft it sounds.

I raise one eyebrow even though . . . even though it almost makes sense. Not the youth part, or the part where Aven's tumor grew back six millimeters in an hour. But my cuts. And earlier in the night, her tumor was almost gone. "And people *believed* him?"

"Well, no . . . That was the point. The search for freshwater was the perfect cover."

"But you believed him," I point out.

"I didn't. Not until this . . ." He bounces, literally *bounces*, over to a small wooden writing desk in the corner and opens a drawer, one that's hidden underneath the tabletop, using a key from his pocket.

He hands me a small glass vial with no more than a drop of greenish liquid in it. ". . . was given to me. By whom, I don't know. I found it in my DI locker during my time there—my locked locker, mind you—with this article wrapped around it and 'Q9' written on the back."

I take the vial in one hand and the clipping in the other, careful not to press too hard. The paper is so old, just pushing down will crack it. I hold it up to the light.

New York, Saturday, June 2048

Modern-Day Ponce or Modern-Day Ponzi?

To some, medical student Harlan Voss's "findings" could be the next step in the biomedical frontier. To others, he is the product of a culture desperate for youth above all else. Twenty-seven-year-old Voss claims to have found the Fountain of Youth, but without the benefit of proof on his side, his discovery has been met with equal shares of skepticism and hope.

"One man discovered penicillin, did he not?" Mr. Voss asks disbelievers.

According to the modern Ponce de León, the storm surge that preceded what has come to be known as the "Wash Out" caused tides to run so low, they resurrected the Minetta Spring, which once ran through lower Manhattan.

After March's meteor collided with the Antarctic's Pine Island Glacier, and high-temperature gases were released, causing a global rise in sea level, Voss was unable to locate the source of the spring. "I went back with diving gear," he stated during the interview. "But someone had been there. It wasn't even a spring anymore—just rubble and mud."

Now, Voss is looking for the spring. But there's a catch: he needs your money.

Two things stand out.

One: 2048. About sixty years ago.

And two: "Our governor's last name is Voss."

"It could be a relative," Callum suggests. "Or—and I know this sounds crazy—but what if they're the same? What if he found the spring and kept enough to keep him alive for a while?"

I look for similarities in their faces, but it's hard to tell. The governor is older. But both have prickly, cactuslike eyebrows, and faces that would make a baby cry.

"Lemme guess," I say, examining the liquid. "You're gonna tell me this stuff is magic in a bottle?"

Or the devil in a bottle, given what it did to Aven.

"Not magic," he answers. "Science. Under the microscope that stuff looked fairly incredible."

"Incredible how?"

"There wasn't enough to run a sufficient number of tests that would yield anything conclusive . . . but it clearly had a regenerative effect on the human cellular structure."

"Okay. So the water is . . . unusual. But why all the secrecy? Why go searching for it behind the back of the DI? Why pretend you're still with them?"

"I thought that you'd be more likely to agree to the search if it came as a direct request from the DI. Had I known about your sister's condition . . ." Callum's gaze suddenly turns serious. "And as for the secrecy, what do you think would happen if the government got their hands on something this big?"

Waving my hands, I spout the obvious. "Oh, I dunno, how

about use it to cure the virus that's killing off the Ward's citizens left and right?"

"You're naive," he mutters, replacing the vial and the article in the drawer before taking out a Core, a shiny, rainbowy disk no bigger than my thumbnail.

I want to argue—no way am I naive, not these days—but I get the feeling he's about to prove me wrong.

He draws the curtains closed, darkening the room. He slips the disk into a slot in his cuffcomm.

"After reading that article, I conducted some of my own research. I figured, if Voss needed money for a search party, he was probably advertising. This is what I found."

An image projects onto the door behind us. The audio is weak—cuffcomms don't have the best speakers—but it's easy enough to see it's a commercial.

Scratchy background music plays, while three kids hold hands and spin together. As they go round, they age. Slow at first, then faster. Older and older they get; their whirling makes me dizzy. When they're too old to keep on spinning like that, the image slows. A man's voice: "For too long, we have accepted one single fact: humans age."

Graphics-morphing software lifts layers of wrinkles from the women's faces like old-school time-lapse photography in reverse.

Another voice-over: "What if aging were just another disease? A disease that could be cured? With your money, we can enter a new frontier—one that is ageless. Timeless. Buy eternity today. Sell eternity tomorrow."

The image dissipates like someone tossing pixilated sand

grains into the air.

"They'd sell it," Callum whispers. "It would go to the highest bidder. Just like Upstate did with their freshwater aquifers—they used to share them with us, back when we were all one state. Especially now, with all the animosity certain West Isle radicals have against the Ward's sick population. You think they'd want to share something this big?"

"What are you talking about? What animosity?"

Callum looks at me like he wishes he hadn't said anything. "You don't know."

"No," I answer. "Most people here don't have electric. West Isle news is hard to come by. We've got radios . . . but then we have to trade for the batteries." I don't add that we never hear them say much interesting, anyway.

"At its most elemental, it's prejudice. They're calling the sick . . ." He pauses, then says the next word like it tastes bad in his mouth. "Subhuman."

My sister. *Subhuman.* I want to curse at him, though I know he's just the messenger. But the more I hear about people on the West Isle, the happier I am that I grew up here. Of all places.

"So as I was saying," Callum continues, "if something like that were to exist . . ."

"We'd never see a drop."

"What's more, the face of this planet would be forever changed. Think of the repercussions. . . . Overpopulation, an even greater strain on the Earth's resources. We're already suffering for water as it is." Callum lowers down onto the floor, sits himself directly across from me. "Immortality is an entirely unsustainable concept."

I'm quiet. There's so much to take in. So much that goes against everything I knew to be true.

Callum doesn't look at me, lost in his own head. After a few moments, "So you see, whatever you found out there, it's imperative that the wrong people never have access to it."

But if Governor Voss is one of the "wrong people," I have to wonder: Who are the right people?

"What, exactly, do you want with it?" I ask.

"I don't want to cure death, that's for sure. I'm a scientist, Ren. I believe that something like this—whatever it is— could have huge potential in the medical sphere. I'd like to examine the water, alter base components. Make it stronger. Ideally, I'd like to use it to develop a drug therapy and eradicate the HBNC virus. But I can't work with nothing."

The ball's in my court.

"Like I said, I found freshwater. A hot spring. But I don't know anything about this fountain of youth you're talking about."

"Just tell me what you found. Everything."

I inhale, and I start with Plan B bunking out on me. I tell him how I had to swim into a building with a big red star, how the place should have been flooded but wasn't, and how under an abandoned subway tunnel, I fell into a pool of water that didn't leave me thirsty.

And then I tell him how it tasted.

He laughs, almost in awe. Mumbles, "Unbelievable," but says nothing more. I get to the part where I gave Aven the water, and for a few hours she was symptom free—better than symptom free—until she collapsed on the floor of the Tank. The grand finale.

The memory physically hurts. Retelling it is reliving it, and the corners of my eyes prickle with salt water. "So if the fresh is responsible for fixing Aven, it's also responsible for making her sicker. How do you explain that?"

"I only have theories. Nothing's certain until I have an actual sample."

"What if I didn't find your miracle spring?"

He grunts, and I can almost see the thoughts clicking into place, the mechanics of his mind landing on an answer. "There's only one way of finding out."

Had a feeling he'd say that.

19

2:45 A.M., SUNDAY

Just as we're about to step out into the tar-black night, Callum stops. Runs back inside the apartment. Returning, he throws me something small and says, "In case you need to reach me."

I catch it—a cuffcomm. Latching it next to my DI-issued one, I realize they look identical. I hold the comm close, inspect its sides, flip it open and everything, but I can't see a difference.

"It's DI issued as well," Callum tells me, noticing. "I snagged it before I left and made it untraceable."

I look at the comm with a nod and make a mental note to ask Callum about that "falling-out" he mentioned. Not one bit do I like the sight of the two side by side on my wrist. My nerves get all jittery.

Then we're out the door again, each carrying one empty rubber sack. The narrows creak the whole half block it takes to reach Mad Ave, but not far down the boardwalk, I see his mobile. Docked and waiting. Callum tugs at the rope, drawing it in.

"You got an Omni?" I ask, awed.

"Of course I do."

Under my breath, I mumble, "Of course he does. Silly me."

"And you're driving."

I do a double take as Callum passes me his keys. You just don't *do* that, offer the keys to your mobile. An Omni, no less. Sure, I'm known, but still . . .

Whistling, I run my finger along the sleek, purple paint job. The wheels that allow for driving on land are tucked inside the body, under the surface. She looks just like a bullet, but with a glass roof. Swankier than Ter's.

"Let's get a move on," Callum mutters anxiously, rubbing the nape of his neck like he's reconsidering getting in with me. "They'll station people there once the freshwater find has been confirmed. We have to move fast, or we lose our shot entirely."

"I'm on it," I say, not liking his tone, but knowing he's right. If Chief Dunn sends the surveillance team early . . . bad news. Don't know how we'd get out of that one.

I push a grooved button on the key and a soft click follows. The roof lifts, revealing two black leather seats, one for the driver, one for a back passenger. Wonder how she goes from water to land. With a classy ride like this, it shouldn't be too hard to learn—you probably just think the word *wheels* and

193

they electromagically grow out of its bum, ready for riding.

We both hop into our respective seats. I click the button on the key again, folding the roof back over our heads. The Omni pressurizes and my ears crackle.

"This is one good piece of metal, Doc," I comment, nodding in approval. "Never know when a floodable airlock might prove useful." Behind Callum's seat in the back is a tiny space where you can enter directly into the water without sinking the boat.

"Could you stop calling me Doc, please?" Polite words, sharp voice. Not sure what gives.

"That's what you are though, right?" I fire up the obviously not-old girl and she sways side to side, sending bubbles round the edges. Now might be a good time to mention that I've never actually driven a fully water-adaptable mobile, which is less like driving a car and more like steering a boat.

Nah. He'd only get nervous. I jam on the acceleration and the Omni jerks forward.

Callum groans. It's a pitiful sound that makes me turn to face him. When I do, he shoos me away and points to the mobile's nose. I shrug and keep driving. It takes a few erratic lurches before I'm able to get the hang of this whole underwater acceleration thing.

"I'm going to be sick," Callum says as I shift the gears and bring us underwater.

"Better not." I turn around to face him again. All the while he's going more and more interesting shades of seaweed. "You're the doctor, remember?"

He shakes his head and points again. "Eyes. Front."

Looking out at the wide expanse of the channel, I realize I don't know where I am. It's a different city down here, full of furry, fuzzy edges. I tap the dashboard screen, hoping there's no actual button. It beeps a few times and then a neon grid lines the black background.

"Quad Nine," I say aloud, feeling mighty foolish. Like I'm talking to myself.

But then . . . *Bingo.*

Green lines mark the way through the rubble to our destination like an antique Etch A Sketch. I set out, steering us as fast as I can, but with each turn, the Omni jolts. It's difficult—following the navigation screen while rushing. After a few moments of silence, I turn around to see Callum curled up with his head hanging between his legs.

"Are you really getting sick?"

"Submarine travel . . . it hasn't agreed with me since I was a child."

"You were fine in the transport sub earlier."

"My mind was occupied. And there were no windows."

"What have windows got to do with it?"

Callum takes a deep breath, presses his head against the window. "I'm guessing you've never been trapped underwater in a mobile, your only way out through a window that's sealed shut."

If he'd said that forty-eight hours ago, I would've been able to say no. "Last night. The race. It was one of the scariest moments of my life."

"I was nine. I'd begged my parents for an underwater tour of the city for my birthday. There was a mechanical failure, something to do with the sub's oxygen tanks. They were leaking. My entire family—all my friends—we were all trapped. The captain had to break the windows. Everyone made it, thankfully. But ever since then, it's been hard."

I don't know what to say. It was terrifying for me, and I'm sixteen. Can't imagine what it would be like to go through the same thing at nine. In the rearview mirror, I see Callum close his eyes. "Open your eyes," I tell him. "You're going to miss the tour."

"I'd really rather not," he groans.

"Give it five minutes. If you don't feel better after that, I won't bother you again till we get to the building." I point out his window, slowing down the mobile. "Take a look."

A shaft of sunlight stakes the water, turns it a golden, muckish brown. Schools of bluefish flick by, white splashes in this brown sea-sky. "It's downright pretty under here." I laugh, hoping he notices.

Callum looks out at the fish, but he doesn't comment. I keep going. "You can almost imagine the city from Before, right? What do you think it was like?"

He takes a glance, followed by a gulp, and then he leans his head against the glass. "I imagine there . . . were . . . very many people."

If I knew him better I might make a joke about that being one *seriously* profound observation.

The red line on the dash makes its gradual crawl to our destination point, just one square away on the screen's grid. "Almost there," I let him know, and I force myself to relax my grip on the wheel since the nav's doing all the work anyway. I'm a sympathy puker. Seeing it, hearing it . . . and, ugh, the smell. If he goes, I go. "Hang on."

As we speed through the water, I can really see the metrop-olis that was, buried in things like gravel and concrete, pavement and sidewalks. Streets that don't wobble when there's an overeager tide swelling in. There's even a whole cathedral down here—I know because the spires are still vis-ible from the surface. It's a rich-looking building, though the marble is covered in green and brown.

Built very differently from everything else, but I've heard the governor's home looks just as stately, with fancy columns and the like. Under my breath, I mutter something about how living on the Isle must not be much different from the city Before.

A dull, unobtrusive beep announces that we've reached Quad Nine.

I bring the mobile up, lifting her toward sea level. "Almost there," I announce.

The Omni dips and nods on the surface, though I try and keep her steady for Callum's sake. I glimpse around, looking for helis in the air or other subs in the water. The glare is wretched out here on the water, so I shield my eyes with the back of my hand. No sign of anyone.

"Looks clear," Callum says shakily. "We won't have much time though, before they arrive."

Pointing east, I say, "That one," and I steer us toward a tall brick building. About as similar looking as I can hope for. In daylight, it all comes down to height. After you've seen one abandoned building, you've seen 'em all.

But there, up in the corner—the red star with a circle around it.

Same one. "We're here. There's the escape ladder I used." I bring the mobile up to the building's side and I don't waste any time getting the roof open.

Like a jack-in-the-box, Callum sticks his head through the roof. He stands on the backseat and the boat sways, sending him onto one side. His legs start shaking—I flip on the prop on the opposite side to give a counterbalance. "Try not to move, okay?" I call up, and slowly turn off the prop. He straddles the seat with his feet quaking, grabbing on to the outside of the roof for stability.

"Sorry . . . I'm a bit uneasy on my legs at the moment." He takes in gulps of the dank Hudson air.

Then, seeing the ladder, "You climbed that thing?" he asks warily.

"Yep," I say, examining it. Tide's even lower than yesterday, so the bottom rung is now a few good feet farther out of reach. "It's easy peasy, don't you worry."

He's clearly not ready. "How safe is it?" he asks.

"Callum. It's a rusty fire escape ladder on a building that's been abandoned for over a century, and it's in the middle of a river. What do you think?"

Together we eye the distance between the Omni and bottom of the ladder.

"How do you plan on getting up there?"

The question strikes me as funny, like it's a given that I've got a plan.

Under the backseat, I find a coiled line of rope. I let out about four feet, the distance to the ladder. Then, aiming for the space between the two bottom rungs, I hurl the remaining line through. When it falls out the other side, I'm able to grab it. I pass both ends to Callum, keeping them taut so we don't drift.

"I want you to step on both ends, okay? Don't let one slip. And no slack in the line, either. I'm going to climb up to the bottom rung. After I'm up, you'll go. Got it?"

"Got it." A pause. "And how will I get up?"

"We'll make it work."

Fighting against the mobile's wobble, I stand, stepping a foot on either side of the roof. I grip the double lines of rope, one between each palm, and coil the bottoms around my ankles, like they taught in DI training.

Just a few feet, just a few feet. My arms strain as I haul myself up, but it's a short distance. Soon the rung is within reach, and I make a grab for it. Then I inch a bit higher and reach for the second rung. "See?" I grunt. When I've got that one, a final pull-up allows me to swing my toes onto the ladder and steady myself. "Like pie." I heave, and I throw the rope back into the Omni.

"What did you do that for?" Callum yells, jumping out of the way.

"There's a reason I didn't tie it to your Omni, Callum. We can't just leave her out in the open. If they come and we're still here, they'll know.

"Take my arm," I tell him, now crouched low, dangling off the side of the ladder. "I'll hold you steady and swing you in."

Callum looks up at me, stands on the roof like I did.

"You're . . . ahhh . . . sure you're steady?" he asks, voice wavering. When he looks up at me, I see what he must have

199

looked like as a little boy, smiling in spite of the sheer terror he's obviously feeling.

"I'm steady," I promise. "As soon as you've got a grip on my arm, be ready to lift your foot to the ladder. I've got you."

Despite our agreement, the trust isn't totally there, but his hand reaches out anyway. I grab for his forearm, wrapping my wrist around it. His palms are slick with sweat, sliding down my bicep. Using the ladder, I stand.

Callum's toes lift off the Omni and closer to the bottom rung.

"Try and swing one leg up," I tell him.

He's able to—he presses the sole of one shoe down on the rung and gasps, relieved. He's probably just realized he'd been holding his breath all along. As he tries to get his other foot to the ladder, though, more flakes of white paint chip off—they catch Callum's eye. His mouth hangs open as he watches the chips sink onto the surface of the channel.

This little thing. It's distraction enough. . . .

"Look at me, Callum. Don't look down," I tell him, but his foot is in midair and he's so busy looking at the water below, his eyes can't find the ladder.

My arm hurts; he's gripping it too hard. It'll come free of its socket if he doesn't get up here soon. I'm pulled toward him, sliding forward off the ladder. I slip just a few centimeters. This turns him into a shaky mess, legs wobbling like they've got no muscle in them.

The one foot he has on the ladder slides off, and he's dangling; the only thing keeping him from the icy channel is my arm.

But there's no grip there, he's too sweaty. "Grab the ladder with your free hand," I shout, annoyed. It's right there, right in front of his face.

Which would be perfect, if his eyes were open.

I bend down, bringing the one hand of his I've got a hold on to the lowest rung, all the while trying to keep my arm looped. "It's right there, Callum."

"I—I—" he stammers. "Swim. I can't . . . quite swim."

You've gotta be joking!

"For real?" I ask him. He opens his eyes, looks at me like a kicked dog.

Good God.

"Grab the ladder, Callum. It's right there."

Slowly, he peels his gaze from mine. It lands on the rung in front of his face and he grabs for it with his free hand. The other arm follows. He uses his upper body to pull himself up one rung, then the next, and at the third, his feet find the bottom of the ladder.

All four limbs, safe and secure.

I exhale, realizing that I too wasn't breathing. Then I pull the key to the Omni out of my pocket and send her back underwater to wait.

Together, we make our way up the ladder and into the building. Without incident, surprisingly.

"Careful," I call down to Callum. "The sill's still covered with glass." I step carefully, trying not to flick any shards out the window toward his face. Once inside, I hold out my hand. He takes it and collapses onto the floor on all fours. "Hope you're in shape," I say once we've both caught our breath. Callum eyes me as he rises to his feet. I can see his legs are still shaking from the climb, but he follows without complaining as I start leading the way to the stairs.

"Fifteen floors. Then back up again. And we've got"—looking at one cuffcomm—"about an hour till oh five hundred. If we move fast, we'll have enough time." I open the door into the stairwell, and add, "We're lucky that rally's going on today, or they'd have had enough manpower to section off the area beforehand."

Callum looks down the stairwell, and I'd bet money that he's wondering the same thing I did when I first saw it. "I know . . . weird, right? It's not flooded." With one hand on the banister, I watch as he pieces it together.

"But these lower levels are below sea level. How . . . ?"

"Someone must've bricked up the windows."

Callum is quiet for a moment. "To keep the spring from going underwater." Then he looks at me, and I get the feeling I've done something wrong without knowing what. "Ren," he starts, "who else knows what you found? Aside from Chief, I mean."

Does anyone else know?

"Well, Aven . . ." I answer, but he just shakes his head, then changes the subject. "Best set the alarm. From down there, we might not be able to hear the helis. And if they come early . . ."

He doesn't have to finish. I want to ask him what he's not telling me, but he's right.

If they come early, we've got no way out.

20

4:15 A.M., SUNDAY

"You hear that?" Callum asks once we hit the bottom of the stairwell.

The dripping that led me to the spring the last time—he hears it too. We're close. "Point the flashlight along this side of the tunnel," I tell Callum. "Over there—"

Right where it should be, the triangle of bricks that looks newer than the rest. I swing my boot into it. A rush of pain tears through my toes, now crunched together at the tip of my shoe.

"*Brack!* My foot." I resist the urge to hop up and down. "It's all been cemented together. They weren't"—I swing again with the other foot—"like that before."

Even though I'm not sure I'm making any progress, I don't stop kicking. "The cement can't have had time to harden yet." Sure enough, as I say that, one of the bricks gives way. You fight with a thing long enough and it's bound to budge. One more go should do it. "Someone was here not long ago."

Callum grips my shoulder. "Who else knows you were here, Ren? Who else have you told?" His voice is suddenly hard-edged.

Confused, I shake him off. "No one, Callum. It's just as much of a mystery to me."

He waves his arms around and starts pacing back and forth in the tunnel. "Well, it couldn't have been the DI—with today's rally, if they'd found freshwater . . . trust me. We'd know. And I doubt your sick sister is responsible. So there must be someone you're forgetting." He takes a swipe at the cemented bricks. They crumble a bit.

I don't like him accusing me, especially when I done nothing wrong. "Callum," I start, through a seriously clenched jaw. "I—" My leg itches with wanting to kick something. "Didn't—" Something like bricks. Bracing my hands against the wall, I ready myself for one final swing, Just as I finish my sentence, my foot connects with the wall. "Tell anyone."

The bricks collapse into a pile, and every ounce of blood rushes to my now-smashed toes. I can feel my heartbeat pounding away straight down to my toenails. "Okay?"

He doesn't answer, just nods and scowls a bit, lowering himself onto his knees. One by one, he moves the bricks away and inches through the crawl space.

"Don't go too far or you'll fall in," I say at the last minute.

And though that would be funny, I still tap him on the back of the thigh to make sure he heard me.

"Damn," he groans. "My knee—I think I cut it open on this effing cement." Some shards of the stuff lie scattered around the floor.

"You need a hand?"

He continues forward. I watch his body disappear into the gap behind the wall. I can hear him sliding farther and farther in, cussing all the while.

But, no splash. No fall. Why doesn't he fall?

"What's going on, Ren? Is this some sick joke?"

Is what some sick joke?

I drop to my knees and start to shimmy through the hole, fighting my gag reflex as I shake a rat from my knuckles. "What?" I ask, poking my head through. "What did I do?"

Callum sits, one knee bent upward, in the middle of the space. He flicks the light from the flashlight around, stopping at nothing.

Nothing. We're sitting on mud.

That can't be—"I swear, it was here. . . ." I scramble to my feet and take the flashlight from his hand, looking in the silliest of places. Behind him. Behind me. Above me. Like a river can flow from a ceiling.

Nothing.

My palms turn slick as eels. I've never understood claustrophobia. That is, not until these tunnel walls start contracting in on me. Breathing becomes an afterthought, a thing to remember to do.

"Without the spring, I've got nothing." I choke the words

out like they're made of glue, and then force myself to my knees, fighting off the feeling of being swallowed from the inside.

The spring isn't here, the spring isn't here. It's all I can think.

And if this wasn't done by the DI . . . The next thought puts me in a tailspin. "What's Chief Dunn going to do when he gets here?" I groan, folding my head between my legs. "I'm so dead. He's going to think I'm lying. . . ."

Callum doesn't speak, just rips the hem from his pants and wraps the fabric around the wound. I shine the flashlight on it for him so he can see. His whole knee is red, the flesh there gaping. "Ugh," he mutters.

"Wait . . ." I say. "Do *you* think I'm lying?"

"No." He's curt. "Unfortunately, I believe you."

"What do you mean 'unfortunately'?"

"Nothing," he says. "It's nothing."

"Oh, no you don't," I snap. "Why is it unfortunate?"

His sigh fills the small, dank space, makes everything feel tense. "There's more you should know about the spring I've been searching for. I didn't want to say anything until I was sure. But the signs are evident."

"Signs?" My voice is low, but in here it carries nonetheless.

"Ren, the reason I accused you back there of having told someone was because I'd hoped it was true. Because the alternative—that someone *else* knows—is worse."

"What's the alternative?" I ask, though I can see he's about to tell me like I'm tied to railroad track waiting to get hit.

"The building. It wasn't flooded *before you told the chief.*

The bricks were cemented overnight. Now a mud pit sits where freshwater should be. Whoever knows you've found the spring is trying to sabotage any efforts you might make at finding it again."

I look around the empty, cavernous space, despite the fact that I can barely see. "Who would . . . *Why?* Why would anyone do that? A spring that heals—in the Ward, of all places," I say. "Why hide it?"

I hear Callum sigh through the dark. "I don't know. I just know, this isn't the first example. During my research I found many other instances of explorers who were close to finding the spring, only to have their efforts thwarted. Sabotaged."

All that useless hope drains out of me, leaves me tired. The spring is gone.

Callum and I sit together for what feels like hours, nothing at all to say. The *drip-drip*ping of condensation coming down from the ceiling punctuates our silence.

I'm about to ready myself to leave—sitting here is worse than useless, it's dangerous—when I hear Callum jump to his feet. "Of course . . ." he mumbles. Then, louder—"Of course!"

"What of course?" I ask, weak-voiced. I'm tired of hoping. I just want to go see Aven, be with her for what time she has left.

He unhooks his satchel from his back, rummages through the bag. "I'm an idiot—how did I not think of this before? Ren. What are you sitting on?"

"Well, I'm not totally sure, Callum—my brain isn't quite at large as yours—but I'm gonna go with mud," I spit, not caring in the least that I'm being rude.

He ignores my snark. "And what is in the mud?" he asks.

It takes me only a second of thinking. *Holy mud balls. Water . . .*

"You can actually do that?" I ask, the words echoing shrilly through the cavern.

"Yes, it's quite simple, actually. I'll just need a cheesecloth and a few . . ."

No need to let him finish. Not sure I'd get it anyway. "Callum, you really are a genius!" I turn myself into a great, big, muddy meteor and blast myself toward him, giving him a bear hug on impact.

"Hey, whoa!" He falls back and has to steady me with his arms so I don't end up in a face-plant on his chest.

I pull myself away and flick the flashlight around. "What do I do? Will there be enough?"

"We start by filling up these." On cue, four glass jars appear from his bags. "At the very least, it will be enough to test with. Remember, I still have to learn why it made Aven's condition worse."

"But once you do—is there enough to make a medicine?" My voice goes high with alarm. We're so close. . . .

"I don't know. I just don't know." His answer is quiet as he lowers himself back onto all fours, starts pushing globs of mud into the first jar. "I'm going to try."

"No," I say, shaking my head. "Not good enough. If you get it wrong . . . it could kill Aven."

"She's already dying, Ren."

The sister in me wants to set him on fire. How dare he say

it like it's nothing. I bite my tongue though, and we pass the next minutes in silence.

When I've filled each of my containers, I stand, still angry. "Hurry up. My boss should be coming soon, if you haven't forgotten."

Callum looks up at me from his spot on the ground. "I'm sorry. That was insensitive. Of course I won't administer anything to your sister without first being sure of its effectiveness. If I can turn this gunk into a cure, I will."

Reluctantly, I give him my hand to lift him up. A peace offering.

But when he takes it, tries to stand, his feet slide on the muck. He reaches for my shoulder. I catch him, and his palm smears brown across my sleeve. "Sorry," he says again, and I shrug.

"It's nothing. And . . . thank you," I muster, no good at apologies—giving them, or hearing them.

Then his foot slips again, hand gliding from my grip, nearly landing him back in the mud pit. The way he wobbles, his feet racing to prop himself up, finding only more mud to slide on—it's like a cartoon, and it sets a crack in my anger.

I can't help but laugh at his *whoa*ing and *uh-oh*ing. As he latches on to my shoulder, we see each other as we are: mud-covered, in a tunnel 150 feet below sea level, looking for the fountain of youth of all nutty, impossible things. And for a moment, the madness of it all, it's like uncorking a bottle of fizzy water and watching the bubbly spritz everywhere. We laugh and laugh and laugh until it seems our abs might split from the hurt, and our cheeks might blow open, and only then could we really, fully 100 percent smile without the boundaries of a body to stop us.

It reminds me of being with Aven.

Our laughter dies almost as quickly as it began. The tunnel feels quieter than it did before, and if for one moment we were someplace else, we're back now. The real world is still dark. We look at each other, we move away, uncomfortable with the silence.

And if it weren't for the sound of nothing, I might have missed the sound of rumbling.

"You hear that?" I ask as we gather our bags and shimmy through the hole in the wall, emerging into the subway.

"Hear what?" Worry ripples in his voice.

"I can't tell." I think I feel a slight vibration, but I could be wrong. If it is the Blues, they're still too far away to be sure. "But let's move."

Callum and I race between the tracks until we reach the platform, both hopping onto it simultaneously. Except Callum's got the advantage of longer legs, so I end up following him into the stairwell.

Together, we dash up the stairs, skipping two, three at a time. At first we're both doing okay; Callum's footsteps echo only a few feet behind me. But somewhere around five flights up, I notice that the clambering noises are solely my own. Callum's fallen behind. No use in stopping, though. It's not like I can carry him.

The distance between us grows, and pretty soon I can't hear him at all. I stop moving, and that's when I'm sure the helis are on their way. "Callum, they're coming," I call out.

Above, the rumbling gets louder by the second. We probably have eight minutes . . . not much more, judging by the vibrations.

"You okay?" I call again when I hear no answer. "Callum?"

So maybe there's no use in stopping, I think, but there's no use in going either. This whole trek will have been for nothing if the doc gets caught. I backtrack a few flights to find him slumped across the stairs sucking down air, on the verge of retching.

"Look, put one arm over my shoulder. We'll do it together." My free hand clutches him on the other side, around his waist. I start up the stairs with him by my side before he has a chance to fight me.

Callum slings a few wheezy insults . . . but strangely, they're not for me. They're for him, something about "needing the help of a girl," like he seriously disapproves of it. But his legs move just the same, and that's the part I care about.

I wonder if all guys are like this?

Why's it so much easier for a girl to take the help of a guy than it is the other way around? Sure, I hated being Derek's damsel in distress, but that's different because . . .

Because, what?

Weird. I don't know. I don't know why it bothered me so much.

Our joint climbing has slowed, but not too far off we both spot a pinprick of light from the floor we came in on.

"Almost there, Callum. You see that?"

The harder I squeeze air down into my lungs, the more

my windpipe constricts. Each time I feel like I need to stop, though, I look up into that light and watch it grow larger and larger. It gives us the last bursts of energy we need to reach the top. When we do finally hit sea level, the brightness—compared to that subterranean pitch black—hits our eyes and it hurts. Always thought it was ironic that something too bright can blind you.

Our feet plant themselves on a flat surface and that's when Callum does better. We run as fast as we can—which is still not that fast—and stop on either side of the window, peering out.

The building quakes. Three small helis' props slice through the air. We can't see them. We don't need to. They circle the whole of Quadrant Nine, probably looking for the building with the red star. Then they start closing in—they've spotted it—and begin circling this building, once, twice. I wait for them to finish the rotations around the building, counting the seconds between the moment one leaves the frame of the window and the other passes into it.

"Six seconds, Callum. We've each got six seconds to climb out the window, down the ladder, and into the Omni."

Callum's still catching his breath, his hands resting on his knees, his torso bent forward. "So long as they keep circling."

There ain't no way he'll make it in six seconds. "After the ladder, you're going to have to jump down," I tell him.

That gets him standing straight. "Into my mobile? No. You're joking." He gives me a look that says he thinks I've lost it.

"Not joking," I say, thinking of those old Westerns where

the guy jumps off a building, onto his horse's saddle. Sometimes it works, sometimes it doesn't. "And . . . you're going first. Totally doable, no more than a four-foot drop."

"Wait, no. You should be first, you'll be better at steadying the thing." He eyes the canal from behind the window.

"Yes, but . . . you're not supposed to be here. *I'm* not supposed to be here, but I'll think of something. Plus, you're the one who knows what to do with the mud." I look past the pane, waiting for one of the aeromobiles to pass. "Soon as you're in, submerge her. Then I want you to check the periscope so you'll know the heli's gone. Got it?"

I don't wait for him to answer. The heli crosses out of view. I press down on one of the Omni key's many buttons, the one that'll bring her to the surface.

"Now! Swing your leg over! I'll drop you the keys after the roof is open."

"Impossible," he mutters.

Don't know if he's referring to me, or to the jump, but out he goes. Without a fight, to my utter surprise. He even thinks to climb down the backside of the escape ladder on his own—a quicker approach. His legs shake, the ladder shakes, while I keep count from above: Four . . . three . . .

The Omni surfaces, but the glass roof is still shut. I fumble with the key, feeling for the button that opens it. "Jump!" I call down as the roof slides open.

Callum listens. He lets go of the ladder and falls into the mobile, sending it side to side. But he straightens himself and looks up. I drop the key.

Catch it, Callum. Catch it.

The key falls into his open palm. I laugh. He's actually pulling it off.

As I spot the next heli, Callum brings the Omni under. Water passes over its roof, and I catch sight of the periscope, brass glinting in the sun. He's waiting for the next heli to pass to resurface, just like I told him.

I hold my breath. Wait for the helis to continue their rotation.

They don't. The heli turns in the sky until it faces the building head-on.

And me.

I can't even tell Callum to get out of here—though the comm he gave me is untraceable, at this close range with the Blues, it wouldn't be hard to tap. Just gotta keep myself hidden behind the window, waiting, watching the periscope.

Callum gets the picture—the brass slides below the surface. His purple Omni shimmers, then submerges till it's disappeared.

He's gone.

And I'm trapped.

21

5:00 A.M., SUNDAY

Pressure overhead from the spinning props churns the water in the canal, makes it look like a storm is coming in. I cover my ears. What was a rumbling before is now a full-blown screeching, and it only gets louder. The heli flies in, then slows. A rope ladder drops from an open hatch on the side. A figure starts to climb down.

I watch, racking my brain to formulate a plan.

This must be happening on all four sides of the building—the scouts each taking a separate entrance, probably planning to regroup in the stairwell.

I could hide—no doubt the building is big enough. But that'd only postpone the inevitable: once Chief Dunn discovers that the spring is gone, he's gonna want to speak with me. At least if I'm here, I can head things off at the pass. Get to him right away, before he has too much time to think me a liar.

The closest heli flies forward, dangles the scout through the air.

May as well let 'em know I'm here from the get-go. I stick my head out over the sill and give a wave to the pilot. I can tell he's seen me; he brings the man on the ladder right up to the window.

As the figure gets closer, I begin to recognize the broad build, the mustache. Even the way he holds himself—too rough, too much authority. He's no scout.

The chief . . .

The man lets go of the rope with one hand and grabs on to the escape ladder, but only once he opens his mouth am I sure of it: "What the hell are you doing here, Dane?"

It's him.

His mouth moves, he yells something else but I can't hear over the roar of the heli as it rises up into the sky. It turns, joins up with the remaining three, and they all head west, probably to wait at the nearby headquarters rather than eat up gasoline in the sky for an hour.

I back away from the window as he jumps through it from the escape ladder.

"Well?" he asks again.

My brain turns to mush—I hadn't thought that far. *Why am I here?*

An answer comes, one that I hope he buys. Stumbling through the words: "I . . . I came to make sure you'd find it— it was tricky the first time. And I wasn't sure I'd remembered it correctly. Head wound and all." I'd point to my temple, but all I've got to show for my near-death experience is a scar. And a barely visible one at that.

Chief Dunn glares at me. I can tell from the slanted look he's giving that he don't know what to make of my answer. All he says is, "Lead the way," and motions toward the stairwell.

Now I get to drop the bomb.

Keeping my eyes downcast: "There's a problem, sir."

He stops midstride. Turns.

I swallow before going on. "Someone's been here," I spit out. "The spring I told you about . . . It's gone."

His demeanor changes. He draws his shoulders higher, clasps his hands behind his back. Marches toward me, each step slow and even-paced.

"What do you mean, gone?" he growls.

"I don't understand it neither. . . . When I went to scout before you got here, someone had cemented the hole in the wall, and all that was left of the spring was a pit of mud. This is the site, though, I swear."

He's quiet. It lasts for miles.

I bring myself to look up, find him dark-eyed and glowering.

Finally: "Show me."

Chief Dunn kicks at the mud, spraying it into the cavern wall.

It takes all I've got not to jump back.

"Governor's not going to be happy," he spits.

I'm left alone with the scouts as he crawls back into the

abandoned tunnel, so I sit myself down, unsure what to do. One of the three men mutters to himself, something 'bout knowing this was a "bunk mission." The others nod their heads. Start talking 'bout another Appeal. They ignore me, which I'm fine with, 'cause that's how I hear Chief's voice through the wall.

"Yes, sir . . . I don't know, sir," I hear him say. He's apologetic—a tone I've never heard him use before. Must be speaking with someone higher on the totem pole. And there's only one person higher up than Dunn.

Governor Voss.

"The girl claims no one else knows. . . ." he goes on, and it doesn't take a genius to figure he's talking about me. "Yes, she's here now. I don't believe she's telling the whole truth either, sir. Absolutely, I'll call in another agent from HQ straightaway. He'll keep an eye out and report back to you. Yes, sir, I understand what's riding on this find." The conversation comes to a halt.

Without thinking, I start gnawing at my nails. They don't believe me, they're going to have me watched. I don't like it, not one bit.

After some more time straining my ears, Chief responds. "A half dozen squads? . . . Within the hour, yes . . . I'll leave right away, sir." Then the tunnel's quiet again, and I hear him tapping the commands into his cuffcomm.

He's leaving? And he's gathering squads. . . .

"Dane!" Chief barks. "Out here, now!"

I jump and wriggle myself through the crawl space, head peeking out the other side. "What's that, sir?" I ask, pretending I somehow missed his yelling.

"The sample came back positive," he begins, not even looking at me. "You were right, it's fresh. As such, I'll be suspending your pay until you can tell me where it went." He says it so easily.

I stand there like an idiot, jaw gaping wide.

"Sir . . . ? I don't understand—I found the stuff, and I'm being *punished*?" The words croak out of my mouth, one by one. *He can't* do *this*.

Chief Dunn spins to face me. In the flashlight's harsh glow, he could be the Reaper. "It doesn't add up," he says in a growl. "There's something you know. And whatever it is that you're not telling, the governor *will* find out. Now is not the time for games."

"Chief," I plead. "I'll look all over the Ward if you want me to. It's just my . . . my friend—you saw her—she's in the hospital. Surgery's scheduled for today. We've got bills to pay—"

Chief Dunn laughs. It's dry and full of meanness. "Well, here's a simple fix, Dane: as of right now, the surgery is no longer scheduled for today. Problem solved. Can't have you running to the hospital, wasting our time." A pause. "And don't think I won't know."

I'm unable to swallow, a slew of curses forming inside my mouth with nowhere to go. I choke them back, feeling like my tongue has grown in size, and all my bones too. I step forward—all 206 of them want to fight. Smash his face to the wall—but I stop myself, when I remember my size. I'm not that strong. I'd get myself killed. "She'll die if you do that," I finally manage.

"Not my priority, Dane! The West Isle is in an uproar. People are afraid of the Blight, and the water crisis has grown dire. Governor Voss doesn't want your excuses, and neither do I. Get me a location, we'll talk about your friend's surgery." Pointing in the direction of the stairwell, "Dismissed!"

I don't even give Dunn the requisite "sir." I just spin away, desperate to be as far from him as possible, and race through the empty subway tunnel, all the way up the stairs.

At the top of the stairwell, I collapse in a heap, head spinning.

He wants me to find another spring? I can't breathe, and I don't even fight off the hornet's nest swarming in my stomach. Only one word repeats itself over and over again in my mind: *No—no, no, no.*

No.

Not after what Callum showed me on the Core.

Especially not after Dunn telling me he's canceling Aven's surgery.

Dunn's a fool if he thinks that will keep me from going to see her. Clearly he's never cared about anyone, ever. Now that I don't know how long she's got, I have to get to her. Have to be with her. He's just made the hospital my first stop.

And after that—Callum's. To bring Aven whatever medicine he's able to concoct from the mud, that won't make her sicker. Reaching for the cuffcomm he gave me, I type in a message:

Can you do it?

It's a ramshackle plan. It's no plan at all. It's a decision to step forward, one foot at a time, for now. But it does the trick.

It's enough. I'm able to pick myself up, force my head thinking again. Focus on how to make the not-plan a reality.

I head back into the empty room on the fifteenth floor. The quadrant is quiet, free of roaring helis, so I know the coast is clear. I rotate the dial to the side of my cuffcomm, trying to decide who to call on.

It's too early in the morning to ask another favor of Ter—he just brought me to Mad Ave a few hours ago, and I doubt his dad would want him running back to the racing district. Once a month for the races is danger enough.

Calling Derek is out of the question. I am "barely a friend" after all. . . .

I find the channel I use to call Benny. I hate to ask him—he already saves my butt on a regular basis—but I've got no choice.

I need to get out of here.

22

5:15 A.M., SUNDAY

I run to the windowsill overlooking the canal, but it isn't the sound of Benny's mobile that brings me there. It's not a sound at all. Across the Hudson Strait, the West Isle city center is crowned in thick, dark clouds, just as the sun begins to rise. The Quad Nine Trade Centers block much of my view—I'm full-on blinded by the glass and steel of One World—but I can see enough.

Billows of black, swallowing the tops of even the tallest skyscrapers.

The rally . . . it must be coming from the rally.

I'm shocked—it was supposed to be a protest. West Isle citizens voicing their discontent, that's what the radio transmission said. But this ain't just a rally.

Smoke means fire.

This is a riot.

Part of me hands it to them for taking a stand. But another part is laughing. A rally, or a riot, or a protest can't fix our issues. Public opinion counts for nothing in our situation. Much as I want to blame Governor Voss for not doing more, he's no magician.

A pink smudge skimming the canal draws my attention back to the water.

It's a Cloud9 Steamer, one of Benny's mobiles, and she's moving much faster than she should. Cloud9s ain't much more than glorified balloons—open-topped, floaty rides sold in pastel colors only. And they're no better under the hood, used for scenic travel. Benny must have upgraded this one, though, 'cause she's hauling like nobody's business.

I climb out the window and onto the fire escape, inspecting the water for the DI guy Chief said he'd send to watch me.

I've got to spot him. And then I've got to lose him.

'Cause I'm about to disobey direct orders from Chief Dunn, something I've never done before. Once he finds out—which he will if I can't lose my tail—I don't know what he'll do. He could make it so I never see Aven again.

I scan the canal even more thoroughly, pausing at every shadow I see below the surface. But the water's dark and murky, and I know this won't be easy. Seeing nothing, I look up and wave my arms. "Over here!" I shout, motioning to Benny.

As he nears, my breath catches. He's not alone.

Derek's with him; no one else has that rusty-colored hair. My body reacts before my head has a chance to remind me that I'm angry. He doesn't deserve that silly, giddy feeling my stomach can't seem to shut down.

"Front door service!" Benny says when he's just below the rickety ladder. I lower myself and Derek stands, holds out his hand for me.

I don't take it.

Instead, I monkey swing myself from the bottom rung, gripping it between my palms, and hover over the mobile. I let go to land in the Cloud9, but the boat sways—my balance staggers. Before I've got a chance to catch myself, Derek's hand is firm at my shoulder, steadying me.

I jerk away from his touch.

I don't know . . . maybe I'm overreacting—but the moment I feel his hands on my skin, I'll go all weak-kneed and googly-eyed. I'll forget he wasn't there for me when I needed him most.

He pulls his hand away, but I still feel his eyes on me.

"I'm happy to see you, Ren," Benny says, letting go of the steering wheel. He wraps his arms around me and examines my temple. Lifting each hand, he looks for evidence of the accident. Even under my nails, which I've torn to pieces.

"You're a lifesaver," I breathe out. "Where were you doing here, up at this hour? Right around the corner, too. It took you, like, ten minutes to get here." Turning to Derek, "And how'd you get dragged along for the ride?"

He avoids my eyes now. No doubt it's from all the warm, fuzzy feelings I'm radiating.

"No dragging involved," he says. "We were close and I wanted to see you. Kent called the others for an early-morning, 'friendly' practice race in Quad Eight—no betting, of course. He just wanted to see if he should buy an Omni, so he swapped mobiles with Ter."

A race—even a "friendly"—and no one told me about it?

The insult stings for no more than a moment when I realize the real reason I wasn't invited. "That's a load of bull and you know it. Kent wants to know he can win with an Omni first. Otherwise he'd just give it a test drive like anyone else."

If I were part of the race, and he *still* lost, he'd never recover.

Derek laughs. "I'm sure you're right. Either way, you're about to see how he does. We're headed back to Eight right now. What are you doing here anyway?" he asks, but I have no intention of answering that question.

"You're headed to Eight? Do they need you?" I whine, unable to stop myself. "I've got to get to Ward Hope. . . ." My skin prickles and all of a sudden I'm antsy. My mind starts tilting away, that feeling of free fall comes back.

What if she didn't make it through the night?

Benny looks at me in the rearview mirror, brows knotted. "We have to drive through Eight as it is. Why don't you take the Cloud and drop us off. I was going to loan her to you anyway."

Exhaling, I'm once again grateful that I have someone like Benny on my side—even though the Cloud is pink.

As I turn around to face the rear, a sunbeam spills over the building tops. The water lightens to a golden brown, and I can even see dark ropes of seaweed in our wake.

And just beyond it, an oblong shadow, trailing us.

I watch the shadow. My throat goes dry, but I say nothing.

Until I've dropped off Benny and Derek, there's not much I can do. Telling them we're being followed will only lead to the little question of *why*—a can of worms I want to keep closed and locked, buried six feet under.

I'm afraid I'll give it away on my own, though. Every few seconds I'm checking the water to make sure I haven't lost him.

At the rumbling of motors overhead, I look up. We all do. Throughout the quadrant, echoes.

"Sounds like they started without you," I say, eyeing the building tops. I don't see anyone, not yet, but this far north in the quadrant the buildings are low enough—six stories high, max—I should be able to.

For a moment, my legs get that itch—same as before the races. It's instinct. I shouldn't want to race, but I do. Mobile metal is in my bones.

But with a head filled to the brim with worry, just thinking about that kind of thrill feels like cheating. Aven could be dead or dying this very moment.

That kills the itch pretty quick, leaves me feeling guilty my bones wanted to race at all.

We boat through a few more blocks, and then one, two, three shapes hurtle off one of the taller building's roofs. The first and third are both Hondas—Jones and Ter, I'm guessing, as Derek said he swapped with Kent.

In the middle, Ter's Omni flashes orange against the bright sky, swerving. As it lands, angled all wrong, it buckles and bottoms out, hard, on the next roof.

Pale sparks from metal scraping brick arc across the

morning sky, dropping and burning out.

I groan, feeling for Ter; Kent's got to have punctured something on the undercarriage.

"The boy's an idiot," Benny howls.

"Which one?" I mutter under my breath. Ter never shoulda switched mobiles.

The orange Omni is out of sight, but reappears just before Kent's about to make the next jump. It sails through the air slowing too soon. He hasn't added enough speed. It lands on the next roof. Bounces. Rear tires catch, spinning over the building's edge. Kent steps on the acceleration—rubber burns brick, but the Omni moves not one inch forward.

Next, we see the rear prop gearing into motion.

"He didn't just do that, did he?" Derek asks, pointing.

"He did." Benny covers his mouth.

"He's going to—"

"*Brack!*" Benny curses.

The propellers chip away at the rooftop's brick edge. No one shouts for Kent to turn them off—he wouldn't hear us.

"The Omni's going down. Drive it closer . . ." Derek says to Benny.

"Closer? And let him take my Cloud down along with Ter's new Omni? I think not!"

"Fine. Bring me over—I'm going up. You can pull back after. If I'm fast enough, I might be able to get to him before he does any more damage."

"You need help," Benny tells him. The two exchange glances, and it doesn't take a mind reader to figure out what they're thinking.

Benny's too old. By the time he makes it up all the stairs, Kent will be ground-up fish food. Which leaves me.

"No way," I say as Benny drives the Cloud around the side of the building. "He wouldn't do it for me."

We pull up beside an escape ladder and Derek grabs the railing. Hopping out, he extends his arm. "You're better than him, Ren."

What if I'm not.

I throw him a glare and stand, not sure if it's because I'm actually a better person, or because I'm fighting the guilt that comes with not being a better person.

Maybe it don't matter.

I take his hand, and we begin the climb.

The building isn't too tall. Less than five stories. The ladder shakes under our feet, so we move fast, scrambling up the rungs. My palms grow red and raw from gripping the metal. Rust cuts the skin. It must be bothering Derek too, but with only fifty feet to go—maybe less—he keeps going, and so do I.

We're close—the whirring of the Omni's props has gotten much louder. Then, the screaming of metal. It cuts out all other noise. I want to cover my ears but I'm afraid I'll lose my balance if I do.

"Jump out!" Derek yells, but he's gotta know there ain't no way Kent can hear him.

At the top, we arrive in time to watch gravity pull the Omni and its driver down into the concrete canyon.

My stomach turns. Kent, frantic, fitful, tries to climb from the mobile's moonroof. I may not love the fact that he's alive, but I guess I'm not so hard that I want to watch him die either.

The props are still spinning, gnawing a gap in the side of the building. Bricks tumble into the canal; the metal slides down, driver half in, half out. Whiplash forces his torso against the mobile's front, then pulls him in the other direction. His back presses against the moonroof, dangerously close to the props.

Derek and I run to the side of the building. More screeching metal; the Omni's nose catches on one of the level's fire escapes. Props spin.

Kent has stopped trying to get himself out.

"I'm jumping onto the fire escape!" Derek yells over the props.

Looking down, I see what a phenomenally bad idea that is. "Don't be an idiot, Derek! The whole thing could give way!" And I can't even hold the ladder steady for him. It's too far down.

What we need is a window.

"I have an idea!" I wave for Derek to follow me, heading back to the ladder we came up on.

I climb back down one level, closer to where Kent's stuck, then hop through the window. Derek sees what I'm doing and together we run across the empty floor to the north-facing window. Pressed up against it—the underside of Ter's Omni.

"Smart . . ." Derek nods.

I open the window and stand on the sill. "Steady me," I say, letting him grip my left arm and leg, freeing me to lean closer to Kent.

He's upside down, black hair dripping with sweat, his face contorted.

When he sees me, that old familiar hatred fires up in his eyes.

"What are you doing here?" he quakes.

I reach out my hand for his, because that's the only answer I have. At the sight of it, his look dies. Out of desperation or thanks, I don't know.

He places one palm in mine—it's so slick and wet. . . . And I thought Callum's hands were sweaty. Kent tightens his grip and lifts himself forward, no longer upside down.

Under the weight of the Omni the fire escape groans. Bolts pop, and the whole thing caves sideways. Kent's still got one of my arms, but I can't give him the other—it's locked in Derek's grip.

"You've got to climb out," Derek says from behind me.

"Shut up." Kent tries to extract his legs from the seat. "You think I don't know that?"

I swallow my irritation, glad to know that he isn't an ass to me alone.

Again the Omni buckles, drops another foot. Kent's arm is yanked from mine. He catches my wrist and freezes, crouched on the driver's seat, not sure what to do.

"Ren—have him take your arm with both hands. When he pushes off the seat, he can make a jump for the window. You can swing him in." Derek adjusts himself to get a better grip on me as my body sways farther over the ledge.

I shake my head. "I'm not strong enough. . . ." My voice is weaker than I've ever heard it, but I'm afraid. I may be strong, but I'm not delusional—Kent is tall. He's got a lot of length on him to be relying on me alone. It's one thing to take risks with my own life, but the life of someone else—even Kent's?

"You're definitely *not* strong enough," Kent chimes in.

"Ignore him. I've got you. You're not going anywhere."

When I look back, I see Derek holding on to my arm with both his hands, one foot on the wall. "You can do this," he mouths.

I inhale, and on the exhale, I count down. "All right. On three." I push my fear away for Kent's sake. He's terrified enough as it is. "One . . . two . . ."

Derek squeezes my arm. At the last moment, Kent nods, looking me in the eye.

"Three!"

He kicks himself up from the seat, both arms clenched around mine in a vise-tight grip. That's all the push the mobile needs. It slides, grates down the fire escape, all the metal tearing and howling, sucked away by gravity.

I try to swing Kent in, but I'm losing circulation in my arm. My hold loosens, and his body flies forward. I have to drop to a squat to keep my grip. He doesn't make it through the window. I'm pulled down, and he's left kicking against the side of the building.

"Use your feet!" Derek tells him, holding my arm tight.

The muscles are tearing in both my arms, a burning all the way to my back. I want someone to let go of me. . . . Slowly, Kent shuffles himself up the brick siding. When he's close, I don't have enough in me to keep holding. Soon as his foot's on the windowsill, I lean back, let gravity do something use-ful.

Kent still on my arm, we fall into the building onto the floor. He immediately rolls off me, panting.

I don't move. All I can do is breathe. If I tried anything more, I'm sure it wouldn't work. Blood tingles back into both my shaking arms. Kent, Derek, and I stay like that, close together, three heaps on the floor.

"You . . . saved . . . my life." Kent forces the words out between breaths, eyes on the ceiling. "Thank you," he says, soft. Quietly, like he don't want me to hear.

Derek says nothing—I guess "you're welcome" makes no sense in this scenario. I decide not to answer him either, but something, a warning in my gut, tells me that I might've made things worse for myself. That my good deed for the day is going to come back and bite me in the arse. So I stay silent.

I listen to the unevenness of our breathing and gather the energy to climb back downstairs, finding life just a little too unfair. That I can save Kent's life—someone who hates me—but not my own sister's.

23

"It's fine, Ren. We'll go with you to Ward Hope and you can drop us off there," Benny says, nodding to Terrence.

I force a smile, except that's the last thing I want them doing—I'm being followed, I know I am, and if we all boat together, they're going to know it too.

Derek leans forward in his seat, touches my knee. I pull my eyes from the water to look at him. *He's so close. . . .* My heart watches him harder than my eyes do—his curls, they dangle over his forehead. Fire let loose in the daylight.

"I'd like to come with, if that's all right," he says, seeming sincere. "To visit Aven. I never should have left the hospital, Ren. I'm sorry. I just . . ." He's pleading, head bent so close to my thigh. "I had to go."

Maybe it was an emergency. Maybe he didn't abandon me

to spend time with his Not-Girlfriend. The next words are out of my mouth before I realize it—

"Sure. Of course you can come," I say, not letting on how thankful I am. I don't want to be back in that place alone.

Ter huffs, lowering himself onto the floor of the mobile. He's sullen, and understandably so. His shiny carrot didn't even make it two full days. He clenches his fist, and under his breath I hear him curse himself for trusting Kent.

"I'd offer to come too," he says, "but I don't want to give my dad more to ream me out about, especially not once he sees I'm home without the mobile."

I pat his shoulder. Can't say I understand, 'cause I don't. Instead I go with, "No worries."

In the curling white trail of waves, I scan for an agent.

Though nothing seems unusual, he must be there. An Omni fell off a rooftop, for crying out loud. If the guy somehow lost me with a bread-crumb trail that size, he shouldn't be working for the DI.

I start to fidget, tapping my fingers on the mobile's siding. The sun is so bright it actually feels heavy. Benny's Cloud is a smooth ride, with floats on either side cushioning each wake—but it makes no difference. Being without the cover of buildings or bridges stirs my anxiety. We've left the racing quadrants, heading north over open waters, so these next two miles are a dead zone: no canals, no gutters. Not even important enough to get a quadrant number. The Wash Out pretty much dunked all these buildings off the horizon.

Every ten seconds, I do a sweep of the area. To distract the others, I call up to Benny, "Hey, you ever figure out what happened to my Rimbo? Why'd she bunk on me?"

He turns to me and his face goes all wrinkly. "Ahh . . . that." He pats the steering wheel.

Derek, Ter, and I all exchange looks, waiting for more.

"You wouldn't believe it—or, perhaps you would." He stops to face the water again. "Evidence suggests that your mobile was, quite possibly, tampered with."

I squeeze the cushy leather of the Cloud's front seat between my fists. "I'd believe it," I say. Of course I'd believe it. Only one person who I can think of, too. "What I don't believe is how I just risked my neck for his—"

"Wait a minute." Derek holds up his arm. "Let's not jump to conclusions—you don't know that Kent had anything to do with it. Mobile systems fail all the time. You dragsters aren't exactly easy on your equipment, right, Benny? It's a little early to be yelling 'fire.'"

I grind my teeth together.

"I'm looking into it," Benny assures me, but I see him eye Derek in the rearview mirror.

"Hey, guys?" Ter says, pointing behind us. "What's that?"

I hold my breath, hoping it isn't what I think—

It is.

Right below the surface, about fifty feet back, we see the winking of light on metal. Then a dark, oblong shadow.

"Looks like an Omni." Derek watches the shape trail behind us. To Benny, "When we hit Six, make a left, okay?"

Benny eyes him in the rearview mirror, hard-jawed. "You think we're being followed?"

I hear Ter laugh at the question and ask, "Who'd be

following us? We're not doing anything wrong."

They're not doing anything wrong. They don't know that they're about to find out why someone might be following our boat.

No one else says anything, and I wipe the sweat from my palms onto the Cloud's leather, swallowing repeatedly till I have to stop 'cause I'm making my throat go dry. *Just play dumb. Pretend you got no idea who's back there.*

Benny doesn't speed the Cloud up, nor does he slow her down. He keeps her steady until Six's best skyscraper, the Gold Pyramid, towers over us. Then we're in view of the southern docks—where the avenue boardwalks end. No longer in open water.

He boats us under Fifth Ave. Sunlight filters through gaps in the planking, but it's not enough. The boardwalk overhead shadows everything, makes the mobile behind us impossible to see. We've all got our eyes fixed on him as he drives, waiting to see which canal he chooses to swing left into. Back in the sun again, we'll be able to see if the guy is following us. And I'm sure he is.

Without warning, Benny guns the engine. The Cloud rockets forward, water sprays everywhere, and just as we're about to pass Twenty-Fifth, he throws the wheel left. We spin onto the canal, but we don't stop there. The Cloud keeps flying—we boat under two more avenues. Benny hurtles her left again, then right. One last left brings us back into the sunlight.

Then, we slow.

Each of our heads turn. At first, for a moment, even I see

nothing in the brack water—I almost allow myself to hope. To think we've lost him. But no such luck.

There, about a hundred feet off—an Omni. Hugging the building, almost out of sight.

Ter surveys the canal, his gaze swinging left to right in a pendulum. "Weird," he says, finally looking up.

"We lost him?" Benny shouts back.

Derek nods his head. "Looks like it." But I can hear in his voice that he's suspicious.

No one sees it. . . . No one else has been trained by these guys, either. I keep quiet all of the ten blocks it takes us to get to Ward Hope. My guy is out there, and he knows I'm headed to the hospital—exactly where I was told not to go. And there's nothing I can do about it. Not without having to explain things that I'm not ready to explain.

I stop checking the water.

Dunn already knows.

24

6:30 A.M., SUNDAY

In the waiting room, the air is tight with electricity. Tense. Every couple of seconds I check the door by the receptionist's desk, waiting for the nurse to call us. And every other couple of seconds, I check the entryway, waiting for a DI agent to charge through.

Then, my foot freezes. Quits its tapping.

A woman in white steps into the waiting room, a datapad clutched at her hip. It's as though my lungs have shrunk a size and my arm hairs lift up, like the moment before lightning. You don't know when it will strike—you only know it will.

"Visitors of Aventine Colatura?"

I begin to lose it, my insides go haywire, and Derek squeezes my hand.

238

We stand up together, and we follow the nurse. She leads us through the corridors, up two flights of stairs, all the way to the HBNC wing. Its double doors swing open, and then we're in the ward where noncontagious patients are kept.

Derek won't look through the windows, into the other patients' rooms, but I do. I look in each one—I can't help it.

A child using only one arm to play with his plastic blocks—the other he can't lift. It's covered in fist-sized lumps, all a blue-black-red. An elderly man, but no older than Benny, with a tumor on his forehead, balled up low and thick over one eye.

Patients whose families can afford to send them here.

The nurse opens the door to Aven's room.

Immediately I can tell—something is off. She's just lying there, body too still in the small cot. I examine her face, pale and waxy, even with daylight streaming through the window. "What's wrong with her?" I ask the nurse, watching from behind us. "She's worse. . . ." Sucking in air through my teeth, I force my hands out of their fists, like unclamping a vise. I'd been holding them so tight, I can actually feel the muscles twitching, clicking as they release.

"You should be prepping her for surgery," I say.

Looking down at her datapad, the nurse shakes her head. "According to her records, she's in no shape for surgery. There's still too much pressure on her brain and so her oxygen supply is limited," she says.

"We both know that's not why," I spit, starting to shake from limb to limb as I glance over at Derek. If he's curious about what the hell is going on, he doesn't show it.

The nurse opens her arms like she has no control over anything that happens in this room. Which, to be fair, she may not. "I know nothing of the sort, young lady," she says, voice stern and monotone. "But Dr. Hartigan will be here in just a moment, and he can tell you more about her condition. I'll leave you three alone until he gets here." She nods over her glasses and slips out the door.

Dr. Hartigan . . . That name, I know that name, I think, crossing the room to Aven's bedside. But anger's made my thinking blurry and I collapse into a chair, wanting only to kick something. There's nothing around, though, that wouldn't get me kicked out in turn.

"Aven . . . it's me, Renny." I take her limp hand in my own and bring it to my cheek.

I wait, but I get no sign that she's even heard me.

However the sky feels after the lightning hits, that's how I feel. Charged up, struck down. I keep my voice sealed tight—lightning might have died, but I'm afraid that once I open my mouth and find myself talking to an empty body, I'll start raining.

Derek squeezes my shoulder. "Speak to her, Ren," he insists. "Even if she's not awake, she can still hear you."

Can she? I want to talk to her, but I can't bring myself to make more words come out if I'm not gonna hear her voice afterward.

Aven, I think in my head. *I need you. You can't leave me.*

Maybe . . . maybe she and I don't need words. You live with someone for so long—love them so entirely—you come to learn how they think.

Don't go and stop using your heart, you hear? Remember

me, and keep living. Just a little longer. I've got a doctor, right now, working on a medicine that's gonna fix you for good.

The penny around my neck dangles on its chain, brushing her bedcovers. I grab it, rub it so hard between my fingers I imagine I've turned it shiny again. My mind goes back to that first night, the night we decided we'd be friends. *You said it wouldn't hurt*, I remind her. *You promised.*

My eyes turn watery, the prickle starts slow and hot, but when Derek says, "Out loud, Ren?" I have to laugh-cry. I can't believe he knew that's what I was doing.

With a sigh, I kiss her open palm, the one still pressed against my cheek. "Feathers?"

I wait to go on, like I'm expecting her to answer. The silence hurts, even more than I thought it would. I try again. "Feathers . . ."

But her quiet unnerves me even more the second time around. It fills up the room—no answer is a type of answer after all, and when I translate what that means, I start unraveling. I bite at my shoulder to keep from shaking her awake. The burn of tears is back, and I move to brush them away.

I forget I'm holding Aven's hand. I watch it drop. Fall into my lap.

My throat tightens, tries to keep me from crying, but when I push my fists against my eyes, they come back slippery with salt water.

The door opens again—the doctor. I turn around to find him waiting in the hallway, one hand on the knob.

"If I could speak with you alone, Miss Dane," he calls to me.

Carefully, I lay Aven's hand beside her on the bed, and walk to meet him. I want to howl. She should be having surgery today, and he's got to be the one taking the orders.

He had her surgery canceled.

When I step out into the hallway, I rub my eyes dry. Nothing's there, though. I killed all the tears with my fists.

My vision's clear and I can see his face just as easily as I could at thirteen. At Nale's Home.

It comes back to me, how I know him—the briefcase. The needle he filled up with my blood. He told me I was *immune*. Told me to keep it a secret. He wanted to keep me safe from the DI, and anyone else who would dissect a small girl in the hopes of finding a cure.

Locking eyes with him, I say the next words carefully, one at a time. "You don't deserve to be called a doctor." As I hear them seethe out of me, I realize I might just have more disgust, more hatred for this man than I do for the chief.

The chief is no more than a bully who made it too high up the ladder for his own good.

But Dr. Hartigan? He was one of the good guys, and now he's runnin' scared.

The man's expression drops. He searches my face. I can feel him recognizing me. "Nale's Home . . ." he says. "I was . . . your doctor, wasn't I?"

"Hers too," I answer, throwing a look over my shoulder.

Dr. Hartigan stares at the door to her room, and I can see him looking through it, all the way to the girl inside.

"She needs the surgery," I say to him. "You know she needs it. But you're a coward. You're their pet. A dog. And instead of 'fetch,' they said, 'murder.' And you're okay with that."

The doctor swallows. For a moment, I see it: like he's looking in a mirror for the first time. His mouth opens, he goes slack-jawed. Even his eyes turn glassy.

The moment ends, and his face hardens, cheeks turning red as they puff out. "You leave me alone," he snaps, growing blustery, tugging at his white lab coat. "How dare you—*you*, of all people—say that. I could've told your secret. I could still tell someone. But despite what you may think, I'm not a bad person. We do what we must, and if I were you, I would go back into that room and spend what time you and that girl have left together, *together.*"

I bite my lip, nauseous all of a sudden, and I look over my shoulder to her room again. "How long . . ." I ask in a voice even I can barely hear.

"Two days," Dr. Hartigan says, and I can hear in his tone how angry he still is. "Maybe less. The rate of deterioration is . . . unusual, to say the least."

I choke. "Days?"

After that, it's all a blur.

I remember turning, finding Derek there, not wondering how he made it to the hallway. I remember fighting him, as though he were the Blight and destroying him might make everything else make sense. But that's the last image in my head—the rest is a series of sounds and sensations, none of which include sight.

I know that I am in an elevator by the ringing it makes. I know that I am in Derek's arms by the feel of the muscle just above his shoulder. I know that I am crying because my face is wet, and from the burning in my throat.

25

7:30 A.M., SUNDAY

My eyes process nothing. I step down stairs without seeing stairs. I'm brought into a room I don't remember entering. Only when I realize I'm not standing does it occur to me that I'm sitting. A dam, high and thick, divides me from the world.

"Ren . . ." Derek's voice is miles away, but it pulls me from myself.

When my eyes shift into focus, things seem off. Like someone's pressed the mute button on life and colored it in shades of gray. Looking around the small, stark space, I can piece together where he's brought me by the objects, if not the colors. A corner mat. Cross-legged statues. Lit, floating candles under a small painting of a blue god. A cross. Stained glass windows. And rows of benches.

The hospital sanctuary.

How long my mind's been gone, I can't tell.

He's seated on the bench beside me, though I don't have to look at him to know.

Gently, he tips my chin and I have no choice. His eyes lock on mine. I notice how his finger is so close to my lip. "She's lucky to have you, Ren," he breathes, tone soft. "Whatever you're feeling right now—guilt, or maybe you're thinking you can do more for her . . . I hope you know how much you've already done."

"You're wrong." I force myself to look past him, over his shoulder. Sliding away, I sink lower into the pew. "There is more I can do."

He'll think I'm talking about the surgery, but I'm not.

Callum. I need to get to him. I need him to know that she doesn't have much time.

In some faraway corner of my mind, I remember that Dunn is having me followed. That I should be looking for another spring . . . but that doesn't feel like what I should be doing. Not at all. I should be trying to get Aven a cure.

I push myself to stand but my head goes black and dizzy— I stumble back onto the bench. Nothing works, none of my limbs will do as they're told.

"Drink—" Derek passes me the metal canteen from his belt. When I can't find the energy to take it, he tilts the cool rim against my lips for me.

My tongue is sandpaper in my mouth, after all that crying. I didn't even realize it. My thirst don't know the word "polite." I chug and I chug until my breathing slows. The drinking forces me to relax. After I've downed half, I pull myself away.

That right there just cost him three square meals of the nonpackaged variety.

"Finish it."

I look at him, guilty, but I don't argue. With a few more sips, my head begins to clear, like stripping dirt from a pane of glass. I wait for the world to hit me with its colors and sounds, but nothing happens. Everything is still at a distance. The glass might be cleaner, but my mind is off in a different room, numb.

Derek takes the canteen, straps it back on his belt.

"How do you do it?" he asks, and rubs at the scruff along his jaw.

"Do what?"

"I called you reckless . . . ," he says, and he watches my hand. Reaches for it. Turns it over, palm up. "All this time you hardly spoke about her. But that's where your winnings would go each month, wouldn't they? You've been taking care of her. Yourself."

I nod, barely.

"So how do you do it?" he asks, my hand still in his. "Love someone who's dying—so much so that, for them you've been willing to risk your own life, over and over again?" Derek shakes his head, and he has the same look I saw on Callum earlier after he noticed the scar.

"What's dying got to do with love?" I start to pull away, readying myself to stand again.

"You're hurting." He tugs me back. Circles my wrist with his fingers, and I let him.

My legs are not quite ready to carry the burden that is me. I'm still too numb, too exhausted.

"Some hurt's worth it," I say, knowing I wouldn't give up the past three years with Aven for anything.

Curling his hand behind my neck, he brings my forehead to rest on his shoulder's soft spot, while I wipe away fresh tears. They've started marching, slow, steady down each cheek. Derek reaches to catch one with a calloused finger. "She's lucky to have you," he tells me again.

I brush my head against the soft cotton of his tee, noticing he hasn't moved his finger from my cheek. "Maybe," I answer. "But she's my favorite part of life."

That's when I feel him press his lips to my forehead.

He lets them rest for longer than I understand and I freeze, confused. Everything is still happening through that glass pane; it feels so far away. *Is this a kiss?* I think. It could be—his lips are touching my skin—so I wait for some flutter, some *something*.

But even my nerve endings have had the mute button pushed on them.

"She's worth the hurt," he murmurs, repeating my words back to me.

I pull away, try to look him in the eye. "You're talking like you've never loved someone." Derek refuses to meet my gaze.

Instead, he palms the nape of my neck and twines my rough curls between his fingers, all the while looking down into his lap. One breathy, quick laugh, and he shakes his head. "I'm just jaded, I guess. I don't want to be—but it happens. You get older. The heart gets tired of good-byes."

He sounds like me, back in the orphanage. Before Aven. I didn't want to be friends with anyone. I knew I'd get left behind.

Then, I feel a second kiss. Again, my forehead. Lighter this time.

What is he doing? It's over now—there's Kitaneh to think about. He'll pull away.

But he doesn't. He traces his lips down between my eyebrows, and I can feel his breath on my eyelashes. When he kisses me there—number three—I feel it. Low in my spine. A fizzy, bubbling itch.

The fourth is different; it doesn't meander, it has a destination. It lands on the bridge of my nose. I start to sink away, I'm not sure I can help myself.

Five and six. My cheeks. One for each saltwater trail still left behind. Slowly, he turns Technicolor—I feel his bright lashes twice, and twice, I feel the fizzing current rippling up to my back.

My body can only react.

One by one my nerves . . . they're waking up. They're waking up to a world on fire, and they like it. I imagine the destination of seven. It makes my face flush hot.

What am I doing? I want to leave, I *have* to leave, have to get to Callum's. But I need to take this with me.

I don't wait. I come up on my knees and with both hands, cup the angles of his jaw. I let my fingers rest at his earlobes, graze his faded tattoo, and close my eyes. Before I can think, I draw his mouth to mine. Like we've done this a million times, he opens up to me and we're breathing each other's breath.

Lips shouldn't feel like this, like swimming through another's body. It's addictive, I could forget things this way. I press closer, wind my arms around his neck. He, in turn, grips me by the hips, hooks his fingers through my belt loops and tugs me into him.

Derek wants me. . . . It's a thrill, knowing that. Makes me bolder. We close all the open spaces between us, and I know my body has never *needed* before. I drink him like freshwater.

Everywhere his hands move, my skin—even under my clothes—hums.

And then, just as quickly . . .

I do it—I riptide myself away from his body. "I'm sorry," I mumble, and stagger to my feet. "I've got to go. I'm sorry. . . ." I don't turn to look at his face as I run from the sanctuary. I don't want to see.

Aven. Aven. Aven. Her name is never far from sight. It circles my brain in an orbit, leads me no different from gravity.

26

8:00 A.M., SUNDAY

I run for the main stairs, still warm in all the places Derek's skin touched mine. Like there's a burner left on, way under my skin, that I can't turn off. I don't want to think about him. I don't want *to want* to think about him. But my mind replays that moment, can't let it go, and then it's too late—

A cold hand grips me from behind. Covers my mouth; I can't yell. . . . *The DI.*

Pure adrenaline pumps my legs alive. I try and shimmy myself out from his grasp, but it's no use. Whoever's behind me has got too strong of a grip. I try biting at the hand—no one likes that—but he's immune to the charms of a slimy tongue.

What will Chief do to me?

So he can cuff my hands with his own, he says, "Let's not make a scene, Dane," as he frees my mouth.

Now that his hands are off my face, I'm better able to have a look at him, but there are no surprises: cropped hair, blue fatigues, silver five-pointed star pinned to his breast pocket. I'm just glad it ain't the chief.

Something tells me he wouldn't be going so easy on me.

The agent hauls me through unfamiliar corridors, all the way up the stairwell. When there are no more stairs to climb—we have to be at the rooftop—he opens one last door. Pushes me into open air.

I'm instantly blinded by the sun bouncing white-hot over the roof's metal drainage system. Behind me, the agent doesn't care that I'm tripping on every damn steel pipe up here. My feet stumble, he jolts me back, only to throw me forward. By the time my eyes adjust to the light, we're dead center of the roof, and he's opening a door.

A door to a house made of glass.

"It is . . . quite incredible, is it not?" I hear a man say, but see nobody.

I blink, and I blink, and I blink again, and even if I couldn't see, I would know—my cells are buzzing, they can feel it: there's magic in this place. Not fairy-tale magic . . . more like the magic of being alive with something built by the world, not by its people.

My eyes don't know what to do with all the green. They've never seen so much of the color in all my sixteen years.

Leaves. Branches and branches of them. Branches attached

to trunks, planted in soil, all growing roots. Right here. Right under my feet.

Trees.

I bring my hand to my mouth, gasp out loud, and then realize I'm able to. The agent—gone, already.

"I hope you know how privileged you should feel to be here—the arboretum is for staff use only, naturally."

Vaguely, like I've missed the cue but my body hasn't, I notice my heart pushing out blood faster than it should. And the hairs on the back of my neck stand higher, even though I hear no threat in the voice.

I turn around to watch him approach—an older man. His feet lazy, unhurried, as he walks the stone path that must wind through the structure. I'm sure I've never met him before, but he has a familiar face. When he's feet away, he motions to the tree at the center of the building with a bench that circles its base.

"Do have a seat," he says, and I listen. Find myself holding the wooden planks beneath my palms. They have a different feel to them than the boardwalk planks, I don't know how.

It occurs to me to be scared. But this place . . . how can I be scared in this place?

"Do you know who I am?" the man asks, lowering himself onto the bench next to me.

When I look at him more closely, something about his features brings to mind that night at Derek's—the autoupdate. I see a hardness, a gaunt line to his cheekbones. This man can't be him, though. . . .

He can't be the governor. "Are you . . . ?"

Crossing his legs and extending an arm, "These last nine years, yes. Governor Voss. Pleased to make your acquaintance, Miss Dane." He takes my hand in his and gives it a firm shake. At his neck, I see the K-dot, white and just applied.

Soon he releases my hand; I'm holding on to the planks again, my life raft.

"All of these trees are different, you know?" the governor says quietly, pointing around the arboretum. "With different names. Properties, too. Medicinal, some of them."

The way he says that, so pointed . . . *It's like he knows.*

"This one," he says as he tugs down a branch from overhead, "is called a hemlock. Natives who once occupied this territory ate the bark." Ripping off a few of its leaves— needly, dark things—he then opens my hand and drops them there.

I close my fist around all the greenness. *Aven would love to see them.* But she's downstairs, barely living. The needles prick at my palm, so I let them go.

I turn to face the governor. He must know that Chief Dunn canceled the surgery. He must.

"What brings you to Ward Hope Hospital?" he asks me, brushing off his hands. "I already know the girl, Aventine Colatura, is a patient, but that's not what I am asking."

Through the dotted green I can see the glass roof, and past that, sky. A twinge at my stomach tells me to be careful what I say. This place is beautiful, but he's brought me here for a reason. On the day of a riot erupting on the West Isle, the governor crossed the Strait to speak to *me.*

"What do you mean, sir?" I ask, keeping my voice soft.

Governor Voss waves his hand. "I mean, who is this girl to you?"

I swallow—*What's he getting at?*—and give him the only answer I have: the honest-to-goodness truth.

"She's my sister, though we don't share blood. My best friend, though the label's too weak if you ask me. . . ." I pause, realizing it as I say it: "She's the first person I ever loved."

The governor nods, and wisps of his steely hair glint as the sun cuts through the glass. "I understand," he says, and reaches for his cuffcomm. When he pushes a button on its side, an image is projected into the air. It's not a hologram—the technology is older. Basic light projection. With no surface for the image to land on, I can barely make out what he's showing me.

As if to catch the light, he raises his other hand. A picture takes shape in his palm. He's holding it . . . her.

A woman.

Darker than I am, but not by much. Freckled. With fuzzy hair cropped close to her scalp. Not particularly beautiful, but she pulls you in with her grin—it's on so wide, you can't help but smile back at her. "Who is she?" I ask, but I think I know, from the press conference.

"Her name is Emilce Weathers," he says, his voice going hard and detached all of a sudden. "She is HBNC positive, still contagious, and according to doctors, she has only weeks to live." He pauses, then adds, "She is . . . my wife."

"I'm sorry," I say, weak, knowing from experience how useless it sounds.

Looking at her image, he smiles, but his eyes stay sad. "You know, she laughed at me when I first asked her out? Not unkindly, though . . . no. In a way that made it seem like she had life all figured out, and I must've missed the memo. I asked her why she refused, and she said, so simply, that it was because I was wearing a tie. She could not date someone who 'chose to wear a noose.' So I took it off in front of her, and never wore another one after that day."

He drops his hand. All that's left of Emilce Weathers's image are the glowing light particles where her teeth would be. "She is the only person I would die for," he says, and clicks off his cuffcomm.

I watch his face as he says that because I understand, and because I want to see what the words look like on someone else. At times I feel like I'm the only one who'd say that sort of thing, and mean it.

"And," he adds, not looking at me, "she is the only person I would kill for."

My stomach twists, recoils like a punch has been thrown— *Is that a threat?* There's such edge to his voice. Layers of it. Brutal honesty, but also desperation. Powerlessness. If it is a threat, it's the worst kind. Not direct, not even indirect. Volatile. As he sees fit, when he sees fit.

It makes me wonder about myself. If I would kill for Aven.

I don't know, but I'm afraid of the answer.

Governor Voss stands and faces me, still on the bench. Looking down, he says, "So you see. I understand why you are here. Truly, I do. And you, in turn, must understand why I too am here."

The spring . . .

I knot my brows and begin to shake my head, readying myself to lie, but the governor dismisses me outright.

"Please do me the courtesy of being forthright, Miss Dane. I saw the sample you gave to Chief Dunn. We both know that spring is more than just a freshwater source. I have done my homework. Miss Colatura was sick before she showed up at the Tank—the chief confirmed it. You gave her the water, not knowing what it was. She then experienced a brief recovery and, for reasons unknown to yourself, is now at death's door."

Slowly, I rise to my feet—looking up so high makes me feel small, and I can't afford to feel small right now. "Reasons unknown to myself?" I say.

The governor reaches inside his jacket, into the breast pocket. Pulls out what looks to be a flip pocketknife, and something else I can't see—it's too small. "Are you surprised? Do you know so much about the water?"

"I know nothing about the water, sir," I answer. It's the truth, and I don't see any amount of bluffing working for me now.

He nods. "No. I thought not. Miss Dane, let me tell you. It is . . . so, so much more than a cure, though that is, of course, a primary concern. My wife's life, your friend's, and hundreds of others depend upon it. It is *the* answer. Not just to the Blight—to all the UMI's problems. All of *humanity's* problems. From cancer to the flu and everything in between. Even when drunk by a *healthy* individual, the results are nothing short of miraculous. For those suffering from disease, with daily, repeated ingestion, the results are life-altering. Within weeks, they'd receive a clean bill of health."

Hope, fizzy and full, rises up my chest when I hear him say that. "So the water can really cure Aven?" I whisper. Callum said he could do it and I believed him—but hearing it twice doesn't hurt.

"Like I said, over enough time. And in the correct dosage. It is a natural antiviral, not much different from ginger root or echinacea. Except far more powerful. In Aven's case, not enough was consumed. Since the virus was not eradicated, she relapsed once the water left her system. But if she'd had more . . ." The governor's voice trails off. "Quite good incentive to find me another source, is it not?"

I nod fiercely. "Yes, sir."

Now I'm even more anxious to get to Callum.

"Don't think I'm the best choice for the job, though."

Governor Voss laughs. As he does, he tosses the object in his hand up into the air, catching it easily. It looks to be some kind of a statue.

"To be fair, *I* didn't choose you," he tells me. "Not that I believe as the natives do, but you found the spring. *It* chose you."

I almost laugh. The spring didn't choose me, it didn't pull out its megaphone and announce itself. My feet just . . . sorta walked there. As they tend to do when they're going places.

Thinking he's done, I open my mouth to object. He cuts me off.

"That, and you know at least one Tètai."

I shake my head and answer, "I don't know anybody by

that name. Sorry, sir. . . ."

He can't make me do this, I don't have time to hunt for him.

"Not a name." He wags his finger. With one hand on my shoulder, he sits me back down on the bench. "A guild, of sorts. The Tètai were established by the early natives with one purpose: protecting that water. And someone you know, though you may not be aware, is one of the last four members still"—he pauses, as if finding the right words—"in existence."

"That's who messed with the spring," I murmur.

He nods, points his pocketknife at me. "Bingo. A friend who knows what you found."

"But only you, Aven, and the chief know."

"We are the only ones you have told, yes. We are not the only ones who know." Governor Voss unlatches his cuff-comm, flips it open to find whatever he's looking for, and passes it to me. "I'd like you to read something."

I have to project the image onto my forearm where the skin isn't as dark. As I begin to make it out, I hear a scraping noise and look up—he's using the pocketknife to whittle the object in his other hand. Sand-colored bits flake off while he chips away at the statue.

It must be wood. . . . It looks like wood. But why carve it like that? Why not use it for something useful?

"It is a translation from the Dutch," the governor says, as though that's what I was wondering about—not the strange thing he's carving in front of me.

Turning my attention back to my forearm, I shake my head, and I start reading.

27

1645

Directors of the Dutch West India Company—

While the tales I have brought you might appear to be the stuff of fancy, I urge you to reconsider my recall from post as Director of the New Netherland region. Interview the men in my militia—they will all attest: the Lenape inhabitants of this region, skirmish after skirmish, do resurrect their wounded bodies, making them impossible to defeat. A native may lose his life one day, yet we will be confronted with the very same face not a month later. Lost limbs have spontaneously regenerated during battle.

To learn the truth, I did send one of my men to search their settlement. He did not return alive—his body, and that of a Lenape tribesman, were found in the nearby woods. Upon inspection of both, a peculiar tattoo was discovered on the native, behind his ear, in such a design. . . .

I suck in air when I see that shape projected onto my skin. Just like a tattoo—a black symbol, or design, or whatever it is. *Derek's tattoo.*

My mind ping-pongs between *coincidence* and *no way*. Because if it's not a coincidence, if he really is one of these Tètai, I can't figure out why he'd ever hide the spring from the sick. The dying.

Governor Voss must hear me gasp, because the pocketknife stops its whittling. When he looks over, he says nothing. We exchange glances, and he nods for me to keep reading.

I continued to send envoy after envoy, each one sabotaged, and turning up in a manner similar to the first, in the same manner of killing. Only one man survived. With his dying words, he told me of the existence and location of the "Minetta Brook," they call it: a brook with unusual, healing capabilities.

The following day, the day I ordered the attack on that area, there was no evidence a spring had ever been there. That was our final skirmish—no natives returned from the dead again.

Admittedly, I ordered the attack without the approval of the Advisory Council, but you must understand: you cannot defeat an enemy that does not die. I was forced to act quickly. That is the tale in its entirety, I beg that you believe me, or I will consider myself shamed.

—Director of New Netherlands, Willem Van Kieft

At the last word, I look up.

"He's my ancestor," the governor explains, and returns to sit on the bench beside me. Not once does he lift his eyes from the thing he's carving. "That letter is how I first came to learn of the spring's existence. Now, Miss Dane . . . I want you to think about what we could do with such defenses on our side. Who could withhold their water stores from us then?"

I'm not listening to him anymore. *That symbol . . .*

As I turn off the comm, my forearm goes blank, no tattoo there. It was too unusual to be coincidence.

Derek must be one of the Tètai.

I bite my lip to keep in all the ugly words I want to say. I'd like to hurl the cuffcomm onto the ground. Why would he keep the cure a secret? Not just from the world . . . but from me. Aven.

The hospital last night . . . I put the pieces together fast, and if I were alone I would be wiping my face clean of all the places where his mouth touched mine. This was why. He left us there in the waiting room with no explanation.

He left to fill the gap in the subway. To close off the spring. To stop me from going back.

I clench my teeth together. Dig my nails to the skin.

"You recognize the symbol, don't you?" Governor Voss's eyes, the same steel color as his hair, meet mine. To himself he whispers, "She's still alive, then," looking away from the statue.

She?

"I knew it," he goes on. "Kitaneh runs in your circle, after all. Friendly with a gambler who works the races. She has kept me from finding the spring many times."

He has no idea about Derek.

I could tell him right now, but some pathetic sense of loyalty makes me keep my mouth shut. "Why don't you go to her yourself?" I ask. "Doubt she'll listen to me."

"If I went after Kitaneh, or any of the Tètai directly, it would only end in death. And I can't afford to kill them off." Rubbing his thumb over what looks like the neck of some animal's neck, he brings the knife there. Narrows it. "No, you're going to talk to them for me."

I stand up and begin pacing back and forth on the stone pathway. *There's no time for this.* "What makes you think I'd get an answer?" I say, frustration cracking my voice.

The governor ignores my question.

He keeps carving that thing. *Scrape, scrape . . .*

All of a sudden the air goes tight again. I want to get out. He said he understood, but I need to leave, and he's still keeping me here.

"Miss Dane, why do you think they've been hiding it?" he asks calmly.

The question takes me by surprise, pauses my pacing.

"I don't know." I speak honestly, and wonder if there's

some answer to that question that could bring me to forgive Derek. I don't think so.

Governor Voss looks up. Makes a fist around the figurine. "Perhaps it is out of fear. Fear of what people in power— like myself—might do with it. They fail to comprehend the real fear." He pauses there, and waits. Makes sure I'm paying attention.

"It is not what I might do with it, but, rather, what I might do *without* it."

Each word is delivered like a boulder, heavy with some threat that I don't understand.

"What would you do?" I ask, unable to stop the words from wavering.

"Only what the people want." The governor reaches up from the bench and takes my hand, opening it up, same as he did with the pine needles. Inside, he places the small wooden statue. "Give this to Kitaneh. She will know it's from me, and she will know its meaning. Tell them that I am giving the Tètai a chance to fix things. But I need to know where to find another location."

Gripping the object in my palm, "A horse?" I murmur. It's more complex than I'd originally thought, but still rough edged. Made like a child's toy, with spokes and wheels at its hooves, even an empty compartment in its belly.

The seed of an idea forms in my mind. I could buy Aven more time. Callum, too . . . "If I do this—if I talk to her, could you have Aven's surgery rescheduled?"

Governor Voss stands up, placing me eye level with his jacket buttons. He rests a hand on my shoulder, firm, and says, "Miss Dane, if you're able to convince Kitaneh, Aven won't need surgery."

Not exactly the answer I was hoping for.

I look around the arboretum—it's too calm in here. No wind . . . *arboretum* is just a fancy word for a glass cage. When I meet his eyes again, I'm fixed by that idea, caught under the steel of his irises. The longer I stare, the harder they look.

"You're to report to Chief Dunn via comm with their answer in—" The governor glances at his cuffcomm. "Four hours. I would not waste any more time."

Four hours? I can't look away from him—I'm an animal, trapped, clutching the strange wooden horse in my hand.

"*Go,*" he hisses.

Are they tailing me?

I lean over the banister in the stairwell to listen for footsteps, but I don't hear a sound. That means nothing though. Could be they're keeping quiet . . . watching. Waiting to see what I'll do.

Well, the easiest place to lose them is here. Right now. In the hospital. And I can think of only one way to do it.

I race up another flight of stairs and into the hall, but instead of making a right toward the main stairs, I keep straight. Straight on to the red double doors at the opposite end of the corridor.

Painted in white lettering on each door: "Contagious."

They'll leave this exit unattended for sure.

I push the doors open and walk through. Find myself

sucking in my air, like I'm still afraid of catching it. So many years pretending, hiding. It's not that I ever forget I'm immune, but I don't always remember it either. *Exhale*, I remind myself. I remind myself to inhale, too, though I'm sure the air's megafiltered anyway.

I take slow steps through the empty hall, my path wide open. I should run . . . but my feet disagree. My heart disagrees.

I can see *every* patient.

All the rooms—made of clear, double-layered glass panes. Visitors can look, but they can't touch. There are never visitors, it seems. Ain't even that many patients. Hospital care is too expensive. Most, like Aven and me, opt for the cheaper route: house calls and black market daggers.

But the ones who are here . . . each of them could be helped by the cure that *Derek* keeps hidden. I want to be sick, and not from the retching noises coming from my left.

A young girl looks up, peers back at me through a room made of glass.

Her hair does me in; not quite as sunny as Aven's, but enough to confuse me. I walk closer, and she brings her hand up to the plastic canopy that surrounds her bed. Holds it there like she's shielding her eyes. But she's not—she's trying to see.

Me.

She's trying to see me.

That hair, that hair . . . She's not Aven—the girl ain't no more than eight—but my insides don't care what my brain knows. Through the blurry plastic and the glass, she's Aven.

Before I ever met her. Before her dad dropped her off at Nale's, 'cause he was dying and couldn't take care of her alone.

I place my hand on the glass, the hand not holding the carved horse, and suddenly I'm back in the Tank. I'm Aven, seeing the world from Before for the very first time.

"Who are you?" a voice asks, tinny and weak, through the comm built into the panels. The sound startles me and I step away, dropping my hand. "Don't go—" She's pleading. . . .

I look around the empty hallway, then back at her glass room and her white plastic door. I could turn the knob. Go inside. Touch her hand.

My palm is on the metal. Then, echoes from the entryway—
The doors . . . someone's coming.

I'm sorry, I mouth to the girl, and I drop my hand. Spinning around, I bolt for the end of the corridor. Every patient turns their head as I race by.

When I swing myself into the stairwell, I hear the static of cuffcomms crackling from behind, but no footsteps. . . . They'll be hiding outside instead.

I clamber down the stairs—if I could, I'd jump the banister, but I'd need both hands for that. The horse grows sweaty in my fist and I'm making a racket, but there's no other way.

Breathless and staggering, I hit the last stair and I've reached my exit. Then I'm out the staff door, onto the narrows.

Planks wobble under my feet, and though the walkway is empty but for me, I don't slow. *Forget the Cloud*, I think, realizing that it's docked around front. *I'll hoof it instead.* They'll have a harder time following me that way.

East. I need to head east, toward Mad Ave. Toward Derek's. Let him tell me no to my face. He kissed me. That must mean something, even if I don't know what. Maybe . . . maybe he cares enough that he won't be able to turn me away. And if he does, Callum is only a few blocks north.

Looking up, I know which way to go. The day is still early—I run in the direction of the sun.

28

9:00 A.M., SUNDAY

I hit Mad Ave at its worst. The vendors are out with their hotcakes and their black market water. I don't want to deal with all the foot traffic, not now. But all those crowds make this the safest route to Derek's, and I can see Lihn's Take-Out just across the avenue.

I swing left, throwing myself into the thick of it.

Like swimming upstream, I push through a pack of neighborhood Derby boys mobbed together this side of the boardwalk. The future roofrat generation, no doubt. They snigger meanly in their shoddy tweed jackets, tossing punches at one another. Every ten seconds one of 'em jumps down on a loose plank, and five feet off, the boardwalk chucks another unsuspecting victim into the air.

This time, it's an older woman, her gray hair neat in a bun.

She flies forward, then falls to her knees. Her bag spills out onto the walkway, and as she reaches around people's moving feet to gather her belongings, the area clears without warning.

I move to help her, but—*Uh-oh . . .*

Stumbling backward, I know full well why a random area of the boardwalk might clear without warning. *Bouncers.* They're testing.

I just need to cross the boardwalk, then I'll be at Lihn's.

But I can't. One makes his way closer, the yellow of his jacket near blinding under this sun. Backing away real slow, I try not to look suspicious. As he nears . . . I recognize him. *It's Ro.*

I exhale and laugh.

He throws me a smile and a nod, and starts to walk over. As if in warning, though, a buzz runs through my muscles and they harden. Ready for something. Ro lifts his cuffcomm to his mouth, and I watch him close. Every twinge around his eyes, every muscle of his mouth—

She's here, I read on his lips. *Quad Five.* He drops his hand. Flashes me another easy smile.

Brack—

Like a powder keg, my legs explode ahead, aimed directly for the crowds. I can't make it to Derek's now; I'd be leading them straight to him. I shouldn't even go to Callum's, but they have no clue about him, and it's probably the safest place to be. Assuming I can keep from being followed.

Knocking into the rush, I fold myself between mother and stroller, doctor and cane. Curses follow me, rounds of invisible bullets. I pretend not to notice them. A man drops his bag as I elbow him to the side—planting seeds spill everywhere. Onto the planks and into water . . . it'll cost him more than if he'd just dropped his change.

He scowls, gives me the finger.

When I look behind me, there's Ro, mouth at his comm again.

Just a few more blocks to Callum's. . . .

Hammering my fist against his door, "Let me in—" I whine through gritted teeth, and glance back at Mad Ave. With so many people, Ro can't have seen me turn onto this block. But right now, one glance to the left and he'd spot me, easy.

The door opens.

I fall in. Straighten myself. Slamming it shut behind me, I lean back to try and catch my breath. "The DI . . ." I manage, panting. "They're keeping tabs on me. . . . Bouncers, too."

Callum's eyes widen. "And you led them here? What were you thinking?"

"No one saw," I insist, though I'm not 100 percent sure—I don't tell him that.

Stepping away from the door, I reach for his arm. "You don't understand, Callum. That cure—I need it. There's no time. The doctor . . . he gave Aven forty-eight hours." My voice breaks in odd places as I speak. Crackles at random.

Callum squints in confusion as he checks his cuffcomm. "She should be in surgery now—I cleared payment with the head doctor and everything. . . ."

I don't know what to say. Back at the hospital, he told me

that he might be able to "do something to help," but I'd had no clue what that meant. No way did I believe he'd *actually* pay for it.

When he sees my expression, he waves his hand like it was nothing. But it's not nothing. It's my sister. "Chief Dunn had it canceled," I tell him.

"I don't believe it," Callum growls, knocking his hand against the table. It shakes, and I hear the clinking of glass though I can't see much—he's kept the curtains closed.

I can make out enough. Everywhere, funnels and hoses. Burners and beakers. An entire makeshift laboratory. And from somewhere deep in this obstacle course, an odd noise—

Coo, coo . . .

Cocking my head, I glance around the room. "Is that . . . Is that a bird?"

Callum just nods. Waves for me to continue, like it's totally normal. Wary, I pull my eyes from the lab and flop cross-legged onto the floor.

"The governor was there, Callum. Waiting for me," I say, shaky. "He told me about the people who protect the spring. The 'Tètai,' he called them. And you were right. I know one. Two, actually. . . ."

He waits for me to go on, but I don't want to speak the rest. Saying it out loud makes it true, and every square inch of me is hoping that I'm wrong. But I know I'm not.

"Derek. My bookie," I say, staring at my lifeline. "And this girl he's friends with."

The hatched wrinkle cuts deep and dark across my palm. Yesterday—*today*—Derek's fingers traced that very skin.

271

Hours ago, I kissed him. And he kissed me back.

But I've never known him, not really.

That realization makes me want to curl up and hide from everyone. That I could be so naive, so foolish. Who, exactly, was I so infatuated with?

I have no idea.

I reach for the carved statue inside my belt pocket. "Then Governor Voss gave me this. To give to them."

Callum takes it from my hand. "A toy?" he asks, and he spins its wheels.

"Don't know, he didn't say." I shrug, watching him fiddle. "A threat, my guess. A message of some sort?"

He finds the belly compartment, flips it open, and lets it swing shut. "I've seen this before," he murmurs. "Haven't you?"

"Never. But he must think it'll scare them bad enough that they'll tell me everything. I don't know what he's planning, Callum, but he's desperate. He showed me a picture of his wife. . . . He wants to save her. He gave me four hours."

Callum returns the statue—I flip it in my hand. Open the compartment, close the compartment. Open, close.

What happens if I don't get it to Derek?

I hang my head between my knees, as the unknown weight of this thing the governor's asked me to do settles in.

Callum looks at me hard. "You can't do it. Ask Derek to give up the spring's location, I mean. I'm sure Governor Voss wants to save his wife. But don't for one second believe that's his only intention. You saw the Core."

I nod and toss the horse up in the air lightly before catching it and setting it on the table. The crawling, spindly legged feeling of fear I get worries me, but the statue and Derek aren't what's important right now. "It can wait. Until after you've made the cure."

At his desk, Callum looks away. Sighs. The sound fills up the room, speaks a language of its own, and I don't like it. It feels too much like padding. Like he's readying me for bad news.

I hawk-eye him. "What's the matter . . . ?"

"Come," he says, waving me over to where a brass microscope sits in front of him. He lays a glass slide under its lens and nudges me in front. "Look."

I peer down, adjusting the focus by spinning the knob on the right. We had one of these things at the orphanage.

Bubble-colored grids and particles of something that looks kind of like a desert wasteland come into view. But I also see other shapes—confetti and extra-long hot dogs, floating around the slide.

"Whoa . . . it's a whole party down there." I keep my eye socket hugged to the rubber. "What is all that?"

Callum laughs, almost. "There's so much, I don't know where to begin. Much of it is useless. Decaying plant matter, a few harmless microbes. The most interesting thing, though, are the chemical compounds I found. They're called 'phytonutrients.'"

"Which ones are they?" I ask, trying to figure out where one shape ends and all the others begin.

"The pattern-like particles," he clarifies, and I nod. Sand dunes. Rainbowy grid. "They're found in all plants. In one apple, for example, there are more than three hundred phytonutrients. And they all do different things for the body. Good things."

I lift my head from the 'scope, because after what the governor said before about plants with beneficial properties, I think I know where Callum's going with this. "Like fighting viruses?" I offer.

His brows rise up, he's that impressed. "Yes," he says. "And reducing the size of tumors. And healing wounds. I've already identified close to two hundred phytonutrients in that sample alone. There are hundreds more, no doubt, not including those that I was unable to match in the database."

"So what's wrong? What am I missing?" I ask.

Callum rubs his temples and folds himself into his chair. "It's not what you're missing. It's what the water is missing."

"I don't get it. You just said—?"

He moves to the window, pulls aside a corner of the drapes. A sliver of light falls in the room, just enough so that we can see each other.

"Phytonutrients come from plants. But there's no plant to be found in that sample. On its own, the water is useless. And it's even more useless because . . ." Callum stops, wears a face like he's ready to throw himself to the sharks. He inhales and turns to watch the springwater being sieved from the remaining mud into a beaker. "By filtering the mud . . . I also filtered out most of the nutrients. A sample that was weak to start—not even strong enough to help Aven long-term—became weaker."

My stomach drops. "Wait," I whisper. "What are you

saying? We've got nothing?" I'm wire taut with the tension that comes from trying really, really hard to keep from bugging out.

"Not nothing," Callum answers. "Not enough, either. Many of the compounds responsible for healing passed through, as did the antitumorals. But the antivirals . . ." He shakes his head.

I don't believe it. . . . I don't believe him. My stomach churns, empty, acidic, and in the background, the dripping slows. Those intervals between one drop and the next stretch longer and longer, as the muddy springwater filters through the sieve.

Soon, the dripping stops entirely.

Callum moves to replace the mud, but not before lifting the large glass beaker and swirling its contents. "Do you see the dilemma?" he asks, emptying one jar into the sieve.

Quickly, I scan the table. Spotting two more, full and waiting, "But you've got—" I start to say.

"It won't be enough." His answer comes quick, in a voice so dark it could swallow gravity itself.

"We could give it to her anyway. That would fix the tumors, right?" I ask, grasping for any possibility.

Callum finds my eyes, serious. "Not unless you want Aven dead by nightfall. HBNC-related growths sometimes return even faster. I told you that back at the hospital. Which is exactly what happened to her the first time. The mass disappeared, but the virus was still in her body. And she relapsed tenfold."

But he said he could do it. . . .

275

"Ren . . . I'm sorry."

No, no, no, no, no—the cure, it's right here. It's sitting in front of my eyes. And it'll fix her tumors . . . but it won't cure her? I can't parse it; it makes no sense . . . none at all. Suddenly, I'm heaving—my body feels like a natural disaster.

I'm earthquake shaken.

Only, natural disasters have nothing on me. I'm avalanche flung, pumping volcano blood. Behind my eyes: Wash Out—the sequel.

And natural disasters, they don't give up. They end when they're good and ready to.

I'm not ready.

29

10:00 A.M., SUNDAY

Emergency. Rooftop, 39 Rough Block. ASAP.

Send.

Then, realizing Derek won't recognize Callum's unlisted comm ID number, I type: "—Ren" and hit SEND again.

"What are you doing?" Callum asks.

"You know what I'm doing," I answer, because he's smarter than that question.

His expression seesaws into warning. "Ren, I don't think that's a good idea. Meeting one of the Tètai so close to the lab . . . You could be inviting trouble in by the front door."

"Look. I'll get there before him, and then I'll watch him leave. Make sure he doesn't stick around. Plus, I'll be up on a different rooftop, and out of sight—Bouncers never check there. Besides," I say softly, thinking back to the sanctuary.

The kisses. If he does care about me, if that's what that meant . . . "I don't think he'd hurt me."

I might want to hurt him, but that's an entirely different story.

I reach into one of my cargo pockets for the horse, but I don't feel it. "Would you pass me the statue?" I ask, gesturing to table. "I can give it to him when I see him."

Callum nods, about to hand it to me, then stops. Examines it. "You've never seen this before?"

I say no for the second time, and he reaches for his datapad. Enters something into it, and waits.

"I should go, if I want to get up there first—"

Holding up his hand, "Just a moment. I think I know what . . ." Then, "*Aha*, look—see?" he says, passing me the screen, pointing to an image.

Front and center, our horse statue. Only it wasn't just a statue.

Big as a building, wooden, wheeled, and with a secret hide-out in the belly—it was a war tactic. "The Trojan horse," I say aloud, reading the caption next to the image. "Used by the Greeks for a surprise attack. They put an army in the belly chamber and called the horse a gift. . . . When the other guys accepted it, the Greeks jumped out and they battled them to bits."

Callum exchanges the horse for his datapad. "That's the story. I knew the statue looked familiar. Basically, any strategy where the target unknowingly invites its enemy into its territory."

I hold the horse in my palm, and walk to the front door. "What does it mean, do you think?" I ask Callum, unable to piece it together.

He shakes his head. "No idea."

I'm about to leave—one hand on the knob—when Callum calls me back. I turn to face him.

"Be careful," he says. "During my research, the guardians . . . the Tètai, they're not known to leave people alive who've found the spring. If Derek is one of them, he won't be happy to hear you asking for the very thing he's sworn to keep hidden. The fact that you're still standing at all might be testament to how much he cares for you. Don't be surprised if he refuses you."

The double-edged blade of Callum's words is not lost on me— that Derek might care enough to let me live, but not enough to want to help my sister. Not enough to want to help *me*.

I wait on the rooftop, my eyes toward Mad Ave so I can spot Derek before he comes. Up here, pigeons bob across the filtration system, gray, pecking for food or seeds that might've spilled from a recent airdrop.

Watching them warble in the sun as they claw the bridge's rope, I squint to see a figure approaching. But ain't him—no coppery hair, no tall, broad shoulders.

It's a *she*. Short. Dark-haired.

I don't need to know more than that. . . . *But what the hell is she doing here? How did she know?*

She must've seen the comm somehow. Derek might not even know I contacted him. Adrenaline surges, angry, all the way to my head—I need Derek right now, not Kitaneh. Kitaneh didn't kiss me, Kitaneh doesn't care about me. I have absolutely no leverage at all.

Trying to seem unfazed, I rise from my perch at the building's edge. She knows I've seen her . . . but she's not slowing.

Kitaneh moves, brisk, across the suspension bridge. Balanced. Poised. Arrow eyed, watching me. The birds scatter. And the closer she gets, the louder the warning bells sound in my head.

"Where's Derek?" I ask, shielding my eyes from the sun, but my voice wavers. *She's moving too fast. . . .*

Something drops down from her sleeve. Falls into her palm. It catches the morning glare, as sharp as any metal. "I know what you want to ask him," she says, five feet away. "He left his cuffcomm on the table while he was in the shower. I did him a favor, deleting your message."

Four—I stick with an utterly ambiguous reply. *Three*—"Okay . . ." I say, stepping back until there's no place to go. *Two*—My heels bump up against the edge of the roof. *One*—

Zero. A blade, tight against my jugular.

I stretch my neck away . . . but she's got me cornered—a fifty-foot drop behind, a slice to my artery in front. My blood rushes everywhere too fast; I can hear it howling against my eardrums.

"And I cannot risk his answer. Derek . . ." Kitaneh pauses, and I think I see her flinch. Hurt somehow. It passes. Granite hardness takes its place. "He cares for you," she says, finally, and pushes the metal farther into my skin. I can see how much she didn't want to say that.

"Stop, please . . ." I whisper, not even breathing, not wanting to move my throat muscles even a millimeter.

A sharp wind whips against us both—Kitaneh's hair sweeps across her face, blood-colored from a shock of sun.

I see it. . . . Only inches from my face, the tattoo. The same faded black circle, just below her earlobe.

"Forget what you found. You have not yet lived long enough for me to want this blade to single you out. But it will. If it must."

She pulls back on the blade. I swallow air by the mouthful, gulping it down before dropping onto the ledge below. The rooftop spins in front of me, and I watch Kitaneh's feet move farther and farther away, like watching a TV hologram that's accidentally projecting its image sideways.

"Wait—" I croak, just as she's about to step onto the planked bridge. At my hip, the horse statue digs into bone, a blunt-edged reminder. But she doesn't hear me. Louder this time, I call her name. "Kitaneh!"

She stops. Tilts her head my way, barely. "What is it?"
"This."

I push myself to my feet. Force the rooftop to even itself beneath me. I walk to her, holding out the wooden carving. "Does it mean anything to you?"

Kitaneh steps backward onto the roof. Turning to face me, she takes the statue. Holds it in her palm. "No," she answers, and I can tell she's not lying. She's about to hand it back to me but, spotting the compartment, looks again. Opens it. Peers inside.

Her mouth opens, her brows go high, her nostrils push out air, and her cheeks redden. She's reading something. . . .

"*Bellum exter*—did you write this in here?" Frantic, she points inside the carving.

I shake my head. "I didn't even know something *was* written."

When she looks at me again, it's with a rage I'm glad I didn't see before—she would've killed me, I'm sure of it.

"I—I . . ." I stammer, suddenly afraid that she'll confuse the message with the messenger. "The governor, it's from him. He said to tell you this is your chance. To fix things. I don't know why, I swear."

Still looking at the horse, Kitaneh says, "You are in far too deep. I don't know how, or why, you've become involved in this. But I hope, for your sake, you have the mind to stay out of it." With that, she pulls the blade from her sleeve and begins to take slices at the wood. The wheels fall off, then the hooves, all the way up to the stomach. "You may give this back to him, if he contacts you again," she says, and she hands me back the legless beast.

I take it from her. Wait for her to leave. When Kitaneh is halfway across the bridge, I look inside the compartment and find the writing. I'm not surprised I missed it before in the darkness of Callum's lab—the letters are small, and in a language I've never seen before.

Bellum Exterminii.

The words mean nothing to me. I don't know what I expected. . . .

My whole body deflates. Wilts. I sprawl along my spot on the ledge as a bone-shaking exhaustion sets in.

I'm left feeling like a cyclone has come and vacuumed away the last of me, physically incapable of understanding how I could be this close, with the end in sight, and find myself out of options.

30

11:30 P.M., SUNDAY

Walking back into Callum's apartment is like walking smack into an old-time newspaper. Direct from his datapad: fuzzy black type projects into the air against a white, pixelated background. Turning around, he quickly shuts the door—the only blank wall space he had to position the article—and continues reading. The headlines send me five steps backward—

THE WARD: A CASE FOR DEMOCIDE

Governor Voss—We no longer have the money to continue searching for a cure. Yet we must stop the spread. We ask you to consider sacrificing the few for the many. Exterminate the virus by any means possible, even by poisoning the host.

The pathogen has overtaken their blood.
They are *the Blight.*

"What the—Callum, what is this?" I ask, my heart gone still in my body, hands suddenly very cold.

He taps his datapad, scrolling down to read more of the article. "A West Isle news report I just received," he answers in a low tone. "You remember my mentioning a group of radicals with serious animosity toward the Ward's sick population? Well, apparently they've grown bolder—and more extreme—since this morning's rally. I suppose with so many people voicing their discontent, today seemed like a good time to come out with their true agenda."

"Poison *everyone*? Every last sick person?" I ask, quiet.

I can't read any more. "Turn it off."

He does. The projection scatters, and the room is dark again, its corners lit by just a few candles. Shaking his head, Callum says, "It would never happen, of course. I doubt the governor would respond favorably to such a plea . . . not when his own wife is suffering from the very disease they're looking to 'exterminate.'"

I nod, agreeing, but I'm silently cursing Derek and Kitaneh. Reading this article only makes it worse—*We were so close*.

It was in *my* canteen.

Callum must see my face, or I'm wearing the day's disbelief like a neon sign. He walks over. Rests his hand on my shoulder. "Derek said no?"

At first the gesture feels awkward . . . uncomfortable. But then something changes. Starts to feel like the very instant when you know you're friends with someone, because you can see—and I mean *really see*—that they care.

"He wasn't even there," I sigh, only to realize a small part of me is actually relieved. If he had been, I would have been forced to look at him. *Derek*. The guy I've spent so much time feeling all gooey about. And I would have had to hold my ground. I'd have done it, of course. But it would've hurt like hell.

Falling into Callum's chair, I show him the new, red mark left across my neck by Derek's knife-happy girl-who-is-a-friend, Kitaneh. "She saw the comm and paid the visit instead. Then she cut off the horse's legs for Governor Voss to see. Basically turned me into her gofer," I say, and check the time on my cuffcomm.

11:45 a.m.

I'm done for, I think, tugging at my hair.

Nearly time to report, and I've got nothing to tell Dunn. If I show up with that legless horse, what will he do to me? Technically, they still own me—I'm a ward of the state. And I know too much to be sent packing.

But if I miss the report, I'm an outlaw. . . . Wanted.

My best option is falling off the grid entirely. Every Bouncer and mole from here to the racing districts will have my picture, and the added incentive of reward money after I'm captured. They'll all come after me. Have me sent back to the DI headquarters, where Dunn will happily make mincemeat outta of me.

And once I'm an outlaw, I'll never be able to get into the hospital.

Not like I have anything to bring to Aven anyway.

It can't end like this. . . . Lifting my head, anxiety-buzzed, I ask, "How do you know we don't have enough? I'm not a scientist. . . . I don't know anything about this, but what if you've done it wrong?"

"Because—" he answers, lifting a black sheet from a small, square object. "I tried."

Again, the cooing. Softer this time. Weaker.

"This is Milo."

Looking out at us through a plastic cage, closed on all sides, is a bird. A pigeon. Gray feathers rumpled, scruffy and white at the neck. He's nestled in a corner, lying on his side. Like he hasn't got enough energy to make use of his feet.

The bird coos once more, but now I can hear . . . it's a cry, not a song.

He's dying.

And his cage—a purplish light shines across a row of airholes at the top, but other than that it's no different from the glass rooms in the contagious ward. "Is he . . . ?" I ask, and find that I'm holding my breath.

Old habits.

"Milo is HBNC positive, and contagious. And what happened to Aven—that is precisely what he's going through. The tumor disappeared, then reappeared. While there may be a sufficient number of the antitumorigenic phytonutrients in the water, there are still not enough antivirals." Callum nods and drops some seeds through the airhole—they go ignored. "It will never work," he says.

His words are a stamp, a seal. Truth. A fact.

He reaches for the black sheet.

The orange-eyed bird watches us . . . *me*. Like I'm responsible for it, somehow. Like I shoulda been able to fix him. My mind wheels around and around, spins my thoughts into a jumble, and I watch Callum send the bird into darkness.

Its orange eyes, its messy feathers—I want to touch them. Lay them flat . . . "Wait—" I croak. "Wait, let me hold him. If he's going to die . . ." I reach out my arm to catch the sheet.

Callum looks at me strangely.

He don't know. . . . "I can do it, I'm immune." I lean my arm on top of the cage, and rest my face close to the glass. I can hear Milo as he rustles his wings. I watch him blink, and realize I've never seen a bird blink before.

"You're *what*?"

Exhaling, I say, "I'm immune to the virus. Born that way. No one knows. . . . I was told not to say anything. People might want to do experiments or something."

As soon as the words are out of my mouth, I'm dumbstruck. *Idiot, how did I not say anything before now?* "Callum—" I start, but he's already on it.

"I don't believe . . ." He's rummaging through his suitcase, tossing aside random sciencey odds and ends. "Ren, this could be *it*. This could be how we can make your sister's cure," he says, pulling out a needle and syringe.

I hold out my arm. "You think it'll be possible?"

Again, I look at my cuffcomm. The numbers tick closer to twelve thirty.

Callum jabs the sharp tip into the soft flesh of my inner elbow—the syringe fills up with red and I barely even wince.

After an armful of VELs, this is nothing.

"I don't know," he says, withdrawing the needle. "But it is absolutely worth a try."

He squeezes a few droplets of my blood into a petri dish, then reaches for another needle. I watch as he lowers it into the glass box. . . . Milo blinks. I think I see his wings shudder, the instinct of fear fully functional even if he can't do anything about it. As Callum sticks him in the neck, just above the shoulder blade—that's when I wince.

Not before, when it was my blood. But now.

Watching a bird.

Callum syringes out Milo's blood into the same petri dish as mine, and lays the glass under his 'scope. Leaning over it, he starts speaking to himself. Words with so many syllables, they may as well be a different language.

I understand when he says, "Holy what—?" though. "Ren, your cells . . . They're practically waging an outright war on the viral cells."

And, "If the dosage is wrong again . . ."

I'd like to see the massacre, but he dives back into another conversation of one, and I guess we don't have the time for show-and-tell right now.

I reach my arm into the glass cage.

Milo's eyes watch me. I don't like the fear I see there. Don't like him thinking I'm going to hurt him. So I keep my hand draped next to him, not moving, and wait. Instead, I listen to Callum—the lilt and the rhythm as he speaks in his own private language. Words that mean nothing to me, and everything.

"Callum—check it out," I call, my finger about to graze Milo's tail feathers. "I think he likes me. . . ."

I'm not expecting an answer—Callum's been digging around way deep in his brain for nearly a half hour now. But I'm kind of shocked. . . . He jumps to meet me.

"Ren, this is it," he says, positioning the syringe inside the cage. I see it's full up, not just with red, but also the greenish brown of the springwater. "The moment of truth."

"Wait . . . You're done?" I ask, sad to have to pull my hand out.

"Leave it." He nods to my arm. "No need to move, especially not if you feel you're calming him." Once more, he brings the needle to the bird's neck—I keep my fingers brushed up against his feathers, hoping to distract him.

Callum injects the concoction into Milo.

Then he pulls back and finds his datapad, which he sets up right inside the box.

I take my hand out to see the screen, and through the plastic, we watch it go black and white, taking snapshots of the bird's insides.

"Look." Callum points to a bunch of massy bubbles along the bird's lungs. "Ren—do you see it? It's disappearing as we speak."

I don't see it at first, but then with each new snapshot, I can track the tumor as it shrinks, millimeter by millimeter. *He's done it. . . .*

I squeak—actually squeak—and drum my feet on the floor.

I'm about to rocket myself up to hug him, but he stops me.

"Wait, I have to take another blood test to be sure. If there's any of the virus left, it will propagate and Aven will relapse again."

For the last time, he reaches into the glass with a needle, extracts more of the bird's blood. Places it under the scope. Peers down.

I'm silent, waiting. Free-fall waiting. Ready-set-*go* waiting. Lightning-rod-in-a-thunderstorm waiting.

Then Callum looks up, a grin splashed across his face, baby blues saying it all. I read it on his face. "Really?" I whisper, the word no more than air in the back of my throat.

He nods. Now I really do rocket myself toward him. I'm a jack-in-the-box, jumping on my toes, clapping, and I throw my arms around his waist. Callum laughs, pats my back kind of stiff, but when he sees I'm not letting go, he squeezes me closer.

I'm so thankful right now, so grateful, that I'm all full up of love for this boy. Even though I hardly know him . . . it doesn't matter.

After a moment, he unwinds himself from me and quickly returns to his table. Pulls out a vial and, counting as he goes, droppers in the greenish-brown. Next, my red. When the vial is full he pushes it into my hand.

He's holding his breath, looking at his comm. "It's not twelve thirty yet. If you leave now, you can still make it into the hospital before they'll be on to you. Getting out will be a different story."

I look down at the vial, so small, so light. Hope roots itself in my chest, pushes out not just shoots and branches, but also wings. This is more than just survival—this is survival of the heart. It draws me out into the open. It will carry me long distances, and I'm desperate to let it.

"I can do it, I'll figure something out," I say, one foot out the door.

I always do.

31

12:27 P.M., SUNDAY

Overhead, thunderclouds smack blue sky, but not even the chance of rainwater calms me. My palms sweat; the vial is slippery—it should go in my pocket, or one of the slots on my belt. But each time I put it away, I find myself reaching. Touching it to know it's safe.

Until it's in Aven's hand, it's staying in mine.

At my wrist, I feel a vibration. Once. Then twice.

Knowing who it is, I look down and I swallow, my throat thick—dry, all of a sudden.

There's no message, but I can see that it's from Chief. The comm contains just one image: me. My face. With one word over it: "WANTED."

Outlawed . . . I didn't think it'd happen so quickly. I'll have to sneak into the hospital. Find some way in.

I round the first corner onto Fifth, dodging gaps in the

planking left and right, while a west wind fights to throw me into the canal. Going through Mad Ave would be worse though, ducking under stalls, risking being seen.

As I run, the planks start shaking beneath my feet. I slow myself. Vibrations creep up through my Hessians. A heli, not too far off—Quad Four, by the feel of it, or in the way north of Five. It could be a regular old Transmission arrest.

It could be.

Still, I'm happy I'm headed in the opposite direction.

Holding the vial tight in my fist, I keep running. Watching the planks. Jumping gap after gap. After a few minutes, I stop and kneel, searching for a shadow underneath. Seeing nothing, I bring my eyes back to the boardwalk.

There, in the distance, boots.

Black pants, military-style.

Black jacket, yellow striped.

Ro.

No . . . not now. I can't go straight. . . . He's too close, I'd never make it onto the narrows. I spin around—*I'll have to backtrack*—except he's not alone. Another Bouncer steps onto the walk. He takes a wide stance, ready, and waits to see what I'll do.

I turn around again. "Ro!" I call, but he doesn't answer.

Slowly, with his hands latched behind his back, he says, "Stay right where you are, Ren," and marches toward me.

My insides twist up, adrenaline gunning through my legs, telling me to *run.* I spin away from Ro only to see the other guy, now much closer than he was before. *No, they can't get me—not now, not with the vial in my hand. . . .*

But they close in, Ro less than ten feet away as he steps left of a gap in the planks. All I can do is spin in circles, eyeing for a way out, when I have an idea—

The planks, I think. *I can drop into the canal.*

Breathing heavy, I look around for the nearest gap, then see the one to the right of Ro.

I don't wait. Tucking the vial into one of my belt pockets for safekeeping, I make a run for it.

Ro sees what I'm doing—cuts me off as I try and duck past. Looking him in the eye, I ball my hand up and ready it behind my shoulder.

"I'm sorry, Ren," he says, and his big, dark fist makes like a knuckly rocket ship, headed for a crash landing with my gut.

Buildings collapse like this: the bottom goes out first, and debris and dust cloud up around it, then everything else follows. I suppose I'm like that too, because my knees buckle though I don't recall my brain giving them the request. All the air, all at once, is gone from my chest. I try to breathe, but my insides have tensed up so bad, I can't get my lungs to work. Then my tongue doesn't work, so I don't speak, and all I see are red lights spun out like veins bursting one after the next.

Coming to, and the light shifts. It haloes. Bends in golden-pink orbs, even around the skyscraper of a body standing over me. My vision is a mess of fog and blur, but the blue fatigues, the boots . . .

"Well, well, well," I hear Chief say, over the chopping of propellers. They're coming from . . . somewhere. I don't know—*Where am I?* A thrum comes up through the floor, grates against my spine. He sets his boot in front of my face with a thud.

My eyesight clears. Homes in on his laces. Up ahead, a cockpit. And between the two seats, an arm. I'm inside a heli . . . but it seems stable. We ain't in the air, I don't think.

I'm shaken awake by the steel toe of one boot.

Flinching, I remind myself of Milo. Without energy to do anything more, despite the fear curdling in my gut. Chief lowers himself down to my level. Looks me in the eye. Shakes his head, *tsk tsk*.

"You missed your report, Dane. Two in a row. Except this time, it was no accident," he spits in my face and waves a small tube—the vial—in front of my nose.

How did he—? Feeling for my belt, I realize it's not there. It's at his feet. *I gotta get the vial back* . . . and then I gotta get out of here. Somehow. I look around the inside of the heli, but the hatch is closed.

"What have we here," Chief says in a low growl. He removes the stopper from the vial and brings the glass to his nose. "Doesn't smell like brack water, that's for sure. Could it be . . . ?"

I shake my head, about to say that it's not, when he re-stoppers the tube and places it under the sole of one boot.

"Don't!" I yell without thinking, reaching for the vial. I'm too slow, though. . . . It's like being underwater. My muscles hurt too badly.

Dunn has time to pull the vial out from under his shoe and step closer. He has time to bring his sole down on my open fingers, and stay there.

I hear myself whimper like an animal, and I don't recognize myself. Not when I'm making these sounds.

"Only one way you could've come by this water, Dane." A

pause. "Someone told you where to find another source."

I can't answer. I can't tell him the truth.

When Dunn sees I'll say nothing, he pulls a black baton from the belt strapped round his waist. I lift myself onto my elbows, trying to back away. Closer, closer, Chief approaches me.

"The governor gave me permission to try some . . . *other* methods of acquiring information, in the event that you suddenly forgot who you work for. Didn't he?" he says, turning to face the cockpit.

Governor Voss?

Chief smacks the baton once against his palm and it makes a loud cracking noise. *Lightning.*

With one foot, he kicks me onto my stomach. Wrenches my shoulders around the baton, then twists like he wants them out of their sockets. It's a bolt of fire that consumes all my air. I groan as he plows his steel-toed boot down the line of my vertebrae. I feel my spine like the serrated edge of a blade.

Chief uses his foot to roll me faceup again. "Where did you get this?"

I'm gasping, heaving. My eyes have started to water and I blink them fast—I ain't gonna let him see me cry. I still got no answer.

Now he crushes his heel down on my sternum, sapping all my energy. I flex my muscles against it and cough, trying to speak, but he won't release any weight from my chest. Physically, I can't. No air, no words.

He lets up, just barely. "Where is the spring?"

"Don't know," I wheeze, the air squeezed from my lungs.

Chief Dunn makes like he's going to strike me. I ball up, braced for the blow. It never comes—

"Miss Dane," a voice croons from the cockpit.

The governor turns around, sees me coiled on the floor. His expression shifts to something like pity. "If you recall, I asked you not to lie to me. And yet, here you are—lying to me. I need a location, Miss Dane. I don't think you quite comprehend how dire the situation has turned." His voice rises, and I can hear the anger there.

Still I say nothing.

Shaking the legless figurine in my direction, "I can see you've spoken to Kitaneh. This is clearly her handiwork. And you had on your person that vial, presumably for your friend at the hospital. Yet you refuse to tell me the truth. Fine. And the Tètai are also not willing to cooperate? Unfortunately, this leaves me without alternatives. Chief Dunn. Prepare to make the announcement."

Announcement?

Dunn, standing over me, slides the baton back into his belt with one hand, his other still holding the vial. One last time, he steps on me. Under his heel the ligaments between my ribs grind together. I have to fight against his weight.

Keeping his boot square on my chest, he kneels down to my level. "Happily, Governor Voss. You know how I feel about it," he says. "I only wished—"

"*Enough*, Chief Dunn," snaps the governor.

Chief scowls, and for a moment I think I see him go for that strike he never got to take, but he holds back. He laughs, scanning my face. "This entire city—it's disgusting. A breeding ground for disease. Every last one of you—" Chief wears a face like he's about to spit. "*Hosts.*"

"Watch your tongue," I hear the governor say from up front,

as he gestures to the pilot. "Miss Dane," he starts, not even bothering to look at me anymore. "I will not regret the events of the next twenty-four hours, because they will not be of my own doing. Tell your friend it is not yet too late."

The hatch opens. A gray sky and a concrete roof wait.

"Now," the governor adds, tired. "Get out."

But the vial—I have to get it. . . . Chief's left hand—I see it, right there in his fist, and I won't leave it behind. I slide closer to him, making like I'm about to stand. Extend my leg. Hook my ankle behind his.

"What the—"

In the cockpit, the governor has started to stand. "The vial!"

Chief looks down at me, steps nearer, and with every bit of strength my quad can muster—I yank him forward. His knees buckle . . . but not enough. I hook my other ankle. Repeat.

This time, he goes lumbering backward.

Jumping to my feet, I resort to the lowest but most effective of moves: Square in the groin . . . That's where I step. Hard.

It does the trick. Chief grunts. Curls up into himself, his face twisted and none too happy.

I lower down, grab the vial.

Chief Dunn starts to rise. Adrenaline hijacks my muscles. With the vial in my hand, I jump out the hatch, not another look back.

32

12:45 P.M., SUNDAY

Sprinting for the nearest suspension bridge, I leap onto it, no care for balance or keeping the thing steady. Behind me, air churns, coughs up roof dust.

But that makes no sense. . . . *The chief's not following?* Only when I've crossed to the other side do I look back. Make sure I'm not crazy.

Despite the vibrations running through the rope in my hands, I don't believe it—Chief's heli roars into the sky. Rises up from the rooftop, one building over.

But I have the vial. The governor should've sent him after me—his wife . . . he'd want to use it to cure his wife, wouldn't he? The aeromobile doesn't even head west over the Strait. Instead, it loops around over to Mad Ave.

Then, dangling out from the airborne beast is Chief Dunn.

Holding a megaphone.

One time . . . One time have I seen this happen—I'm thirteen again, back on the Empire Clock with Benny before my first race. When they announced the Health Statutes, locking down the Ward and making Transmission of the virus illegal.

"Attention, citizens of the Ward!" Chief's voice booms through the air.

The announcement . . . This is what the governor was talking about. I don't breathe. I imagine no one's breathing right now.

Across the roof, another man steps quickly off a bridge. Holding his hat, he looks up to the sky, then over to me. As if I know what's going on.

"Attention," Chief repeats, body half in the air. "Between the hours of twelve and two a.m., a squadron of pilots will fly through the city. Do not be alarmed. After that time, we ask that all HBNC-positive citizens gather on the rooftops of your respective sickhouses. No arrests will be made. There you will find shipments containing a new drug in development that has been proven effective at eradicating the HBNC pathogen."

I can hear a hundred breaths catching in a hundred throats, it's so quiet.

"I repeat." A pause. "We have a cure for HBNC!"

With that, the heli rises into the air, the chief and his megaphone swinging back into its cockpit. As it spirals out in the direction of the West Isle, headed northwest toward Central Bay, the howling it makes against the blue is the only noise for miles.

Three unsure seconds pass.

Then, the city erupts.

But they don't have the cure. . . .

From across the canals and gutters, manic yelps ring out in the crisp air. Hoots, high-pitched and frantic, echo all around. With a bird's-eye view of Mad Ave, I can see everyone who'd ducked under an awning or behind a storefront stepping out. Looking around. As though they're walking outside for the first time. People hug—people who don't know one another.

If they don't have a cure, what are they giving out?

I become my own island, fighting against the dizziness in my head, refusing to move.

"You hear that?" a stranger shouts, and rushes closer. When his eyes land on me, a heady grin splashes across his face. Without a word, he throws his arms round me. He picks me up, lifts me right off my feet. "A cure, they've made a cure! It's a gift from above!"

I push against the stranger's shoulders, a trapped animal. "They haven't. . . . It's not a gi—"

Gift. It's not a gift, I'm about to say, but he doesn't hear, or notice, or believe. I wouldn't believe either, and then the pieces click together too quickly. . . .

An attack, disguised as a gift . . . *the Trojan horse.*

A CASE FOR DEMOCIDE.

The gift is the cure.

"Put me down!" I cry as he swings me through the air. I'm a mouse in a mousetrap. A roach on glue. Any living thing about to be exterminated. *Eradicated.*

I'm a host.

"What'sa matter?" The man shakes his head, *tut-tut*-ing. I grapple against him, legs straining to touch ground until finally, he lowers me down. As he walks away he mutters, "Ain't she happy?" to himself. Looks back at me. I can see him feeling sorry. Pitying me.

All this wasted joy . . . I begin to feel hysterical with its wrongness.

Their cure isn't a gift.

It's a poison—it's their extermination plan.

33

1:00 P.M., SUNDAY

All around me, the city is a madhouse.

Little balls of light fizzle in the hands of the neighborhood kids running across suspension bridges. *Sparklers.* The skyline bursts with them. Dozens of stars shooting from roof to roof, then dying out.

It makes me sick, all this prettiness right now.

Would he do it? Would the governor really poison people just for being sick?

If the West Islers are actually rioting 'cause they're so scared, I think so.

I have to stop him. . . .

My knees can barely hold up the rest of me, amped and shaky as they are. In my veins, blue fire. I tuck the vial—the real cure—into one of my belt pockets and run toward the building's escape ladder. Now would be the perfect time to get it to Aven; the hospital will be in an uproar, no one paying attention.

After that, Callum's. Together we can figure out a plan.

As I'm climbing down the ladder, only a few rungs from the bottom, my cuffcomm vibrates. Buzzes once, then again. I pull my palm away from the rail to read the message, expecting to see two from the same sender, but I'm wrong—the first message is from Callum, sent ten minutes ago. I must have missed it in the chaos. I can't make sense of it, either:

HE

That's all it says.

HE . . . *then what*?

Confused, I flip to the second comm, and my feet stop working. It's from Derek's number. But I'm even more shaken by the message than I am by its sender:

Kitaneh knows about the lab. The doctor isn't safe.

Gripping the rail, frozen on the ladder, I reread his warning over and over. In the back of my mind, I recognize that it means something, him sending me this. But right now it's a drop in the ocean. I hardly care. *Callum's in danger?*

I flip back to his message:

HE
HELP

Callum's not just in danger, he's in danger *now*.

I jump onto the boardwalk, then stop, tugged in two directions. The vial, miraculous and tiny and waiting, is burning a hole through the fabric of my pants. I don't even feel it in my pocket anymore. It's eating straight through to my chest.

But I'm only minutes away from the lab.

I'm too close to do nothing.

Spinning onto the Rough Block narrows, everything in me fires off warning shots. And then I see his door at a distance, already half open, swinging on its hinges in a sudden gust of wind.

Kitaneh's already here. She might already be gone, too.

Holding the knob, I push.

It rebounds. Sent on a direct course for my face. I go stumbling onto the narrows, knocked backward.

My stomach drops—I'm too late—and as I'm cupping my nose, groaning, a figure rushes past. Hooded, dressed all in black, strands of dark hair blown to the side. Then an arm is on my shoulder, pushing me. . . .

Within seconds, I'm tottering on the brink of the narrows, heels balanced in the air.

One more blow, aimed just above the kneecap—it does me in. I fall into the gutterway, brack water filling up my nose and mouth. *This can't be happening.* I don't even know what *this* is, but instinct does.

I dog-paddle, I spit out the water, and surface, expecting the person to be long gone.

I'm wrong.

Kitaneh pulls down her hood. She wants me to see her face

as she stands over me on the narrows. Watches as I grapple with the Hudson. "You . . ." She stops herself. Fists clenched, she looks away from me, letting her hair curtain forward.

When she turns again, there's no anger. Just a stone sadness to her eyes and a frustration. Like I ain't never gonna understand. Slowly, she lowers herself to a crouch.

"You all want the same thing," she says, pointing to the sky. "You desire an all-encompassing cure. But the spring is not a medicine. Even if it mends your cuts and heals your sick, it is not a cure. Not unless humanity is a disease." Her voice is even. "The spring is sacred; it is so much more than a cure. But used to the wrong end, it is a curse. You must understand." Kitaneh looks at me as she rises.

"I told you not to come here," a voice growls. I see Derek running up to her, out of breath, winded, his face lined with fear. He spots me in the canal, and he relaxes some.

I hate that I notice it. I hate how clear it is on his face. I can see the concern, the *caring* there, when I couldn't before. But I don't want him to care about me, not now, not when I know what I do. It makes my anger that much harder to hold on to.

Because if he actually does give a damn about me . . . then he's got it in him to give a damn about everyone else, too.

"Are you all right?" he asks. Kneeling down, he reaches for my hand, and in one easy swing he lifts me out of the water and onto the narrows. My anger is too slow. It doesn't even have a chance to make it to my face, at least not in time for him to see it. Quickly, he positions himself between me and Kitaneh.

I wonder if maybe I wasn't safer where I was. Back in the water.

"You knew what the doctor was doing," she barks. "All along. And you were going to let him do it. I, however, refuse to take any chances. Especially not now, after *that*," she says, pointing in the direction of the announcement. "This girl has no idea what she's dealing with. See that she leaves it, Derek. Or I'll have no choice."

Kitaneh eyes me one last time and shakes her head. Tucking her hair under her hood, her hands in her pockets, she turns on her heel. And then she's gone, walking briskly down the narrows.

Soon as she's out of sight, Derek—with just a look—nudges me toward Callum's apartment. I hold on to the words I want to say to him, because through the crack, I can see just how well Kitaneh did her job.

"Callum . . ." I whisper, afraid to open the door.

"Check on him . . . ," he says, something black in his voice. Now I'm more afraid not to. *What if he's hurt?*

That does it—I push it in but stop, unable to go farther.

Papers torn from nails. The faint smell of smoke. When I look down, ashes snake across his floor. Glass triangles litter every surface; all the beakers lay in pieces. Sharpness everywhere.

And his desk . . .

The samples, destroyed. His research, destroyed.

I'm soaking, dripping water onto the floor, spinning around in circles. Disbelieving. Just as bad as Ro's fist to my gut, I'm out of air again. Derek walks into the room behind me. I hear his breath catch too.

"Callum, you here?" I call out, glass crunching beneath my sodden Hessians. There's no sign of him up here, so I begin toward the staircase that leads downstairs.

I open the bathroom door.

Covering my mouth, I look away. I can't help but gag.

Callum.

In the dark room, a red pool gathers around the shower drain. It spreads over the tiles—he's lost so much. I can make out his body, curled up, limbs bowed out at unnatural angles. I need more light—I can't see him enough to help him. On the sink, I spot a match, which I strike, then bring to the candle on the counter.

The smoky smell eases some of the nausea I'm feeling. I drop down beside Callum, blood painting my leggings a color not much darker than my leather jumpsuit, but I don't retch. I look for the wound. It ain't hard to find—his shirt's soaked through.

On the right side of his stomach, a gash the size of my hand. Gaping flesh sliced straight through to muscle. "No . . . *no, no, no.* Callum," I say, his name hard as nails in my mouth. Pressing my palm to the spot, I try to slow the blood. "Look at me. You've got to look at me."

He doesn't. And the way his head lolls to the side—I don't like it. There's no movement in his chest, neither. I grip his jaw, one hand on the wound, and gently shake him. His skin is cold and clammy against mine. "Wake up. Wake. Up."

Is he . . . ?

My hand pressed to his flank does nothing. The warmth of his blood sticks to the spaces between my fingers.

I can sense Derek standing there, in the doorway. Eyes can touch, too. My back may be turned, but every one of my vertebrae understands. Cringes. *I just want him out.*

"He's dead." Derek's words are sure. Certain.

Callum's not moving, and the color's mostly gone from his face. His skin is a waxy, sallow white.

You hardly knew him.

Even as I think the words though, they feel irrelevant. The boy on the floor was somebody's son. Somebody's brother, maybe. I'll never know. One day, he might've been somebody's husband. Then somebody's father.

Somebody's doctor. So many people's doctor. The lives he would have saved.

Who'll help me stop the governor?

Derek steps closer and kneels just behind me. Once more he says it, repeats the ugly words like I missed them the first time: "Ren, he's *gone*."

So easily. So quickly. I feel all of my hurt at once. Wild. No cage.

"*Stop* saying that!" I snarl, cheeks burning, eyes hot in their sockets. On the counter, the candlewick sizzles. I watch its light draw orbs around the room. I won't let my hand up. "Life may mean nothing to you, Derek. But I'm not you."

"What—?" he starts, but I cut him off.

"You and that girl. You kill. Don't sugarcoat it," I say. "Death toll thanks to you two is probably higher than anyone else's, come to think of it. Ever. In the history of the world. Because you get to add the lives that water would've saved, too. Not least of all my own *sister's*."

Derek's face twists, as if I've said something horrible.

I don't see how it ain't true.

"And you thought you could *kiss* me?" My voice shakes, all the sounds colliding together. I'm speaking too fast, and I'm not even close to finished. "I could never want you, Derek. What's there to want? *You care about no one.* A person who cares about no one is no person at all."

Soon as the words are out, I'm left shivering.

I hear him inhale. Feel him shudder and pull back, and I'm glad I can't see his face. I wouldn't be able to say the rest if I could see any hurt there.

"The 'cure,' Derek. I know it's a poison," I say, Callum's blood still in my hand.

Derek shakes his head but doesn't try to deny it. "How do you—?"

"Could the water work against it? Could it stop the poison somehow?" I ask, realizing how little Callum and I actually know it. "It might not be too late. You could still stop Governor Voss."

Prove to me that I know you, Derek. Please . . .

"The water can, Ren, but—"

"All the poisons, Derek. You know this?"

"Yes. The water protects the body from any number of things while it's in the bloodstream. But *I* can't do anything. You know I can't."

In my lungs, a beast wants to howl at him. And then that beast in my lungs *does* howl at him.

"*No, I don't know!* Why not?" I cry. "How could you keep living after this?"

He can't do nothing.

Derek rises to his feet. Yells, "People die—it's what makes

you alive!" His breath hits the candlewick. The flame flickers, bounces light around the room, and I realize something—

"People die. And people are *murdered*. It is not the same thing!" I shout back. I almost stand up, forgetting that I'm the only thing holding Callum's blood in his body.

I don't, though.

"Ren . . . you would have me give up the spring to a man who'd exterminate hundreds just to find it? The death would never end there—what would happen after that? How many wars, do you think, would be fought by others so that they could get to the spring? People like the governor are *exactly* the reason why the spring must stay a secret."

The death would never end.

Derek is right . . . it wouldn't. All we wanted was more water, back when New York City launched the Appeal, and so many people died.

"Your friend is gone," he says again, weary. He walks to the door, knees drenched in red. "Let the spring go with him."

My next words roll out, thunderclouds thick in my mouth—"I want you to leave, now."

I don't remember thinking them, but looking up, I know it's true.

Callum can't be dead. . . . I won't believe it.

The room falls quiet. Shadows cover everything. My clothes are soaked, though I no longer feel it.

For a moment I think Derek's left. My head feels so heavy, I have to close my eyes. But his footsteps come up behind me—

"I'm sorry," I think I hear him whisper, and then he kneels

again, inches of electric space between his kneecap and my spine. Electric miles separating him from the vial tucked in my back pocket. He leans forward. Tells me, "Not *no one*," and when he does, I swear I taste ashes on my tongue.

34

1:30 P.M., SUNDAY

I'm left alone with Callum's head resting on my lap and a pool of blood beside us. When I tell myself to breathe, I can hear my insides as they rattle apart. Slowly, I rise to my knees.

I haven't forgotten what's in my back pocket. . . .

But what do I do?

I reach around, keeping my legs bent just enough so Callum's head doesn't slide.

Then, I take out the vial.

My hands shake—*Don't drop it*—but that just makes me tremble more. So I force another breath of air in and out, and wait until I'm steady. My fingers hug the tube, red-stained, but I try to ignore that. Inside, the water looks inconsequential.

But the water would fix him.

What do I do?

On the floor in front of me: Callum Pace. Someone I hardly know.

I lower back onto my heels, find myself wishing I knew him better, this boy whose head is sitting in my lap. I brush a few shaggy, brown strands out of his eyes, and end up smearing his forehead with blood.

In my other hand I hold the vial. *Aven's vial.* So one day we can walk outside together on Mad Ave. Or visit a roof garden. It's for our futures together. Our microscopic futures, important to no one but ourselves.

If Aven lives, nothing changes.

But if Callum lives . . . If Callum lives, so much could change. *Everything.*

Derek said the water would keep the poison from working, and Callum knows how to make the real cure. . . . Plus, we've got my blood.

We would figure out how to stop the governor, together. Get the real cure to everyone. First, tonight. Before the squadrons fly through. We'd have to find more water, but we could do it. *We could end the Blight.* And it's only even remotely possible if Callum is alive.

My sister.

Callum.

Two lives, one hand.

My mind can't piece it together, this choice—it rips my core in half. I look around the room, as if I'll find an answer hiding in the shadows, but I'm only reminded of how alone I am in this. Not even Aven can help me now.

This is not a decision I can make.

Of course . . . if Derek's right—Callum is already gone. There's no more choice. It's just Aven.

Is it sick that part of me hopes he's right? For fate to leave me with one card and pull away the rest?

It's time.

I reach for his wrist to feel for a pulse. It's not a choice until there's a pulse. I'm scared of hurting him, so I rotate his palm carefully and place two fingers on his vein. Though I've done it before, it's never been like this. All that learning means nothing, not when my own racing heartbeat makes it almost impossible to check for someone else's.

I wait for some movement through his veins, but all I feel is the hammer of my own heart.

Focus. Breathe. Focus.

I try again. Two fingers on the vein. I wait, and I wait, and then, after seconds of no movement—

The slight *bump-bump* . . . I feel it.

My heart's got no clue where to go—it rises up into my throat, it barrels down my chest. Relief don't feel like this. But neither does remorse. More salt water beads up behind my eyes.

I'm ashamed of myself, but this choice . . . it's too much. I can't do it.

The room begins to spin, hard and fast.

When I blink, everything dims and my stomach heaves. I'm going to retch. I gasp for air, but I can't hear the sounds I make. Just a white, static rush between my ears.

I wish I'd never found the water.

I can't do this. . . . I can't leave Callum to die.

But I can't give up on Aven either. Not when I'm so close.

In my head I hear the governor: *My wife is the only person I would kill for.* Hours ago, I asked myself if I would do the same for Aven. Now I have an answer.

Hating every cell in my body for what I'm about to do, I begin to remove my hand from Callum's side. It's doused. The blood is hot, burns worse than if it were on fire. I move my palm in millimeters, reaching across his body—for a moment, the vial presses against his cheek.

Even more red, now. There's so much of it. . . .

I ease away, release the pressure from Callum's muscles. The hole in his flesh gets wider.

But so many people could be saved. The girl in the contagious ward, with hair bright like Aven's—

More and more red. I don't know when it will stop. I watch and wonder, anxious. Unable to take my eyes away, unable to get that girl out of my mind.

She's not my Aven. She's a stranger. They all are. And who decided that life was a numbers game? What if some people deserve life more than others? People like Aven. She deserves it more than anyone I know, and I'd rather have one of her than hundreds of strangers.

That girl ain't my Aven, but she is somebody else's Aven.

My eyes flood up with that thought and I keep ripping. Splitting in two.

And then, he breathes.

A groan, barely audible, so airy it's lost right away. Almost too quiet for me to hear. Almost. I shake my vision clear and look down to meet his eyes, like I should.

Except he's not looking at me. I follow his gaze. His eyes are barely open, just a sliver of blue there. He's looking at the vial.

"For Aven," he whispers, and I choke.

He understands. . . . *He understands.* He's ready to let me give it to someone else. A girl he don't even know. She's not a genius, and she can't develop miracle serums. *So why?* I don't understand—it wouldn't even be selfish for him to want it for himself.

His life equals many lives.

It strikes me hard—Aven would do the same thing. Callum isn't her, not by a long shot, but . . . The Ward needs more people like Aven. And here I am, ready to leave him to die. The horror of it is a bullet to my chest.

I unstopper the vial—

How much do I use? Split it in thirds, that's what I'll do. A third on the wound, a third over his broken bones, and the last third he can drink. Hope the serum works better—and faster—than what I gave Aven.

"Here goes," I mutter, ripping his shirt to expose the slit along his abs. I use the cloth to wipe away what I can of the blood, and hold the vial over the wound. I make sure to pour it deep.

Next I move to reset the bones in his arms. "This may hurt like hell," I warn, but he's gone unconscious again and can't have heard me. Still, the sound of my own voice helps keep me sane, so on I talk. "Emergency first aid. Never had to use it on myself, which is why the Blues taught us, but it's sure going to come in handy right about now."

I lift the left arm, snap it back into its rightful position.

His face contorts, he groans louder now, but I keep going. Right arm, right leg, left leg, until it's time to apply the serum locally.

I pull off his black leather shoes first, then I undo the fancy buckle around his waist. Lifting him up, I start to remove his trousers, making sure the boxers stay on. The pants get caught at his knees and so I lower him, sliding them the rest of the way. At the sight of his bare legs, I blush and look away.

Shirt. He's in no condition to be moved, so I decide to rip off his shirtsleeves. Using the knife I keep strapped in my boot, I slice off one, then the other, exposing long lines of muscle in his arms. I raise a brow, somewhat surprised, and rush to add more drops onto each.

"I've saved the last of it for you to drink, okay?" I don't expect a reply; I just lift his head and bring the vial to his lips.

His blue eyes watch me from my lap. I see his brows twinge—he's confused. He doesn't understand why the vial is over his mouth, and not Aven's.

In that instant my guilt is a twisting knife. Only his goodness, his confusion, reminds me I must be doing the right thing. "It's for you now," I tell him, and feel my eyes turn wet. I leave it at that—he's in no shape to hear, or understand, why I'm doing this.

I tip the vial over his mouth again—he tries to swallow. I

watch his throat move, but he coughs, and blood trails from his mouth. I pull away, wait for the spasm to end. Once more, I tilt the vial. I pour the serum. I make sure every last drop finds its way down.

Too soon, it's gone. "And now we wait," I whisper, eyes glued to the empty glass as Callum drifts off into a fitful rest.

I continue to hold his head in my lap, brushing away his hair. I used to do this to Aven—my breath catches at that, and the candle flickers, *yes*.

With that comes the tidal, catastrophic truth: I've exchanged the two. Callum for Aven.

How could you?

Fat tears begin to brim over, and the lump in my throat is a brick I don't know how to swallow. Callum, a boy I hardly know. I choke on the brick, try for air. Palm to forehead, palm to forehead, I run my fingers over the scalp and all the way down—I don't stop. It's automatic. I even find myself searching behind the neck for that spot that always seemed to be growing larger. The lump.

I don't find it. And the ears, too low. The strands of hair stop short too soon. My fingers tangle free too early. This is hearing your favorite story—the one you know by memory, you've heard it a hundred times—suddenly end differently.

I don't stop. Over and over, I shock myself on every different ending. And when I close my eyes to the shadows, try to lose sense of it in the dark, I can't. I can't even pretend I haven't done this.

35

The spigot's steady dripping becomes the second hand on a clock I don't see, the only reminder I have that time moves forward.

When I can't do it anymore, when holding his head becomes a betrayal so sharp I can't stand it, I lift it off my lap and lower him down. He can't be moved now, but when he can, he'll need a place nearby to lie. I drag the mattress from the cot to the bathroom door. Then I take his hand in mine and lie on the mattress myself.

I'm alone. I chose it, too. Chose to lose the one person I called family—who was better than family, really. My own blood dropped me on a doorstep. Aven was—*She's not dead yet.*

Drip, drip, drip.

"Ren . . ." Callum sounds stronger as his voice echoes against the bathroom tiles, but hearing my name in his mouth—it's like hearing my shame speak directly to me. It makes me want to resent him for being alive. Using the life I gave him.

I swallow the feeling and crawl off the mattress. The choice has been made, and I made it. He will save people. *We will save lives, together.* "I'm here," I say, lifting his wrist and wrapping my fingers over his veins to check his pulse again.

I can feel it, the beating of his heart. It's stronger now. "You're going to be okay, Callum," I whisper, and wait for more words, signs of life, but he's silent again.

He's going to be okay, I tell myself. *It won't have been for nothing.* Keeping his hand in mine, I return to the mattress.

More drips. Time passes.

"I'm not dead. . . ." Callum whispers, and my eyes snap open.

I must have fallen asleep. Sliding toward him again, "Callum?" I say, and I squeeze his hand in mine. It's warmer. Hot, even. When I look down, his eyes are open. Big and blue and clear and awake. "How do you feel?"

His eyes dart around the bathroom, land on every corner. "I'm not dead," he says again, which I guess is answer enough. And then, looking up at the ceiling, "How am I alive?"

He must not remember.

On the counter, the candle—wick almost at its end—flickers, hissing into wax. The sound catches his attention, and he watches the shadows in the room like they're ghosts.

Follows their haunting all the way to his side. To the vial, now empty.

Callum looks at it. Moves to sit up, but clutches himself, face in a grimace. "Why?" he asks, twisting to look at me head-on.

I wait to answer, not knowing where to start . . . but then I hear him inhale.

Like he's breathed in the answer.

Through teeth gritted in hurt, "The cure," he says, forcing his back against the wall. "It's not—"

"I know. It's an extermination plan. A poison pill," I fill in for him. Don't want the words, or their meaning, on my tongue too long. "And with the extremists and the protestors on his back—"

"He'll go through with it," Callum finishes for me.

Pushing his back farther up the wall, face flushed, "We can't let it happen," he says.

"No. We can't."

Callum nods. Closes his eyes. "Which is why you saved me."

"Yes."

He's silent, then opens his eyes to stare at the ceiling. "Do you have a plan?" he asks, monotone. I can hear it in his voice; he don't know what to do with it. The knowledge that I saved him not for *him*, but for what he can do.

I didn't think about how that might make him feel.

"Get the cure out first?" I offer weakly. Now that the serum actually worked, and Callum is here—alive—I shake my head, realizing how weak of a plan it is.

"We have no more water. And I have no notes," he counters,

groaning and throwing a fist into the tiled floor. "Not to mention that the cure is a poison. Who's to say the water will counteract it?"

"It will. I asked Derek. He said so." I take his hand. It's clammy in mine as I unball his fist, one finger at a time. "And I know where to find more."

That bath I took . . . Derek had enough water to draw me one, then another, with no worries about rationing. And where else could he constantly keep an eye on things?

Callum's eyes flicker toward his hand. My hand. Our hands together. Shifting himself toward me, "Let me guess. Derek. Your bookie."

"My bookie," I answer, exhaling as Callum closes his eyes once more.

My bookie. Derek.

No, I correct myself.

Someone who would sit by and watch as hundreds are killed.

A murderer.

Callum walks upstairs after his shower, a towel wrapped carefully around his waist, loose, avoiding the wound.

"Let me check your side one more time," I insist, and then realize that as he's no longer on death's doorstep, that request is a tad more awkward. Especially the half-naked bit.

He rolls his eyes—this is the fifth time I've asked him that. But he walks over anyway and turns to the side, showing me the flesh under his rib cage. "You need to leave," he says.

"Not until I'm sure you'll still be alive when I'm done," I

answer, leaning down to get a better look at the wound. I try my best to look at him without *looking* at him. I feel my face start to burn, but as soon as I get a better look at the almost-mortal wound at his side, the embarrassment kind of dies. A gory flesh wound tends to do that sort of thing.

By now, the bleeding has stopped entirely. The two folds of sliced skin are taut together, and dark maroon crusts along the line. I whistle my amazement, timid as I press my fingers around the worst of it. "Well," I say, standing up. "The serum definitely works on wounds. Enough of those phytowhosits, it would seem. Faster than the original stuff without a doubt."

Callum smiles and looks down at his torso like he's pleased with his work. "And with pure, unmuddied water . . . I'll be able to do even more, I think." He walks over to his suitcase to pull out clean clothes.

"Will you still need my blood, do you think?" I ask, turning away from him so he can change. I walk over to the mess by his table, and with my fingers wrapped in a washcloth, I try to collect half-broken test tubes and droppers and whatever else looks even remotely usable. I'm only slightly worried about him needing my blood to make the cure. With a few hundred sick to heal, I don't know if I have it in me—literally have enough blood in me—to be up to the task.

Callum looks at me and inhales. "As all of my notes have been destroyed, it's hard to say. But, Ren . . . after you left, I ran more tests. The way your blood interacted with the virus—I've never seen anything like it. Not only did it break down the viral cells but somehow—and I'm still foggy on this point—it stimulated Milo's own immune response. And, if my observations are correct, your blood actually improved how the recipient was able to synthesize the springwater's chemical compounds."

A pause. He raises one brow like he don't understand it himself. "Your blood is . . . different."

"Different how?"

"I don't know." He shrugs, then says, "But your blood has served you well these sixteen years, so clearly it's nothing to be concerned about."

I nod—*If he says so*—and pack away the last of what was salvageable into his suitcase. He's ready to take off. The lab is still a disaster—glass shards on the floor, tubing cut into pieces. . . .

It's as good as it's going to get.

"Comm me when you have a new location," I say. He throws me a look that reads *Of course, now get out of here?* I take the keys to his Omni. "Can I ask you to do one more thing for me?"

He meets me by the door, and I turn to find him holding something in his hand. "Anything," he says, and I can see he means *anything*, though what I'm about to ask doesn't require that much.

"You're a doctor. The hospital knows you. If you asked for Aven's status, they'd tell you the whole truth, no sugarcoating. I want you to contact them for me and find out how she's doing."

Callum nods. "Absolutely, I'm happy to. I'll get an update from them soon as you leave, and I'll comm you straightaway. Anything else?"

"Nope," I say, one hand on the doorknob. I'm about to step out, when I feel his arm on my shoulder.

"Wait, Ren." He pulls me back gently, and when I turn around, there's an openness to his face that I'm not sure I've ever seen before. Not that he's always closed off. . . . He's just the serious, bookish type. Head always off someplace, figuring out confusing things.

"What you did before . . ." Callum starts, shuffling his feet and shaking his fist. It's still holding something that I can't see. "We don't know each other, and you didn't have to do it. It wasn't for me. I know that."

He waves his hand to dismiss me before I even have a chance to speak, then continues.

"You saved me because I can save others. *We* can save others," he corrects himself. "I just want you to know—I'm going to make it worth it. For you. Aven's not lost. You didn't choose me over her. . . . You chose both. I promise."

I smile, but his words . . . they make me want to cry. The happy kind, but also the not-so-happy kind. I don't like him thinking that he's just a means to an end. I do care about him, of course. Though I don't know him well, he's a good person. That much I can see.

I make my hand into a fist just so I can bite it to stop the tears.

Callum turns up his palm. In it, he's holding a shiny copper penny.

"I saw at the race you already have one." He glances at my necklace. "Nonetheless. Thank you," he says, gesturing for me to turn around so he can add it to the chain I'm already wearing. "It's store-bought, unfortunately," he goes on. "Not like the other you're wearing. I don't expect it's any less lucky, though."

I open my mouth—

"Not that you need luck, of course," he adds casually. "I'm quite certain you get along perfectly well without it."

Good skill—I can almost hear Aven saying it to me right now. Like she's speaking to me through him. Or maybe . . . maybe it's that they just think the same. For the first time in days, I smile, with Aven's voice right there.

"Thank you," I say, rubbing the penny between my fingers. "Thank you."

Good skill.

36

A red path mazes across the screen of the Omni's dash. Remnants of the old city pass by in the windowpane, and it's like someone's taken out time's batteries. Left everything frozen in place.

The underwater city is always like this. I imagine it's different over in the West Isle, where so many people have mobiles that the canals actually get congested. Here, though, it's dead quiet.

My cuffcomm buzzes. It must be Callum getting back to me about Aven. I pull one hand from the steering wheel, still there despite the autopilot. I read the message:

She's stable, and though the mass's rate of growth has slowed, it's dangerously close to damaging her long-term brain function.

Translation: Fine for the time being. Not fine if we can't help her soon.

I swallow and pretend that the world is frozen—no ticking—above the surface. Aven has days that don't become hours, that don't become seconds. *Soon.*

I'm holding in my breath. Like holding in life.

I sit back. I do nothing, my hands on the wheel nonetheless. Though the Omni moves easily through the water, I'm not used to letting a machine make all the decisions. But right now, it's a blessing to be able to turn off my head. I don't want to make any more decisions.

Focus. I need to stay focused.

After a few minutes, the VoiceNav announces that I've arrived at my destination.

The spring could be anywhere, though. Can't just walk in—what would I say? *Please pass the fountain of youth, thanks!* Not going to work.

I'm just gonna have to look around—but down here, nothing is familiar. There are no obvious landmarks. My sense of direction has flown out the window. If I knew the difference between this pylon and that pylon, maybe I'd have some idea. But they're all brown, covered in green gunk.

Nonetheless, VoiceNav doesn't lie.

I turn right into an alleyway flanked by two buildings' brick foundations. The space between is so narrow, I couldn't lie down sideways without having to bend my knees—the buildings are maybe only four feet apart.

Callum's mobile better be small enough. It's a later-model Omni, putting it at about three feet, nine inches, so I should be good, but I still drive slow, gripping the wheel too hard. The mobile shakes. Nearly bangs into the brick siding.

Why is she shaking so bad?

I look down at my grip—my fingers are the problem. His Omni's just answering the command.

My hands never get the shakes during a race. Before, sometimes. But not during. Now, though, my nerves physically hurt. Every last one is a razor, ready to slice. *Breathe.*

I force air into my mouth, down my lungs, repeat, repeat, listening to the sound.

It's because there are too many people at stake. Too much responsibility. I don't like it, don't know where to put it. And Aven's life is riding on this, too—my one more shot at saving her.

I turn off the headlight in favor of the belly lamp, not wanting to draw too much attention. Actually, I'd rather keep the lights off entirely—it's safer—but then I really might run into the building's side.

Everything under me turns bright green as the Omni hovers alongside the walls. I search for a window, or anything. Just a way to make it inside the building and get scouting.

But then, *there*—a glint of silver?

What would be silver down here? You could store a mobile, I guess, but it would be hard to get at when you needed it. And if it weren't being used on the regular, it wouldn't be silver. Metal, plastic, you name it—it all gets covered in green underwater funk almost immediately.

I hit reverse, trying to catch the light again. Nothing, nothing—

There.

And it disappears. The alley is no more than algae and concrete blocks and brick turned green. Seaweeds move with such sway, if I weren't so adrenaline-amped, I might find it soothing.

Again.

I'm along the Strait's floor now, and I've lost sight of the glint. But, over there, caught underneath a pile of rubble, I think I see a tangled fishing net.

Normally this wouldn't catch my eye, but there's nothing else like it down here. And it's the perfect place to cover something metal, something silver.

This wasn't exactly in the plan, but then again, nothing was.

I know what to do next, but I'm not looking forward to it.

Dimming the belly lamp, I hop into the backseat, then dig around for the neoprene suit that I know is back here. After all, this baby has an airlock hatch.

When I find the neatly folded suit, I quickly strip out of my clothes and slide myself into the skintight fabric. It was obviously made for a guy: long in the legs and puffy in the shoulders and groin. The thought of Callum's *thing* having been right here makes me snicker. I can't help but pat the bulgy space. *He must've had it made special order.* The rest of it may be small enough, but this space . . . *not small.*

Tucked into a net on the roof I find a rubber storage pack. I pull it down and throw it on like a backpack, then fold the extra neoprene underneath itself. Last, I crank at the hatch in the back, crawl into a space no bigger than I am, and curl into a ball.

How would a guy fit in here?

Then again, Callum is pretty slim. Derek couldn't fit. Who knew they made mobiles that came in a size small?

My head and hands are gonna be exposed, but so long as my core stays warm, my temp should be fine. I know I should take off my Hessians—they'll only weigh me down. But we've been through so much together. I can't abandon them now, when I'm finally doing something worthwhile.

I leave them on, and push the red button and take a deep breath. The bottom retracts.

I'm back in the water.

After the second or two it takes to shake off the pesky feeling of being knifed by ice water, I focus myself. My Hessians drag me down and I don't have to swim to the floor—a happy accident thanks to my stubbornness. I reach out for the net, but it's slick, slippery, and coated by algae, and we grapple with each other. I defeat the monster though, in the end, tossing it to the side once I free it from the bricks.

Then I see the thing that glinted.

Another hatch.

An underwater entrance for docking Omnis or subs is unusual but not unheard of. Still, it warrants some poking around.

I brace myself, steadying my legs against the wall, and with both hands I try to rotate the latch. Air bubbles drift away from me—*How long can I go without breathing?*

The latch won't budge.

To the right, I see a small device glowing neon green under the water. I flip it open, and on the screen a series of shapes appears: square, triangle, circle, dot.

What do I do?

Seconds float by, each one seeming longer than the last. I'll need air soon.

I look at the shapes again, then—to see what happens—I tap the square. It slides down onto the middle of the screen, blinking, waiting for me to do something else. I drag it back to the row of shapes, because I know it's not right.

I need the circle. Using the pad of my finger, I drag the circle down. Next, the dot. But there's no line. Without a line, how can I draw the tattoo? I look closer.

The square—

Dragging the bottom line, I lay it directly over the dot, across the middle of the circle.

I'd hold my breath . . . but I already am.

Air bubbles drift up from the circular hatch in front of me. *Must've done it right.*

I try twisting the wheel-shaped handle again and find myself spinning it to the left. In a rush of air and water, the latch makes one final rotation, and with a heavy click it automatically rises. Suction pulls me into an indoor pool.

I can almost breathe.

Behind, the hatch lowers. I try to get some air but the Hudson water hurdles over the closing door in a waterfall, pushing me down. I can't stand until the airlock pressurizes and there's no more water coming in.

When the door finally locks, suctioning closed with a heavy sigh, I'm standing waist deep in the pool. In front of me is yet another latch. I inhale the dank smell a few times. If I weren't so short on air, I'd be plugging up my nose. The swampy rankness ain't exactly pleasant.

I inspect the other circular door—it's got no latch. No way to open it.

Below my feet, the metal flooring groans. It slides away, and I'm left standing on a grate, allowing the water to draining away. Soon as the last of the water disappears, the hatch opposite slides up, and, wasting no time, I step through.

37

4:40 P.M., SUNDAY

Dust-covered black pianos. Gold-painted chairs stacked high, leaning to the side on top of a plush, velvet sofa. Rolled-up carpets in every corner. Trunks with brass handles, destinations papered to their sides.

Stuff, *everywhere*.

The space is huge, probably bigger than the inside of the Tank. I'd call it the base-base-basement, but basements don't look like this, even if that's what it is. This room looks kinda like how I'd imagine the inside of a dragon's lair.

I know I shouldn't waste time, but my eyes don't know what to do with everything. I wanna know what all of it is. When Derek got it, since you can't buy most of this stuff nowadays. I can't help myself—I pick my way through, until I see a small desk leaned up against the exposed brick.

On it, albums. Stacks and stacks of albums, all dusty and worn.

I find the one that looks the oldest, and open to the first page: a faded black-and-white photo. It's not dated, but the somber faces tell me this was taken before people started smiling in pictures.

Three men stand beside three women, all dressed to the nines. For the men, waistcoats and tall hats. The women, though, wear half–American Indian garb, half-white-settler fashions. Poufy, embroidered dresses, but also strands and strands of beads. Feathers dangle from their hair while pearls dangle from their ears. Moccasins for their feet, and stockings for their legs.

I lean in closer.

The first and second couple I don't recognize at all, though one of the men looks a lot like Derek. But the last . . . Even without color, I know the distinct glint of his copper hair.

I almost drop the pack dangling over my shoulder. Why the *brack* is he still alive?

Guardian of a magical healing spring was one thing, but this? This is . . . this is *immortality.*

Maybe I should have known. Maybe I did know. Somewhere, in the way, way back of my mind. It's just . . . Seeing him like this. It changes everything. I can't deny it, or ignore the possibility.

I choke, cough, and in my stomach, a snake pit. I can feel it writhing. *I'm* writhing—he guards the water from people like Aven, who need it, and yet here he is . . . alive. *For centuries.* No wonder he's quick to let us die—he's juiced up on a spring that keeps him young. No expiration date.

But the picture shows me more than just that. I keep looking, hunched over the album. Next to Derek, a woman stands straight. Fearsome and commanding despite her lack of height. Glossy, pin-straight liquid metal. It's Kitaneh, and his hand rests on her shoulder.

His hand. Her hand. Gold bands on the fourth fingers—

They're married.

My eyes water, but like watching some horrible accident, I keep riffling through the album. Page after page, Derek and Kitaneh. Him in the militia, her the good colonial wife. Decade after decade. She's smiling, sequined; he's got a floppy grin on—New York City in the nineteen twenties. Thirties. On and on.

I slam the album shut and start opening drawers left and right, looking for . . . who knows what. More of the story. More answers. Forcing myself to breathe, I push down the feeling that I'm about to be sick. *He kissed me. . . . How could he?*

The drawers are mostly empty, or filled with papers.

Except for one. In it, a small wooden box with words carved on the lid: *"Bellum Pesti—"* I can't read the rest, so I reach down.

Brack. Crisscrossed red laser lights web across the drawer. Overhead, a siren sounds. *But the water?* I've found nothing. . . .

Except, there's no time.

Beelining to the airlock, I push aside ottomans and guitar cases, framed paintings and old leather trunks. The hatch is closing all on its own even though I left it open specifically so I could make a quick getaway. The alarm must've triggered it. I duck low to the floor and, sticking my feet through first, wiggle myself back into the pressurized room—

With only two inches to spare. And still in one piece. I get no chance for relief though.

My feet . . . they're losing their balance—

The grate slides away. Opens up to a cavernous water-filled space below. I fall to one side, avoiding the gap. Pretty soon, though, there's gonna be nowhere left to stand.

Then, from a dozen nearly invisible vents, clouds of vapor fog up the room.

What the hell is that?

I hold my breath as long as I can while trying to keep my footing. Looking down, I notice that not only is the grate moving, the water that drained down earlier is now rising up. I reach for the handle on the first hatch and turn, expecting it not to budge.

The wheel rotates easily.

This makes me stop—*too easy*. It makes no sense. Unless whatever just came out of those vents was supposed to do something to me, but failed.

Something tells me not to take the bait. Something also tells me not to stand around like an idiot. Call it a hunch . . . call it intuition. I think there's a spring down there, wherever that water is coming up from. I brace myself, glad I'm wearing Callum's neoprene suit, and kneel at the edge.

Then, I dive-roll in.

My forehead, and after that my cheeks, are the first to burn from the freeze. Neoprene keeps the rest of me warmish, but it's still a shock.

A few feet down and light's just a memory. I flick open my cuffcomm and activate the laser light on the side. It's small, not made for this sort of thing, but bright enough to shine a path.

Too bad my frog stroke ain't exactly conducive to keeping a beam steady. Every time my left wrist pushes through the water, the light shines backward in the opposite direction. I wish I had one of those silly flashlights that you attach to your head.

Though I know I'm swimming deeper, the temperature doesn't seem like it's getting colder. Warmer, maybe. But definitely not colder. My eyes start to burn from the brack water, but this tunnel is too small for me to want to keep my eyes shut.

Then the first pang of air hunger hits.

I swallow the gasp my body wants to take, and keep on.

Eventually, my fingers stop grazing the sides. The space widens. I wave my wrist ahead, just in time to follow the change in direction. A curve, and I'm swimming back toward the surface. My Hessians drag me down. I should leave them, kick them off.

Never. Now we've *really* been through too much together.

Air hunger pang two . . .

I open my mouth a bit, let some air escape. That helps, like there's less pressure inside me. As I close my mouth, I notice the water—it don't taste salty.

Once more, I take in the tiniest bit.

Sure enough, the taste is sweet. Somewhere in this tunnel, the water went from bitter brackish to fresh. I must have hit another pocket that bleeds into the Strait, mixing together.

Then, all of a sudden, I'm warm. Warmer than warm. The neoprene has locked in my heat, and I'm actually sweating. I must be close, but even with the light from my cuffcomm, there's no way to be sure.

I keep pulling myself up and up.

Through the blur—*I must be imagining it*—the sides of the tunnel seem to be glowing. *Bright green?* Dots of speckled neon. Just as I grapple with air hunger pang three, my head breaks the surface.

I gasp, sucking down air, fighting the wave of dizziness that follows. My arms flail, exhausted, and my beloved boots keep trying to drown me—but looking around, I see I was right. Under the surface, all around me, the walls of the cavern are spotted with the stuff. I dunk my head again and swim closer.

Through the underwater blur, the stuff is unidentifiable . . . some sort of plant, I think, but what do I know? So I pluck a few from the side of the wall's slick mushiness, and swim back for air. Once I'm breathing again, I look down into my palm.

The neon-green spots—they're tiny, glowing mushrooms, with droopy tentlike caps and nearly invisible stems.

So, basically—aliens.

These must be the plants that the phytothingies come from. I should take a whole bunch of them, 'cause if I'm right, they're probably going to have the antiviral goodies that the spring water was missing.

And . . .

I guess the jury's still out on whether Callum will be needing my blood for this evening's science experiment.

I swipe a few fistfuls of the extraterrestrial buggers from the tunnel walls for him, then pull the waterproof sack from my side to fill up with fresh. The weight of the sack, plus the liquid inside, drags me under slightly. The trip back will take longer for sure.

I don't wait.

Sliding the sack over my shoulder, I take one final breath of air and dive under, following the cavern back the way I came. My cuffcomm lights the way, enough so that I don't swim into the sides. I keep my feet kicking and wait for the air hunger pangs.

Every few strokes, I stick my tongue out. The longer I taste the sweet, the more anxious I become. *Return trips always pass quicker*, I remind myself.

This time, when the temperature shifts suddenly to cold, I feel it like a glacier. I'm chilled straight through despite the neoprene, and soon, my fingers are numb. Then, the first hunger pang hits.

I'm ready for it. I know how to swallow it, choke it back down to where it came from. I feel the round of the curve, start to swim up again. When I stick my tongue out again, the water finally tastes normal. Like brack.

I'm close.

Time passes—*I'm gonna make it*. I can see light coming from the pressurized room's ceiling, and the tunnel has started to narrow. My fingers graze the sides. *One final push forward . . .*

I reach for air—the light's right there, right on the ceiling. But instead, my fingers graze metal.

I'm touching the ceiling.

How am I touching the ceiling?

Then I remember . . . when I dove into the tunnel, the space filled up after me.

I open my mouth; I swallow gulps of brack water because there's no air in the room. None at all.

38

5:00 P.M., SUNDAY

My chest spasms. A burning spreads throughout.

Backpedaling through the water, I reach for the first latch. Using hands I can't feel, I rotate. The door lifts up, and I shimmy myself underneath, finding myself outside the building once again. A hundred plus feet to the surface.

Not too far off, the thrum of an engine stirs the underwater silence. As the dull sound grows clearer, I'd bet money it's not just everyday canal traffic. A bright beam of light like a neon-green laser cuts through the murk. Whoever's in that mobile is cutting beneath the boardwalk—not a good sign, so I swim upward, again fighting the weight of my Hessians. I kick and kick but they weigh me down like boulders.

You're staying on my feet, y'hear? I tell the both of them, pulling myself closer to the purple Omni. That bright beam closes in, shines on me directly. I feel like an underwater Santa, with this big red sack over my shoulder. Whoever is manning that other mobile will see me, too.

The engine thrashes my way.

I dive under Callum's mobile, where I pull myself into its belly and close the bottom barrel door. At the telltale muted click, I push another button—green this time—and immediately start gagging, retching up water, while the water trapped in the hatch gets sucked out a series of one-way pipes.

It drains away in a rush, and I damned near have a make-out session with the roof, I'm so starved for air. Within moments, only an inch or so of water is left in the airlock crawl space, but I've got no time. A tide sweeps by, rocking the Omni, and I open the hatch into the pit.

The floor will flood slightly. So be it.

Just then, my neck jolts forward, whips back. A garbled crunch, then I see the other mobile— also an Omni, sleek and black—lurching from the collision.

Oh no.

I shove in the key and hit the acceleration, not caring about a case of repeat whiplash.

My Omni jolts forward, but it feels heavier—like it's dragging in the back. Bright neon draws my eye to the dashboard. On the screen, an outline of Callum's Omni flashes. The airlock hatch flashes, too. Both red.

That crunch I heard wasn't just external damage. The airlock is filling up with water—it's gonna drive slower than it ought to. I check the steam and gas levels; both are in good supply. Still, I hope it can get up enough speed.

I keep driving straight, knuckles bone white against the wheel. Above, a circular brass button. If that is what I think it is . . . I push it.

Yes—a brass periscope extends downward. The lens falls to about eye level. For someone *not* five feet tall. I curse all the non–vertically challenged Omni manufacturers out there.

If I lift my butt up, I can easily see the other mobile behind me.

I force myself to ease my grip on the wheel, notice I'm holding my breath. Again. I exhale, willing a slower rhythm onto my heart.

Whoever's riding me, they're maybe only fifteen feet back.

I can do this. I've made it so damned far. I'm Santa. I have the water.

I remind myself of that fact, thinking it'll comfort me, but instead it sets my nerves wild. I've just reminded myself how much there is to lose.

Now it's not just Aven—it's every HBNC-infected person in the Ward.

But the very thing that set my nerves off is the same thing that calms them. I think of Aven. How she'd scold me first for landing myself in this mess, and next give me a kiss on the cheek for finally doing something she'd approve of. That makes me laugh.

The other mobile and I are both stuck in this narrow alley, brick walls on either side and only a few inches of wiggle room. One sideways rip and I'm crunchy toast. But I have to turn soon. If I keep straight, I'll end up in a suicidal brick maze of gutters like this one. Not smart.

I need to get under an avenue.

I tear my eyes away from the periscope and buckle myself into the seat.

This is gonna hurt.

Turning off the back props entirely, I wrestle with the wheel as the mobile slows. "Don't hit the walls, now," I say out loud, and flick on the belly props. The Omni shoots up to the surface.

I still need to get out of here though, and the nearest avenue is behind me. There's also no room to turn around.

Looks like I'm going to have to steer upside down.

The teensiest, most minuscule part of me is excited; I've always wanted to do this. Never could, what with my Rimbo and all. I just wish it didn't have to happen now. There's a bit too much on the line for me to be entirely comfortable with death-defying mobile stunts.

But it's the quickest way out.

I pull back on the steering wheel, angling her up, up, and over. Soon enough, I'm dangling from my seat. The belt digs into the tops of my thighs—I feel myself slipping, but my butt will hold me well enough. At the beeping noise, I look around the pit, then realize it's coming from my cuffcomm. It's gotta be Callum—I can't look now, though. I jam on the accelerator. Propelled forward, my Omni grazes over the other's domed glass roof.

I won't slow down—*I'm not that stupid*—and really, I don't need to see her face. I only need one guess. The girl looks up through the glass and even if all I saw was her long, straight, black hair, I'd recognize her. But I see the eyes too. Coal dark, set beneath high, arched eyebrows. It's Kitaneh.

Shocking. Anger snakes through my chest. *The girl tried to kill Callum. . . .*

She watches me hurtle past.

Maybe I am that stupid.

I blow her a kiss, then shove my middle finger up against the glass of the roof.

My Omni takes off for Mad Ave. If I can get her to follow me underneath the boardwalk—the super-crowded-with-innocents boardwalk—I'm hoping that she won't want to risk an accident.

I'm just hoping that there's a heart in there. Somewhere. Even though she kills people by protecting a spring that could save people. I know what she said, about it not being medicine. But she gave me no reason. *Why not. Why can't it be?*

Either way, alls I know is that she wants back what I've got in my rubber sack.

I race to the end of the building, aiming to cut an L around it and lift the Omni closer to the walkway. Blood rushes to my head and I feel like gravity is going to drop me out of my seat, but the belt holds tight. This move is a gamble, but Kitaneh is way closer than she should be. Clearly, I've angered the beast.

Then I feel the waves rocking behind me, even with my lead. A quick glance in the periscope shows me that she's pulled the same upside-down whirligig.

I wheel to the right, or left, since I'm upside down. In the semi-open water beneath the boardwalk, I straighten out the Omni. The veins in my head—practically mountains growing out from my forehead by now—return to normal size, and the relief of all the blood flooding back to its proper places nearly blacks me out.

I'm only a few feet below the walk when I see the shadow of her Omni behind me.

On the dash, my VoiceNav screen lights up, shows me TV snow. *But I didn't turn it on . . . ?*

"Omni-to-Omni comm request. Do you accept the transmission?" the nav system's synth voice asks me.

I look at the gray screen, unsure. This is not a feature my Rimbo has, nor is it one I want Benny to install, ever.

Do I accept? All she's going to do is try to convince me to give the water back. That, or she'll tell me that she's going to kill me. Neither of which I care to hear.

But . . . I'm curious.

"Yes," I say, and it still feels strange speaking into the air.

The snow flickers in and out, is replaced by Kitaneh's face, cool and unfazed, on my dash. "You accepted," she says, arching her brows. Then, with a nod, "Thank you."

Not quite the reaction I'd expected, I think, realizing how little I know about this girl—this *ancient* girl. And all of a sudden, I feel bad for her. I feel bad that she married Derek, and that he would go behind her back kissing girls like me. Who are, like, 3 percent her age.

"You're welcome . . . ," I answer, quietly.

The screen goes gray for a moment, then all I hear is her

voice: "Please . . ." she pleads, and I'm sure I look as shocked as I'm feeling. She's saying *please*? Then her voice grows harder. "You think you're doing the right thing, and perhaps . . ." She cuts out, but it's not because of the connection. She's stopped speaking. When her face returns to my dash, she looks desperate. Tired.

"Perhaps you're right," she says. "But the risk is too great. Governor Voss is no fool. Until the airdrop happens, he'll be waiting for us. He'll be on the lookout to see what we do."

Though Kitaneh is probably right—he will be—I'm too close to give up. The sack is full; my sister's life is in there and so are all the other sick. "I'm sorry," I say, reaching for the button to drop the call.

Just before I press it, I hear: "Forgive me—"

The line goes silent.

I check the periscope again.

She's still way too close—*I have to lose her.* So I zigzag, the best thing to do when someone's coming after you like this. You can't *just* zigzag, though, 'cause then that becomes a pattern, and they'll just catch on. I weave between the boardwalk's pylons, mixing it around—one, one, one, then skipping two or three and crossing over to the other side's row.

I can't keep this up.

The tank holds only enough gas to keep the steamer boiling water. It'll be empty soon. Is that her plan? Skunk me out till I got no place to go but hell in a handbag? Her Omni don't have laser guns or anything, so it's not like she could blow me outta the water.

Then it dawns on me.

That's exactly what she'll try and do. I know full well she'd like to end me—all she's gotta do is keep tailing me until *I* blow me outta the water. Collide with something. A wall. A pylon. Anything hard enough to make smithereens of me.

Okay, I think. I can work with that.

Once more I reach for the periscope. I bring my eye to it, but I'm too late—all I see is the bullet-shaped nose of her Omni clipping my tail.

My own Omni careens forward—I twist the wheel away from pylons, but one of them swipes my side anyway. If this were above water, I'd be setting off in a tailspin to the moon right now. But we're not, so the mobile just reels out, then slows.

I regain control, but something feels off kilter.

At first, I hear a hiss. Like there's a water snake trapped in the mobile. Then, from the battered side that took the blow, a spray of water shoots through. I'm struck in the jugular by so much pressure, I don't know how it doesn't pierce skin.

I need to end this. I need to end this *now*. And I can think of a perfectly good, possibly suicidal way.

If Kitaneh wants me to smash myself into a brick wall . . . well, that's exactly what I'll do.

39

5:15 P.M., SUNDAY

I swallow so loud, I can hear it in my ears. This better work—and by "work" I mean, in one hour I get to hear Callum ream me out for pancaking his Omni. That right there?

Best-case scenario.

'Cause if I'm listening to him yell at me, it means I'm alive. I can't believe I'm doing this. Of all my plans . . . this one is by far the craziest.

I veer left, into the open channel.

Turning off the belly props, I bring the mobile down a few feet, though we're both still too close to the surface for my comfort. Closer to the canal's floor means farther from Mad Ave and all those people. At worst, the explosion will send a few people in for a dip. Better than burning them to death.

There's a building back behind me that should do the trick.

Of course, ain't no need to be picky when it comes to blowing myself up. I jiggle at the wheel, veering the sub left and right, making it look like I've lost control.

Chief, Governor Voss, and Kitaneh all need to think what happens next is an accident. If she's right and the governor is keeping an eye out, my being dead can only help what Callum and I are trying to pull off. Governor Voss will never expect anything from a dead girl.

I gun the engine.

Kitaneh follows me out a hundred feet or so. Then I shift 180 degrees, turning back the way I came, aiming to cross beneath Mad Ave at a perpendicular.

"Autopilot. In fifteen seconds, shift speed to a hundred and thirty miles per hour," I say to the VoiceNav. "Then shift angle to forty-five degrees downward." I'd just autogun her right away, but I'll need those ten seconds to get into the airlock without the Omni sliding me around. And a forty-five-degree angle should be wide enough so that Callum's Omni will hit the building. I'm no Benny, though—I never liked playing pool.

I'll need to jump ship before she hits. *I could do it now. . . .*

Checking the periscope again, I see Kitaneh. *Not now, too soon.* She'll spot me for sure.

I look around the Omni, sit back down. All of a sudden it's no longer an Omni—the phrase *buried alive* comes to mind, though these days we just weight the bodies into the canal or burn them when we can. Or, if they were important enough, we'll send them down the Strait on a boat. We don't put our dead in coffins. But that's exactly what this Omni's starting to look like. A coffin.

It closes itself around me, and my insides start to shake. The soles of my Hessians drum against the floor, and to kill the nerves in my hands, I squash them both under my butt. I've been nervous before, but this is different.

The sack. All that water . . . it's sitting right there.

Too much. Too much responsibility. Looking at it, again I wonder if every life is equal. If every life carries the same weight, has the same value.

Take that sack. What's in there can save a few hundred lives. Then take me: one person. If every life is equal, then that sack is more important than me, if only 'cause it holds more lives.

But what if everyone in that sack is evil? Murderers. And I, not knowing, give my life to save them. What then? Are we all still equal?

It's the most confusing word problem in the world, where every number changes depending on what you do or don't do. My head spins. "Get it together—" I moan to the dashboard, because I have to stop the panic before it disables every ounce of courage I ever thought I had.

"*Brack,*" I curse to myself. "You *can't* die. It's just Aven. Forget the others."

It's just Aven. I have to make it—if not for the other numbers, for her.

And like someone's opened a window, that does it. I can put the math problem aside, I can breathe again.

Never liked numbers anyway.

"Countdown to autopilot, please?" I ask, steeling myself for the next . . .

"Ten seconds."

Ten seconds. She says it so kindly. Ladylike. Classy. Makes me think I'm headed for a ball, not a brick wall.

Turning off the headlight and the belly lamp sends the mobile pitch dark. *Gotta get a move on.*

I walk back into the airlock hatch, still dripping, and wait. Crouched in a ball, I'm the same size as the red rubber sack swung over my side. *I'm the same damn size*—except I'm just one life. Numbers pop back into my head again—that thing has to count for hundreds. Thousands, maybe.

Just one.

"Seven seconds."

Just one.

"Six seconds."

Can't jump now—have to wait until the sub shifts to the new speed. That'll take three seconds, at least.

"Five seconds."

Then, when I feel the sub shift down, I'll know I'm out of Kitaneh's line of sight. She'll be above me. That's when I'll hit the red button and land myself back in the brack.

The seconds drag on, each longer than the next.

I clutch the sack by my side. Hugging my knees in this curled-up position, I imagine the one life in there that matters: Aven. I picture her next to me. She's telling me I'm doing the right thing. That she doesn't blame me for choosing Callum.

That thought though, it kills me. My eyes sting and I blink

away a tear that starts on a path over the bridge of my nose. There's hardly enough room to wipe it away. I inhale and exhale. I realize my nails are digging into the sack.

Fear freezes me up. I loosen my grip and breathe out all the air in my lungs, prepping for the dive and the air hunger.

"Three seconds."

I'll push the button. Swim out, then down. Under Kitaneh's sub. Behind her. Up. Get myself dockside, onto Mad Ave.

"Two seconds."

Then, back to Callum.

Kitaneh will think I'm dead. Then she'll tell Derek, who'll tell Terrence, and the chain of gossip in the Ward will spread faster than the Blight. Everyone will know.

"Zero. Shifting to speed one hundred and thirty miles per hour, shifting to angle forty-five degrees."

The Omni bucks and sways; the damage has made scrap of it. *Not just yet*, I think. *Let's go out with a bang.* I know it's only metal. It can't think. But this is all I can do.

We jerk from side to side and I feel the nose dip, angling itself toward the building. It's pulling the speed, all its belts and cogs on the inside straining against the added weight— a low layer of water already slicking the floor. Faster. It's getting faster. One more jolt and it'll really be moving. Propulsion pushes me back. I claw the floor with my fingertips. Now is no time to screw up.

I push the red button.

Water rushes in, a shock of cold everywhere. Have to wait until the airlock is mostly full before I swim out, otherwise the water will just push me back in.

Soon, I'm submerged. One last chug of air, mouth pressed against the roof. I realize the last thing on Earth my mouth might ever touch is the roof of Callum's Omni.

I push myself out of the doomed mobile, sack hauled over my shoulders. Seconds later, orange headlights shine directly overhead, as Kitaneh's Omni sends a rush of water my way. I'm thrown into a somersault. The weight of the sack slows me some, and disorients me more. I try to keep my lips tight together, imagining that they've been sewn shut, but they open, and my own air bubbles drift away from me.

At first I hate myself for being weak, for letting them go. But then I realize . . .

They are my compasses. When the somersaults stop, down is up is up is down. . . . These bubbles are the only thing that remind me which way ain't lying.

I follow them, not sure where I am under Mad Ave.

Don't care.

Again, I find myself frog stroking for the surface with my body fighting a thousand icy jackknives, each one telling me to stop moving. To stop moving means to stop fighting, but I'm so far away, and the sack is so heavy, and my boots . . . my boots are also dragging me down.

Almost fifty feet to surface and it's taking too long. Callum's Omni will hit any second now, and if I'm in the water when it does, that's it. Underwater explosions are even more dangerous than ones on land—the blast from the pressure wave would turn me into a ball of ruptured junk. I'm fuzzy on the science, but it's bad. Of course, that's for, like, a hand grenade. Who knows what happens when a mobile explodes.

I drag my toes against my heels, lifting the soles of my feet out of my boots. One drifts off, then the other, and I can't even afford to spare a glance at my beloved Hessians as they sink to the floor. Nor will I tell myself that they're just shoes. They're not.

They were like a second pair of feet.

The upward haul goes slightly faster, now, with the boots gone. I've still got the weight on my back to deal with. Only twenty feet or so away. Ears crackle as I close the distance, and then my temples flare under the pressure.

That's when I feel the first wave.

It pushes me to the side, takes the rest of the air from my lungs.

I open my mouth—I don't want to; I know not to, but I swallow the greenish-tinged water by the mouthful. I'm only four feet, three feet. . . . Fingertips break the surface—they hit hard wood. My head comes up too quickly. *Boardwalk*, I remind myself, but the need to breathe trumps all. A thwump to my cranium, and outer space has direct mailed me every one of its stars. Planets too, free of charge. I see black, black, and more black. I won't go under again though, and I grip the planks, keeping afloat.

After a few retching gasps, I can actually begin to start breathing again instead of just hacking up water. I swim under the boardwalk till I reach the dockside. Wet and bedraggled, I haul myself over the edge.

First things first—I reach around my back, feeling for the rubber pack.

It's there. Setting it down, I look for any holes in the rubber.

Seeing none, I decide a little jig is in order. In honor of the sack, and me.

People start circling around the edge of the walk, about thirty feet off, where a chunk of the wooden planks has gone missing. Someone calls the DI: "A huge collision under Mad Ave, yes," I hear them say.

Any other day of the week, the Blues wouldn't care less about that sort of thing. They'd ignore the call till the monthly arrests. Then, *maybe* they'd send over divers.

Today, though, they'll be on it.

And they'll find my shoes.

Soon enough, I'll be off their radar for good.

My cuffcomm beeps its reminder and I glance down:

Q5/6. B-sickhouse on the Strait. Apt PH305

Callum's new address . . .

I hardly believe it.

And not because it's all the way west, practically in the DI's backyard. Or because he's chosen to hide out in a sick-house. Both those are either brilliant moves or sheer idiocy.

But they're not why I'm standing still. That sickhouse— the only one in Hell's Kitchen—is the last place on earth I want to go back to. That's where I found Aven after my DI training was up. Seeing her alone, looked after by strangers who could do nothing for her 'cause she had no money for daggers—I still feel the guilt of leaving her behind three years later, though I was snatched up, no choice in the matter.

She's alone right now. *She could die like that.*

My chest holds in a boulder, one that keeps getting pushed up- and downhill, and the only thing that seems to make it better is being near her.

Yet here I am.

I should be with her—I *want* to be with her. But I'm so close . . . so, so close to getting her a cure.

Starting the shoeless trek back to Hell's Kitchen, a cure in reach, I wonder why my guilt feels no different today than it did the day I found her. Like nothing's changed.

Maybe nothing *has* changed. Instead of being *with* her, I'm always off someplace else. Off far, far away, thinking that I'm big enough and strong enough to fight her death for her—

And win.

PART THREE

40

6:00 P.M., SUNDAY

The suspension bridge sways under my feet, heavy with me, and the sack, and other things like life and love that you simply can't touch with your hands.

Overhead, quiet and perfect like nothing could ever go wrong in the world, I see the stars. Out in full force.

If Callum and I can pull tonight off . . . My brain don't even know how to think that kind of thought—it can't imagine it. The borders will open—I'll be able to see the West Isle for the first time. But would I even want to? A city with people who'll push *for* genocide?

Maybe, when you're not fighting to survive, you can afford to think about wiping others off the map. Either way, it's not important. Tonight isn't about getting tourist visas so we can take vacations to the Isle.

I'm here—I see the roof of the Hell's Kitchen sickhouse only feet away, but I stop moving. Stop crossing the bridge.

Below, the wooden planks creak, and ahead of me the Strait splashes between us and the Isle. The Ward isn't silent tonight, though. Not too far off I hear the high-pitched whistle of a firecracker. Then its thunderous finish. Like it is its own exclamation point announcing itself to the sky.

Telling the world to get ready for what comes next.

Tonight is about Aven, and the girl in the contagious ward, and everyone else afraid to go outside. It's about putting *us* back on the map—as people, and as a city.

We're not *hosts*.

I let go of my fist, tight around the suspension rope, and jump onto the rooftop.

Opening the door out of the stairwell into the top-floor hallway, I nearly gag. Have to hold my nose as I walk. The smell . . . it's worse than the dying stink of the hospital.

Rank viscera. Old, decaying flesh. Blood loss, coppery and acrid.

This high up, and they usually just weight the bodies before tossing them into the canal below. But sometimes the flesh is dying and the body's still alive. The smell is the same.

I can taste it all in the air, passing room after room. My stomach twists, and though this isn't the floor I found Aven on, it may as well be. All the doors look the same, and I can almost see myself pushing them open. Frantic.

Yelling for anyone who might've seen the girl with the near-white hair.

I come up on apartment 305, my footsteps quiet and even. Candlelight flickers under the door, and I don't even have to knock. It opens, and there's Callum.

He pulls me in. Wraps me up in a hug. Seeing the sack, his face is a mixture of wonder and even more wonder. "You made it. . . ." he says, and kneels beside it. "Is this really it?"

Disbelieving, he lifts it up by the straps to feel its weight.

"To the brim," I say softly, and I pat the rubber, a little bit proud. Then I look at him—really look at him—give him the once-over, two . . . three times. "You're *whole*," I say, wide-eyed, and he manages a weak laugh, nodding.

Even with the cure . . . everything is tense. There's too much dying.

As he carries the sack to a corner of the room—a huge room—I see all the big furniture's still here from after the Wash Out. Everything else, though—picked clean.

"That I am," he answers, lowering the sack onto a bulky wooden table. Careful not to spill, he pours the water into a glass basin, shaking his head as he watches. He murmurs, "Only you," then glances at me with that strange, awed look again.

I avoid his eyes; each time that happens, I find myself going more and more red in the cheeks, like I'm *too* unusual.

As he pours, the tiny green mushrooms fall out too. "What's this?" he murmurs, leaning in to get a closer look. Then he answers his own question. "A bioluminescent fungus . . ."

I don't know much about that first word, but I nod anyway. He's talking about the aliens, all right. "It's the plant you were talking about, right? It's how the water got those phytothings," I ask, but he don't answer.

He's totally absorbed, filling an eyedropper with the springwater. "Amazing," he murmurs.

Through the tube, I see now that the water is darker than I thought. A brownish, reddish color. Flecked with neon. When he swirls it around, a glow-in-the-dark galaxy whirl-pools in his very hand. He droppers it onto a glass slide, then adds a dye or something. He lays that under his 'scope's lens. For a moment I'm surprised—I'm thinkin' the 'scope got lucky. Survived the ransacking of the first lab. But then I see Callum hold a super-duper bright flashlight over it: Kitaneh's handiwork must've included bulb smashing.

"Shine it here, please?" he asks.

I take it from him, trying to beam the light where he wants while he looks through the lens. After a few moments of him lifting his eye, moving the slide, adjusting the focus, and repeating the process about a half dozen times, Callum stands.

In a whisper, eyes glazed like he's way too happy: "This is . . . I have no words. The fungus—it grows underwa-ter, and the hot spring seeps out its nutrients. Kind of like a tea. You know, I've heard of something like this before." He pauses, recalling as he looks up. "There's a place called Siberia where a tree-growing mushroom exists, one with similarly beneficial properties. Antiviral, antitumor, anti-bacterial, et cetera. Locals make tea out of it. Still, this one blows it away. Far more potent. Take a look." He nudges me in front of the 'scope.

Peering down, I see a half dozen other patterns, similar

to the desert dunes and the bubbles. One looks like a fence, all Xs and diamonds. Another ripples like the Hudson on a windy day.

"The antivirals, along with all the other necessary chemical compounds, are there. We can cure the Blight with this," Callum tells me, tapping the table. When I look up he adds, "Along with your blood, that is."

I laugh, nervous. "Again?" I say, gesturing to myself. "Remember, Callum, limited quantities only."

He chuckles and walks over to me, syringe in hand. Motions for me to roll up my sleeve. "Don't worry, I won't need much."

I step back—I don't believe him for a minute. We're talking enough for at least eight hundred people. "Why? I thought with the mushrooms we'd have enough antivirals. . . ."

"We do. But, like I said before, your blood does something to jump-start the recipient's immune system. With it, we only need to administer one dose. Follow-up doses would be necessary otherwise, and we just don't have enough time— or water—to do that."

I nod. Without another thought—we've come too far to get tripped up over a little blood donation—I extend my arm, exposing my inner elbow. The tip of the needle pierces flesh. I watch my blood go away. And away. And away . . .

"Okay, mister," I grumble after even more time passes. "Leave some for the girl in the body, will ya?"

Callum laughs, but doesn't move. Only when *he* feels he's taken enough does he steps back. Then he looks at the desk.

On it, three glass bowls. All different sizes. The first and smallest (thank goodness) holds my blood. In the second, our alien mushrooms. The springwater is in the third bowl, swirly and neon.

Biting his lower lip in a smile, Callum double punches the air. I'm fool-grinning too. "We're going to do it," he says. We stand there, our eyes first caught on the bowls, then on each other, because hope has the perfect face.

"We need a plan. To get it to everyone . . . and Aven," I say softly, afraid of sounding too selfish.

Even with all the others, I want to get her the cure first.

"Yes. We do. And we will. But first I need to figure out what 'it' is," he tells me. "There's still so much we don't know."

"True," I say. I'm about to say more, but I stop. Cross my arms. As soon as *his* name entered my head, the writhing came back. The anger. All of a sudden, it's like I'm holding that album again, filled with Derek and Kitaneh's joy, centuries of love-dovey, gooey-eyed crap. *Derek.* Who kissed me back. Who would drink the water for himself, and let me watch my sister die.

"The Tètai, Callum . . . They're not just guardians of the spring. They've *been* the spring's guardians. All along. Centuries. I saw pictures. Actual old-school flash photography."

Callum eyes me, but not with disbelief. Then he laughs, brows sky-high, and scratches his head. "I'd suspected that was possible, to be perfectly honest. But without seeing it in the water, I couldn't even attend to the possibility." He points back at the 'scope. "I still can't see how, actually. We know that, for someone who's sick, the water has restorative properties if administered in multiple doses over time. But immortality? That's a whole different ball game, I'm afraid."

I walk back over to the 'scope to have another look. "What if . . ." I start, and peer down into the lens. Just in this tiny microcosm of a swab, there are dozens more patternlike phytothingies than there were before—ones that look like hologram images of grassy fields, or rainbow feathers, or cords and cords of twisty rope. "Maybe there's a new nutrient in here that does it. Or maybe if you're not sick, drinking it regularly stops you from getting older. The governor did say something about the results being 'miraculous' when a healthy person drinks it every day."

Callum's hand is firm on my shoulder as he says, "You're kidding, right? You never mentioned that—"

"I dunno," I answer, standing up and turning to face him. "He said a lot of stuff. It was hard to keep track."

I'd also just found out Derek is part of a secret guild, responsible for hiding a cure that could save my dying sister, so there's that. . . . I was kind of distracted.

No need to mention that bit, though.

"I'm going to have to run tests. Many, many tests. So we don't accidentally hand out doses of immortality . . ." Callum has started to look a little dazed.

"*After* you've figured out the cure part," I remind the absentminded professor in him.

"Naturally." He casts me a glance like he didn't need the reminder. "And I still don't understand how the spring would protect against the poison. Your bookie didn't happen to mention that, did he?"

I shake my head. "Nope. Just said it would."

"Hmmph," Callum grumbles, scratching his ear. "I admit that there's still quite a bit we don't know about the water. I don't like it, but we're going to have to take it on faith that he knows what he's talking about. And, considering he's been around the stuff for more than five hundred years . . . I think it's safe to assume he does."

Together we turn to face the West Isle skyline, still visible through the dirtied, cracked window. Callum watches it like he's waiting for something to happen at any moment. Which, if we wait long enough, it will.

"Then, the last order of business: distribution," he says, leaning up against the bare white window frame. "I've been thinking about how best to get Aven the new serum once it's made. I figure you'll have some tricks up your sleeve as far as the rest of the Ward goes." Callum says it to me so naturally. Like, of course I do.

Like it's not a plan to prevent the government-sanctioned extermination of hundreds.

I almost laugh out loud, but then I realize it's kind of a compliment—Callum *trusts* me. He barely knows me, and he thinks I can do this. *I kind of like it.*

"You first," I say nonetheless, looking over at him. Just 'cause he thinks I have tricks don't mean I *actually* have them.

At least not yet, I don't.

Callum flips closed his cuffcomm, and the Ward Hope Hospital schematics he's projected onto the wall disappear. The wall goes back to blank, with its peeling paint and cob-webbed corners.

"You really think that'll work? Will you have time to make two separate batches?" I ask. "What if the night guard catches me? Tampering with the water supply is probably one of the biggest crimes around. . . . I know from experience. It's how I ended up in the DI jail."

"Don't worry," he insists. "I already know how to make the water stronger—I can make enough for just the hospital within the next few hours, which is all the time we have if you're going to put it in the water system before the final night rations go out at ten. It's making the serum for the hundreds of others that will take time. The hardest part for you, Ren, will be getting in. I'd give you my ID badge, but it's too risky," he insists. "The receptionist will have seen your image from the Wanted broadcasts. You can't just walk in through the front door."

"I'll figure it out," I say, confident.

I've totally got tricks up my sleeve when it comes to sneaking into, and out of, places.

"All right." Callum eyes me before sitting down in front of his scope. "Your turn," he says, and glances at his comm for the time.

I do the same and have to remind myself to breathe. My stomach goes all knotty—time just keeps passing, faster by the second. I've got no plan, and I've got to make it to Ward Hope by ten. . . .

"All right," I repeat slowly, hoping that an idea magically appears in my brain. "Distribution."

Come on . . . come on. Think.

Of course, it's impossible to think when you're telling yourself to think, 'cause all you're doing is saying that one word over and over. Not actually *thinking*.

"Well . . . we've got to find a way to get enough vials of the cure onto every sickhouse rooftop in the Ward. All before . . ." My voice trails away; I sink into the thinking part.

There are sickhouses all over the U. We can't just walk around, handing out some magic cure to everyone. . . . That would take forever. Not to mention that people might be suspicious of taking some strange medicine they've never heard of.

I scoff to myself. No one gets suspicious when they hear it from officials.

"They have to think it's their 'cure,'" I say aloud.

Callum looks up. Nods. Waits for the rest.

I go on. "We can't swap one for another—whatever poison they're giving out will be down people's throats as soon as it's on the roof. Everyone's gonna be waiting in their stairwells at least an hour beforehand, guaranteed. So we've gotta get to them before the squadrons come through. Late enough that everyone still thinks our cure is coming from the government, but early enough that we're not around when the actual aeromobiles arrive."

"That's less than six hours away," he says. "And it's going to take me half that long to make the cure. How do you propose we do it?"

Rooftop distribution. Countdown clock. Quick getaway.

Uh-oh.

"What if—" I start, excited. But then my fingers start fidgeting. I press what's left of my nails into my palms and begin pacing the length of the room. I've got an idea all right, but no way is Callum gonna like it.

Spit it out.

"We need the other dragsters."

I let the idea hang in the air, and wait for him to grab it. Or swat it. And . . .

I think I see a swat coming.

Callum's mouth takes the shape of *Oh, hell no*, so I cut him off before he can object. "It's the best way—they're fast, and once they learn the truth, they'll want this plan to work as much as we do."

Shaking his head, "No, absolutely no. I just don't think it's safe, Ren. On so, so many levels. One, you'll be on the U, an entirely residential area, piloting those *death traps*—which, let's face it," he says, waving his hands around, and I know I'm not going to like what comes next, "are really no more than scrap metal excuses for mobiles."

Say what? I shoot him a glare made of so much evil, I think I actually see him step back, afraid. Raise his hands in surrender.

"I'm sorry," he says. "Perhaps that was uncalled for. But they're dangerous, and dragsters are notorious adrenaline junkies, yourself included. Not to mention how many people we'd be trusting with incredibly sensitive information."

"Callum, this was never gonna stay a small operation. Not with so many sick. And . . . though I know it's not the same on the Isle, those of us who live here in the Ward—well, we all know someone who's sick. Someone we love is always dying. That's just the way it goes. Curing the Blight is probably the only thing that we'd ever be on the same side for."

I can only hope that it's true. The Ward's also got a "survival of the fittest" mentality that could get in the way.

"Answer honestly: Can you depend on them?"

I don't know.

Would Kent ever be on my side, for anything? Even this? He owes me. "I think so," I say. I saved his butt today. "And I don't have an idea that's better than this one."

I flip open my comm, punch in Ter's number, then type my message:

Dragster meeting, ASAP—Derbies too. Bone Vault. Bring Benny. —R.R.

Even though this is an unregistered cuffcomm, I use my racing initials, short for "Red Rider."

"You sure they'll show?" Callum asks, watching over my shoulder as I flip the comm shut.

Not in the least, I think to myself. Especially not if they know that I'm the one calling the meeting.

I open the cuffcomm again and send him another message:

Keep me dead, will ya?

Terrence will know what I mean.

"Now they'll show," I say, nodding. *Hoping.*

41

The Bone Vault is a dismal place. No one ever comes here, and I don't blame them.

Light would help, though—I glance around the space, then up at the chandelier. It's pieced together outta decades-old clavicles and smooth, gray skulls that look like they died laughing.

I decide against touching the thing and curse the insane architect whose idea it was to decorate a house of the dead with *the actual dead*. Even after the Wash Out floated new and old bodies to the surface, but left us with no more land to put them . . .

Really? This was someone's brilliant solution?

Joke's on me, though, I suppose. When the Blight hit, the Ward had a place—ready and waiting—to stash our bones.

Reluctant, I reach for the skull to my right and pluck a candle from one of its eye sockets. When I strike a match from the pack in the jaw, an orange glow turns the Vault into a bona fide nightmare.

Now I can see too much. I wish I'd left the candle alone.

All across the ceiling hang bony odds and ends. Worn molars, sharp, white knuckles, strung up side by side.

Without warning, the same way you imagine your own death—a mobile crashing, a racer knifing you in the gut—I imagine every one of these bones belonging to Aven. Each knuckle grows muscles and skin and fingernails. Becomes a hand, her hand, and it reaches out from the ceiling. For me.

I'm socked into nausea, ready to vomit. I double over the stone bench, head between my legs, and heave. Sliding off the bench, I huddle close to my knees on the dusty floor. I use my palms as blinders to block out the bones—I can't look at them. Clutching my gut, I wait for the sick feeling to pass.

A slight wind sets the candle flickering. Shadows grow and shift. Some rustling sound kills the dead quiet, but I see nothing. In here, I'm swallowed whole. It's not just Aven anymore. This place is a monster. I've landed myself in its belly. Keeping me company is every body it's ever eaten, every body it will ever eat.

Imagining the overflow of bones come tomorrow morning—that plants my feet. I'm standing on the barbed wire of guilt. I want to run, find Aven, but it'll just follow me. It fences in every choice.

"You in there, Ren?" I think I hear Ter call.

I peek my head out the window to check, and I see him

standing there, face pressed against the glass. I inhale and slide down to the floor again with relief, watching my imaginary beasts scatter. Now all I'm left with are the real ones.

"I am," I call back, hearing his footsteps as he enters the Vault.

He finds me hunched on the floor, like I'm hiding from something. Quickly, I stand up. Brush off the floor's grime.

He folds me into a great, big bear hug.

"Ter?" I say, my voice muffled, nose pressed into his armpit. "Umm . . ."

"You're alive," he sings, holding on a few seconds longer before backing away.

When I'm able to breathe again, "I commed you, didn't I?"

He starts laughing—it bubbles and bubbles and doesn't stop until he has to slow down for air. "The rumors were insane, Ren—you scared the hell out of everyone. I found out from Derek." Ter breathes out, solemn all of a sudden. "He was pretty messed up about it, actually. Which kinda surprised me, you know?" Seeing my face, raised eyebrows and pursed lips, he waves his hand. Adds, "Not that he shouldn't have been upset. But, I mean, he was just your bookie." Then Ter pauses. Looks down at me. In the dark of the Vault, with just candlelight to see by, the whites of his eyes are glowing.

I can only guess at what's coming next.

"You guys didn't have a thing . . . did you?"

Like hell we didn't. Thank goodness. I shake my head, about to open my mouth when Ter and I hear the sounds of feet shuffling, and the tail end of a conversation.

". . . divers found her boots and everything. Even left a calling card—"

Can't tell who's talking—they're too far away—but they're definitely talking about me. I wrinkle my nose. Mouth the words *"Calling card?"* at Ter, who points to my bare feet.

"A photo, inside your boots?" he mouths back.

Then I remember. The picture I took from Callum's place. I'd stuck it in my poor Hessian and forgotten about it. Bet I was walking on that photo all day and didn't notice.

"Someone saved my boots though, right?" I ask, raising my voice.

Ter rolls his eyes, pulls me into his arms again, and actually gives me a noogie. In a whisper, "They're *boots*, dummy. I'll buy you a new pair."

". . . whatcha think this is about, anyway?" the voice asks, now just outside the window.

It's Jones, definitely. Antsy. Worried. Nerves of glass.

Throwing me a sideways glance, Ter mouths the same question, but I don't answer. No time.

"Daresay we'll find out soon enough."

That'd be Kent. I'd know the breezy sleaze of his voice any day. Just hearing it, and the hairs on my neck bristle.

Craning my neck around the alcove, I watch as they enter the Vault and exchange easy armshakes with Terrence.

He's not a girl. They don't hate him. A few more steps bring Kent into the main sanctuary. He sees me, and his face twists in disgust.

Still? Has he forgotten already? I could've let that Omni plow into the canal, left him stuck there in the pit.

"What is she doing here?" he snarls as he presses the black derby farther down his forehead. Nudging a stray dark hair behind his ear, he looks to Ter, vexed.

A dozen slurs are batting against the roof of my mouth, wanting out. I swallow every last one of them. I breathe deep. "Boys," I say, walking into the sanctuary with my gaze to the floor, my hands at my sides. Any other day, I'd come out fighting. Today, the first round is theirs.

I won't fight them with my eyes.

I won't store a fist in my pocket for later.

I open my mouth, about to begin, then realize someone's missing. I look at Terrence. "Where's Benny?" I ask. He's going to be the hardest to see. . . . I don't like anyone worrying about me, him most of all.

"Said he'd show later. I'm sure if he knew you weren't dead, he'd be here right now."

"But you are dead," Kent interrupts. "There was a party and everything." A dark smile worms across his lips.

My fingers twitch, fighting to take position, but I keep 'em pressed down.

Ignoring him, I go on. "Thank you all for coming. I've asked you to meet me here tonight because what will happen over the next three hours affects each of us," I begin.

The three pass unsure looks like hot potatoes.

"Tonight, at half past midnight, Governor Voss plans to eradicate the problem of the Blight. Only it won't be happening how we think." I pause to make sure I have everyone's attention.

I do.

"The announcement you heard was a lie."

Ter is the first to speak. "You're saying they *don't* have a way to cure the Blight?"

From his tone, he doesn't disbelieve. He doesn't believe though, either.

"Oh, they'll get rid of the Blight all right. But it's not how you think. The cure won't just destroy the virus—it destroys carriers, too." I watch their faces, wait for my meaning to sink in.

"His plan is extermination."

The Vault absorbs each and every word into its bones. Maybe they remember life. There are no echoes of what I've spoken, only speechless digestion. I'm met with faces serious and grim, eyes downcast as they consider.

Of course, since Ter was the first to give me the benefit of the doubt, it should come as no surprise that Kent is the first to laugh.

"Insane," he scoffs. It breaks their thoughts. Turning to me: "How do you even know this?" He looks at Jones, then Ter. They hear his doubt and now they're raising their brows, suddenly on the fence. "You guys believe her?"

But no one knows how to answer, because no one else has heard the West Isle news. No one *ever* hears West Isle news. And I bet it goes both ways. Sure they can pick up the signal, but what news of ours would they care enough to listen to?

"Look," I tell everyone, taking off my cuffcomm. I flip it open and, sliding my finger across the screen, bring up the West Isle newspaper article Callum showed me. Then

I project the headline onto the wall: "THE WARD: A CASE FOR DEMOCIDE."

I let them read the first few sentences of the column, and inhale, preparing to tell them the rest of the truth: how I know.

I'd rather not, of course, but if they were to find out after the plan was already in motion, it could upset everything.

"And I know about this because . . ." *Brack, here goes. I can't believe I'm telling them.* I hold my breath as I look at Ter. The others already hate me, but Ter? This is going to cut him up the worst. "Because I used to work for the DI. Freshwater scouting, that's all—"

Someone cuts me off, but it's not Kent.

"You've been working for the Blues?" Ter asks, and I read hurt on his face in a hundred ways. He feels betrayed.

"I'm sorry—" I start to say, but Terrence raises his hand to stop me.

"I don't want to hear it. Not now." He refuses to look at me. "Later."

I can't lose Ter. . . . My chest starts to shake like I've got wings in there, beating away at the air, pushing me to run to him. They want me to make it better, and that's all I want to do.

But he's right. Not now.

Kent scoffs. "You expect that we'll believe you after you tell us that?"

"Yeah, I do. 'Cause I just love pissing off the people I work for, for no reason at all. Brilliant plan of mine," I spit back at him, probably harsher than I should, but I'm shaken by the thought of losing Ter too. After realizing who Derek really is, and now if I fail Aven . . . ?

I can actually feel the threads of myself spinning out into nothing.

The Vault is silent.

When Jones opens his mouth, we look at him, stunned. Kent most of all.

His sandy hair flops in his face, and he pushes it out of the way. Softly, he says, "Why'd you bring us here?"

He's not asking meanly, but with curiosity.

Keep it together. I inhale, and grip on to the new air with my lungs. *Focus.*

Somehow, this next piece is harder to say, even though I've seen the serum in action. I lift my eyes, finally, to meet theirs head-on. I want them to know the truth of what I'm saying.

"A cure does exist."

I leave out the fountain-of-youth bit. Something tells me it makes the story a little less believable. And now that I've dropped the conversational (opposite) equivalent of the atom bomb, I wait.

Jones makes no movement—he's thoughtful. Kent laughs through a breathy snort, and Terrence waves his hands.

"Whoa, whoa, whoa." He steps a few feet outside of our semicircle. Paces, crosses his arms, but finds my eyes again once he comes to a standstill. "You're serious."

"I am."

"Can you prove it?" Jones asks.

If it were ready, sure.

"Yes," I answer, firm.

"Really." Kent watches me carefully, like everything depends on my next words. "You can prove it?"

"Yes," I tell him again. "But first we come up with a strategy."

He nods once. "Then my father will get some, right?" he asks, about to reach out for an armshake. He holds back, though, and I can see that his answer is dependent on this.

I grip his forearm, just below the elbow, wrapping my hand tightly around it.

"Your dad will get it," I say, trying to keep the giddy out of my voice. I'm bubbling over twofold—this right here is our first armshake. Ever.

Plus, he's the first domino. Kent's the one that sends the rest of them over.

And right before my own two eyes, I watch the balance tip in my favor.

42

8:00 P.M., SUNDAY

"Why couldn't we just drop it into each roof's rainwater drainage pipes?" Ter offers. "Seems easy enough."

Ter would make that suggestion. The Trump Card filters their rainwater before it gets rationed. "Most of the sickhouses are older buildings, Ter," I tell him, trying not to let on that by "older" buildings, I really mean "poorer." "It's the same filtration system as the 'Racks. We do it ourselves, with sand. Put the medicine through the system and you'll end up with decent drinking water, but not exactly a cure."

He goes quiet. "Didn't realize that," he mumbles.

"That, and people need to think it's the cure, or who knows if they'll take it. They might not drink it beforehand, and that's the only way it'll protect against the poison."

Nodding, everyone is quiet for a moment.

"We could route it like a roofrace," Jones says as he looks down at a map of the Ward projected onto the floor. "Except . . . instead, we'd all start—and end—on a different building. How many sickhouses are there?" He pauses, then realizes something. "Do we even know how many people are sick?"

"Just around eight hundred, I think," I answer quickly. DI stats come in handy so rarely, and information like that is kept under wraps. Especially with a population of only a few thousand. "As for sickhouses—twenty, each with about fifty beds."

That I know from my time spent searching for Aven.

"Some beds must be empty, then," Jones says. We all go silent. Statute One, ruthless and irrational as it is, served its function: it reduced the sick population.

"So that makes . . ." Ter does the math in his head. "Around forty patients in each sickhouse."

Jones nods. "Okay. What if we have your doctor friend," he says, nodding to me, "put the cure in packages? We could make rooftop drop-offs at each sickhouse. Then we'd just have to divvy those up between the four of us and make up routes according to distance and what our individual mobiles can do."

Kent, Ter, and I all exchange blown-away looks, because I don't think any of us thought Jones had that in him. Just as I'm about to chime in, remind everyone that my Rimbo might still be out of commission, we hear a noise coming from the outside.

It's got to be Benny. . . .

I jump up and run to the window, peeking around the corner. I didn't realize it, the thought of seeing him—it's like new air fills up my lungs. As though it's been years, not hours. He'd probably scowl if I told him this because he's not one for cheese, but with him on my side . . . there ain't nothing that feels impossible.

When I see his white, wiry head of hair bob past, I rush out the archway and half tackle him. And when he sees me, his eyes go wide, then they narrow. He squints. Drops his bag. Covers his mouth, and then laughs until he cries, arms open.

For someone who doesn't hug, when Benny gets ahold of me, he keeps a pretty tight grip. But then again, so do I. "You're going to be the death of me, Renata," he says into my curls.

I laugh but shake my head. "Sure hope not," I answer.

"I'd have it no other way."

At that—I can't help it—I'm crying, and it's not from sadness.

Benny drapes his arm over me and we walk down the narrows, back to the Vault. But just as we're about to step inside, he slows down. Stops. "Renata," he says, and I turn to face him.

"What is it?"

I don't like his tone. It's too grave, considering that he just learned I'm alive.

"It's about your mobile. I wasn't able to uncover anything, but I returned to the first roof to see if anyone had video footage of the race with their comm. Turns out someone did. And you're not going to like what I saw."

"What did you see . . . ?" I ask, tripping over the words as they leave my tongue. I don't know what I would do with more bad news. . . . I can only handle so much.

"The footage showed Derek. Underneath your Rimbo. Right near the Plan B wiring. He's the one who tampered with the mobile, not Kent."

My arms drop. My breathing stops. My own heart knifes me in the gut.

He tried to kill *me?*

It doesn't make sense—*Derek kissed me.* Something is missing, some piece of information. "Are you sure?" I whisper.

Benny nods, but he doesn't avoid my eyes. That's how I know how sure he is.

When we walk back into the sanctuary, we're quiet. Solemn.

I don't believe it. But I have to. Benny wouldn't lie. *There's something I don't know.* I'm praying that I'm right about that. And until I know what that something is, *if* there is a something at all, I have to keep myself sane. Focus on the moment at hand.

The other racers tip their chins to him, even Kent. Because Benny's a champ no matter how you slice it, and he gets respect even if he's *my* mech.

We bring him up to speed, and when he hears the part about my being a mole, he says, "Renata. Did you honestly expect me to not notice you installing that filter before each race? I knew what it did, and had my suspicions about who it was for. But the search for freshwater has always been an honorable one."

While grumbling to myself, pretty sure I've gone red in the

face, I think I see Ter look at me. Reconsider how much he hates me . . . Maybe.

Jones tells him about the plan so far, and Benny nods, agreeing that it's a good one—until we get to the part where I don't have a mobile. Callum even offered to let me take his before I left; I had to tell him what happened to it at that point, though I'd been avoiding it. He took the news pretty well, though he did say telling his mom was going to be the worst part. Then he actually said that he was "just glad I was safe." It was pretty big of him.

"Do you think you can have it ready?" I ask Benny. He could do it. With anyone else that kind of request would be impossible.

Benny touches his chin, scratching his whiskers. "I think so."

Then, "Yes. Yes, I believe so," he says, surer.

For the next hour, the five of us grapple over maps, divvying up routes.

"I call this building," Kent says, pointing his finger over Quad Two, and we all look at one another like he's nuts. When he adds, "My dad's sickhouse," we understand, and drop our heads, quiet.

Still, we can't let Kent take his dad's building. He drives a Honda. Souped-up, yes. But it's got no speed over the water, and we tell him so. His face flushes. Says he wants Jones to do it for him—but that doesn't work either. The two of them drive basically the same mobile.

"Terrence. You promise you'll get it to him?" Kent insists when we decide Ter's the only one who can do the job. Since he'll be taking the Cloud—and the Cloud can cross Central Bay—he's getting all the northern quads. Including Kent's dad. The mobile's not as fast as ours, but she's good with distance, and sickhouses up north are few and far between. Most are in Midtown, in Quads Five and Six.

"Yeah, man," Ter says, sincere. "I got it covered."

If only that were the last thing Kent goes head-to-head on, though.

We argue over every detail:

Whose mobile is *actually* faster.

How to drop off the packages: out the floor latch, or by slowing down and tossing them out the moonroof.

If we should all start at once, or stagger the start times.

We bang our heads together over each possible outcome, and when that's done, we get to the real hard stuff: calculating headings between roof jumps. But with Benny and Ter here, they're able to breeze through the math, so soon it looks like the worst is over.

"Wait," Ter says, and he points to a building in Quad Six. "We're forgetting one thing."

I see where he's looking and shake my head. "It hasn't been forgotten." Standing in front of the map, I black out that spot with my shadow. "Ward Hope is mine."

The guys give me the same look they had for Kent.

"But it isn't on your route," Benny says, confused, and he passes his finger in the air over the zigzagging line I've been assigned.

I was hoping no one would mention the hospital until after I'd made the delivery, but no such luck. As I glance at

Kent, something in my gut warns me to tread lightly. He's not going to like this.

"And it isn't going to be. The Ward Hope drop-off has to be done first, anyway. It's not like we can just dump a package on the hospital roof and expect that it will make it to the patients. Drugs need to be administered. So Callum had the idea to add the serum to their water supply. Kind of like what you suggested at first, Ter," I say, nodding at him. "But it has to be added after the water is filtered, and before it's rationed. Callum's showed me maps of where it needs to go. Then, during nightly rations and when nurses change IV bags, everyone will get it."

Quickly, Kent looks up. Soft all of a sudden. "I'd like some too."

Here it is. This is what my gut was warning me about. Knowing he's not going to like why I've got to say no makes my blood pump a little bit faster—everything is so fragile. We can't do this without him.

"First off," I say evenly, "it isn't made yet. Callum's working on that as we speak. Second, it isn't going to be dosed per person. Callum knows exactly how many people there are in the HBNC wing, and he's making one whole batch that he'll give to me. The cure will get dosed properly in the rationing pipes. If you take out even a tablespoon, that'll be one less drop for everyone else. And then the meds may not work." I look at Terrence, hoping for some backup, but he can't help with this.

Kent jerks back, then strides up to me. Gets in my face. "This is brack and you know it." The muscles in his neck ripple out, clenched tight.

"It's n-not," I stammer, and look around, but no one has a life raft to throw me. "I'm sorry."

The tension in the Vault puts everyone quiet.

Jones and Ter stand, ready to leave, but I don't think anyone wants to end on that note. And no one wants to go up against Kent either, so I'm on my own.

I wish I could tell him different. We'd made progress, armshake and all. Why is it that everything I decide ripples out in ways I'd never imagined? Even the good choices, if those exist, have a way of hurting someone. Sorrier than he'd believe, I watch him pass through the archway made of femurs.

His whole body's hardened like a boulder—for a moment I worry that he won't help us anymore. Quickly, so he can hear, I say to the others, "Callum will show you guys how the cure works once you guys get there. I'll comm you the address." I tap my wrist before everyone steps out into the night.

The city is quieter than before, the revelry's died some, but not that much. It seems everyone's got their windows open tonight, hollering between apartments or sitting in fire escapes. It's a night unlike any other.

I follow the guys out onto the narrows, expecting Ter to be waiting for me so maybe we could talk. But he hasn't—I'm alone.

I'm not alone.

Waiting, back up against a building, is Kent. He's holding in his rage, I can see that clearly. Whether or not he lets it loose all depends on my answer—and I still can't tell him what he wants to hear.

"One more time, I'll ask you," he growls. I look at him and step away. Didn't know his black eyes could get any blacker, but that's what they do. The look he gives me could cause earthquakes. Put a 9.0 on the Richter.

"I—I can't," I stammer, my back pressed against brick.

Kent throws his fist into the building—I jump to the side. He's an animal, roaring away his anger, but under it, I can hear something else: he's sad. Plain and simple. He kicks the narrows, storms away, and I slide onto the planked sidewalk, feeling guilty even after all that.

When I can't handle the sound of my heart in my ears any longer, I force my feet to lift me.

They hammer against the wooden sidewalk.

They don't wait to see if more guilt catches up.

43

8:50 P.M., SUNDAY

No one will recognize me.

I bring the scissors to the final, frizzed-out black corkscrew that's left on my head. The last man standing. The kinky lock falls to the floor, a fuzzy caterpillar, and joins the rest of the wiry mess that's piled up there.

The last thing I do is nick off the fuzzy patches that stand taller than their neighbors, brushing against my fingers when they shouldn't. Then—

I'm done. Finished.

I exhale. I drop the scissors in the sink and rub my scalp clean. Stowaway strands float off in shaggy, black clouds. And then, between my feet . . . I see the bathroom floor.

And I choke.

It's a crime scene. Except, instead of blood, my curls.

Clinging for dear life to every possible surface—the toilet seat, the towels, the shower curtain. My hair is the victim. *I'm* the victim. All of that is me. Little pieces of myself, dead on the floor.

I want them back. I know I've trash-talked those fuzz balls before, but I was wrong. You don't get more than one Trademark Characteristic, and mine's gone.

I pull my eyes away, tell myself that hair grows. Remind myself why I did it, who I'm doing it for. A lifetime supply of hair-dyeing sessions and eye rolls, and getting to hear Aven say "good skill" before every race.

But it still hurts.

Then I look up.

And if I thought the crime scene was down there, I was deeply mistaken.

Gripping the porcelain sink, I gasp. My heart falls down a dozen flights of stairs.

I wish I didn't care, but . . . *whoa.* Tears brew behind my eyes and I have to blink them away so I can examine my handiwork. Who gave a sixteen-year-old the scissors anyway?

I tip my chin to the side, brush my hand over my scalp and down to the nape of my neck.

My head . . . it's so much rounder than I thought. Darker, too. And my forehead. I have a really, really wide forehead. I never knew that. *Am I ugly?* I never thought I was, but whoever's in that mirror, it isn't me. She's hardly a she at all.

But then I see my eyes—actually *see* my eyes—and I wonder why that feels new. It's probably an optical illusion (less hair, more eyeball). They look darker. Like the leather of my drowned Hessians. Yes, they still sort of look half-closed, but in an entirely new way.

Very come-hither.

I like them, I think, and as I do, I realize how funny it sounds in my head.

I've always had these eyes. *Has Derek noticed these babies?* The thought dissolves straightaway, though. Leaves me heavy. Even the writhing is gone. In its place, something still. Noiseless. Dull and worn-down, like broken glass churned up by the Strait. Nothing sharp, nothing raw. He's no longer Derek, whoever that was.

He's an obstacle. Same as Kitaneh.

Taking one last glimpse in the mirror, I tip up my chin at the girl I don't recognize. She's stronger. She's not weak in the knees.

Not for a guy who'd cheat on his wife of a few centuries.

He's older than the Statue of Liberty, for crying out loud.

I step out into the main room. Callum scans me like a portrait, from all angles.

"It's gone," he says at last, gulping back his shock. Then: "It's perfect."

Perfect? For a moment I think it's a compliment—I feel the blood as it beelines for my cheeks. And then I realize what he means. . . . It *is* perfect. No one will recognize me.

He walks to his desk and lugs over another rubber sack. Smaller this time. Black. "Turn around," he says, his voice suddenly serious. I do, and he tucks my arms under both straps. "There you go. Enough for the entire wing."

This sack isn't heavy. Certainly not as heavy as the red one. But I feel the weight of it with every cell in my body. My muscles want only to put the thing down. I'm wrong, it is heavy.

Too heavy.

Not too heavy. Aven's in there.

"Do you want any more soup?" he asks, pointing to the bowl of rehydrated broth I left sitting on the moldy mattress box. He had it ready and waiting for me when I got back, and I just about kissed his feet. "And don't forget to fill up your canteen before you go. I don't know how you're still standing, to be perfectly honest."

Now he reminds me of Benny. Rolling my eyes, I touch the closed cut at my temple and then examine my arms and legs. I shrug.

From a chest of drawers pushed up against the far wall, he pulls out a folded pair of light blue scrubs.

"Here. It won't get you in, but it's something. Avoid the main entrances—the receptionists get updates from the DI and they'll have seen that you're wanted," he says, pushing the pile into my hands. "I wish I could come with you. . . ."

"You've got to make the cure," I say, punching him in the shoulder. I hardly know what I'm doing when I catch myself pulling him in for a hug. It's like my arms just horseshoe-magnet themselves around his body. "We're a team. Don't worry. I'll find a way in."

Callum laughs, nervous, and pats my back. Just as I start to wonder when he'll be comfortable around me, it happens: the muscles in his shoulders unwind; his chest loosens.

He relaxes.

"This is it," he promises, chin resting on the top of my shorn head. "You're the only one who could pull it off. It'll work."

I don't know what to say back. . . . I refuse to let failure sound so easy, so possible, by saying something weak like, *I hope so.* But I'm not about to go jinxing it by saying, *You're right*, either.

Silence, then, I think. *He'll know my answer's in the silence.* And without knowing when or how this trust came about, I let his breathing, steady and sure, give my heart the rhythm it can't seem to find on its own.

44

9:30 P.M., SUNDAY

Ward Hope Hospital's windows glow like animal eyes. A beast that's eaten Aven, and I have to kill it from the inside. I check my cuffcomm and run a hand over the base of my skull, warming myself. A sheen of sweat has gathered on my scalp, lost in whatever's left of my hair.

Thirty minutes—I've got thirty minutes to get the serum into the right spot in the filtration system before evening rations. *I better find a way in fast.* If I waste too much time, I'll be caught by the night attendant.

As I jog closer to the staff-only entrance, I spot an emergency transport sub bubbling up to the surface, red-and-white lights blaring as they spin. A shiver slides behind my ears and I jump back, out of sight behind a garbage Dumpster along the boardwalk.

Brack. The sub's drawing too much attention.

I'd hoped to find a nurse on a cigarette break or something. . . . It'll do, though.

Crouched low behind the Dumpster, I slide my way closer to the sub. Its rectangular airlock hatch opens, and a Bouncer lifts himself up, onto the dock. Must be an HBNC emergency—they've found someone who's contagious.

But the Bouncer moves slow. Takes his sweet time, like he's got no place to be.

Only one reason why he'd be doing that—whoever else is in that transport sub has got no place to be either.

'Cause they're dead.

Not at all their good luck . . . but definitely mine.

I jog toward the submobile and climb onto it, then down into the hatch.

Sure enough, I see a stretcher with a white sheet laid over it. That's when I rethink that bit about luck. There's nothing lucky about this. Lifting the sheet, I gag—

It's a man. Older. Frail and slight, except that his chest has ballooned out. He looks like a pregnant woman, but one whose baby formed over where the lungs should be.

Wriggling myself onto the stretcher, I position the sack between my knees and I lift the man's arm. When I touch his skin, it's still warm, and my whole body cringes. Swallowing the acid from my stomach, I try to shift his torso. Pretty quickly though, I realize I can't. He's too heavy.

I reach for the sack and slide back off the stretcher. Though I'd rather go facedown on the stretcher, if I do that, I'll never be able to get the sheet over us. So I loop my arms under his shoulders and shimmy myself under him. With the sack positioned behind his kneecaps, I lay my back on the stretcher.

Last, I shift the rest of the man's limbs so he's directly over me, and even the sheet over the both of us.

I'm gonna vomit. . . .

It's his weight, the way it presses down on me. And his hair. I can feel each strand shake against my nose when I move. I can't breathe. I don't even want to—the man may not have the scent of death on him yet, but I can smell it anyway. I've got too good of an imagination. My stomach fights to free itself from my body. I close my eyes, try to will away the nausea.

Against the submobile's roof, the clang of footsteps.

More clanging as the Bouncer makes his way down the ladder. The foot of the stretcher jostles in his hands as he lifts me and the dead man up through the airlock. "Heavy guy," I hear him grunt as we go higher.

At the top, the stretcher starts to move sideways—he must be pushing it onto the dock. And then, after a few more moments, the light through the sheet goes bright.

We've been wheeled into the hospital . . . through the hospital. The Bouncer doesn't stop.

Now, the dangerous part. I keep myself so still, I feel like I could be dead along with the man.

No one better decide to examine him, or they'll be mighty surprised.

I hear a door click open. I hear it slam shut. Again, click open. Again, slam shut.

In an instant, I've got goosebumps. The room is freezing.

I'm in the morgue.

I wait just a few moments longer before attempting to get off the stretcher, just to make sure the Bouncer is gone. Soon as I know I'm alone in here—the only sounds come from the air-conditioning that's keeping the bodies refrigerated—I push the man off.

As fast as I can, I snake myself away from the stretcher.

I'm so close to retching, I'm actually dizzy. So without air 'cause I didn't want to smell him, or his hair. Everything spins. I'm shivering down to my hair follicles.

But I'm in. I've made it in.

Slipping out of the cold room, I try to find my bearings without wasting too much time in the hallway. Callum drilled the schematics into my memory before I left, but he never showed me how to get to—or from—the morgue, so I'm at a loss. My only guess is that I'm in the contagious ward . . . assuming they store the contagious and noncontagious bodies together.

I follow the hallway straight for a few minutes. Eventually, I'll have to hit a stairwell. And if I am where I think I am, I should be able to take it to the rooftop, where the filtration system is.

As I keep on, I hug the wall though I know it'll do no good if someone recognizes me. Voices echo through the corridor—I don't like it. It's too loud. They bounce around and I start to think I've come upon an area for visitors. Like the waiting room.

I slide up to a corner, and just as I was afraid of, I see the waiting room. Quickly, I duck away, afraid of being seen.

But when I peer around again—

Walking up to the receptionist's desk, hair glinting like stupid, useless copper pennies . . .

Derek. *He's here. . . . Why is he here?* I pull myself away, out of sight, but down to my toenails, I can feel him. And for some reason, I can't stop my confused head from thinking it should be happy. I've made a habit out of worshipping him.

He wanted you to give up on Callum, I remind myself. *On everyone.*

Still, my body betrays me. I peek my head out into the hallway and search for him.

He turns.

Our eyes meet. *Idiot, move!* But it's too late. He cocks his head.

Cursing myself for being so weak, I pull myself away for a third time. *It's okay. . . . He didn't recognize you.* But I don't know that for sure, and I won't forget the sack I'm wearing on my back.

The serum. Aven. Everyone in Ward Hope Hospital.

I check my cuffcomm: only twenty minutes left. *Brack.* I've wasted too much time already.

Ungluing my legs, I shuffle back the way I came, brisk, but at a hospital-appropriate pace. If Derek is following, I don't hear the footsteps.

Moments later, I pass the morgue on my right and I keep going. Then, at the end of the corridor—the stairwell I was searching for.

In I go.

I clamber up it, all the way, until I reach the top. Breathless, I open the door.

45

9:42 P.M., SUNDAY

Just like I remember, the rooftop is a steel maze of gutters and piping. I hear city pigeons, hidden away. They're cooing, shelved for the night, deep in the filtration system's nooks. As I step over a line of tubes, their warbling follows after me, but none of the birds move.

Calling to mind Callum's schematics, I start searching for the HBNC wing's water funnel. The most western one. Up here, the roof slopes in sharply angled geometric shapes, kind of like they dug upside-down pyramids into the ground. It was designed that way to increase the roof's surface area and catch as much rainwater as possible. And though I'm all turned around up here, landmarks are easy to find. To my left, the Strait—West.

Overhead, the moon shines a flashlight on every surface she can. You'd think there were a hundred of her, it's so bright.

Altogether too much wattage for a night like tonight, me up here sneaking a miracle drug into hospital water.

When the ground beneath shifts, slopes down, I know I'm at the funnel. I start sliding, no traction. I quicken my step, feet clanging against metal, tugged along by gravity.

At the bottom of the pyramid, a hollow square chute.

Can't just drop the sack down, or it'd get diluted in the giant tank and be useless to everyone. It needs to go into tonight's rations. Which means down I go into the water tanks. Not at all excited for that. I pull off Callum's scrubs, wearing my own leggings and buckled shirt underneath, then stuff them into the dry sack he gave me. I seal it shut, and it goes back in my belt pocket.

Here goes.

Filling myself with air, I hold my nose and swing the black pack around to my chest so it hangs frontside. Then I crab-walk to the square. It's pretty wide—good for my backside—and I release my grip.

Down I go: half slide, half bump, half free fall.

No chance to enjoy the free-fall bit though, because of the first two. Mostly the second. Clutching the rubber pack like a baby, head down, I notice too late my arm unwrapping itself.

One elbow smacks the side of the chute; I ping-pong—metal side to metal side, sending my right knee smacking too. My joints throb. I howl twice, then shut up. *What if someone is down there?* That thought puts the buzz in my blood. Every nerve starts humming. Callum said the room should stay empty between the morning attendant and the night shift, but still. It's the water tank, after all. The place is a gold mine, and people steal.

No time to come up with a plan if someone is down there.

Soon my stomach starts to really feel the drop, to rise up into my chest, and that's when I come flying out the chute—

Back in the water.

Cannonballing myself, unfiltered rainwater splashes up around me like a tent. Toe to head I'm soaked. *Don't let go*—I cling to the rubber sack like a life raft.

Which it is, in its way.

I'm dunked underwater; I kick, I sew my mouth tight, but I wasn't ready for the fall so I'm a moment too late. I push myself to the surface, taking gulps of rainwater, using only my legs. The pack in my arms may be weighing me down, but I'm not letting go.

I kick and I kick, and then—

Air.

I gasp, eyes darting around the giant space. I'm looking for a way out, making sure no one's here.

Behind me, I see what I'm looking for and I exhale.

A ladder.

I swing the pack around to my back again, freeing my arms to swim. Limbs pull the water, and I frog swim through the tank. The rainwater is cold, but it ain't nearly as bad as the Hudson; otherwise I would've grabbed Callum's wet suit. This is nothing. I cross the tank easily, legs burning only a little.

At the ladder, I grip the rails and pull myself up.

Okay, maybe not nothing. My legs wobble—my knee hurts so bad I can actually feel the creaking as it bends. I'm almost sent tumbling back into the tank, but catch myself, and I come down the other side, no incidents.

At the bottom, I collapse to all fours, dripping wet.

I need to breathe.

I count to five to collect myself. One—peel myself out of the wet clothes. Two—back into the scrubs. Three—find the exact spot Callum wants me to put the serum. Four—slow down my heart rate, 'cause this I *have* to get right. If I put the serum in the wrong place, this whole thing will have been for nothing. Five—see nothing, and freak out, frantically scanning the room. I don't need to hit six. Just like Callum had described, I see it: *the robot arm.*

A nickname, but I see it's pretty accurate, and it makes me laugh. Barely.

From one side of the tank, a super-sized, metal-plated arm one might imagine belonging to a robot. Of course, it ain't an arm. It's just the main pipe. But the similarities are uncanny. It starts out thick, steel sheets bolted in places. That's where the water gets filtered, Callum said. Not with sand, like us at the 'Racks, but with metal meshing and chemicals.

Attached to the arm is a wheel. Don't open it.

I see it, a great big captain's wheel. *Check, do not open.* That would be bad. The wheel opens and closes the tank valve. Opening frees the water into the pipes. That's the attendant's job, and he does it only three times a day to keep the rest of the water safe in the tank.

I follow the steel arm, since the wheel is not what I'm looking for. It extends downward, hovering over the floor. Then it starts to narrow, shrinking and shrinking, until the material changes, connects to a different part of the arm.

Jackpot . . . sorta.

The basin.

After the attendant turns the captain's wheel, that basin right there then gets filled with everyone's rations. Then it's inspected. That is also *not* where the serum is going. But it's close.

I walk to the basin and pull off the sack.

A click, and I jolt upright at what sounds like the ID scanner at work. Someone's unlocked the door. I look at my cuffcomm—less than fifteen minutes. The attendant shouldn't be here. . . .

Quickly, picking up the sack again, I follow the basin to the pipe that it feeds into—that's where I need to get the serum.

My hands move like two hummingbirds, fingers flying to twist off the cap at the top of the pack. Across the room, footsteps echo, somewhere behind the water tank. I'm out of sight, hidden by the robot arm, but there's no time to waste.

Soon as the rubber pack is open, I hold it over the pipe's mouth and position it. Then, I let it pour.

"Ren—"

That voice—

He's here. Even timbre, warm, though I can hear the crackle of frustration in it. Derek's found me. . . . I still don't look up. The sack continues to empty into the pipe.

"Please, Ren. Where are you?" he calls again, insistent. I can hear it—he's behind the water tank, on the opposite side of the room—he don't see me. I won't let him see me.

I tilt the sack's mouth so every bit drains out, then crane my neck to find Derek.

When I don't see him, I watch as the last of the serum

rushes away, following the line of tubing. A few drops get stuck on the sides, but I don't worry—tonight's rations will pick up whatever was left behind. When it's all gone and the sack is nothing but rubber, I throw it over my shoulders.

"Down the drain," I type into my comm—our cheesy code for things going off without a hitch—and I send the message off to Callum.

Ducking myself under the basin and freezing, I strain my ears to listen for more footsteps. I need to know where not to step. Except, I hear nothing.

The serum gurgles down the pipe. Stops right before the next valve.

There it'll wait till the attendant gets here. Twelve minutes from now.

I've gotta get out. But it occurs to me—if Derek came up from the opposite side of the room, my only exit is probably there too. *I can't let him see me.*

I have to leave. *Now.*

Crouching under the arm, I shuffle to the tank's wall. My back hugs it close, but doesn't touch. One brush up against the metal cylinder and it'll squeak. Keeping my footsteps light underneath me, I follow the base. When I pause, listen, I think I hear the scuffle of footsteps, but I can't tell where it's coming from. I keep rounding the base, until I have the exit sign in sight.

I don't wait—I make a run for it. My soles scrape the concrete floor as I close the distance. With my nerves amped and roaring, pushing me to the door, only one question takes over my mind: *Would he hurt me?*

46

9:51 P.M., SUNDAY

My feet fly down one flight and then another, rounding each corner with a jump. He's behind me, barreling down the stairwell. I don't stop on the fifth floor, or the fourth, or the third. But when I hit the second floor, Aven's floor, that's when I pause—*I have to see her.*

Checking my cuffcomm, I've still got nine minutes till rations go out. Probably a few more before someone stops by to change her IV. Which means she won't be awake. . . .

That pause is all the time it takes for Derek to catch up. He slams against my back. The momentum hurtles me into the metal door, and an ache, sharp and hot, spreads down my arm. "Damn you—" I bite my lip to keep from whimpering.

Derek pulls away. Props himself against the wall as I slide to the floor, slack-muscled.

"It's you," he whispers. "I thought it was you. But you look so . . . different." He eyes my not-hair, kneeling in front of me. Makes like he's about to touch my shoulder. "Kitaneh . . . the crash?"

"Don't," I snap, recoiling, like he's made of pure fire. "I know what you did to my Rimbo. And I know about Kitaneh. *And I know about you.* You don't get to touch me."

The way his face contorts, you'd think I was the one made of fire. That *he'd* just been burned. Derek closes his eyes, turns away. "What happened to your Rimbo—it was an accident. . . ."

"What? *That I survived?*"

He shakes his head and collapses down onto the stairs, keeping his back to me. I don't like it. I may not want him touching me, but I do deserve to see his face right now.

"You were supposed to see the malfunction before the race. You weren't supposed to race at all," he murmurs.

"Look at me." Angry echoes of my words travel up and down the stairwell. "Tell me to my face why I almost died because of you."

Derek shifts uncomfortably. With his back up against the wall, he says, "My brother and his wife live on the Isle. They learned what that doctor Callum was up to. They informed us. I never wanted you hurt. . . . And I certainly never wanted you dead."

I exhale, realizing I've been holding my breath this whole time. What he's said . . . maybe I should feel comforted by it. He didn't want me dead, after all.

It's just the other hundreds of sick people he'd see murdered.

Not quite enough, I'm afraid.

"Your brother and his wife," I start. I'm remembering the photo album—there were six of them. "Are they . . . are they like you?"

"You mean are they still alive after too many years? Yes. They are."

Now he looks at me, and I wonder how his eyes can seem so damned soft while he's telling me these things. I'm suddenly very aware of my weakness.

"And what about your *wife*?"

I can hear him swallow. The muscles in his throat tense up, and he looks away. "What about her?" he asks. Each word drags, ending and beginning like some far-off thunder.

Forget this. I shouldn't be here, drilling Derek about his epically eternal love life.

Not with Aven so close, about to wake up.

I don't wait for him to answer—don't even want to hear it. I lift myself up from the linoleum and reach for the door to the second floor.

Before I have a chance to turn the knob, he spits out, "How are you going to get those patients follow-up doses? Most of them will need more. Did you think of that?"

"Callum . . . He developed a serum so that it requires only one dose," I tell Derek, pushing myself through the door just in time to hear him say, "That's not possible," in a whisper.

I can sense his awe as he steps closer. "We've tried. There's no substance in existence that allows it. . . ."

I exist.

I make for Aven's room.

"Ren, wait!" he calls after, but I don't hear any more—

I'm already gone, rushing down the corridor.

He follows. And when I pause a few feet from her door, he's only steps behind me. I feel him reach for me, and I also feel him stop. His palm hovers over my shoulder before he pulls it away. "Go inside," he says softly.

I turn around—

He says it like he's been to see her.

I turn the handle and walk in, every atom in the room feeling different to me than the last time I was here. *Good different.* Even the smell.

Flowers. Real, live flowers. Must've been expensive, too. Yellower than Aven's hair, shaped like cups on six-petaled saucers. Soil grown probably from a rooftop hothouse in one of the northern quads, where fewer people live. They sit on her night table in a pretty, red-painted pot, roots and all, smelling too delicious; I want to eat them like food. *Who . . . ?*

"Renny?"

I snap my head toward the bed, and watch, no words, as Aven looks at me from her pillow, pale as the linens she's been sleeping on. She squints her eyes to see better. Using her elbows, she props herself up. Squints some more.

"That you?"

She's awake.

She's awake, she's awake—I blink a hundred times, and each time it's true—she's awake. She shouldn't be, not yet, not for another three minutes, but she is. I had no time to expect this moment. It's as though the world, broken into bits around me, has suddenly pieced itself together again.

"It's me, Feathers. It's me," I say, hushed, and run to her bedside. Lean over her. Run my hand across her forehead, pale and bluish under the harsh light. Then her white-blond hair. She looks up at me with eyes that have never seemed so hazel. They're the color of the canals on a good day, sunlit and golden-green.

"Where'd your hair go?" she asks, rubbing her eyes at me like I'm an alien. Then, her face softens, and she lies back in bed. "You're still so pretty."

I laugh, and choke down a sob, new water at my eyes. Good water.

Only a few times before has my heart not felt like it fit in my body. Like it belonged in a bigger body, a giant's, maybe. One with a rib cage that had more compartment space to it. It's a strange feeling of feeling too much. Wanting to cram it all in and then make room for some more.

"You're just saying that," I mumble, and I kiss her knuckles over and over again. "You, on the other hand. Even in a hospital bed, look at you. Blooming prettier than those flowers." I nod in their direction, all trumpety and yellow.

"Aren't they wonderful? Derek brought them," she says, grinning, pointing back at him.

Derek was here . . . when she woke up? And here I'd forgotten he was even in the room.

"He was here when I woke up! They were the first things I opened my eyes to."

I can land on a possible explanation, but it makes no sense. If he wouldn't give the water to anyone else . . .

"Did he give you a medicine, Aven?" I ask, and look back at

him standing by the door. He's running a hand through his curls, now he's avoiding my eyes.

Aven nods. Bites her lip. "I think he likes you," she whispers, and winks.

I don't know what to say to that. With all my cells, I want to hate him. *I do hate him.* My heart wants something entirely different. But this still isn't enough.

Just as I think the question, *Why—?* Aven opens her mouth with an answer.

"He thought you were dead, Renny. He said he was going to miss you, and that since you told him *I* was your favorite part of life—which I thought was very silly—he wanted to get to know me. Like he was getting to know you, through me."

I don't know what to think anymore, but I'm happy. Happier than I've ever been, maybe in my whole life.

Our microscopic futures . . . they're ours again.

"I can't stay," I tell Aven, looking down. "But I'm coming back tonight. After I'm done, I'm coming for you. I'll sneak in. I'd take you with me now, but you're still too weak." I pause, and take her hand in mine. "I'm about to do something big . . . something almost impossible."

I want her to know the rest—the governor's plan, and what we're doing to stop it—but I gotta leave before the attendants realize I broke in. The hospital will go on lockdown and I'll never get out.

Aven nods like she understands. "If you say it's impossible, it must be hard." Reaching for the necklace dangling against the bed, she notices the second penny. "Where'd you get this one?" she asks. Then she looks up at me, grinning all the way to her eyes again. "Is it from another boy?"

I open her palm and laugh into it, kissing her lifeline.

"It is."

Aven eyes Derek still standing by the door. "I bet he's not cuter than that one."

Oh my goodness. My sister . . . who is she?

I can't wait to find out.

"You still wear this," she mumbles to herself, touching the penny she gave me. When she looks up, she sighs. "And I'm still holding you to your promise. If I'm going to be healthy soon, you'd better stick around long enough to see it."

Without hesitation, "I promise. No dying allowed," and I stand up. Head for the door.

All the way there, I battle a fear so old, it's beginning to feel like a friend. That someday, the only promise I ever make might become one I can't keep.

47

"**W**e need to leave. Now," I say to Derek in the HBNC hallway.

He grabs my wrist, turns for the stairwell we just
came from, but I pause. Any minute now, rations will go out.
If more patients wake up as fast as Aven did, the nurses will
put it together that the water in the HBNC wing might've been
tampered with. And the first place they'll look for the culprit
is the stairwell leading to the western water tank.

"No . . . I don't think that's a good idea." I shake my head,
looking toward the entry doors.

"And you think that's a better one?" he scoffs. "Nuh-uh.
We're taking the stairwell." He tugs me in the opposite direction.

"Derek—you're gonna have to trust me on this one. You
can't catch the virus, right?"

"No . . ." He narrows his eyes at me.

"Okay. Well—I have a secret. Neither can I." I spin on my heel and start down the corridor. Hearing no footsteps behind, I turn around to find Derek standing there, looking like I bludgeoned him with a hammer. "I'm going through the other ward," I call back. "You can come or not. Your choice."

He jogs to me, in a daze, and we keep on going straight, since I'm the one in the scrubs.

Together, we exit the noncontagious ward, crossing from one end to the other. At the red double doors, I glance around, making sure no one sees us. One hand to the lettering that reads "Contagious," one hand on the handle, I swing the doors open and usher Derek in behind me.

Then, we run.

Through the corridor. Past the glass and the patients behind plastic. Past the girl who looks like Aven. Down the stairwell.

At the staff exit, I shove open the door. Too much moonlight waits there, like a spotlight.

I'm sent careening onto the narrows, unready for a night without cover.

"Follow me," I say, pulling Derek toward Mad Ave.

I want to get the hell out of here—I'm meeting with the other racers in thirty minutes—but first, I need to know where Derek stands. What kind of person he is.

Would he try to stop me if he knew what we were planning?

We sprint through the narrows, me in front, mulling over that question. But there's only one thread to pull that could unknot the others—Aven.

I slow down. Tug that first thread. "Why save her," I ask, panting, "and not the others?"

But Derek doesn't answer. His eyes are someplace else, tracing the curve of my scalp. I look away, embarrassed. "What? You ain't never seen a head before?"

He tears his gaze away, shakes off whatever feelings he had about me and my new do.

"Ren . . . that water," he begins, no louder than the waves splashing back and forth beneath our feet. "You saw the album. You know it's not just a cure. As soon as you turn it into one, the spring's other . . . *properties* . . . are in danger of being exposed, too."

"Immortality, Derek." I watch him, shifting and pacing along the narrows. "Call it what it is."

"Fine. Immortality, then," he says, and meets my eyes. "You found a way to make a cure with one dose. . . . I don't know how, but I believe you. And that's good. It doesn't change the facts, though—*everyone* will want it. First the water will be a cure, but once the people are healthy, it won't stop there. There will be wars. *More people will die fighting for the water than it could ever save.*"

"Maybe that was a good reason to keep it hidden in the past, but with Callum's serum . . . things are different, right? And it'd just be the Ward—you could help me get it out before the squadrons fly through."

"We follow rules, Ren. Rules that don't change on a case-by-case basis. Even when . . . feelings . . . are involved. Any one of us breaks those rules, our life is forfeited. Drinking the water may keep us from aging, but that doesn't mean that there aren't ways for us to die.

"Kitaneh and the others—they'll find out what happened here tonight," he says, pointing back to Ward Hope, "and they will come after you."

"And you'll let them."

He smacks his palm against the brick siding. "The Minetta must stay guarded! Life doesn't exist without death. We protect one, we're also protecting the other."

Nodding, "Oh, I get it now," I say coolly. "You'll *kill* to protect life. Makes perfect sense. Then why save Aven? Why not just let her die with the rest of them?"

"Ren . . ." he begins. Then he loosens, defeated, and it's as though he can hardly hold himself up. "I thought you were dead. And I'd only just begun to know you. To *see* you. Not the you that everyone else knows—but who you are when you're alone. You're not who I thought you were—you're even . . . *better*."

Right before my eyes, my heart undoes itself—I lean back against the brick. Under my feet, the narrows buck and sway and I tilt with them. "What are you saying?"

"I know what you saw. You saw the photos . . . but they're not what you think."

I look to his hand but see no wedding ring. He's never worn it in public, if he wears it at all.

"Kitaneh and I . . . we were married as part of a contract," Derek continues. "That's how things were done in the early days. It's a longer story. One for another time. But my point . . . When you kissed me, for the first time in ages—I felt something *like* love."

He falls into me then, head hung low, and catches the wall. "I'm not saying you love me. But . . . you love the right people.

I see that with Aven. And I thought that if you ever could, if *you* ever thought I was worth it—maybe it could be true. That I could be worth it."

I'm caught, bridged between both his arms. Frozen, listening as he tells me these things I never could've imagined he'd say. I want to reach for him. I don't let myself—*nothing's changed; I still don't understand him*—but in my mind, my hand is coiling itself in his bright hair. Next thing I know, it's no longer in my mind. I'm touching his scalp, tracing my fingers down his nape. His hair bristles.

His breath stops short; I like hearing that—*No.* Dropping my hand quickly, I fold my arms behind my back. I don't want to touch him. It just adds fuel to my weakness.

Derek's brown eyes hold me to the wall. "Ren, you live harder . . . you love harder than anyone I've met. I wanted to earn it. And then I thought you were gone, and that it was too late. For me. For me to love you back," he says. He drops his forehead against me so it's cradled by my neck.

My tongue is blank. In my mouth, no words. The thoughts I had—all stunned away. I vaguely recall not wanting this—*him*, but all I'm left with are my vertebrae—each one a trigger, counting down to *closer.*

"Saving Aven was like saving a part of you. The part that you loved the most. The part I wanted to get to know," he breathes, shaky.

Word by word, I'm unfolded. I wish my heart were made of paper, so I could write each one down where it belongs. As he traces his nose up the line of my neck, all the way to my ear, I know my heart will never be paper. Paper's way too quiet. Bullet rounds, maybe. Rapid-fire.

Then, he pulls away. He searches my face. Eyes my mouth, thirsty. Like he's never had a drop in his life. Leans in. With only millimeters to go, he stops. Miles and miles of millimeters, charged, electric power lines—"I don't want the same regret twice."

His lips are on mine, slow at first, hesitant, almost a tremble to them. Like he's afraid. A moment later, he's not. He's the tide under a megawatt moon and this kiss is the ocean. Surge, then rush. No end to it.

Until, *beep*—my cuffcomm trills.

Looking down, I've got a message:

Serum's made. Racers are here. Showed them Milo's stats. Where are you? Vials are almost all filled.

"*Brack*," I whisper. "I have to go."

Derek looks back at me, his face drawn and hard—I can see it in his eyes. He's read Callum's comm. "Please, Ren," he pleads, arm muscles tensed on either side of me. "I see what you're planning. Once the others find out, I don't know if I'll be able to stop them."

"Can I ask you a question, Derek?"

He searches my face, not sure what's coming. "Anything," he says finally.

"Forget the others. What do *you* think is right?"

"It's just not that simple. . . ."

I open my mouth, though I can't believe what I'm about to say. *What am I worth to him?* . . . If he was just telling me the truth before, then my next words should mean something.

"Earn me."

Derek looks up, runs a hand through the hair that's fallen in front of his face.

"You said that's what you wanted, right?" I go on. "Well, now you have your chance."

I wait to see his reaction, but his face stays hard and I read nothing. I'm not sure if I should speak these next words. . . . They make me feel like I'm standing out on the highest rooftop during a summer's lightning storm. Defenseless. But they also just might be exactly what he needs to hear.

"And I hope you do, Derek," I say, a stillwater calm to my voice that surprises even me. "Because I could have loved you. Once upon a time."

Spinning away from him, I don't wait to see his reaction to *that*. I continue along the narrows, and when I hear him call my name, I turn off my ears and my head. All the places I hurt. I rip the paper in my heart to shreds, and I dry my mouth of the kiss. That's harder, though. Salt water is everywhere. It's below my feet and it's behind my eyes. I run above it while wiping it from my face. I curse oceans, every one of them, until the moment my cuffcomm trills again.

?

That's all it reads.

Faster. I pump my legs so hard my breathing goes thick.

The other racers are waiting.

48

10:35 P.M., SUNDAY

In Callum's apartment, a shaky energy fills the room. Circling a glass basin: Callum, Kent, Jones, Terrence, all seated cross-legged on the floor in front of me.

"If I left now, I'd have time," Kent says as I walk in, eye-dropper in one of his hands, a small plastic tube in the other. A pile more of each lie at everyone's knees. Pointing to me, he adds, "But she gets to bring it to some girl she's not even related to?"

"There's no way you're getting all the way up north and back again before we start. Not even if you run. Your dad's on my route, man." Terrence's voice turns serious. "I'll get it to him. Swear."

The guys turn to look at me, and glancing around, I realize Benny's not here. Wanting to change the subject, I'm about to ask where he is, when one by one I watch as their eyes outline my new look—blue scrubs, no hair. Comments range from "Whoa" to "Different."

Boys really know how to drop a compliment.

Then, with his eyes back on a dropper, Kent growls, "You missed the best part."

Clearly, Kent was thrilled to get Callum's comm asking for help with filling up the eight hundred vials of serum.

"Where's Benny?" I ask Terrence, and search his face to see if he's forgiven me yet.

He doesn't look up, not even between drops. "He offered to bring the finished packages to our mobiles, since he's the only one with fins—ours are all roofed already. Save us a trip," he says.

For the bazillionth time, I realize how lucky I am to have Benny for my mech.

Looking for an opening in the circle, I decide to squeeze in next to Callum. I don't even try to sit next to Ter. If he needs more time, I'll give him more time. I just hope that he can forgive me before the race—it'll be dangerous, after all. *What if one of us don't . . . ?*

I push the thought away.

Callum moves over, making room for me to sit. Under his breath, he asks, "How is she?" as he hands me a dropper and a vial.

I give him a smile small enough that only he can see. No need for Kent to hear. "Awake," I answer. Our eyes meet, and I can see he knows how much more is behind that weak grin I'm giving him.

"Should we review the game plan?" Callum offers, screwing on the lid of the last tube in his pile. "I can quiz you if you comm me your maps."

They're gonna love that, I think, looking around at the others. Him. A West Isler. Taking the lead. Poor guy. He's been here, alone, for an extended period of time with a bunch of dragsters. What a deadly combo.

But the others say, "Thanks, man," and nod their heads like he's just offered them his kidney, and I realize something else: even with a pampered, silver-spoon-fed West Isle boy in the room, I'm still at the bottom of this totem pole.

Because I'm a girl who races.

Unbelievable.

Well, despite the boobs, I still have important things that need hearing—"Guys," I start, taking a breath. At my side my fist balls all on its own. My nails, sharp in my palm, make it feel like I'm holding fire. I won't let my voice crack when I say this, though I still can't believe it—Derek might not hurt me, but the other racers? And Kitaneh will have no problems doing away with any of us, me least of all.

"Before we do that, there's something you should know."

They all stop what they're doing and look at me. All except for Kent.

"We might have company out there," I tell them, fast.

Kent's eyes shoot up at that. "What?"

Waving him quiet, I go on. "Unfortunately, there are a few people who'd rather we didn't give out the cure, and I just don't know how far they'd go to stop us. They could be waiting for us." I pause. "At least four of them."

"Are they dangerous?" Jones asks, just a hint of fear in his voice coming through. He coughs—he heard it too. "So we can be prepared, is all. . . ."

I nod. "They're a threat, yes."

"Why the hell would anyone want to stop the cure from going out?" Ter shakes his head, glancing around the room.

I mumble, "Who knows," and shrug, but I'm sure if I told him that the cure was also the not-so-mythical fountain of youth, it might clear things up. Derek was right about that—accidentally handing out immortality would be bad on so many levels.

I change the subject. Don't want to be thinking about Derek any more than I have to. "Benny said my Rimbo was good to go?"

"Good enough," Ter tells me. "When I stopped by the garage, there was just body damage left."

I wince a little thinking about it, but give Callum a nod.

"All right. Maps, please?"

Four cuffcomms flip open as we send him the image files.

He stands up and walks to a corner of the far wall. "Let's start with Jones, shall we?" Callum says, and he projects the first route map onto the wall. It's hidden from him, but visible to us. On it, the ten sickhouses on Jones's route are outlined in green.

"Target buildings' and sickhouses' height differentials, bearings off each roof, and optimal speed for making each jump. Go."

We listen as he goes, probably each thinking the same thing: Callum would make a killer dragster.

"One last thing remains," Drill Sergeant Callum informs us, all headings bored into our skulls, nine hundred tubes capped and ready to go. He points to a pile in the corner: dozens of copper boxes with brass locks—the boxes that Benny couldn't take since they weren't finished. "These are what you'll be dropping on the rooftop of each sickhouse. Please fill every box with fifty vials."

"That's more than the number of patients," Ter comments, reaching for one.

"I've rounded up. The cure might bring some sick out of the woodwork. Unaccounted-for contagious patients, or even untested ones who've been ducking the law, might send family."

Like my neighbors, the Bedrosians. With images of the raid brewing in the back of my mind, I add my fifty vials to my remaining boxes and put them in my sack.

When we're done, all the racers stand, individual packs clinking with the sound of cheap metal, and walk to the door.

Something's off—I'm uneasy. A twinge in my gut. "Odd, though, right?" I ask everyone, just before opening the door.

"What?"

"It's just . . . An extermination that hasn't accounted for a hundred percent of the contagious population? The Blues raided my neighbors—they know that people avoid testing."

The room goes silent.

"They're calling it a cure, Ren. I bet they're banking on it making its way around," Kent says, looking at the others to gauge their reactions.

No one else seems bothered by it, so I nod. Still, his answer doesn't settle me.

"All right, everyone. First squadron flies in less than ninety minutes, so be off your last roof at least five minutes before midnight," Callum says. "I think it will be too risky to meet immediately following your drop-offs, so let's wait until first thing tomorrow morning—six a.m.—at Benny's garage to reconvene. Together, we'll listen to the radio for news of the 'cure.'"

One after another, the guys nod and line up single file behind the door. Jones reaches out for an armshake, which I take without smiling. Not on the outside, at least.

Next comes Ter, shuffling his feet and still avoiding my eyes. Then, just when I expect him to turn out the door and leave me without another word, it's as though all his anger drops away. He opens his arms. Hugs me. Even kisses my forehead.

"Benny spoke to me," Ter whispers. "He seems to think that if I'd found out under any different circumstances, you might deserve my anger. But since you're trying to save the Ward and all . . . it wouldn't kill me to cut you a break."

I laugh and snort into his jacket.

"Be safe out there," he says seriously.

Pulling back from him, I see the worry behind his eyes. We're not sentimental, but I've got it behind mine also.

"Same for you," I tell him, and as I open my mouth to say

something else—what, I don't know—Ter pats my shoulder and turns away. We don't need to say anything else.

Kent's turn.

No arm. He just towers over me, a disgusted look curling on his face. He holds his derby close to his chest, faking sincerity, and leans forward. "How's your sister?" he asks, hissing into my ear. But by the time I open my mouth, he's out the door.

As I close it behind me, I fall back. Lean my head against the wood. Try to shake away the feeling that the pieces aren't all in place, though Kent always acts like that.

I hope he drives off a roof.

Immediately, I unthink it—this is one race where I'm even denied the small pleasure of wishing death on the boy. I remind myself that, for the first time, we're fighting on the same side. I won't win or lose alone. If he skids out, doesn't recover, dozens of people lose along with him. Each of us dragsters no just longer equals one person—we're a sum total, all wheeling from roof to roof, hundreds of lives at the finish line. Not just Aven's.

My breath starts to go ragged, inhales pushing against exhales, neither one really doing its job. How in hell will we pull this off? There are too many people. . . .

From across the room, Callum must sense my freak-out. "It's going to work," he says, and walks closer. "You've done this a hundred times. This is just a hundred and one."

I'm grateful he's trying to make me feel better, but we both know that's not true. This is not like every other race.

Without warning, Callum folds his arms round me, and

rests his chin on my head. I don't expect it, but arms always know what to do when it comes to a hug, so a moment later they're wrapped around his waist. I lay my cheek to his chest, and he rocks me side to side like we're old friends. Old friends who don't totally know each other. Yet.

"Just in case something happens, though . . ." he says, arms still around me. "I'm standing here because of you. No one else. Even if it's only because of my brain." Coughing, "Large and sexy though it may be . . ."

I laugh—Callum's funny. Didn't know that.

He continues, his voice serious. Full and breaking all at once. "I owe my life to you. And if this works, I won't be the only one. No thank-you will ever be enough."

Same goes for "you're welcome," I think to myself, and I squeeze him tight. I can't figure out the words to say—how can you put any feeling into words, really?—so I hope he'll know what I mean.

Callum exhales heavily, like a blowfish. "I can't believe we're doing this. I can't believe we're about to pull this off." Then, finding my eyes with his baby blues, he says, "I'll see you at the finish."

"See you at the finish," I echo, and as I close the door it occurs to me that for the first time, the finish line ain't even a place. It can't be charted, or graphed, or put on a map.

This time, the finish line is people.

I jog quick-paced along Mad Ave, and not far off, a few beggars have taken up residence for the night. One of them's lying huddled under a rough woolen blanket, legs sticking out. He wants people to see, he's not your everyday beggar. I don't slow as I pass, though I can't help but stare at his knees, skin stretched out, high and thick.

His shins are bowed, muscles and bones making room for the tumors. I shudder and cringe in a way my mind doesn't understand. Fear, I guess.

Running by, I read the chalk writing on the boardwalk: *HBNC+ Not Contagious. Homeless. Spare a drop?*

"Just a sip from your canteen!" he calls to my back, but I try to ignore him. I can't though . . . because something occurs to me. He's a hundred feet back by the time my feet begin to slow.

Homeless.

Roofless.

I spin around. Race back the way I came.

When he sees I've returned, he smiles, shows off the gaps in his teeth. "Thank you, miss," he says, and holds out his hands.

"You—" I start, kneeling down. "Can you get to a sickhouse? How will you get the cure?"

He takes back his hands. Looking at me like I've asked him the silliest question imaginable, he scrunches his brows and closes one eye, considering. A moment later, "I suppose I could find one in the morning, if my legs feel like doing the work of it." He hoots. Pats his thigh. Then, he points to my belt. "I'll be sure they do if you wanna pass me a drop from that pretty canteen I see?"

Like he's doing me a favor.

I choke back a cry, a yell. I want to stomp my foot, scream

at the world. How did we not think of this? So much time ironing out the details. Every one of these last forty-eight hours has hurt me, in some way—even he was part of the payoff, though he don't know it.

More holes in the plan.

More holes in the plan?

An extermination plan that doesn't account for the homeless. It makes no sense. In my gut, the twinge is back. A wavering feeling, a compass that has lost its north.

"Well?"

I shake my head and pull off my sack, taking a vial from one of the copper boxes. *If Kent knew . . .*

This ain't fair; I know it ain't. It's not his fault that he had no time to hand-deliver a vial all the way to a northern quadrant. But it's not like his dad won't get the cure at all. . . .

I uncork my canteen and pass it.

The beggar pours too long, smacks his lips at the sound of the splashing water. I have to tip the thing away from him, or he'd probably drain it.

While he downs the water from his own canteen, I give him the vial. "Drink this, please?" I ask, but he won't answer, or even nod. I have no time to waste on an argument. Checking my cuffcomm—twenty-seven minutes till the squadrons fly through—I tell myself that this changes nothing. The water is still going to people who need it.

Keep moving.

Keep moving.

49

11:40 P.M., SUNDAY

Focus.

My breath catches when I see the metal bosun's chair Benny used to roof my Rimbo. It dangles against the facade of a narrow, redbrick highrise, like any other pre–Wash Out remnant. I give silent thanks to the ancient nutjobs who rigged chairs to most of these buildings so they could have their windows cleaned. With fresh. For windows.

Shaking my head, I look up. The Milky Way stretches over the Ward, like asphalt and snow flung to the sky. Aside from the Isle—electric, blue-white, needle-sharp towers—and Ward Hope, it's the brightest thing out there. And sitting right in front of me, nearly invisible . . . my Rimbo. It's real, we're really doing this.

My heart does a jig.

I hop over the bridge's last few planks and onto the roof, right up to it. The boiler's rattling away, a steam engine sending out heat good as any fire. It's the only noise up here, and the only noise for miles. Before, the city was abuzz. Now, you can hear everyone waiting.

It's eerie. Shakes my breath—no checkered flags, no spectators, no jeering. A roofrace no one knows about. Ironic, that the race we keep secret is the first to really matter.

I lift the roof and climb in, sinking into the familiar seat, breathing the pit's smell. Old and musky. Puts the feeling of home in my bones. I breathe out, and finally feel like I know what I'm doing.

Then I see them—the packages—stacked up atop the dash next to my headset. Three more copper boxes. One for each sickhouse roof along my route. And I do exactly the thing that I shouldn't—I imagine the people. Hundreds of them, like a hundred Avens. Her number's not in there anymore, and I'm so thankful, but without her to focus on . . .

That feeling I had at the hospital, of being so full up?

Just one of those boxes holds fifty times that feeling. Five boxes, two hundred and fifty times. And when I think of everyone—eight hundred times that feeling?—I want to hurl.

One drop-off, I remind myself. Even just one is worth it.

I can't stand to look at all them, the faces—the life count. 'Cause I'm not Aven or Callum. They can see the numbers. Giving is a part of them. If life were a numbers game, they'd count for infinity.

They're the ones you can count on, because they never count themselves.

They're too good.

I've never been too good. And that's my saving grace.

My mind relaxes, my grip eases on the wheel—because I can handle one.

I reach for my headset to sync it with my cuffcomm. Earbud in my ear, mic by my mouth, I'm ready as I'll ever be. "I'm in," I say to the others, and take a swig from my canteen while my hands are still free. The static comes back in rounds, our signals linking up.

"Took you long enough," one voice crackles.

Oh, Kent. I'm going to love having you in my head this race.

"Whoo! Drop-off one—down!" Terrence yells.

When Jones calls out two seconds later that he's made his second drop-off, I say into my mic, "B, I'm putting these guys on mute. Too many voices—it's gonna drive me bonkers."

I think Ter actually boos me. Then it's only me and Benny. Strapped into my Rimbo, everything comes into focus. Liquid nerves shift to metal. Breathing turns metronome even. This is the only place where I know what I'm doing. Everything else may have changed, but not this. Not here.

One last time, I project a map of the route onto my lap and face it westward, the direction I'm headed. Neon-green, yellow, and red lines warp over my thighs, but the refresher is enough:

Yellow—the eleven rooftops, total.

Red—my five sickhouse drop-offs.

The entire route is no longer than half a mile, and my cuffcomm reads T minus nineteen minutes. Nineteen minutes till the governor's squadron flies through, dropping off their "cure." Eleven jumps . . . I should be done in less than five minutes. Seven, max.

Depending on what Derek's chosen. Will he tell Kitaneh I'm alive?

Slow and steady, I ease against the acceleration—not one of my cargo will I let get destroyed 'cause I jumped the gun. My Rimbo rolls forward. I lean in, give it more. The wheels drag against a thin layer of undrained water covering the copper rain-collection panels.

Into my mic, "I'm off, Benny."

I'm moving faster now, but I'll need to gather enough speed to make the jump. I step on the acceleration—the mobile jolts forward and I watch my water tank drop a notch. The edge nears and I check for my heading on the steering wheel's rotating compass globe—270 degrees. I'll need a bearing of 263, so I angle left before giving a propulsion boost.

I watch the black slide closer. Once more, gunning the steam engine—here it comes.

My Rimbo sails over the side. With a lurching stomach, neck tight to the headrest . . . A smile creeps up. This next moment, right before the drop—I live for it. Despite the fear brewing in my head, my body goes giddy. The mobile hits the highest point of the arc.

Ain't nothin' but now.

For not even a fraction of a second, I'm weightless. I'd stay this way forever if I could, holding in my air like a balloon. 'Cept I'm no balloon.

My Rimbo begins to fall. Up and up, my stomach rises

into my chest. Out of habit, I reach for my favorite button: ROCKIN'. Another pre–Wash Out classic spills from the speakers, this time chosen by Benny.

"Nice, B." I laugh-snort into the mouthpiece. He's passing me a not-so-secret message via the lyrics.

"Just want you to be careful, that's all," he answers, and the line goes quiet, just in time for the chorus.

Low rider, don't use no gas now, low rider, don't drive too fast.

Ten feet over the second roof, I lean forward to keep the rear from bottoming out.

Too late I see it—the main gutter, smack where I'm about to land. My Rimbo skids—*You brackin' idiot, how did you miss that?* One rear wheel in the gutter, I'm at a sideways slant. Now I've got to get outta the ditch.

I watch my water level drop even more as I step on the acceleration and then hit the propulsion button. This time, I give it everything. Full speed ahead, I angle the wheel toward the fourth roof instead of the third, 'cause I won't be touching down there.

My first delivery may be on that roof, but I'm going over it.

The edge is nearer, nearer, and I forget how to breathe. Just this one drop, just one—

Then I'm hurtling over the side. In midair, I reach for the first box. I slide open the weight chute using my foot, and a gust of cold floods the pit.

I look down. Between my feet—drainage pipes. Here goes. I drop the box.

Like a vacuum, it blows through the chute, then out of

sight behind my mobile. I crane my neck. *Land on the roof, just this one.*

And there it is—bouncing along the rooftop. Into the mic, "Drop-off one complete!" I burst, and exhale so hard, I can feel my lungs tugging together. It worked. . . . It worked.

Too soon, my stomach pitches, lungs sucked dry by the drop. I look down. Under me, Mad Ave—no, no, no. A good thirty feet too far.

Was my speed wrong?

More propulsion—head folded between my knees, I peer down the chute, willing the mobile on in my head. She listens. I watch as my Rimbo closes the gap. . . .

And forget to drop the second box.

"Brack!" I curse, teeth clenched. Fast, before landing, I chuck it through the opening. My Rimbo touches down, and a handful of gravel sprays into the pit. Pings my face, stings my tongue. I shut my trap with a whimper and look left.

Three feet over, I could've landing on metal paneling.

I realize something else: the open chute . . . it's why I almost didn't make it to the fourth roof. Air in the pit was dragging my Rimbo—*What are you, a rookie?* I scold, and cut the wheel at a hard right, for a heading of 340 degrees. Off the northeastern corner toward the fifth roof on my route I go, hating myself for not being more careful. I'm so in my head, I almost miss them—

Beamers . . . ? Only three hundred feet away. By Central Bay. Can't be Ter, he's probably at Quad Three by now. The mobile jumps from roof to roof, closer. Headed straight for me . . . This is not good. Flipping on the comm line. "Come in, come in, Benny—" I say into my mouthpiece. "You see what I'm seeing?"

He should have a clear view of this from the Empire Clock—I wait.

"I am, and you're not alone. Four of you, four of them," he tells me through static, but now I'm not paying attention. Rear first, I'm whipped down. My Rimbo bottoms out—I forgot to lean forward—and even my suspension system turns against me.

I curse myself yet again as the steering wheel throws itself to the left and my tires spin out beneath me.

"Did you just bottom out, Renata?" Benny asks.

Even through a headset, he knows.

It's enough to nearly set me off. . . . Everything is going to pieces.

Then, like a Slinky on steroids, the shock coils decompress. Send my butt flying. I'm thrashed upward into the glass, without even my hair to ease the blow. A throbbing ache closes my eyes for me, and when I do open them, I still can't see.

Before my Rimbo touches down again, I straighten the wheel. Where does the roof end?

Landing, I hammer on the brakes, eyes open. Whited-out vision turns to purple, to brown, then tall rectangles fill in my blind spots. Tall rectangles, and . . . something else. Like a bullet. Black. Beelining for my Rimbo, headlights blinding in the distance.

An Omni—

One of the Tètai.

But it's too soon for things to go so wrong. . . . I've only made two drop-offs. In my chest, panic starts shredding my nerves. It turns me stupid, tempts me to look through the window. Just to make sure . . . it could be Derek, not Kitaneh or the others. But that's a terrible idea—my Rimbo's slowed to a standstill. I'll be squashed. Clumsy, disoriented, I spin my torso in all directions trying to get my bearings even though my instincts are telling me to move, any direction.

Then I look down. On my steering wheel, the compass sphere has stopped revolving—at precisely the right heading. I'm arrowed toward my third drop-off.

The hardest on my route. I laugh. A belly-full whoop of a laugh. This small bit of fate . . . it's like the universe is forgiving me for tonight's muck ups. Keeping me afloat for the next jump. I'm reminded that it ain't game over, not yet. I gun the steam engine and I don't lift my foot. Not even as the tank dips below half.

My Rimbo plows ahead, aimed for the sloped plates. I'll use them as ramps for picking up speed, but not because the next roof is far. Worse. The jump is a rise, not a drop. Meaning up. Glancing right, northwest, I search for the Omni—spot the headlights twenty feet away.

But it's not Kitaneh in the driver's seat.

Copper hair, sparkling and obvious despite the Omni windshield's dark tint.

Derek? I don't understand. . . . All those things he said—he could never hurt me—were they even true?

If he's here to stop me . . .

The muscle of my heart wants to rip itself apart and fight, all at the same time.

I understood what he was saying before, outside the hospital. A part of me even agrees. People dying from a disease is horrible, but it's nature. Sitting back, not trying to stop a genocide from happening? That's an entirely different beast.

I don't want to go against him. But I will.

"Come in, Ren—" Benny calls through my headset. "The others . . . something's happened. I'm syncing you up again."

A broken stream of static hits my ear, and below my tires I feel the incline. I hold down the rear propulsion, allowing for drag caused by the chute. It'll burn a trail behind me. The Omni will see my path like I've drawn him a map.

Plating disappears. I'm riding on air.

And then . . . Kent's voice: "No! Ter, you can't head back—My dad . . . the vial!"

"I've got no choice. . . ." Ter answers. Screeching metal, then feedback. I can't breathe for a moment—Is Ter hurt?—and then I hear his voice again. "I'm on three tires as it is—they took out my fourth. . . . I have to, man, I'm sorry." More feedback, more metal, all of it high-pitched and grating.

Like in free fall, I feel my stomach drop, far far away. Not the others too . . .

"Dammit, Terrence. Jones . . . you can do it, you're nor—" His voice cuts out. "Brack," I hear him grunt. "What the—? Where'd the package go? It just disa—"

The other Tètai have got to be here too. . . .

I've still got a job to do. Let them come after me.

I shift my weight till my Rimbo's nose up. The distance

shrinks away. Thirty feet becomes twenty, then ten. Open chute—holding the third box, I wait. At five feet, my stomach knows what's coming—the apex of the jump.

Last minute, I look around for the Omni. My skin itches; I can't find it.

Eyes back on the chute. When the metal-plated roof is about seven feet below, I let go of the box.

Fountain of youth superserum—away.

Spinning around to watch it, I lean on the wheel and even out the nose. The box is sucked backward. It dips down, and I wait for it to hit the roof.

And wait.

And wait.

Meanwhile, my Rimbo lands easily on the copper plating, only a slight skid to grapple with. I kill the propulsion. The pit darkens. Why'd it get dark? My gut knots, and looking up, I see . . . an undercarriage?

Covering the right half of the moonroof's dome—the black bullet, sailing overhead. Derek's Omni can fly. A steam-powered, 100 percent metal-clad aeronautical mobile.

Brack.

When I turn, looking over my right shoulder, I pound my fist against the glass. The third box. Dangling in midair. It's been caught in a net with magnets sewn into the wire meshing, which is attached to the Omni. Suddenly, I can't move—my rib cage actually hurts my lungs. With my nose pressed to the right curve of the moonroof, I watch as the package floats away, like magic. It's raised up and up, then into the mobile via the open chute.

442

Fifty vials, Fifty Avens. Gone. Just like that.

I can't believe he's doing this. . . . It's worse than betrayal. He warned me. I should have known.

That don't make it hurt less, though.

I need to try and stop it. Stop him.

But do I have time? I can't check my cuffcomm—I need both hands on the wheel. "Benny," I call into the mic, knuckles tight to the wheel. "How long before the squadrons come through?"

A few moments later, "Twelve minutes," he says. Then, "But, Ren, Terrence is back, and so is Jones—Kent . . . we don't know where he is. But this is not a competition. No one made it to their last drop-off. It's dangerous out there. I want you off in seven."

Very rarely does he go so far as to try and tell me what to do, so I know he's serious. Doesn't mean I'll listen, though. Depends on what I can do in seven minutes. I try to veer right, but my Rimbo refuses.

The metal groans—I'm jolted forward, thrown from the seat. Turning my head, I do a double take: the black Omni.

It's behind me . . . ?

I look up—

It's also above me. Now I'm really confused.

They must be tag-teaming, Derek and Kitaneh.

One Omni roars at my rear, gains speed. Next thing I know, it's by my side, our metals screeching together. Sparks firework between us. That driver who wants to kill me . . . must be Kitaneh. She sideswipes my Rimbo so hard, she's gotta be trying to flip it. Half the mobile lifts.

I look left, fuming. . . . Benny worked too hard on this job for me to watch it undone in a matter of seconds. But when I look through the glass at the shock of rusty, brassy hair . . .

I nearly choke.

It's Derek.

I knew he might try to stop me. But this? It's like all of a sudden he wants worse than that—he wants me dead. As I look again, though, I realize I'm not so sure. His features are off, somehow. The jaw is too square. Shoulders, too thick. This guy looks like Derek, but something is different.

So there's a Derek look-alike trying to kill me to my left, and another black Omni overhead, who could be Derek or could be Kitaneh.

Out of nowhere, I feel my Rimbo being pushed down. I look up through the moonroof, and see the undercarriage of the other Omni staring back at me.

It's keeping me from flipping over.

No way would Kitaneh try to help me, ever.

That must be Derek above. He's trying to help me. . . .

For a moment, the realization almost undoes me. That he could be against the others . . . because of what I said. It feels too big, and I try not to think about what it means.

Turning once again to the front, I see a silver cord dangling—the netting's metal tail. Smack in the middle of my windshield. The package. It's dragging behind my mobile, skidding and throwing sparks of its own. So close, if my roof were open, I could reach for it myself.

Still gripping the wheel steady, my palms grow hot and begin to cramp. I accelerate, and watch my water tank drop to a third. The Derek look-alike accelerates. I pull back. So does he. He's my echo—I can't stay locked like this forever.

I rotate my left wrist to find my cuffcomm: nine minutes till the Blues get here. Four to finish my route. Assuming I take Benny's warning.

In my head I do the math. My last drop-off lies a full five boardwalks west, not including diagonals. I can't make two more. Not under six minutes. Not with Kitaneh and Derek around.

Out the back of the moonroof, I watch the copper box ricocheting behind the engine.

In nine minutes, those fifty people will be given a "cure"— a drug they believe will save them. The thought adds metric tons to my bones, my muscles. Like there's something inside me so empty, so barren, that it actually has a weight. The fifty faces paint themselves against my mind, all in shades of Aven. This time, I look.

And then I decide.

I'm leaving it.

I step on the pedal and flip the propulsion boost. The combination of a steam engine plus the thrust sends my Rimbo barreling forward. Barbs of guilt prod, but I don't try to pull away. I feel them all. They deserve that much.

The Omni overhead lifts up, the other trailing behind.

With the building's edge in sight, I hold the wheel steady, then race nearer and nearer to it. Then, I'm over it.

In midair, I get my bearings by looking straight ahead to the West Isle, and above the electric city, clouds muddy together in oranges and purples, all ink-tinged. Smoke from the riot still hides the tallest buildings, and a wispy fog rolls in across the Strait.

Through it, I can see white specks, probably from people's windows, but . . .

The specks—they're moving.

Just as I'm about to land on the seventh roof—

"Ren! Come in, Ren!" Benny's voice is tinny in my ear. A stream of white noise spits from my earpiece. He gives me no time to answer—"Get out, now," he says. "The DI . . . they're here!"

They're early.

I touch down on the seventh roof, metal clunking as it rebounds. Through the fog, what were specks in the sky moments ago are quickly becoming a full-on light show. Vibrations shudder my mobile, make me clamp my jaw tight with understanding: it's not the squadron with the governor's cure. Those are straight Blues helis, and they're circling the Ward in swarms.

Correction: circling *me* in swarms.

50

11:42 P.M., SUNDAY

The helis fly out of the mud-colored clouds as if they were born there. I feel acid-filled. I'm poison that I want them to drink up. In my ear, our signals mix—my mic shrieks, they're flying so close now. Several hundred feet away, their high beams and spotlights cast broken circles everywhere— the sickhouse rooftops . . . they're landing on each of 'em and gathering the packages.

I'm cut off from my two last drop-offs. The final sick-houses on my route.

Now at a standstill, I glance over my shoulder. The two Omnis—can't lose sight of 'em. Scanning the quadrant, I find them five bridges southeast. Two black mobiles and a fountain of orange sparks. One races over the planked sus-pension bridge, the other hovers alongside. Every time one

Omni jerks forward, makes like it's about to head west—for me—the other mobile cuts them off.

Derek's been keeping the other Omni away.

In the sky, spinning propellers remind me that I'm a sitting duck. But I don't move, yet. I watch them there—one by one I count the ways in which I hurt. The thick skin of all my angers turns hot. Fighting that cloud, not stopping—it's about more than just tonight.

It's about my life.

And not just mine, all of ours. Being told we're getting a cure when, in fact, we are getting a death sentence. Funneling rainwater from our rooftops, when across the Strait, the wealthy buy fresh black market.

It's about being hated for no reason.

I face the cloud. I won't give up, not now.

Flooring the pedal, I shoot toward the swarm. My fingers shake as I grip the wheel, and I can feel the burn at my cheeks.

Just as I meet the end of the roof, a high beam grazes my side. They've seen me. My headset shakes static in my ear. I hear a *click-click-click*-ing, like someone changing stations, then more static, like all the other channels have died.

Leaving only one.

"It's over," Chief growls through my earpiece.

Throwing my wheel right, dodging out of the beam's way, I see my heading for the next is now out of whack.

My Rimbo careens over the building's edge, and Chief's voice is back in my head. "Tell your boy Kent that Governor Voss would personally like to thank him," he says.

"I don't understand. . . ." I whisper into the mic, stomach muscles cementing together, and not just 'cause I'm currently sailing over a boardwalk. "My boy Kent?"

"He called you in, told us you were alive." Chief snorts. "Wanted to see that his father got the stuff. Didn't exactly turn down the reward money, either."

Of course not.

I imagine pulling him to pieces, limb from limb. We were never on the same team. Stupid of me to think that we were.

Then, steely through the comm, "Last chance, Dane. Where can the governor locate another spring?" Chief Dunn asks.

It's a question I'll never answer.

"I'll take my last chance," I say into my mic, looking ahead. *Why haven't I landed already?* Right, left, I look . . . and I see nothing. No roof to catch my fall. Not even a building facade that I could aim for. I've completely overshot my next roof.

I'm in free fall.

Buildings tower past. They grow larger. Wider.

Punching my fist to the steering wheel—it's over. It's over. I can't make the other drop-offs. A curling, constricting rage forces its way out my throat. How do you know when to give up? How can this be the end?

Like yawning forever, I'm thrown down into the center of the earth. My stomach wants out of my body so badly, the drop has made me sick. I can't even relax my jaw; my tongue's latched to the roof of my mouth. This is the longest jump I've ever made, and still I'm falling.

When my Rimbo finally hits Broad Walk, it thuds and screeches, clobbering the planks. They groan and smoke under my tires, and the sharp, coated smell of rubber wafts in, even though the weight chute is closed.

"Have it your way," Dunn says.

A spotlight pins me. I'm a fly needled to a wall.

I watch a heli carve through the black and glance at my water tank—almost empty, but I floor it anyway. Under my tires, the wood rattles and shakes, not made for mobile travel. Jamming on the brakes, I spin the wheel to face east again, closer to Mad Ave.

I need to hide. Right now, I'm just too easy a target.

As I'm wheeling down the boardwalk, time turns to sludge. The seconds rush by, but minutes take forever. Then, the first net falls.

I remember from when they netted me before. The edges flap like impatient wings. Electronic, motion-detecting pulses keep the nets open, and magnets woven into them are attracted to any mobile's steel frame. They'll jam your props if you get caught.

I turn the steering wheel left and push RETRACT, folding the wheels into the underbelly. My Rimbo hurtles in an arc off Broad, and within moments it's living up to its name. It skips along the surface of the water, and I flip on the propellers to give a boost.

Once I'm closer to the end of the gutter, I risk looking behind me: about a hundred feet up, and one block over, I watch the net float down, looking for motion from my Rimbo. When an easy wind sways the suspension bridge, the net gets caught on the zigzags, its motion sensors confused. *Don't watch—go.*

I steer left under the Mad Ave boardwalk, so I'm out of the helis' sight. Since the walkways were built with tides in mind, the canals are high. My Rimbo skips under the walk, leaving me a good foot of clearance between the roof at its highest skip and the planks. Can't keep this up though—it's not made for so long on the water. I weave through two pylons, and check to see if the air is clear. Tonight, though, everything is bright. Two flashlights shine on the Ward: the moon, and that heli's spotlight flooding the canal with light.

My Rimbo's bounces begin to fall short, each one closer than the next. It slows even as I steer, rallying the bullet blood in my veins. I need to dock it fast—

Forget it. Just get out.

I'll have to go by foot from here. It's my best chance for avoiding the heli above. My Rimbo slows even more. When it makes its final skip, I pop the roof and reach up. Clutching the support beams on the underside of the boardwalk, I climb out, dropping into the water.

I don't have a chance to feel the cold.

"Miss Dane—" a voice crackles in my ear.

Not the chief—this voice is too subtle, too many undercurrents. Governor Voss.

"Since you are not willing to share the spring's location with me, I thought it only fair to withhold a location from you. Something equally valuable. Do you have any idea what I'm talking about?"

The hairs on my neck know what he's about to say before my mind makes any sense of it. "No, sir," I answer, still clinging to the boardwalk's beams. But my stomach knows the feeling before the drop. Before the downhill.

"One thing of value for another. Only fair." The governor pauses, and I hear him tapping. "I'm referring to the girl you call your 'sister.'"

451

The edges of my eyesight go black. "You have Aven," I whisper. Like burning, the black curls at the periphery, working its way in, until all that's left is the memory of what was there. My body tries to extinguish itself, but no amount of salt water will ever be enough. "You can't hurt her. . . ."

"But clinical research is so important to understanding the spring's exact properties. Recall my ancestor's letter. Entire limbs . . . regrown. I imagine it's painful—the loss, and the regeneration."

He wouldn't. . . .

Behind the smoke and blur, I look for her. *Where are you? Where are you?* My only answer comes from the wailing heli as it hovers, waits, and the animal noises I make that have no name.

Outside of me, I hear tapping. The governor—through the comm. "Well, well, well. It's nearly one a.m.. The evening has been . . . very successful," he says lightly. "You, Miss Dane, have exceeded all my expectations."

I shake my head. Where are the squadrons? "What do you mean . . . ?" I mumble, pressing my fists into my eye sockets, fighting them.

"What do I mean . . ." he repeats, like a riddle. "Honestly, Renata. Democide? Really? Hardly the best way to win over the people. Especially not after this morning's riot. I'd thought, this time, perhaps the Tètai would try and stop me. They did not. Smart. You, however . . . you accomplished for me far more than I ever could have on my own.

"My wife will be cured. I'll be hailed as a hero for

weakening the Blight's hold on the Ward. And after you share the spring's location, the United Metro Islets will return to the thriving, prosperous metropolis it once was, with freshwater for all.

"This city will never die again."

With his pause, a hard, rotten pit of fear bursts wide in my chest. My body heaves, like it's trying to get rid of something on the inside, but nothing comes out. The pieces that didn't quite fit, the twinge in my gut that I was too stupid to understand—

All along . . . a lie?

"All that's left: my location," Governor Voss continues. "Today's riot cannot happen again; I must have access to more. Aventine Colatura is waiting. Till then—

"Good night, Miss Dane."

The line dies.

A lie. A trick.

Every choice I made in the past twenty-four hours—I want it back. I should have chosen Aven. . . . It should always have been Aven. Life is not a numbers game. *Just one, just one.*

Energy, raw and volatile, is all that's left. I pull myself to the edge of the boardwalk, kick my feet over. Forehead pressed to the planks, heaving with an exhaustion I can no longer feel, I come to standing.

Face-to-face with the aeromobile, its spotlight cuts a hole in the night's darkness like target practice. Each of my nerves is a lit, fraying fuse, begging for zero. Every cell is a bomb, and they detonate with one singular need: *do anything.*

In the air, the heli howls metallic death.

I run toward its light.

It's waiting for me.

The beam scalds.

City dust tornadoes around inside it, shaken by the heli's props, and simpler enemies, like wind. Everything moves in slow-motion.

I watch.

Somewhere in the subway tunnels of my mind, I know this makes no sense. And at the same time, it is the only thing that does. Nothing else is real. Every choice, false.

Shielding my eyes, I shout up at the sky to the mindless, gutless aeromobile.

"Take me! I'm immune!" I yell. "I'm here! I'm right here!"

My words fall to pieces, collide with the propellers and the water churning from the pressure. The man in the heli doesn't see or hear me. And that feels right, too. Appropriate. I've become invisible, my choices no longer about me. I wave my arms. I throw myself up into the air.

I say it again. "I'm standing right here!"

Time stops. What was slow-motion is now freeze-frame.

Above, the heli circles and I catch a glint of metal. A man inside loads a net—this one for people—into a long-barreled gun. I've been here before. Three years ago, this same scene.

And so I know what happens next.

He loads the gun. Shoots the net. It'll hit and it'll hurt no worse than getting punched. You're folded into its diamond-meshed wings and carried away, dangling through the air like any other package.

When the gun sounds, I hear nothing.

I see stars. . . .

The net's twinkling border.

And then, hardness. In the way of hands gripping around my waist. In the planks that I fall onto, rough and splintering.

I'd expected the next minutes to exist in verticals—the net should be lifting me by now. Instead, everything is horizontal. Thick pylons lying on their sides. Nails and splintering wood. Close up on the chopping waves. No stars, no tossed-asphalt Milky Way. No beast in the sky.

Freeze-frame—*off.*

The shift hurts, makes no sense. Dust. Propellers. The water churning. My eyes are too slow, too small for the world. They can't process. Even the smell, ocean salt and stale brack, hurts my nose. Sharp at the back of my throat.

Around my waist, nothing stings as it should. Not the way the nets should. There's muscle there. Thick, unyielding flesh, forcing me out of the beam.

"Get in," Derek's voice tells me.

We're dockside at a black Omni—*how did we get here?*

"Let me go." I push and pull, in a tug-of-war of arms and legs. Looking up, I again notice the slight freckling along his cheeks, eyes rusty-red and brown. The beam finds us. His hair becomes a straight shot of fire, sparking to life.

That last color—it sends me into overdrive, crosses all my wires.

I'm a schematic with no lines, I'm an ocean with no body, I'm words without letters. A numberless value. I am senseless and I am crying, holding on to and throwing back anything that comes too close.

Derek lifts me by the waist. I struggle, but can't remember why. He lowers me down. The corner I sit in fits like a hard shell. He shuts the roof. I twist, I have a body of snakes. A pit of them. I forget to breathe. I cry. Too hard. My body breathes for me. Repeat. Repeat. I quiet.

It ends. It begins.

It ends again, and it begins again, because we think in circles.

And then, one final time, it really is over—

I'm over.

51

When the shaking stops, when I open my eyes . . . it's like waking up to find that I've fallen off a map. The world I thought was round is flat, and nothing is as it was before.

A dull ache has taken Aven's place inside my head.

She is gone, and so am I.

Under the canal's surface, Derek steers the Omni east, high beams lighting up abandoned cars and buses. The waterways are empty like always. Even more empty now.

Vaguely, I feel the cloth of my leggings and the thick fabric of my vest holding in water from the canal. I think I'm cold. I *know* I'm cold, and for the first time, I understand what it feels like. Separate from the discomfort. I don't care that I'm cold, or that my knees are scraped and raw and bloodied.

Without feeling any of it, I watch the sunken city through the window. I remember Aven's face at the Tank when she saw it all for the first time. Like the machines, in all their useless glory, were the greatest things in the world.

"Ren?"

Even my name feels far away, fragile in his mouth. He's just as afraid of saying it as I am of hearing it.

I turn my head. That's enough of a response.

"Where should I take you?"

For a moment, I forget that there was a plan. It all got so derailed. But there is a plan; it hasn't gone away just because the governor was lying. "Garage," I answer. Then, quieter, head tucked between the seat and the window, "I'm a fool," I whisper to myself.

I know nothing.

Except for regret. But for what, exactly . . . I'm not sure. Could I have left Callum, and all the others, to die? I don't know. But somewhere along the road, I went left when I should have gone right. I made the opposite choice.

And so I regret. Something.

Not being a better sister, maybe.

"You and Kitaneh knew not to do it. You knew not to play into his hands."

Derek looks at me. He shakes his head. "You're not a fool. We had no idea that he wasn't going to go through with it— so really, we had even more reason to have done something." He sighs, leaning back in his chair. "*I* should have done something," he adds, his voice heavy, and that's how I hear them: regrets.

He has them too. And they have nothing to do with me, or *earning* me. They're for his own sake. Which is all I could take right now—I don't know if I feel worthy, or good enough, of being earned.

"I saw you out there," I say, mustering something like sympathy. I'm too empty for this kind of talk, but I manage to add, "You did something."

"I was too late. I couldn't stop the others. My brother, he almost . . ."

"I thought he was you."

Derek slows the mobile, begins bringing it up for air. "Kitaneh must have found out on her own that you were alive, then told him and the others." His voice rises. He's afraid I might not believe him.

But I do, and I tell him so, and then we're silent. The Omni's headlights cut lines of gold alongside the boardwalk as we break the surface.

"Did you know . . . the word *Tètai* in Lenape—Kitaneh's native tongue—means *between*."

He doesn't need to explain. "Between life and death," I murmur.

"Between life and death," he repeats, glancing at me out of the corner of his eyes. Then, barely audible: "But not for long."

"What do you mean?"

"I acted against my family, in opposition to the order." He swallows hard, his jaw squared to the windshield. "Against Kitaneh, my wife by contract, and also my single remaining blood brother, Lucas. They'll come after me. His wife, too.

They have to. It's our punishment."

When I look at Derek again, I see him differently. No longer through the rose-colored lenses I once wore. He's made mistakes . . . centuries of them. I see his history laid out in front of me. The same family keeping the same secret, forever.

I see what he's lost tonight.

We've both lost tonight.

"Then come with me," I say, and I push down on the button in the center console that opens the roof. I don't want to move—I'm sluggish and heavy as we bob sideways in the black water. But a gust of wind sweeps through the pit, shakes me from my stupor, and I stand.

I just want tonight to end.

"I thought I was coming with you anyway." In his voice, equal parts fear and hope. He searches my eyes with his. "We have to find Aven."

I nod, letting him take my hand to help me out of the Omni. I can feel every ache and hurt my bones are carrying as I step onto Mad Ave. Derek lifts himself out after and rests his hand low on my back.

As we walk toward Benny's garage, I reach for my necklace out of habit, just to make sure it's there. Attached to the chain, my two pennies—from Aven, and from Callum. Without looking at them, I can't tell who gave me which.

And then I think of her. *Alone*. I see where I made the wrong choice.

"We have to," I whisper, watching the stars overhead, slowly tracing their paths through the night sky. All of them alone on their orbits, together. All of us alone on our orbits—together, too.

EPILOGUE

7:00 A.M., MONDAY

"*As of two a.m. this morning, Governor Voss has successfully eradicated the HBNC virus in approximately seventy-five percent of the Ward's sick population. Unfortunately, the remaining twenty-five percent of the sick population was not administered the cure due to a pharmaceutical recall in a number of the shipments. An unknown percentage living in private homes also remains uncured. Until further notice, the Ward will remain under quarantine. Entry and exit regulations will not change, nor will laws regarding Transmission of the virus. A city-wide celebration will be held at the following times in the following quad—*"

This is what I wake to: a radio crackling the news in Benny's garage.

I'm not allowed one moment of forgetting.

Even in sleep, there was a far-off hurt that I couldn't place.

But I could feel it everywhere.

I shift on the spare cot Benny set up for me in the office. It's a small room; I've only been in here once or twice; it's barely bigger than the cot. I like the smallness right now, I realize, and I pull the cool, white linens closer.

When I shift again, this time the springs lodge themselves between my ribs; I groan. In the other room, all voices go silent.

"You think she's up?" I hear Callum ask after a moment.

"We should wake her."

"Let's let her rest."

"She should see it, though. . . ."

See what? I wonder, but the voices are too muffled, too far away for me to tell who else is speaking. Now I'm curious. Swinging my feet onto the cool, concrete floor, I inhale. Prepare myself to meet the others.

As I stand, the radio transmission starts over from the beginning. It must be on a loop. *"As of two a.m. this morning, Governor Voss . . ."*

I take a few steps forward. Too achy for a lot of movement, I step slowly into the garage, find Benny, Derek, and Callum huddled around the radio, their faces drawn and tired. Terrence and Jones are sitting in the Cloud, docked—and floating—in the open pool Benny had built into the center of the garage. He made it so you could exit under the boardwalk and ride out onto the canal.

"What will I see?" I ask, and every guy in the room meets my eyes.

Except Jones.

He looks a bit like he feels he shouldn't be here. Keeping

himself too quiet, gaze flicking around the garage, landing anywhere but my face. If I had a friend like Kent, I'd be feeling guilty too.

If it hadn't been for Kent calling the Blues on us . . .

"You really think it's smart to be here right now? After what your best friend did?" I glare at him, shaking my head. "I wouldn't be able to look at myself in the mirror if I were you."

"Jones didn't know—it's not his fault. . . ." Terrence jumps outta the Cloud. He blocks off Jones like he knows how close to the edge I am.

"He didn't know his friend is scum?" I scoff. "I thought everyone knew that—"

But then, faintly, in the background: *"As of two a.m. this morning . . ."*

My eyes get hot. Tears start to build, and next thing I know, Ter's got his arms around me. I don't want to fight anymore, especially not Ter, so I just drop my head to his shoulder. I can't see the others; everything becomes blurry, but all I want is to turn around and run back to the cot.

I don't want to see anyone.

"We failed. . . ." I say. Ter rocks me side to side, cradling me tight, his palm brushing what's left of the hair on my scalp. I'm no different from an infant right now.

"She needs to see it," Callum says, and something in his voice makes me turn.

"See what?"

Callum lifts himself from the chair and walks over to me. Places both hands on my shoulders. "We didn't fail," he whispers, trying to catch my gaze as I look away. "Not even a little bit."

With that he strides over to the garage door, and lifts.

The air is thick with sunlight. It falls into the garage like a blanket, making all of us warm. Even me, almost. For a moment, we watch the Mad Ave crowds go about their business like usual . . . but nothing is like usual. The colors. The clothes. A young girl in a torn lavender tutu runs past, holding the hand of an old man. He's grinning and sporting a shiny black suit with a bow tie around his neck.

I don't say a word, though my jaw drops a little I'm sure.

Derek comes up behind me. I feel one of his hands on my shoulder, the other at the nape of my neck. "Look down," he says into my ear, and I do.

And I stop breathing.

Littered in front of the door to the left—Benny's doorstep . . .

Pennies. Dozens. A hundred, maybe. Their copper catches the light perfectly, and it's almost as though we've got a Milky Way's worth of tiny suns shining up from Benny's worn-out welcome mat. I laugh, and wipe my nose with my sleeve. They're too pretty, and my heart starts to hurt.

I can't believe that they mean what I think they mean. "I don't get it. . . ." I whisper.

"Renata." Benny laughs lightly, resting his hand on my other shoulder, squeezing it. "The people are not dumb. They saw the Blues removing our packages, and they saw that nothing was replaced. Rumor counts for a lot in this city, you should know that. Word of the infamous Red Rider and a team of dragsters dropping off the cure on sickhouse rooftops is newsworthy on any day."

This is too much. . . .

"A hundred thank-yous, Ren. A hundred people wishing you luck."

I choke on the last word—*luck*. Aven should be here right now. "Will I need it this time? To find her?" I ask, thinking no one but myself can hear.

Callum turns me around to face him. His blues are bluer than ever. "Never," he answers. "You have us—all of us. We're going to find her."

Jones nods, along with Derek and Terrence and Benny, and I choke again, this time on the mixed ball of feelings rolling around inside me. Looking down at the galaxy of copper stars lighting up the doorstep, I start to get that fullness in my chest I had at the hospital, like my body simply don't have enough room in it. There's too much to feel. *They have their Avens back.*

And all of a sudden I'm able to do it . . . hold in my head all the numbers, even the ones that didn't get the cure. Aven's there, and it hurts, but I don't dam myself off from it this time.

We'll find her. We have to.

In the morning sky, the sun—the real sun—is its own shade of copper. Getting ready to shine for other people. Share its warmth across the globe.

For now, all I can do is watch it rise for everyone else. For the hundred others at my feet. 'Cause I know I'll find my own again.

AUTHOR'S NOTE

There are a few things I'd like to bring to the reader's attention in the hope that by separating fact from fiction we might honor the historical truths in this novel, which were both brutal and unprecedented.

In order to do this, what follows will look a lot like a history lesson.

If you grew up in the tri-state area, chances are you've heard of the Lenni Lenape. They were a peace-loving people who once inhabited much of the mid-Atlantic region, including New York and New Jersey, and were known by other Algonquin tribes for their diplomatic ability to settle disputes.

When the Dutch arrived in the early 1600s seeking to profit off the land's many resources, the two cultures clashed; the concepts of profit and property were as foreign to the Lenape as the Europeans themselves.

In 1645, a man named Willem Kieft (sound familiar?) became the director, aka governor, of the region soon to be called New York City. Shortly after taking the position, Willem Kieft tried imposing taxes on the nearby native populations. The tribes resisted.

Kieft, angered by their refusal, launched a massacre.

That massacre, later known as Kieft's War, ultimately got him fired from his position as director. Not only were most of the settlers against the movement, but the Dutch West India Company (which had chosen him as director) had never given him permission to attack.

It's important to make clear here that Willem Kieft—the man who inspired my villain—started a war not because he believed the Indians would "resurrect," but because they would not submit to colonization and taxation by foreigners. Kieft was not seeking a miraculous water source with healing capabilities. He wanted money and power, and upon this attack, no Lenape or any other tribesmen were inexplicably brought back to life. Though highly skilled warriors, there were hundreds of deaths, and each of them was final.

The Tètai—the guardians of the spring in the novel—are the product of my own imagination. The design for their tattoos, however, was adapted from images in the controversial Walam Olum—a historical narrative of the Lenape published in the 1830s by antiquarian Constantine Rafinesque. The document's authenticity, however, has never been verified.

Lastly, though the Minetta Brook of *The Ward* is the stuff of fancy, a real two-mile-long Minetta Brook actually did run through Manhattan, emptying out into the Hudson River. You can even find Minetta Street on a current map of New York City. It's a lovely, narrow little road in the West Village that the stream once traversed during its heyday.

The Minetta Brook may or may not still exist today, hidden deep beneath the city's foundation.

WANT ANOTHER
HEART-RACING READ?

When Miki Jones is pulled into the game—pulled through time and space into a thrilling and dangerous alternate reality—her carefully controlled life spirals into chaos. There is no training and no way out. What Miki and her new teammates do now determines their survival, and the survival of every person on this planet.